The TEMPLE AND THE CROWN

KATHERINE KURTZ AND DEBORAH TURNER HARRIS

A Time

WARNER BOOKS EDITION

Aspect® name and logo are registered trademarks of Warner Books, Inc.

Cover design by Don Puckey
Cover illustration by Greg Call
Handlettering by Carl Dellacroce

Warner Books, Inc.
1271 Avenue of the Americas
New York, NY 10020

Visit our Web site at
www.twbookmark.com

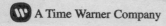 A Time Warner Company

Printed in the United States of America

First Printing: April 2001

10 9 8 7 6 5 4 3

To
Ken Fraser,
recently retired as Head Research Librarian at
St. Andrews University,
with profound thanks for putting your encyclopedic knowledge
of Scottish history, culture, and folklore at our disposal.
We couldn't have managed without you!

The TEMPLE And The CROWN

1306:
A Historical Foreword

IN THE SPRING OF 1306, THE CROWN OF SCOTLAND HAD but recently been vested—precariously, to be sure—in Robert Bruce. He was the survivor in a dynastic wrangle among no less than thirteen contenders for the crown briefly intended for a child called Margaret, commonly known as the Maid of Norway, granddaughter and only direct heir of the last Canmore King of Scots.

On the strength of a childhood betrothal agreed in treaty but never consummated by even a casual meeting of the two principals—the Maid and the Lord Edward of Caernarvon, son and heir of England's Edward Plantagenet—King Edward had used the premature death of the little Maid as license to adjudicate the Scottish succession, with an eye toward at last absorbing young Margaret's kingdom into the realm of England. A client king, John Balliol, had been chosen from among the contending thirteen—deposed but three years later, when he dared to assert Scotland's independence.

Then had come Sir William Wallace, hailed by some as an Uncrowned King—of common blood, but one whose life and death had given new hope to the Scottish nation and enabled the present king to come forth: Robert Bruce, in whose veins, by way of distaff, also ran the ancient blood of the Canmore kings. Not only had Bruce at last risen up against King Edward, but against inhuman forces that might have charted an altogether different course for Scotland.

Behind and at the bedrock of this struggle had been an ancient and power-full artifact called the Stone of Destiny, or sometimes the Stone of Scone, for the place where it was kept: mystical palladium, sacred altar-stone, relic of Jacob and of the saintly Columba—the high seat of Scotland's high kings since the time of Kenneth MacAlpin, nearly five hundred years before. Earmarked for seizure by King Edward's men, its power waning, the true Stone had been spirited away and a lesser copy left in its place, saved through the agencies of men who wore white robes: tonsured servants of the gentle Saint Columba, who followed a form of Christianity predating the supremacy of Roman pontiffs and practices, and crusader Knights of the Temple of Jerusalem, whose Inner Circle guarded secrets harking back to the wisdom of King Solomon himself, who had built that Temple in the land where Christ later walked.

Upheld by these seemingly disparate allies, the Uncrowned King had laid down his life and so reempowered the Stone—the Stone upon which Robert Bruce subsequently had undergone a mystical enthronement that had wedded him to the Land by ancient Celtic rite, bracketed between two public inaugurations upon a lesser throne.*

But being crowned king and actually *being* king were not necessarily one and the same, as Robert Bruce would soon learn. And not only Edward of England would be seeking to destroy him, as the deed became known. Enemies of the Temple had long been searching for ways to

---

*Related in the novel *The Temple and the Stone.*

bring it down. Discovery of the Knights' involvement in Scotland's struggle for freedom was likely to place both the Temple and Scotland in grave danger . . . and also Scotland's new king. . . .

Chapter One

Late April, 1306

G OD SAVE KING ROBERT! HAIL, THE BRUCE, KING OF Scots!"

The roof beams of the smoky great hall in Castle Cupar reverberated with the cheers, and shadows leapt on the lime-washed walls, as men rose from their benches and lifted their tankards in honor of their liege lord, who occupied the seat of honor at the high table.

Robert Bruce, lately lord of Annandale and only a month ago acclaimed as King of Scots, returned the salutes of his followers with a flourish of his wine cup. As the cheering subsided to good-natured banter, he rose and turned to his host, seated at his right hand: the venerable and ever-faithful Robert Wishart, Bishop of Glasgow. Gradually, a semblance of order settled on the hall.

"My lord Bishop," Bruce declared, bowing slightly to Wishart and pitching his volume so that all could hear him. "I present my compliments again on your newly discovered skills as a man of war. In wresting this keep from English hands, you once again have proved yourself one of Scotland's staunchest champions."

The men signified their endorsement of this declaration

by thumping cups and beefy hands against tabletops, and Wishart's gray head bowed in gratitude. For two tumultuous decades and more, since well before the time of John Balliol, he had spearheaded the legal and political battle to secure Scotland's independence. Now owning more than seventy years, he had only lately taken to arms in the field, with a degree of daring and initiative that would have done credit to a man half his age.

He gave a droll grin to the Bruce. "While you're handing out commendations, Sire, let us not neglect Edward of England, who so thoughtfully provided us with the means to breach the castle's defenses."

A roar of laughter rose from the hall, for the bishop's statement was precisely the truth. Having received a grant of English timber to repair the bell tower of his cathedral, Wishart had ordered the wood converted into siege engines, which he then had turned to less pastoral employment than the ringing of bells. Following a successful assault on the fortress at Kirkintilloch, the bishop had marched next on Castle Cupar, in the ancient kingdom of Fife, whose English garrison had offered only token resistance before surrendering, utterly daunted by the prospect of heavy bombardment.

"Well said, Bishop," said Christopher Seton, Bruce's close friend and brother-in-law. "But it doesnae hurt to have a pair of engineering experts on hand, either." He cast an admiring glance at the two white-clad men seated beyond Bruce and Wishart. "It seems to me that the good Sir Arnault and Sir Torquil also merit no small vote of thanks for their parts in our recent success."

A murmur of approbation rippled through the hall as all eyes shifted toward the two men named, both of them bearded and white-clad in a room full of mostly clean-shaven men dressed in the harness of war. The elder of the pair merely smiled and inclined his head in acknowledgment, but the younger, a Scot called Torquil Lennox, grinned self-consciously as he raked a big-boned hand through short-cropped red hair going gray. Though the two customarily went about in well-worn leathers and mail like those around them, tonight they had donned the distinctive white livery of their true vocations as Knights of the Temple of Jerusalem, in honor of the day's success. The crusader crosses splayed across the left shoulders of their white mantles much resembled splashes of blood.

"Och, anybody can build a catapult," Torquil said with a self-deprecating shrug. "Besides, Brother Arnault and I have been doing it for a long time."

"That's as may be," Bruce allowed, "but *we* haven't. Once you've *built* a siege engine, the trick is getting it to hit what you aim for. For that, we are much indebted to your crusading expertise—both of you."

Arnault de Saint Clair, the second Templar, chuckled good-naturedly. He also made light of their contribution, his manner much at variance with the pride and hauteur displayed by some of his more worldly Templar brethren.

"If the truth be known, my own experience lies more with trebuchets," he said easily. Though fluent in Scots and English and half a dozen other languages less useful on this island, he had never lost the accent of his native Brittany. "Fortunately, the principles of range-finding are pretty much the same. Consider any debt handsomely offset by Bishop Wishart's hospitality—and by the luxury of having a roof over our heads for tonight!"

"I thought you Templars made a virtue of sleeping rough under the sky," said Thomas Bruce, one of the king's younger brothers.

"Aye, but it doesn't rain much in Palestine," Torquil pointed out, "and never the way it rains here." He grinned. "Why do you think I joined the Temple?"

Hearty laughter greeted this rejoinder, followed by another round of toasts in honor of the king's Templar allies, and then more toasts to the future they all were seeking for an independent Scotland.

At least a start had been made in the four weeks since Bruce's inauguration as King of Scots, duly affirmed by a Pontifical high Mass on Palm Sunday. Immediately thereafter, he had dispatched messengers throughout Scotland, proclaiming his kingship and calling upon all loyal Scots to pledge fealty to their new liege. He and a fast-mounted escort had followed in their wake, defying the rough weather of uncertain spring to make a royal progress through the northerly reaches of his kingdom.

With so much ground to cover, and the speed of an English response uncertain, the company had been obliged to press forward at a grueling pace, rarely halting anywhere for more than one night. But the hardships of the journey had been well repaid by the loyalty of the townsmen and villagers who flocked to greet their new king. Now, after a brief sojourn in Aberdeen, Bruce was on his way south again, to rendezvous with friends and allies and make preparations for the inevitable reaction from the south, once Edward of England fully comprehended what they had done.

Tonight, however, the bloodless taking of Cupar Castle had left everyone in a festive mood, and the firelit hall buzzed with eager banter as heaped platters of beef, bread, and cheese, and pitchers of ale passed from hand to hand. Farther down the table, another of Bruce's allies, Sir John of Cambo, sampled the claret just poured for him by a kitchen boy and lifted his cup in the direction of Bishop Wishart.

"My lord Bishop," he called, "there canna be doubt that you have got the better part of the bargain, by letting the English garrison march away unmolested in exchange for leaving us the castle stores. I can assure ye that the castle cellars are particularly fine! I say we set ourselves the task of doing justice to this noble vintage, and drink to Scotland's freedom!"

This toast was heartily seconded by all, amid much whooping and further pounding of fists on tables. But neither Bruce nor those closest to him had lost sight of the very real difficulties that still lay ahead.

"Well enough, to speak of Scotland's freedom," the new king said to Arnault, Torquil, and the others close around him, as the uproar subsided to convivial converse and serious feasting resumed. "But we need time to consolidate our position. I had hoped Edward would be dead before I made my move. God willing, he will prove too weak to make us much opposition—and the son is not half the man his father is. But we cannot count on that."

"Indeed, not," said Bishop Wishart. "I'll not be surprised if we hear that the news has killed him—but if it has not, we must be prepared."

"Aye, the English won't stay away forever," said Edward Bruce, the king's eldest brother. "We've done well in securing the support of the folk of Aberdeenshire—we mostly control the approaches to the Firth of Clyde, in the west. But as long as the south remains divided, we're vulnerable there. It will be difficult to defend the border."

"Best not forget about Galloway, either," Seton observed sourly, "and that's well within our borders. Despite everything we've done, that district is still a hotbed of support for the Balliols and the Comyns."

Mutters of agreement bracketed Bruce from either side, sprung from varying degrees of knowledge of the true extent of danger from that quarter. Both families had been powerful contenders for the crown he lately had taken up. John Balliol, head of the Balliol clan, had managed to wear the crown of Scotland for only two years before being stripped of his titular sovereignty by Edward of England. Though he had since retired to comfortable exile in France, vowing never to return, some of his adherents still cherished the illusion that he—or his son—might one day be induced to a change of heart.

The Comyn link was even more dangerous, and came, in part, from the marriage of one of Balliol's sisters to the father of the Comyn slain by Bruce a few months before at Dumfries Abbey—a Comyn whose alliance with infernal forces had nearly cost Bruce his life that day. As it was little known that the Comyns, father and son, had dabbled in the black arts, or that they had based their bid for Scotland's crown on an alliance with certain demonic entities out of Scotland's pagan past, the majority of Comyn supporters simply viewed the killing, within the supposed sanctuary of a church, as sacrilegious murder.

No matter that it had actually been self-defense, and Bruce had been absolved of the killing within days. Comyn loyalty would always back the assertion that Bruce, and not John Comyn, had been the aggressor, violating sanctuary; and absolution by a bishop known to be a Bruce supporter was hardly to be accepted. Small wonder that Galloway, long loyal to Comyn interests, continued to be recalcitrant.

"Aye, that's true enough," Bruce replied, toying with his cup, perhaps recalling some of the circumstances of that killing—for without Arnault and Torquil, his Templar protectors, he himself might have been killed instead of Comyn. "The Gallovidians can be a shortsighted bunch, with old loyalties and old grudges. An alliance with King Edward is always a possibility, especially if they stand to profit from it. I've little doubt but that they'd throw in their lot with the devil himself, if he offered them my head on a platter!"

His glance at Arnault and Torquil confirmed that he was well aware of the deeper implications for the few who knew the true story.

"It's a pity we had to dismantle the castles at Dumfries and Ayr," said Sir Simon Fraser, who was not among those few. "A strong garrison in either place would have put some protection at our backs."

"Aye, but we haven't the men to spare," Torquil pointed out. "And we daren't leave anything behind that might be useful to our enemies."

"Even if it would be useful to *us*?" Fraser replied.

"No, because we might not be able to hold it, while we're spread so thin," Arnault said. "Believe me, Brother Torquil and I have seen such tactics used to good effect against *us* in the Holy Land. After the fall of Acre, in 1291, Sultan al-Ashraf's troops swept up and down the Syrian coastline, leveling orchards and villas and wrecking irrigation systems. When they were done, nothing remained to support an enemy invasion force—for that's how we were regarded. The tactic has enabled them to hold Syria uncontested for the better part of fifteen years."

"So there you have it," Bruce said briskly. "Any fortress we can't defend must be pulled down; any supplies we can't carry with us must be spoiled. The point is to make the English feel so unwelcome that they'll give up the fight and go home."

"Amen to *that*!" Bishop Wishart signaled his steward to bring more wine. "And now, let us do justice to this very excellent fare provided by the English!"

Again, servants passed along the tables with ewers of wine and platters of food. Torquil, when he had let his cup be filled again, stretched across to spear a gobbet of succulent spring lamb with the point of his dirk.

"How long d'you think it's been since we've seen food like this?" he asked. "Or until we see such again?"

"Too long," Arnault replied. He tore off a chunk from a loaf of fresh bread and dunked it in gravy before stuffing it into his mouth.

"If we ate this way too often," Torquil responded, around a mouthful of lamb, "we'd probably get fat and sloppy. Probably best that we're vowed to poverty. But if we were allowed to have any personal wealth, I'd give it all to know what's in King Edward's mind right now."

"Aye," Arnault agreed, "one of the hardest parts of this job is waiting, not knowing when the enemy will strike next, or where."

"D'you think it would make any difference to him, if he knew what's really at stake?" Torquil asked.

"Edward? I very much doubt it." Arnault drank from his cup as his gray eyes roamed the hall. "Remember that there are good reasons Edward Plantagenet is known as the Hammer of the Scots—and he recognizes no authority but his own. Maybe not even God's.

"As for what *we* do," he added in a lower tone, "sometimes I'm not even sure *I* understand it. How would you even begin to explain something like the Fifth Temple to a man like Edward?"

Torquil shook his head, returning his attention to the meat on his dirk, and both men lapsed into companionable silence amid the buzz and bustle of the feast. The truth was that on this isle of Britain, far darker forces were at work than paid any mind to the wranglings of English or Scottish kings—and the prize was no mere earthly kingdom, but a realm that dealt with the life and death of souls.

Safeguarding that realm was the hidden purpose of Arnault and Torquil and others like them, even though the Temple's avowed public purpose was to win back the Holy Land and safeguard the pilgrim places where God once had walked. Within the Templar Order there existed a hidden inner order called *le Cercle,* heir to ancient wisdom turned always toward the betterment of humanity's spiritual condition. Its members had worked toward that purpose from the time of the Order's inception, secretly guiding certain of the Order's work toward a higher purpose than merely retaining a Christian foothold in the Holy Land.

But if the Holy Land once had represented the perfect symbol for the physical and spiritual battlefield whereon the greater struggle of Light against Darkness was being played out, that seemed no longer to be the case. The first intimations of this shift in focus had begun to emerge in the past several decades, as it became clear that physically restoring the Temple of Jerusalem—rebuilding the so-called Fourth

Temple, in succession to the Third Temple destroyed by Titus in A.D. 70—was not likely to be possible in the foreseeable future.

So a new home for the Order must be found—and a new battlefield for the forces of Light against Darkness. The superiors of the external Temple had their plans for the greater Order, by means of a new Templar state hopefully to be carved out in France, but the Inner Temple must make its own arrangements—and not only in the physical plane. By means of prayer and meditation and the employment of diverse divinatory gifts sometimes accessible to various of their number, the leaders of *le Cercle* had been vouchsafed certain signs and portents pointing to Scotland as the Order's new home—and the future location of a spiritual Fifth Temple, which would anchor the forces of Light in Scottish soil.

Arnault had been instrumental in discerning these signs; and despite the increasing opposition of dark forces that would have prevented it, he and Torquil had been key players in achieving the first step toward that goal: reviving the ancient power of the Stone of Destiny, focus of the Celtic sovereignty of Scotland, which power had since been vested in Robert Bruce as rightful King of Scots.

Now in progress was the task of making Bruce's kingship effective in practice as well as in law and in declaration, recognized outside Scotland as well as within. Failure would mean the end of Scottish identity and a foothold for the forces of Darkness. But if Bruce succeeded in winning the battle for Scotland's freedom, it was *le Cercle*'s intention that the Stone of Destiny, the Palladium of Scotland, would become both a physical and spiritual cornerstone for a new Fifth Temple enshrining the mystical wisdom of King Solomon himself—a temple not built with human hands.

The clatter of fresh logs being piled on the fire jarred Arnault from his contemplation, and sent waves of heat billowing across the room. Stifling a yawn, Arnault gave himself a shake and pushed his half-empty wine cup to one side.

"I think I'll step outside for a few minutes," he said to Torquil, pivoting to swing a leg back over the bench where they sat. "If I don't get a breath of fresh air, I'm apt to nod off and fall facefirst into my trencher—though God knows when we'll be this warm again."

"I'll join you," Torquil replied, for the combination of warmth and wine was also making him heavy-lidded.

But before either one of them could rise, a muffled disturbance from outside the hall heralded the appearance of a guard from the outer baillie. Murmured speculation grew and followed the man as he threaded his way toward the head of the hall, subsiding as Bruce signed for silence and nodded for the man to speak.

"Two travelers at the gate, Your Grace, with news," the sentry reported. "Templars," he added, with a glance at the two seated near the king.

"Then, fetch them in!" the king ordered.

The sentry bowed himself out, leaving a murmur of tense expectancy. When he returned a few moments later, two closely muffled figures accompanied him, shaking back the hoods from mud-bedraggled dark mantles that parted as they walked to reveal the conspicuous white livery of the Order of the Temple.

Both Arnault and Torquil stiffened as the two approached, settling back onto their bench, for the elder of the pair was Frère Luc de Brabant, their *le Cercle* counterpart from the main Scottish preceptory of Balantrodoch, south of Edinburgh: a wiry, silver-haired man in his still-vigorous sixties. Bearded like the younger man who accompanied him, Luc looked tense and somewhat preoccupied as his blue gaze swept the room, evidently searching out Arnault and Torquil, for he looked visibly relieved as he spotted them. His younger companion was one of Arnault's Scottish cousins—Aubrey Saint Clair, still very junior in his service to the Temple and to *le Cercle*—who bore himself like a man braced for a possibly hostile reception.

"I can't say I like the look of this," Arnault muttered, with an apprehensive glance aside at Torquil—for only a matter of some urgency would have brought the aging Luc in person, all the way from Balantrodoch.

Silence settled on the hall as the newcomers made their way toward the high table, Luc in the lead, and inclined their heads to the king, who signed for them to speak.

"I fear that the news we bring is not good, Sire," Luc said, with another glance at Arnault and Torquil. "Would you rather hear it in private?"

A flicker of misgiving showed in the Bruce's eyes, but his gaze was steely. "Secrecy won't soften the blow," he said. "No, speak out where all can hear."

"As you wish." Luc squared his shoulders, half-turning to address the assembly as well.

"I regret to report that an English invasion is on its way," he announced in a carrying voice. "By all accounts, King Edward has put not one, but two armies in the field. The eastern contingent, under command of Sir Henry Percy, is expected to arrive at Berwick within the week, with an estimated six hundred horse and two thousand infantry."

As a murmur of consternation rippled through the hall, he paused to glance back at the king, whose face was set like stone.

"Continue," Bruce said quietly.

"The second army, in the west, is commanded by the Earl of Pembroke," Luc said.

A flattened silence followed this announcement, and Arnault and Torquil exchanged troubled glances. No one present needed reminding that Aymer de Valence, Earl of Pembroke, had a personal axe to grind. Half cousin to the English king, he was married to the sister of the slain John Comyn. A few of Bruce's supporters had been witness to his killing of Comyn at Dumfries, but only the four Templars knew the truth of what had provoked the killing. Young Aubrey, standing close to Luc's shoulder and a good hand taller, had not been present, but by his scowl, Arnault could make a good guess as to what was probably on the younger man's mind, imagination doubtless having embroidered the account he had heard.

"Fortunately," Arnault murmured, leaning a little closer to Torquil, "I very much doubt that Pembroke knows anything about Comyn's . . . shall we say 'darker' involvements. As Comyn's brother-in-law, however, he does have a family obligation to avenge his death. This is apt to put a personal edge to the coming campaign."

"Pembroke himself is not the worst of it," Luc warned, before Arnault could say more. "It is what we all have been dreading. Not content with naming a commander known for his ruthlessness, Edward has given the order to *burn, slay, and raise dragon.*"

Torquil, a native Scot, went a little pale, and several of the men at table crossed themselves while others muttered darkly. The red dragon banner of the Plantagenets was England's most terrible standard of war. Its unfurling on a field of battle signified that no mercy would be shown, no quarter given to anyone on the opposing side, regardless of age, gender, or infirmity. Hearing of Edward's leave to raise dragon, Arnault found himself recalling other English atrocities of which he himself had firsthand knowledge, like the sacking of Berwick and the carnage at Falkirk.

And then there had been the mock trial and grisly execution of Bruce's spiritual predecessor, Sir William Wallace: hanged by the neck until near unconsciousness, then cut down and emasculated, disemboweled, his entrails drawn from his living body before the removal of his still-beating heart. And though, by then, Wallace himself would have been beyond caring, the ignominy had not been ended even by the headsman's axe—for they then had cut his mutilated body into quarters, which were sent for eventual display outside the gates of four Scottish towns, as a warning to other would-be traitors. His head had been piked on London Bridge.

No, temperance, mercy, and even humanity were not in the lexicon of the English king; and allowing his armies to raise dragon would not endear him to the Scottish people.

A sullen mutter spread through the hall, quickly swelling to a rumble of anger.

"If the Plantagenet thinks he can terrorize us into submission, let him think again!" an anonymous voice shouted from the ranks.

"Aye, we'll not be bullied!" another cried.

A roar of agreement went up, and Bruce rose to his feet, his gray eyes as hard as flint.

"Brave words," he called back, "as long as they come from your hearts, and not merely from wine!"

His words brought immediate silence to the hall. "If we have learned nothing else these past ten years, we have learned the high price of freedom. You have only to ask William Wallace of *that*!

"And the cost will be higher still, before this fight is over," he continued grimly. "Are you prepared to follow me where Wallace led?" He leaned both hands on the table and leaned closer to them. "Are you prepared to risk a death like his? Are you prepared to hazard the lives of those you love, for the sake of this land and the welfare of future generations?"

A heated murmur started to rise, but Bruce stilled it with a raised hand.

"If you are not," he concluded, "go now and make whatever peace you can with our bitter enemy. But if your answer is yes, then let us pledge loyalty to one another from this moment onward—and make ready to defend ourselves and this land with the longest and strongest stick we have!"

He swept a challenging look over the now-silent sea of upturned faces. Arnault could detect no sign of flinching or wavering among them as they boldly returned the king's gaze. Slowly the harshness faded from Bruce's face, to be replaced with an expression of pride and even tenderness.

"So be it, then, my friends," he said quietly, nodding. "Henceforth, we must count ourselves as dead men, and every earthly thing we hold dear as lost, trusting in God to crown our sacrifices with victory. Be assured that this land of ours is as sacred as the Holy Land, and the war to preserve her liberty is nothing less than a crusade." His gaze flicked pointedly to the four Templars, in their white robes of purity touched with the red of martyrdom.

"We fight to maintain not only the sovereignty of our Scottish crown, but also the integrity of our traditions. Remember that both the crown *and* the traditions are wedded to the land itself—and while we live and breathe, I see that it is, indeed, true that the land shall not lack for defenders!"

A burst of acclaim answered these words, every man on his feet to salute the king with drawn sword or dirk, and it was a long time before the rafters stopped ringing. Meanwhile, the two newcomers were bombarded with anxious questions, given space at table before trenchers mounded high with food.

Much later, after most of the company had fallen asleep, Bruce drew Arnault aside, withdrawing into the shelter of a window arch. Torquil was conferring with Luc and Aubrey, closer to the dying fire.

"I must confess that I hardly dared to hope for such a show of loyalty as you witnessed here tonight," Bruce said. "It grieves me more than I can say, to know that many will pay for that loyalty with their lives, once we come to grips with the English. I know you cannot make me any promises, Brother Arnault, but I would be grateful for any support that your Order can give us. I *am* grateful, for what you have given already."

"I shall convey the message, Sire—and add my own appeal."

Bruce raised an eyebrow. "You *are* leaving us this time, then?"

"Not for long, I hope," Arnault said. "I should have gone weeks ago, as soon as I saw you crowned. I've yet to confer privately with Luc, of course, but our superiors in Paris must be informed of these latest developments—and in light of some of the things you and I have seen, it is hardly anything that can be committed to writing. That means someone—either Torquil or myself—has to relay the information in person."

"I am loath to lose you—or Torquil, either, for that matter," Bruce said. "Could Luc himself not go?"

Arnault shook his head. "If there were no one else, of course he could. But he has not been witness to all that Torquil and I have seen. Besides that, I think he can better serve if he remains our liaison with the preceptory at Balantrodoch—which must maintain at least the appearance of neutrality. If King Edward were to complain to the pope . . ."

"Aye, there is *that*," Bruce said with a wry grin. "It appears that I cannot dissuade you, then. When will you go?"

"At first light—and so must you," Arnault replied. "Your best strategy will be to stay on the move."

After a beat, the king gave a nod. "I had already planned to do that."

"Excellent. And since Luc has brought young Aubrey along, I'll ask if he can remain with Torquil, in my place. He's a good man. Another Saint Clair, as it happens."

"Is he?" Bruce glanced in the direction of the other three Templars. "Related to you, by any chance?"

Arnault smiled faintly. "A distant cousin. I hope you will not be disappointed."

"Well, if he's half as useful as either you or Torquil, he'll earn his keep," the king said. "When do you think you might return?"

"It may be some weeks," Arnault replied, "perhaps even

several months. By then, if things go well, the war might even be won."

"God grant that it be so!" Bruce said fervently. "But if it takes a bit longer than that," he added with grim humor, "just look for us wherever the fighting is!"

Chapter Two

Late April, 1306

IN THE BLEAK, SILENT HOURS BEFORE DAYBREAK, LIT ONLY by a few sputtering torches, a small armed company wearing the king's livery slogged through the rain-drenched streets of Paris, making for the great royal fortress of the Louvre. In their midst staggered four bound and hooded prisoners, one of them a woman. Their escort chivvied them roughly through the west postern.

After splashing across a sodden courtyard, the soldiers halted before a portico set deep in the face of the north wing, where their leader rapped smartly against the metal of a shuttered spy hole with the pommel of his dagger. After a moment, the shutter withdrew, and a bleary blue eye glinted at the opening.

"Who's there?" the owner of the eye said crossly, before subsiding in a fit of coughing.

"Sieur Bartholeme de Challon," came the curt reply. "Open up at once! I do not relish standing here in the rain!"

Following the hasty clatter of bolts being drawn, the door swung inward to spill a sullen swath of yellow light across the swimming cobbles. Sweeping the sleepy porter aside, Bartholeme strode imperiously into the anteroom, shaking back his hood from a helmet of dark hair above a bronzed, hard-angled face.

"The Magister will wish to question these prisoners in person," he informed his sergeant over his shoulder. "Lock them in the guardroom and keep close watch. I will return to fetch them presently."

"Oui, monsieur."

A groined arch in the right-hand wall gave access to a spiral stair which Bartholeme ascended to the top floor, taking the first few steps two at a time. Torchlit passageways branched left and right off the landing, and Bartholeme set off along the left-hand corridor toward an oak-paneled door, where a servant waited to admit him. Divested of his dripping mantle, he proceeded through an intervening anteroom to a larger chamber lit by the commingled glow of four hanging lamps and a goodly fire blazing on the hearth.

Beneath the lamps, nine men sat assembled around a heavy oak table that dominated the center of the room—the full complement, now that Bartholeme had joined them, of what was known among them as the Decuria. The man seated at the table's head did not rise as Bartholeme approached, but fixed him with a heavy-lidded look of inquiry.

"We expected you earlier," he said mildly. "I trust there were no unforeseen difficulties?"

The speaker was a slight, stoop-shouldered individual who might have been any age between thirty and fifty. His wispy dark hair was yet untouched by gray, but thinning at the temples, emphasizing the height of his forehead. With his pasty complexion and slightly protuberant gray eyes, Guillaume de Nogaret looked more like a scholarly ascetic than a powerful minister of the French crown. Ruthless and devious, and with his own secret agenda, he had been the king's principal minister for more than a decade, defying even popes to advance his royal master's interests. He was probably the most dangerous man in all of France.

"Your instructions have been carried out, Magister," Bartholeme said neutrally, and with due deference—for the full range of Nogaret's sinister abilities was a matter for speculation even among his closest confederates. On this occasion, Bartholeme could only guess at his superior's veiled intent. "The prisoners are in custody, and await your pleasure. I thought it wise to search the house before we left. We knew what to look for."

"But you found nothing," Nogaret said—a statement rather than a question.

"Nothing we were not expecting—and nothing we were looking for," Bartholeme replied.

"Very well." Nogaret's thin lips curled. "It appears we must do this the hard way. Secure the room, then take your place."

Without demur, Bartholeme stripped the glove from his left hand to expose the handsome gold signet ring he wore on his third finger, set with a lozenge of polished jet. Engraved thereon was the image of a swan—the *Cygnus Hermetis,* symbol of alchemical transmutation—a sigil adorning similar rings on the left hand of every other man in the room, and betokening the oaths and constraints that bound them together in sinister fellowship.

The seal of this ring Bartholeme touched to the lintels of the door with a muttered phrase of empowerment. At once, a curious deadness stole over the room, muffling the sound of the rain drumming on the roof and leaded windowpanes and even faintly dimming the firelight and lamplight. As Bartholeme then made his way to the vacant chair at the foot of the table, a florid, silver-haired man spoke up from two seats away.

"All members of the Decuria being present, Magister, may we now hear the reason for this summons in the dead of night?"

Nogaret transferred his hooded gaze to his questioner. "I make no apology for interrupting your nocturnal pleasures, Lord Baudoin. Do you imagine that I would call a full assembly at such short notice for anything less than a matter of dire importance? I have received certain information to suggest that an enemy we thought we had left for dead may have found a route to recovery."

Uncertain glances skittered up and down the table.

"And what enemy might that be?" asked the cautious voice of Count Rodolphe de Crevecoeur.

Nogaret's pale eyes burned with a deep-seated glint of malice as he pronounced each word of the name in a low, flat tone: "The Knights of the Order of the Temple."

This revelation elicited a flurry of startled glances and mutters of incredulity.

"There must be some mistake!" Baudoin blurted, his protest heralding echoes from other parts of the table.

"Impossible!" came the emphatic agreement of one of Baudoin's neighbors, the Chevalier Valentin de Vesey. "The Templars are a spent force. The Christian West has been expelled from the Holy Land. Whatever danger to us they once represented, surely their powers are now in decline. If they could not summon the resources to retain their grip on Acre fifteen years ago, I very much doubt there is anything they can do now to hamper our plans or imperil our prospects."

"Aye, the crusades have failed, and so have they!" Baudoin agreed. "Their desert castles lie in ruins, and their reputation likewise. In another decade or two, there will be nothing left of the Templar Order but a name in the annals of the past!"

Nogaret shook his head, raising a ringed hand for silence. "I have had a vision," he announced grimly. "Unfortunately, it suggests that nothing could be further from the truth."

Stunned silence greeted this declaration. Then everyone began talking at once, until Count Rodolphe's voice cut across the clamor.

"Gentlemen!" he rapped. "Have you forgotten in whose presence you are speaking?"

This reminder immediately brought the room to order,

with a few furtive glances cast in the direction of their superior. With a deferential nod, Rodolphe turned to Nogaret.

"Magister, we all know the signs by which to distinguish the phantasms of sleep from an event of revelation," he said. "Perhaps you would give us your account of this vision, so that we may weigh the matter of interpretation."

"That was always my intention," Nogaret said mildly.

His fingers moved to caress the magnificent ruby ring he wore on a chain about his neck—a gesture subtly calculated to remind all present of his capabilities. Four years earlier, nominally at the instigation of the French king, Philip IV, Guillaume de Nogaret had stormed the papal palace at Anagni and physically assaulted the troublesome Pope Boniface VIII—an action which simultaneously had rocked the courts of Europe, earned him an excommunication yet to be lifted, and won him the leadership of the Decuria.

The elderly pontiff had subsequently died of shock, and Nogaret had recovered Boniface's ring as a trophy of his success. The man who now wore the papal tiara as Clement V was a creature put in place by Nogaret himself, ostensibly at the behest of the king, and would serve as their tool when the time came—whether or not he wished to do so.

"Mere hours ago, as I lay sleeping," Nogaret said softly, "a voice stirred me from my slumbers, warning that great powers were on the ascendant. I have had this part of the dream several times in the past month, but never have I been able to pursue it—until tonight.

"Leaving my body where it lay, my spirit rose up and moved to the window, where I beheld a star like a comet, its fiery tail trailing westward like a bridge of light."

He watched their rapt wonder as his tale unfolded, and could feel himself gathering the strands of their focus.

"Following on wings of shadow, I set off along that bridge," he went on. "Over land and over sea I flew, until the path at last bowed to earth, its glow overwashing a great cathedral, whose roof and walls became as transparent as crystal. There, deep in its vaults, I espied three knights in the white robes of the Temple, assisting in the enthronement of a king."

A stir of consternation greeted this announcement, but Nogaret lifted a hand for silence as he continued.

"Nor was this any ordinary throne on which they attended, but a great block of stone encompassed by a pillar of fire. Graven on the stone were words writ in an angelic tongue, and seated on the stone was a man robed in white, who bore the aspect of both king and sacrifice.

"Others were present as well, also robed in white, and as one of them placed a crown of greenery upon the man's head, I heard a voice cry out, *Worthy is the king who has Jacob's Hallow for his high seat! The house erected upon that rock will long endure.*

"With this utterance," he concluded, as uneasy murmurs briefly swirled around him, "an overpowering stench of sanctity filled the room, and a cloud of confusion surrounded and blinded me and hurled me from that place. I awoke some little while later in the darkness of my room, but there remained a lingering resonance of power in the air, to confirm that what I had just witnessed was far more than a dream."

The stunned silence following this declaration was almost palpable, until at last Count Rodolphe signed for leave to speak.

"Magister, there can be little doubt that you have, indeed, been vouchsafed a portent," he said uneasily. "But there is no profit in it unless we can strip away the veils of obscurity to confront the threat in its true guise. Have you any notion as to the meaning of the vision?"

"I have," Nogaret replied, "but I wish to hear the Decuria's observations before I reveal my own impressions."

"Then I say that it bodes ill," said another knight, Thibault de Montreville. "Whoever this king may be, it is both unprecedented and unacceptable that the Templars should be acting as kingmakers."

"Yet by this act," said a thin, nervous man called Jervis Fonteroi, "it would appear that they have taken an active interest in the establishment of this kingdom, whatever it might be. Have we any clues as to the identity of this new-crowned king, or where his crowning may have taken place?"

"We have the reference to Jacob's Hallow in connection with the king's coronation seat," said Rodolphe, his gaze narrowed in thought. "Whatever this object may be, it would seem to represent some sort of bridge between the ancient realm of Israel and some future goal that has yet to be accomplished: a goal that can *only* be accomplished," he concluded, "in association with this king whose name still remains hidden from us."

Baudoin eyed Rodolphe askance.

"Are you suggesting a connection—some kind of alliance—between the Templars and the Jews?"

"That is not beyond the bounds of possibility," Nogaret said briskly. "The Templars have always had mystical links with Solomon and the Hebrew kings and patriarchs. On the strength of a kindred supposition, I have had the Sieur de Challon procure us the services of an individual who may be able to read this riddle more clearly than we can."

He glanced at Bartholeme. "Fetch the seeress Zipporah—and her family as well. I wish her to understand quite clearly that all their lives depend utterly upon her cooperation."

Valentin de Vesey came with him as far as the door, to suspend the wards. Clattering swiftly down to ground level, Bartholeme relayed Nogaret's orders to his men and watched as the cell door was unlocked.

Quickly, without resistance, the bound and hooded prisoners were hustled back up the steps, stumbling as they went. Leaving the three lesser captives under guard in the anteroom, Bartholeme conducted the one he knew was Zipporah into the main chamber, one hard hand clamped firm on her elbow. He could feel her trembling.

All eyes turned in their direction as the pair entered. Valentin resealed the room behind them. Without comment, Nogaret rose and came to meet them, signing for Bartholeme to pluck the hood from the prisoner's head. She flinched at the sudden glare, blinking round at her captors in bewilderment. She was round of face and body, of indeterminate middle years, with the dark eyes of her race and dark hair going gray, where it showed from beneath the goodwife's kerchief binding it. In her youth, Bartholeme thought, she might have been somewhat attractive.

"Look at me," Nogaret said, menace in the very mildness of his tone. "I am an officer of the king, and you may consider this a royal tribunal. Your reputation as a prophetess and an interpreter of oracles precedes you. Hence, you are here to give us a demonstration of your craft, so that we may determine whether or not you bear the taint of Satan upon your soul."

The woman drew herself up stiffly—she stood hardly as high as Nogaret's shoulder. Her bound hands still were trembling, but she did not flinch from his scrutiny.

"Pardon, my lord, but such matters are not within my control. I do not seek visions; they come to me of their own accord, or not at all."

"Then we shall take measures to assist you," Nogaret said briskly, with a curt nod toward Bartholeme. "Bring her to the table."

Hustling the woman forward, Bartholeme saw that preparations had been made in his absence. On a pall of ivory silk before Nogaret's own chair lay a large leather-bound Bible, several sheets of vellum, and writing implements. To the right of the book were set a brass goblet and a small flagon of wine. To the left, mounted in a brazen candlestick, a thick taper flickered and burned with a faintly cloying scent like spikenard mixed with opium.

Signaling Bartholeme to untie the woman's hands, Nogaret moved the book before him and opened it at a place marked by a slip of parchment.

"I am told that you can read and write the Hebrew tongue," he said in a matter-of-fact tone, not bothering to look at her. "I am going to read you a passage from scripture. I shall translate it from the Latin into French, and I require that you render the verses into the Hebrew tongue and set them down in your own script. See that you make no mistakes," he warned, "for I am as learned in these matters as any rabbi. You will speak the words as you write."

Her face had gone still and pale, and Bartholeme could feel the tension in her shoulders as he bore her down into the chair at the table.

"What purpose is this meant to serve, my lord?" she asked without expression.

"*My* purpose," came the icy reply. "Question my instructions again, and one of your sons loses an eye."

Zipporah flinched, but drew one of the vellum sheets in front of her and, with trembling hand, selected a quill from the assortment Bartholeme offered. When she had dipped it into a silver-mounted inkpot, Nogaret glanced at his text.

"The passage is from the twenty-third chapter of the second Book of Kings, relating how the king of Babylon took Jehoiachin prisoner and appropriated the treasures of the Temple of Jerusalem. I shall read a phrase at a time, and you shall write it in Hebrew. Do you understand?"

At her nod and murmur of assent, he began.

"And he carried out thence all the treasures of the house of the Lord. . . ."

"*Vayotsay . . . misham . . . es-col-otsros . . . bais Adonai. . . .*" She spoke the words as she wrote them down.

"And of the treasures of the king's house. . . ."

"*V'otsros . . . bais ha-melech . . . vay'katsaits. . . .*"

"And cut in pieces all the vessels of gold . . . which Solomon

King of Israel had made for the temple of the Lord . . . as the Lord had foretold. . . ."

Bartholeme watched over the woman's shoulder as she wrote out her translation with painstaking care, pausing now and again to select a word. Her hand trembled slightly, but the letters were well formed. Bartholeme had not thought that women received such training; certainly, Christian women did not. When she was finished, he handed the vellum wordlessly to his superior, who scanned the tremulous lines of Hebrew script.

"Nicely done," Nogaret said, though he scarcely glanced at his anxious captive. "Precisely what was required."

Smiling faintly, he set down the parchment and rummaged somewhat distractedly among the writing implements, selecting a little silver knife used for sharpening the quill pens. Then, before she could react, he seized her left hand and drew the blade smartly across the palm, holding her fast when she would have pulled away in pain and shock.

The hiss that accompanied his glare of warning made her freeze as he tipped the bleeding wound over the parchment she had just written, letting blood drip on the lettering until all the characters were obscured. Then, releasing her hand so that Bartholeme could bind a cloth around the wound, Nogaret plucked a hair from his own head and laid it across one of the larger splotches of blood. She gasped again as he held an edge of the bloodied vellum to the taper's flame until it caught.

His lips began to move as the parchment began to burn, and a choked sob rose in her throat, her fingers curled hard around the chair arms, as all of them silently watched the flame eat its way up the sheet toward the carefully penned lines—the men dispassionately, the woman fearfully. As the page crumbled and embers started to fall, Nogaret deftly held the burning parchment over the goblet to collect them. When the last fragment had turned to ash, he reached for the flagon of wine and poured some into the cup with a few more murmured words, swirling the cup until the ashes were suspended.

"Drink!" he ordered, presenting the cup to Zipporah.

Instinctively, she tried to shrink away, but Bartholeme's iron grip clamped down on her shoulders from behind and held her fast.

"I will not ask again," Nogaret said, again presenting the cup.

He had not raised his voice, but his tone was heavy with menace. Shuddering, Zipporah obeyed. When she would have lowered the cup after a single gulp, Bartholeme seized her by the scruff of the neck and locked his other hand over hers, holding the cup, forcing her to drain it.

The woman gasped and choked as she was forced to swallow, subsiding weakly as the cup was taken away. Over the next few minutes, as her breathing steadied, she began to look a little glassy-eyed, her pupils gradually contracting to mere pinpoints.

Watching without comment, Nogaret finally signaled Bartholeme with a jut of his chin. At once Bartholeme turned the woman's chair to face his superior, with a screech of wooden legs on stone, hard hands locking hers to the chair arms with an iron grip when she would have shrunk away—for Nogaret was taking up the ruby ring on its long gold chain, leaning close to press its stone against her forehead. She stiffened at its touch, her breathing coming shallower and faster.

"By the rubrics of Zosimos, *Princeps Artificorum*, I charge you to See what I have Seen," he commanded, as the others leaned nearer to hear what she might say. "Bring to light that which is hidden and speak with the tongue of truth!"

As a little cry escaped her, Zipporah's eyes rolled back in their sockets so that only the whites could be seen, and her lips and hands began to twitch. A bout of shivering seized her, and a grimace contorted her face. Then, abruptly, she went limp, with her head resting awkwardly against the back of her chair.

"Excellent," Nogaret breathed, drawing back slightly. "She is ready now."

A hectic flush had risen to his sallow cheeks, and he gazed at her avidly as he crouched down beside her chair, the ring now closed in his hand. Bartholeme moved round to support their victim from behind, heavy hands resting on her shoulders.

"I require answers to certain questions," Nogaret said sibilantly. "You will supply these answers truthfully or you will die—and all your family, make no mistake. Tell me, firstly, this: What is Jacob's Hallow?"

"A stone . . . a sacred stone," she whispered dazedly. "It is the pillow where the patriarch Jacob laid his head and dreamt of the ladder of angels."

The other members of the Decuria leaned closer, straining to catch the exchange, but uttered no sound.

"And where is Jacob's Hallow to be found?" Nogaret asked.

The woman hesitated, as if some inner part of her were resisting the compulsion to answer, but after a moment she whispered hoarsely, "It lies now in Scotland."

Surprised glances flew around the table.

"What foolery is this?" Baudoin growled. But Thibault de Montreville gestured for restraint.

"Perhaps no foolery. The Canmore kings of Scotland formerly had a stone for their coronation seat," he reminded them. "Some of the legends surrounding this so-called Stone of Destiny claim that it came originally from the Holy Land. Most legends have some basis in truth."

"But the Canmore dynasty ended with the Maid of Norway," said Valentin de Vesey. "And did not Edward of England seize all the royal relics of Scotland some ten years ago and remove them to London?"

"Apparently, not *this* relic," said a fair-haired younger man named Artus Beaumaris, thus far silent. He added, with a wry grimace, "To uninitiated eyes, one block of stone must look much the same as any other."

"You're suggesting that someone substituted a fake?" asked Peret Auvergnais, another who had not spoken hitherto.

"They must have done, if my lord Nogaret's vision is true," said Euraud Bassegard, seated at his left.

"Aye, and the issue of Scottish sovereignty is still far from settled," Thibault noted. "And if the Stone and Jacob's Hallow are one and the same, and the Stone is still in Scotland, that means that the Scots possess the ability to crown a true king—and perhaps to invest him with power on higher levels, power that might be of use to the Temple."

"A sobering and disturbing thought," Rodolphe agreed. "Such an alliance would not be useful to our cause." He paused a beat. "Will it be the Bruce whom they have crowned?"

"Who else?" Thibault retorted. "Earlier this year, he eliminated his closest rival, Red John Comyn—murdered him before the altar, they say. It could well be that he has taken to himself the crown of the Scots."

"Little would it mean, be he not enthroned upon the Stone," Rodolphe retorted. "But according to your vision . . ." he said to Nogaret.

"Aye, it is possible," Nogaret agreed. "Perhaps the Jewess can tell us." He turned to address his prisoner again. "Who is the man crowned on the Stone? Speak," he demanded, when she did not answer immediately.

"He is . . . successor to the Uncrowned King," came her halting response.

"The Uncrowned King?" Euraud repeated.

"Wallace," Nogaret supplied, under his breath. "And what is the name of this new king? Answer me, woman!"

Zipporah's brow furrowed in uncertainty, her closed eyelids flickering. "King . . . Hobbe . . ." she murmured at last.

"What kind of a name is that?" Valentin muttered.

"The only name we seem likely to get," Nogaret retorted. "But Hobbe . . . Bobby . . . Robert. . . . It's clear who she means. She cannot lie under this compulsion." Considering, he abandoned this line of inquiry and switched to a more direct line of questioning.

"Besides Jacob's Pillow, what other treasures of Israel are known to the Templars?"

"I—may not say," Zipporah managed to murmur, after an obvious internal struggle.

"On the contrary, you *must* say," Nogaret retorted. His pale eyes registered a glint of excitement—and challenge. "Name them!" he commanded.

The woman stiffened, her fingers curling like claws around the ends of the chair arms as her head slowly moved from side to side. Her lips moved, but no sound came out.

Rodolphe arched an eyebrow. "She may not be able to lie, but she's putting up a fight. . . ."

"And *that* is a mistake!" Nogaret muttered through tight lips.

Roughly he yanked the kerchief from Zipporah's head and caught her by the hair, again applying the ruby to her forehead. Its touch evoked a choked cry as the seeress tried to wrench herself away, but Bartholeme tightened his grip, and Nogaret held the stone ruthlessly in place.

"*What—other—treasures*—do the Templars have at their disposal?" the master demanded through clenched teeth. "The Ark of the Covenant, perhaps?"

"No!" Zipporah gasped.

"The horn of Joshua?"

"No. . . ." The answer trailed into a moan of anguish.

"The Breastplate of Aaron?"

Zipporah writhed in her chair, panting.

"Answer me!" Nogaret snarled, and gave the ring a twist.

A rending shriek of pain escaped the prisoner's lips, but it failed to move her listeners.

"The Templars have access to the Breastplate, don't they?" Nogaret persisted, unrelenting. "Who are its guardians, and where are they keeping it?"

Blue veins bulged at the woman's temples, and her jaws clamped shut, trapping her lower lip between her teeth. Blood welled down her chin. From somewhere at the back of her throat came an ugly strangling noise.

Instantly Nogaret ceased his ministrations with the ring and seized her by the jaw, trying to prise open her mouth.

"She's swallowed her tongue! Someone give me a knife!"

Bartholeme was already proffering the dagger from his belt, trying to hold her steady as Nogaret snatched it and attempted to force the blade between her clenched teeth. He succeeded in cutting her lips, but nothing more. As they struggled, Zipporah's contorted face grew increasingly livid, her heels drumming against the floor as violent convulsions racked her from head to foot. A final shudder died away, leaving her slumped suddenly limp beneath their hands.

Hurriedly, Bartholeme felt for a pulse in her neck, then shook his head. "She's dead," he said almost in disbelief.

With a grimace of disgust, Nogaret turned away from the body, tossing Bartholeme's dagger on the table with a clatter and wiping his hands against his thighs, a look of vindictive intensity passing across his pale face.

"Summon your men to remove *that*," he ordered Bartholeme, with a vague gesture in the direction of the dead woman. "Tell them to dispose of it—and the members of her family—so that no trace of them will ever be found."

Baudoin gazed after the soldiers as they carried the woman's body out of the room. "You might have stopped short of using killing force," he said sourly. "It's possible she could have told us more."

"What more is there to tell?" Peret Auvergnais countered. "The worst forebodings of Magister Nogaret's vision stand confirmed: The Templars have some hidden agenda in Scotland, almost certainly in opposition to ours. With ancient Hebrew artifacts at their command, they could well prove unstoppable."

"Not if we can find these treasures and appropriate them to our own use," Bartholeme said from the doorway.

Nogaret turned to survey the younger man with heavy-lidded interest, motioning him back to the table with a jerk of his chin.

"I quite agree," he said. "Do you see a role for yourself in achieving this objective?"

"I do—and not only to help redeem the treasures, but to settle an old debt."

"How so?" asked Rodolphe de Crevecoeur.

"I see a chance to prove myself worthy of the name I bear," Bartholeme replied. "Over a century ago, a distant kinsman of mine joined the Templar Order to spy on their activities and sow the seeds of destruction in their ranks. His name was Thierry de Challon. I would like to help finish the task he began."

"Admirable," Baudoin murmured, as several of the others also nodded agreement.

"Let me go to Scotland and confront the Templars there," Bartholeme continued. "It occurs to me that the English king perhaps has need of a physician, he being aged and ailing. I am not unacquainted with certain oriental medicines. And from the bosom of his court, and with the assistance of our patrons of shadow, I will undertake to find this Stone of Destiny and remove it from the game."

"Very well," Nogaret agreed. "I place the matter of Scotland in your hands. See that you do not fail.

"Meanwhile," he went on, picking up Bartholeme's dagger to fondle its blade, "I have another use for the Jewess's kindred. If they cannot provide us with access to their Hebrew treasures, their wealth may serve to ease the king's fi-

nancial embarrassment while we continue to work toward
our own goals.

"And one of those goals is the downfall of the Temple.
That may be closer than we think. The king is near to persuading the pope to summon the Grand Master from Cyprus,
ostensibly to launch a new crusade but also to discuss amalgamating the two military orders. The Master of the Hospital is otherwise engaged in Rhodes, and will not come, but
the Templars' Master has no such excuse. I am working on
a plan that will eliminate him and his troublesome Order,
and leave all the wealth of the Temple in our hands."

Chapter Three

May, 1306

IT TOOK A WEEK FOR BARTHOLEME TO ORGANIZE HIS departure for London, by way of Calais. He had expected the buzz of gossip at the Channel ports to be focused on the resurgent rebellion in Scotland, and preparations for King Edward's coming departure for the North—and, indeed, he gleaned a great deal of valuable intelligence pertaining thereto, especially once he arrived in Dover.

Of more immediate interest than the coming war, however, was news of a more domestic nature: that King Edward first planned to celebrate Pentecost at Westminster Palace, with a feast of unparalleled magnificence. This celebration would also honor the knighting of the king's son and heir, the Lord Edward of Caernarvon, together with almost three hundred young men of noble birth whose names thereafter would be added to the king's retinue.

Nor, according to a garrulous royal butler overseeing the unloading of fine wines at the port of Dover, was any expense being spared to mount this royal extravaganza.

"I tell you, it's going to be bigger than anything *I've* ever seen—and I served the king's father before him," the man said, as servants secured crates and barrels on a succession of carts. "When I ordered this lot, I thought it would be plenty—but then I saw the guests arriving as I rode down from London. There's just enough time to get another shipment in—and if you don't already have lodgings secured, you might just as well get back on the boat and return to France, for you'll find no bed here."

Upon hearing that Bartholeme had, indeed, made adequate domestic arrangements, the butler went on to elaborate on the formidable logistic requirements for accommodating so many guests. Food and drink of every kind was being requisitioned to garnish the tables in the king's banqueting hall. Cartloads of timber, paint, and canvas had been diverted from the shipyards to construct stages and backdrops for a parade of court pageants. Warehouses were being emptied to provide furs and fine fabrics for new robes of livery. Acrobats, jugglers, and musicians were being recruited in droves for the entertainment of the royal guests.

With the event but a week away, evidence of these preparations became increasingly apparent as Bartholeme rode into London at the head of his own modest retinue. He had been to London many times before, and knew it well, but he had never seen it so crowded. Riding past the Temple's complex near the Lud Gate, where he was told the buildings had been requisitioned to house many of the guests, Bartholeme saw that temporary tents and pavilions had even been erected in the gardens there—adequate lodging in May for the spillover from inside.

Bartholeme made his way through the bustling city streets to a handsomely appointed town house in the vicinity of Lincoln's Inn, its use secured for him by one of his most trusted agents. Dismounting in the stable yard, he surrendered his vicious Andalusian charger to a wary groom and briefly beat dust from his sleeves, then left his servants to unload the sumpter mules and baggage wagons while he proceeded indoors to inspect the accommodation.

The first member of the household to greet him was the

resident chief steward, who showed him to the principal apartments with uneasy deference.

"Yes, these rooms will serve," Bartholeme acknowledged coolly. He briefly drew aside a heavy drape to glance into the courtyard below, where a particular trunk banded with iron was being unloaded from one of the sumpter mules. "Where is my servant, Mercurius?"

The steward's placid face did not change expression, but a gleam of resentment flickered in his hollow eyes.

"I believe Master Mercurius is supervising the installation of new wall hangings in another of the guest chambers, my lord," he said stiffly. "Do you wish me to summon him?"

"Inform him of my arrival," Bartholeme replied, "and bid him attend me when he has finished. In the meantime, fetch me some wine and see that a hot bath is prepared for me. I do not propose sitting down to dine with the dust of these English roads still reeking in my nostrils."

The steward departed with a bow. Wine came at once, followed shortly by a brief flurry of activity as members of Bartholeme's traveling retinue transferred his personal baggage upstairs. Among the items deposited in his sitting room was the trunk he had looked for in the yard below, but he waited until the porters had left before opening it to remove a small, brass-bound medicine chest.

This he set on the counterpane of the canopied bed, unlocking it with a small key from around his neck. Opening it, he quickly examined its contents: diverse vials and philtre bottles, each carefully labeled with an alchemical glyph, all organized within the cushioned niches of a cunning array of compartments. False panels concealed several more compartments, and their contents the Frenchman also inspected, satisfying himself that everything was in order before relocking the chest. This he stowed next to the bed, within reach of his hand, just as a knock at the door heralded the entrance of an outlandish figure scarcely taller than a six-year-old child.

Hunchbacked and grotesque, the newcomer was garishly arrayed in parti-colored silks of peacock splendor—turquoise and vibrant rose and poison-green; his stubby legs were clad in silken hose of sapphire blue. A shock of coarse orange hair made a bristling frame around a lumpy face like the mask of a malignant goblin, though the eyes were of extraordinary beauty: a pure, crystalline blue fringed with lush, dark lashes. Bartholeme greeted this apparition with a raised eyebrow and a sardonic grin.

"My compliments on your powers of transformation, Mercurius. You have managed to render this house tolerably habitable."

"The work is not yet complete, Master," Mercurius demurred in a reedy voice. "These English servants are sullen and inept. If we were at home, I would have them all beaten and then dismissed."

"You have borne a great deal in my service," Bartholeme said. "One day, that debt will be repaid in full. Meanwhile, I bring you a small token of my gratitude."

From an inner pocket of his tunic he drew out a disk-shaped gold medallion the size of a walnut, trailing a spill of heavy chain like molten gold. The engravings on the disk were nearly worn smooth with age and polishing, but the gold glowed pure in the light from the room's one window. This Bartholeme dangled before the dwarf's bright blue gaze.

"Unless I am much mistaken," he drawled, "this is an heirloom you have been coveting for quite some time."

Mercurius gaped in recognition, the goblin face contorting in what passed for a grin of delight.

"The Crusader Besant!" he croaked excitedly. "Saint Louis bestowed it on the founder of my family, after the storming of Damietta! But, how did you get this away from my brother?"

Bartholeme let the medallion and its chain fall into the

dwarf's greedy hands, smiling thinly as the little manikin caressed it and devoured it with his gaze.

"I bribed a servant to leave me alone with his corpse on the night before his burial."

"Etienne is dead? How did he die?" Mercurius demanded eagerly.

"He contracted a sudden fever of the blood," Bartholeme said in a voice devoid of expression. "It caused his heart to swell until it burst. I am told he died screaming in agony. Regrettably, that agony was all too brief."

Breaking briefly into a spontaneous jig step, Mercurius gave a cackle of malignant glee.

"Hee-hee! So much for his fair face and his tall, straight limbs!" he crowed. "The Devil take him—and my father's soul likewise, for casting me aside to set my brother in my place!"

"All that was theirs shall be yours," Bartholeme promised, "on the day that the Stone of Destiny comes into the hands of the Brotherhood of Ten."

"The Stone of Destiny?" Mercurius hardly batted an eye. "Do we steal it from the Abbey, Master?"

"No, we find its hiding place in Scotland and use its power to defeat the man who now calls himself King of Scots," Bartholeme replied.

The identity of that man was as the Decuria had surmised. In the fortnight since their meeting, the name of Robert Bruce of Annandale had become the focus of a storm of debate and speculation throughout the courts of Europe, as news of his crowning at Scone became known. Briefly Bartholeme reviewed for his servant some—though not all—of what he had learned.

Mercurius screwed up his face. "But, if the Stone is in Scotland, Master, then why are we here in London?"

"Because we need allies," Bartholeme answered, "preferably unwitting ones. We are not the only ones interested in this artifact. Certain highly placed Knights of the Temple have already secretly attached themselves to Bruce's cause. It is probable that they were instrumental in setting him on the throne, however unsteady that throne may be. If we are to stand any chance of snatching the Stone from under their noses, we are going to need an army to keep the Scottish rebels occupied. I propose borrowing King Edward's, since he stands to benefit from our labors."

"Borrowing Edward's army," Mercurius mused. "That will be quite a coup."

Bartholeme's faint smile was one of cunning rather than of pleasure.

"Tell me," he said, pausing to pour himself a measure of wine, "what is the state of the king's health at present?"

"Rumor has it that he has been somewhat ailing," Mercurius said promptly. "Some say it is an attack of spleen engendered by this latest Scottish uprising. Those who fear it might be something more serious confine their opinions to a whisper."

"But plans for the Pentecost Feast are still going ahead? Good," Bartholeme said, at the dwarf's nod. "That's all I need to hear. Tomorrow we shall go to Westminster Palace to seek a royal audience. As delegates of the King of France, we are assured of a prompt reception. And I have a gift for King Edward that cannot fail to win me the royal favor."

"A gift, Master?" Mercurius said eagerly. "What kind of a gift?"

"It comes in two parts," Bartholeme replied, pausing to sip at his wine. "The first is a book of . . . illuminations. A pretty thing—and one I daresay he has never seen the likes of, though I myself find its wrappings far more interesting. It will be your task to ensure that those wrappings disappear after the book is presented. Very shortly after that," Bartholeme went on, "King Edward will swiftly discover that he has an urgent need for my services."

* * *

The following morning, with the help of Mercurius, Bartholeme de Challon arrayed himself meticulously in a short coat of crimson silk over a close-fitting undertunic and breech hose of fine black wool. Over this he donned a sumptuous mantle of crimson velvet trimmed with sable. Shoes of soft black chamois, gloves of crimson-dyed doeskin, and a cap of quilted black velvet completed his court dress. Adorning the cap was a brooch of nine rubies set around a larger one in the center, securing a fanned cockade of black swan feathers.

"Eminently suitable, Master," Mercurius commented, after adjusting a fold of the crimson cloak. "We cannot fail to attract admiring glances." His own garments had been fashioned to match, though his cap was plain.

"Which is the point of the exercise," Bartholeme replied. He tugged critically at a gauntlet-cuff as Mercurius angled a looking glass before him. "It is well-known that the Prince of Wales, unlike his father, has a taste for eccentric conceits of fashion. It will do us no harm to pique his interest now, in the event that he ascends to the throne before our work here is done. Yes, this will do nicely."

The illuminated book had been placed in a richly gilded box specially constructed to hold it. Consigning the box to the dwarf's care, Bartholeme unlocked his medicine chest and plucked out a twisted bit of parchment, which he secreted in a pouch at his waist.

"I believe that concludes our preparations," he observed to Mercurius, when he had locked the chest again. "Now it's time we were off to Westminster."

It was customary for the English king to hold court in the lavishly decorated hall known as the Painted Chamber. In preparation for the coming feast, however, the Painted Chamber had been turned over to an invading host of carpenters, drapers, and scene-painters, so King Edward was holding court instead in one of the lesser halls.

Bartholeme sent a liveried manservant on ahead to announce his coming. Consequently, when he and Mercurius arrived, they received the preferential distinction of being ushered into the royal presence after only the briefest of delays.

As they approached across the expanse of polished floor, Bartholeme took the opportunity to study the man seated on the dais at the end of the room, coolly noting the ravages that age and ill health had inflicted on the English monarch's once robust frame. Now sixty-eight years old, Edward Plantagenet was gaunt and sallow, his thin lips drawn tight over yellowing teeth. The sunken cheeks were bracketed with lines, but time had not quenched the cold, acquisitive gleam in the depths of the brooding eyes.

By contrast, Edward's queen was young and fresh: Margaret of France, the half sister of Philip IV and Edward's second wife, a plump blond woman with the pouting lips and protuberant blue eyes of her Capetian forebears. Behind and around them were ranged various courtiers and ladies-in-waiting, all of them richly garbed.

Doffing his cap with a flourish—which also showed off the cockade of black swan feathers—Bartholeme made a sweeping bow before addressing the royal pair.

"My lord, I bring you greetings from my royal master, Philip of France—and to you, madame, I bring the loving affection of your good brother. He trusts that both of you are in good health and spirits, and wishes me to convey his felicitations in honor of this season of Pentecost. By the same token, he offers congratulations on the fair prospects of the Lord Edward. May the achievement of his knighthood be auspicious for the whole kingdom."

"The knighting of my son," the king said, "signifies his coming of age." His tone was one of bitter rancor. "He will prove himself my worthy successor when he has crushed the rebels of Scotland under his heel and brought Robert Bruce before me in chains."

"When that time comes," Bartholeme responded smoothly, "all your friends and loyal subjects will rejoice. Until then, I pray you to accept this modest gift to lighten the days until your final victory."

Taking his cue, Mercurius stepped forward to present the ornamented book box with a flourishing obeisance. The calculated clumsiness of his performance elicited titters of laughter from the queen and her ladies, and grim amusement plucked at the king's mouth as well. Beckoning the dwarf closer, Edward leaned down and took the box from Mercurius's stumpy fingers.

"Knowing that you soon will be setting out to war, Sire," said Bartholeme, "it seemed appropriate to present you with a copy of the books of the Maccabees. I have always found that they speak eloquently of the honor to be won in an honorable cause."

Edward's grizzled brows lifted as he opened the box, itself a work of art, and folded back the silken wrappings in which the book nested. When Mercurius had helped him remove the book, the king turned a few pages at random, his lip curling within his beard. No one noticed the dwarf wad up the wrappings with gloved fingers and tuck them into a hidden pocket in one trailing sleeve.

"This is a fair gift," Edward acknowledged, turning another page to admire the color and gold leaf adorning an illuminated capital. "I accept it with pleasure, and send thanks to your master. I, too, admire the heroic exploits of these ancient Hebrew kings. This will remind me of the virtues of warfare when I am far from my own halls." His gaze shifted back to Mercurius as he closed the book, a thumb caressing its cover. "And is this manikin of yours also part of the gift, Lord Bartholeme?"

"If you wish it, Sire," the Frenchman said lightly. "But perhaps you might find my own services more useful."

"Indeed?" said the king. "In what way?"

"My poor Mercurius is nothing but a jester," came Bartholeme's response. "I, on the other hand, am a knight well schooled in the arts of war. Though I have fought in many engagements, no opponent has ever bested me, either on the tilting ground or the battlefield. If you have any use for a seasoned warrior, I would esteem it an honor to place my sword at your service."

"Indeed," Edward said, looking vaguely uncomfortable as he shifted slightly in his chair. "And why should you, a subject of France, wish to hazard your life on behalf of the English crown?"

Bartholeme shrugged elegantly. "When a nation rebels against its rightful overlord, as the people of Scotland have done, it is an offense against all other sovereign monarchies."

He might have said more, but at that moment an expression of extreme discomfort came across the king's face, and he caught his breath with a gasp. As an involuntary grunt of pain burst from his lips, his face went suddenly ashen, and he doubled over in his chair. The queen bounded up with a gasp of alarm, and cries rang out across the hall.

"The king has been taken ill!"

"Call his physician!"

Edward shuddered and groaned aloud. As the book slid from his lap, Mercurius caught it in gloved hands and returned it to its box, glancing back at Bartholeme in feigned dismay. As courtiers fluttered about the throne, the king slumped lower in his chair, gasping now and trying unsuccessfully to stifle another moan, both fists pressed hard against his lower abdomen.

"Help him!" the queen cried, wringing her hands. "Someone, please, help him!"

Calmly Bartholeme shouldered his way to the fore, easing next to the queen, whose anxious glance registered vague recognition as he addressed her softly and urgently in Norman French.

"Madame, I have seen attacks of this kind among Crusaders in the Holy Land. If these spasms grow worse, the king could suffer a fatal rupture of the bowels. I have a medicinal powder about me which will relax the gut—I use it myself—but you must give me leave to administer it."

A fresh paroxysm wrenched a hollow cry from the king's lips, to the dismay of his servants. Slowly, despite their attempts to ease his pain, he slid out of his chair and curled in on himself, still clenching his abdomen as he was lowered to the floor. His face was contorted in a grimace, his eyes screwed shut, his skin cold and clammy. Margaret of France hesitated no longer.

"Help him!" she begged in a tight voice.

Instantly Bartholeme rounded on the other courtiers pressing in from all sides.

"Stand back, all of you!" he ordered. "And you," he added to Mercurius, "fetch some wine—quickly!"

The dwarf disappeared, returning within seconds with a brimming goblet, half of which his master instantly dashed onto the floor.

Meanwhile, Bartholeme had retrieved the twist of parchment from his pouch. Deftly, after handing the goblet back to the dwarf, he made a show of opening the twist and spilling its contents into the cup. It would, of course, counteract the drug impregnating the wrappings of the book.

"We must give him this immediately," he informed the queen, swirling the contents of the cup to dissolve the powder. "Have them sit him up, so he can drink it."

At a signal from their royal mistress, two gentlemen of the court hastened to haul the stricken king vaguely upright, though he still was clawing at his gut. Kneeling beside his patient, as all watched anxiously, Bartholeme bade Mercurius hold the king's head while he tipped a small measure of the potion between the stricken man's bluish lips and stroked the wattled throat to induce him to swallow, repeating the procedure several times until the goblet was drained.

Setting it aside, he then took the king's hand in his and gently chafed its back, watching.

The change, when it came, was dramatic. Within only a few minutes, an almost beatific look of relief stole over Edward's taut features and his breathing began to ease, the tension starting to drain away. As Bartholeme watched the color return to the king's face, he released the royal hand and bade Mercurius withdraw. A moment later, Edward roused to his senses with a sigh, eyelids fluttering.

"It is almost like a miracle!" the queen murmured.

The king's gaze was feverishly bright—that intense Plantagenet blue—but he appeared otherwise in command of himself as he allowed his courtiers to assist him fully upright and then back to his chair, beckoning Bartholeme to approach.

"I owe you a debt of gratitude," he said a little thickly. "What was the medicine you gave me?"

"An opiate powder made by the Arabs," Bartholeme answered. "I would be happy to instruct your own physician as to where he can obtain the necessary ingredients. I myself sometimes suffer from the same malady, which is why I carry the remedy always with me."

Smiling, Edward held out his hand to Bartholeme in thanks, his overly brilliant gaze gravitating to the Frenchman's signet ring as their hands clasped.

"An interesting ring, my lord," he observed. "I do not believe I have seen that insignia before."

"It is the *Cygnus Hermetis,* the black swan," Bartholeme said casually. "Among scholars of alchemy, the *cygnus* or swan denotes the triumphant culmination of the alchemical work. In heraldic terms, it is a symbol of victory. Perhaps," he added, "that is why the men of my family have always been fortunate in battle."

"A black swan . . ." the king repeated. He paused for thought, then asked abruptly, "You will attend our Pentecost revels?"

"With the greatest of pleasure, Sire."

"Good," Edward said. "Your coming here today was assuredly fortuitous. Perhaps my son and I should adopt your bird of good omen. With this insignia as our rallying sign, perhaps this time our armies will secure a final lasting victory."

"I cannot answer for that, Sire," Bartholeme said smoothly, "but you may be assured that I am your good servant to command."

Chapter Four

May, 1306

TWO DAYS LATER, A GIFT ARRIVED FOR BARTHOLEME FROM King Edward: a rich robe of wine-red velvet, enriched with embroidery of gold bullion and silk and lavishly trimmed with ermine. Mercurius tested the quality of the fabric with knowledgeable fingers, a malicious grin creasing the goblin face as he turned to his master.

"My lord would seem to have won high favor with the English king," he remarked.

Bartholeme smiled faintly. "Indeed. Pandering to a king's self-interest has long been an effective way to secure advancement." He paused. "But he has not yet taken me to his service." He considered briefly, then got to his feet. "We must visit the palace straightaway, to thank the king for his princely gift."

Bartholeme wore the robe for his audience. Afterward, he was invited to attend the king on a private walk around the gardens.

"Tell me, my lord, how much longer do you propose to remain in England?" Edward asked.

"That depends entirely on Your Majesty's good pleasure."

"Then I hope you will bide a while yet," said the king,

"for it would please me to see you a frequent visitor amongst us. And you will join us, I hope, at the festivities in honor of my son's coming of age. . . ."

"That would please me as well, Sire," Bartholeme replied, with a courtly bow—though he still had not yet been offered the position he sought.

In the several days remaining before the Feast of Pentecost, Bartholeme deftly insinuated himself among the other courtiers who gathered daily in the halls of Westminster, his dwarf always at his side and dressed like his master. It soon became clear to the pair of them that there existed three separate factions at King Edward's court.

The first group comprised the king's personal advisors, mostly senior knights of baronial or comital rank: mature, clear-thinking men of proven loyalty whose versatile capabilities had earned them their places in the king's esteem. Shrewd statesmen and able administrators, these household officials formed the core of Edward's government. To them fell the practical burden of keeping the country in order.

"These men are dedicated to upholding their king's interests—as, indeed, they should be," Bartholeme observed to Mercurius. "But we shan't find any allies amongst their ranks."

The second faction revolved not around the king, but around the Prince of Wales: a coterie of young noblemen as arrogant and frivolous as the prince himself. Handsome, pleasure-seeking, and self-indulgent, the members of this faction devoted their days to hunting, hawking, and other forms of courtly entertainment. Their nights were often spent in debauchery.

"Popinjays," Mercurius muttered contemptuously under his breath, as he and Bartholeme observed one night from a minstrel gallery. "But could not some of them perhaps be turned to serve your purposes, my lord?"

"Easily," said Bartholeme, "but what would be the point? Not one of them has any true mettle. Such creatures make poor tools." He gave a snort of contempt as his eye roved the hall below them.

"The Lord Edward himself is more like a play actor than a prince," he went on. "He revels in all the stage trappings of royalty—the wealth, the pomp and circumstance—but conceives little of the burdens of kingship. With no head for strategy and no stomach for hardship, he will make a poor substitute for his father when the time comes for him to take the throne. But by then, I hope to have the situation in Scotland well in hand."

The dwarf cocked an eyebrow at his master. "Then you have found some suitable allies?"

Bartholeme nodded. "Aye, indeed. Among the exiles and adventurers hovering about the English throne are a number of dispossessed Scots—men who have pledged service to Edward in the hope of regaining their lost lands and honors. Unless I am much mistaken, we should have our pick of candidates vying for the pleasure of knocking Bruce off his precarious throne. And *we* will be free to deal with the Templars."

The Feast of Pentecost arrived at last, its celebrations to begin with Mass and the knighting of the Prince of Wales and nearly three hundred other young nobles of the realm in the chapel at Westminster. That alone would have been cause for note, since so large a knighting had never taken place in England, but the banquet that followed would be talked about for generations.

By mid-afternoon, the day's more solemn tasks having been concluded, invited guests had begun to gather outside the Painted Chamber of Westminster. The halls of the palace resounded with gay laughter and the music of pipes and timbrels. Tapers and torches cast a dancing golden glow over the revelers, who were decked out for the occasion in a riot of silks, furs, and fine jewels.

When it came time for the feast itself to begin, the doors to the Painted Chamber were flung open to admit the guests.

The tables had been arranged to leave an island of open
space in the middle of the floor for the performance of various entertainments. Bartholeme arrived in his court attire,
and was shown to a place at the king's own table, among the
great officers of state and the highest lords in the land. Ignoring the haughty glances directed his way, he settled himself comfortably with Mercurius behind his chair and waited
for the king to appear.

A flourish of trumpets heralded the entrance of Edward
and his queen, with the newly knighted Prince of Wales following in close attendance. All present rose as royal heralds
escorted the king and his family to canopied chairs at the
center of the table. At a nod from Edward, the Archbishop of
Canterbury offered up a prayer of grace and thanksgiving,
after which a second trumpet flourish announced the formal
commencement of the meal.

A small army of pages and servants dispersed through the
great hall, bearing laden trays and steaming platters. In the
course of the next few hours, Edward and his guests dined
on a sumptuous array of rich and exotic dishes: geese stuffed
with quail, lampreys stewed with oysters, and larks baked in
honey, in addition to more commonplace staples such as
roast beef and venison and succulent spring lamb.

While they ate, the guests were regaled with a succession
of pageants presented by members of some of London's
prominent trade guilds, drawing their inspiration both from
biblical sources and chivalric romance. Between one pre-
sentation and the next, while scenes and drops were being
shifted, the performance area became the stage for jugglers,
tumblers, dancers, and puppeteers. And throughout it all,
music floated down from the galleries above, mingling the
music of flute and recorder with the pulsing beat of tabor
and tambourine and the silvery, broken sound of the psaltery
and the harp.

As the meal gradually drew to a close—though drinking
would continue far into the night—servants returned in

droves to carry away the leftovers and trenchers of bread to be distributed among the poor. Shortly, the Archbishop of Canterbury rose to deliver a somewhat ponderous discourse on the virtues and obligations of knighthood. Somewhat to Bartholeme's surprise, the Prince of Wales seemed to be making a sincere effort to attend to the speeches being made in his honor. Following the last of the exhortations, the master of the king's revels struck the floor of the hall three times with his rod of office.

An expectant silence fell as a procession of footmen entered from the wings, clad in livery of black velvet quartered with cloth of gold and ushered by heralds wearing tabards of King Edward's arms. The footmen carried on their shoulders a silk-draped bier on which reposed a pair of life-size swans sculpted from ebony, each sinuous neck engorged of a golden and jewel-studded crown, the beaks fashioned of gold and the eyes set with bright-flashing rubies. The sight caused Bartholeme to sit forward with keen interest, for the statues clearly had been fashioned in the likeness of the *Cygnus Hermetis* that adorned his signet ring.

These the footmen bore to the royal dais, where the heralds placed the ebony swans on the table before King Edward's high seat, within easy reach of his hand. The king looked very tired after his long day, but got to his feet when the footmen had withdrawn and turned toward Bartholeme, singling him out with a sweep of a beringed hand.

"My lords," he said in a voice that had lost none of its power, "we commend to your esteem the Sieur Bartholeme de Challon, of the court of King Philip of France. Since his arrival, Lord Bartholeme has done us great service through the offices of healing. He professes to have learned this wisdom through the arts of alchemy—the symbol of which you see before you, manifested in these swans. Therefore, in salute to Lord Bartholeme, we take to ourself these swans as a sign of lasting triumph against all caitiff enemies of our crown!"

Laying his gnarled hands shakily on the heads of the twin swans, he continued.

"Hear me, and bear witness!" he declared. "By the God of Heaven and these swans, I hereby swear that I will take no rest until the Lord has given me victory over the crowned traitor Robert Bruce and the perjured nation of Scotland! I further swear that, when the traitor has been dealt with, I shall again make crusade to the Holy Land, so help me God!"

This oath provoked an outbreak of cheering and cries of affirmation and support, such that the Prince of Wales likewise was moved to come forward and lay hands on the swans, affirming his father's oath and swearing never to rest two nights in the same place until he reached Scotland.

"Hear, hear!" came the shouted affirmations.

"By the swans we swear!" cried an anonymous voice from somewhere in the hall, followed by like cries of, "Death to King Hob!" and "Damnation to all who follow him!"

As other voices took up the cry, the hall resonated to a noise like thunder as men stamped their feet and pounded on the tables and cheered, many others crowding forward to lay hands on the swans and add their affirmation. Only when the cheering at last subsided did Bartholeme rise to stand silently at his seat, his action stilling the commotion.

"Sire," he said, with a slight bow from where he stood, "while this occasion is still upon us, I beg leave to ask a boon of you."

King Edward was still standing behind the swans, his face waxen with fatigue, but the gaze he directed toward Bartholeme was gimlet-sharp, and his reply fell into utter silence.

"You have my ear, my lord," he said.

Swift-moving as a hunting cat, Bartholeme approached the royal dais to lay his hands on the heads of the two swans between them.

"My request, Sire, is this," he proclaimed in a voice that all could hear. "I ask that you accept my service, as you have accepted the services of these many new knights of your household. Give me leave to accompany you when you take to the field against King Hob, and I pledge to harry your foes to the brink of death and beyond!"

This declaration brought a gaunt smile to the king's lips and a pounding of hands and cups on the tables as Edward's men registered their approval, though Bartholeme knew they had no idea how literally he had meant his pledge. Their acclamation died away as the king lifted a hand for silence.

"There is no boon you could ask, Lord Bartholeme, that I would more willingly grant than this," King Edward declared. "If you can swear to me that you are free of all prior obligations, then I shall be pleased to accept the offer of your sword."

"In all save loyalty to my own land and king, Sire, I do so swear," said Bartholeme. "Your enemies shall be my enemies."

Edward's smile broadened. "Then I decree that from this moment, you shall be counted among the knights of my personal household—and glad am I of your company!"

A faint smile of satisfaction curved at the Frenchman's lips as he bent to kiss the king's hand.

Following the events of Pentecost, the visiting families of the newly fledged knights gave up their lodgings and began dispersing to their homes, and the young knights themselves made ready to depart with the king and the Prince of Wales on the march north into Scotland. There they planned to rendezvous with the English forces already in the field, after which young Edward of Caernarvon would assume overall command of the English army on behalf of his father, whose health remained precarious.

Bartholeme de Challon also prepared to leave for Scotland, and on the eve of their departure invited two young Scots nobles to dine with him at his lodgings, both of them from families with a history of personal rivalry against the Bruces of Carrick. John Macdougall of Lorn was a first cousin to Bruce's late adversary, John Comyn, and considered himself honor-bound to avenge the death of his kinsman. Sir Alexander Abernethy still professed allegiance to the deposed John Balliol, and bitterly resented Bruce assuming the Scottish crown. Big, bullheaded, and ruddy, Abernethy arrived in a belligerent mood, barging ahead of Lorn as Mercurius admitted them and then retired.

"We have just come from having words with one of the prince's posturing companions," he growled, as Bartholeme directed both him and Lorn to seats in the snug before the fire. "That strutting popinjay had the audacity to throw the name of Toom Tabard in my face, claiming Scotland to be justly subject to England by nature no less than by law."

Bartholeme controlled a smile as he turned away to pour wine into two pewter cups. "Toom Tabard," or "empty coat," was the nickname derisively applied to John Balliol, after he had been publicly stripped of his kingly rank and regalia by King Edward. Ten years after Balliol's submission, the name still rankled among those who came from north of the border.

"I was minded to crack his empty head for him," Abernethy continued in the same resentful rumble, "but Lorn here would have none of it."

"Aye, and lucky for you that I dragged you off," Lorn retorted, "for yon lady-faced prickasour was none other than Piers Gaveston, the Lord Edward's favorite."

At this Bartholeme intervened, passing filled cups to both men.

"Gaveston is nothing more than an empty codpiece," he said dismissively. "You might as well take offense at a bitch breaking wind under the table as give ear to a word he says.

You won't win back your lands by thrashing lapdogs. Save the strength of your arm for taking on Bruce."

Abernethy's brow darkened at this mention of their adversary.

"Bruce!" His tone laced the name with contempt. "Aye, the sooner we march north, the better. And when we get there, we'll see who does the lion's share of the thrashing— the likes of us, or the Lord Edward and his parcel of dandies."

"I would not dismiss the prince out of hand," Bartholeme said. "He will be your next king, and he *has* won his share of tournaments."

"True," said Lorn, "but he's nae the general his father is. Someone ought to warn him that real battles are nae fought by the rules of chivalry."

"Especially not when you're dealing with a back-stabbing traitor like Robert Bruce," Abernethy grumbled.

"Like him or not, Bruce will not be easily beaten," Bartholeme pointed out. "To get the better of him, you may be forced to fight fire with fire."

"And what is that supposed to mean?" Lorn asked.

Bartholeme affected a look of surprise. "You *are* aware, are you not, that Bruce has been receiving assistance from the Order of the Temple?"

"We've heard reports of Templars being seen in Bruce's camp," Lorn said cautiously. "We understood that they were acting merely as observers."

"Doubtless that's what they'd like the rest of the world to believe," Bartholeme said. "But let me assure you that the Templars' interest in Scottish affairs is far from impartial."

He paused to replenish their cups before continuing, relishing their looks of question as he took up his own.

"Since the loss of Acre, all the military orders have been forced to redirect their activities," he said, after taking a sip. "The Teutonic Knights have found a new theater of operations in the Baltic. The Knights of the Hospital are poised for action against the pagans and heretics on the fringes of the Byzantine Empire. For the Templars to launch a new crusade against the Saracens to the south would be rankest folly. With their rivals already on the move toward the north and east, where else are they to go, but west?"

Lorn's brow darkened. "Are you suggesting that the Templars want to make a new home for themselves in Scotland?"

Bartholeme nodded. "And to ensure that they find welcome, they are said to be placing the Order's resources at Bruce's disposal. *All* the resources," he added with emphasis.

"Stop hinting and make yourself clear," Abernethy snapped impatiently.

Bartholeme lowered his voice to a conspiratorial whisper. "You have probably heard rumors condemning the Templars as sorcerers and heretics?" He nodded in echo of their startled nods. "I very much fear that those rumors are not without foundation. Through trafficking with the Jews and the Muslims, they have gained access to powers above and beyond the realms of nature. If Bruce has consented to become their puppet, they will use these powers to defeat King Edward and secure their own interests."

Lorn and Abernethy exchanged glances, and the latter set down his cup.

"If what you say is true, what can we do to stop them?"

Bartholeme smiled coldly. "I have crossed swords with the Templars myself before now, and I tell you that the only way to combat Templar sorcery is by invoking supernatural forces hostile to those at their command. I can teach you how to harness such powers . . . but I do have my price."

"Name it," Lorn said coldly.

"I want something which the rebels have in their possession," Bartholeme replied. "I want the Stone of Destiny."

"You're too late," Abernethy said. "King Edward has already taken it."

"Perhaps you are not aware that the stone at Westminster is a fake," Bartholeme said carefully, "and not a very good one at that. Let the king keep his trumpery trophy. When we have disposed of Bruce, I claim the real Stone as my reward."

"What is the Stone to you?" Lorn demanded.

Bartholeme took a sip of wine and lounged back in his chair. "What do you know of the science of alchemy?"

His two listeners exchanged nervous glances, but their uncertainty was laced with respect.

"I have heard," said Lorn, "that those who practice it seek a secret knowledge by which lead may be changed into gold."

"That tale embodies only as much of the truth as the vulgar mind can understand," Bartholeme said. "There are always pretenders, of course, willing to cheat the credulous, but true alchemy is deeply rooted in mysteries older than Christianity. And the transformation of base metals is only a trifling expression of a far greater power."

Abernethy looked somewhat skeptical, but Lorn leaned forward with narrowed eyes.

"Nothing in the world exists," Bartholeme continued, "without some flaw or weakness which contributes to its destruction. The Church would have us believe that disease, infirmity, and death are the consequences of Original Sin. The prelates preach that Man's only recourse is to seek salvation from God, who alone has the power to confer eternal life. But I tell you now that, for those daring enough to seek immortality on their own terms, alchemy offers another way."

"How?" Abernethy asked.

"By means of the philosophers' stone," Bartholeme said, "which causes all things in nature to conform to their ideal of perfection. The physically whole and perfect man is a man immune to the ravages of mortality. That is what makes the philosophers' stone the ultimate object of the alchemist's quest—and that is what the Stone of Destiny is: a philosophers' stone, a *lapis philosophorum*."

Both the Scottish lords looked startled. It was Abernethy who first found his tongue.

"What makes you so sure of that?" he asked.

"I belong to an alchemical brotherhood who have made the Stone an object of lifelong study," Bartholeme replied. "In some ancient traditions, the philosophers' stone has another name: the *lapis exillis caelis*—the Stone Fallen from Heaven. We have reason to believe that the Stone of Destiny and the *lapis exillis* are one and the same." He paused a beat. "Shall I go on?"

Abernethy seemed to have trouble swallowing, but Lorn was slowly nodding.

Bartholeme inclined his head with a faint smile.

"The Judaic scholar Flegetanis first established the connection whilst deciphering a stone tablet from the Arabian Desert. The inscriptions belonged to a lost codicil to the Book of Genesis, concerning the war in Heaven. According to this codicil, Lucifer himself tore one of the foundation stones from the throne of God and cast it to earth as a gift to mankind. Since then, all those who would become initiates in the mysteries of alchemy take Lucifer as their patron. His name, of course, means Light-Bearer, though it is not the light spoken of by Christians."

He eyed his two guests expectantly, waiting in the breathless silence. Finally, Lorn spoke, clearing his throat and then choosing his words with care.

"You do not frighten me, Lord Bartholeme. Many folk of my blood have been at war with Christianity since the time of Columba. I owe no allegiance to any God who demands that a man must bow the knee in abject servility to those who have done him injury. Nor do I turn the other cheek."

"Nor I!" Abernethy agreed.

"Then you have nothing to lose by embracing the mysteries of alchemy," Bartholeme said. "And there is a very great deal to gain. If you are willing, I can begin your instruction this very night."

Lorn and Abernethy traded somewhat wary glances, then looked again at Bartholeme. "How?" Lorn demanded.

Smiling thinly, Bartholeme produced from beneath his sleeve a stiletto, its hilt curiously wrought in the form of a bird. The eye was set with a cabochon ruby, and the thin, serpentine tail disappeared into the weapon's narrow blade, the tip of which he set against the finger that wore the black swan signet, applying increasing pressure.

"Do you find it disturbing—the thought of binding a pact with blood?" he whispered.

In that instant the blade punctured his fingertip, blood suddenly welling up like a garnet-glittering jewel, in echo of the bird's eye. Both Scots flinched, tight-jawed as Bartholeme calmly held his wounded finger over the remaining wine in his cup, squeezing out several drops.

"Know that blood is the essence of life," he told them, "the *via sanguinis,* by which power is conveyed."

It was also, though he did not say it, the offering by which to appease the demon he lately had installed in the ring he now pulled from his finger and deposited in the cup with a murmured cantrip. It was a lesser demon than the one that served Nogaret, but like most demons, it demanded oblations of blood in exchange for favors granted. Sometimes a mere taste was sufficient; payment for greater favors required a greater contribution. And for large favors, only a sacrifice of life-blood would suffice—if not a surrogate, either animal or human, then sometimes the alchemist himself.

"You dare much," Lorn said, as Bartholeme laid the dagger beside the cup and wiped his wounded finger on a clean cloth.

"I seek a rich prize," Bartholeme countered. "Will you dare as much?"

Without speaking, Lorn picked up the blade and deftly

pricked his own fingertip, adding his blood to the cup. Abernethy followed suit, if with somewhat less enthusiasm. When he had done so, Bartholeme took up the cup, briefly swirled the contents, the while forming his magical intent in his mind, then lifted it to his lips, glancing pointedly at each of his companions before drinking deeply.

"Now, finish it between you," he said, pushing it between them on the table.

Lorn's hand was steady as he also drank, but Abernethy looked nervous, and passed the back of his hand across his mouth when he had handed the empty cup back to the Frenchman. Bartholeme was smiling faintly as he retrieved his ring.

"Now are we bound to one another in the sight of Lucifer, the Light-Bearer," he informed his new recruits, as he wiped the ring on the blood-spotted cloth—which he would keep, for their blood gave him power over them, if needed. Their blood also bound them to the demon, which might prove even more useful.

"On the day when we cast down the warriors of God," he went on, "you shall share in the rewards that alchemy can bestow."

Chapter Five

May, 1306

THE NEAREST PORT FROM WHICH ARNAULT DE SAINT CLAIR might take ship for France was the town of Berwick-on-Tweed, situated astride the border that separated Scotland and England, and long in dispute. Early in the summer of 1306, once again occupied by the English, it was the staging area for yet another war taking shape between the two kingdoms, being both the mustering point for the Earl of Pembroke's invasion force and its main provisioning depot.

Arnault had traveled there by way of Balantrodoch, the Order's main preceptory in Scotland. There he had parted company with Luc de Brabant and acquired the company of a staid and pious brother knight called Grigor Murray, who was charged with the duty to deliver revenues from some of the Order's Scottish properties to the Paris treasury. At Balantrodoch, Arnault also lingered long enough to obtain a travel permit from Frère Walter de Clifton, the Master of Scotland. The papers were intended to facilitate procurement of the English travel documents he and Brother Grigor would need to cross the Channel to France.

That was the theory, at any rate—and once arrived in Berwick, the pair did not hesitate to employ all the clout that usually accompanied Templar livery. Grigor even resorted to Templar arrogance, to no avail. With the streets of Berwick swarming with troops and the harbor teeming with ships, the town's resident English officials were too busy trying to keep order to deal speedily with a trifling matter of travel documents for a pair of neutral Templar observers. It took more than a week to obtain the necessary signatures and secure passage aboard a Flemish merchant ship bound for Dieppe.

They made port on the ninth of June—Saint Columba's day, it occurred to Arnault, as he and Grigor swung up on their hired horses and set out for Paris. He had hoped that was a good omen, but on the second day out, just south of Rouen, a heavy storm compelled them to take shelter for two nights at the Templar preceptory at Prunay. By the time the weather improved enough to venture forth, road conditions had become so atrocious that they abandoned all thought of continuing by horse and instead took passage aboard a river barge bound for the French capital.

The barge made periodic stops along the way to take on and unload cargo. Venturing ashore at one of these landing stages, in hope of something besides the scant and monotonous fare aboard ship, Arnault found the local inn abuzz with somewhat agitated-sounding converse, which subsided to furtive whispers as he entered. The tavern keeper minding the kegs behind a counter littered with tankards wore a look of surly irritation.

"If you mean to have a meal, first make sure you can afford it," the man warned, as he wiped at the counter with a filthy cloth. "You'll pay like everybody else!"

It was not a response to which Arnault was accustomed, when traveling openly as a Knight Templar, but he schooled his expression to one of benign surprise and produced a silver coin worth twice the cost of any meal likely to be available in such an establishment.

"Are your prices as high as that?" he said mildly.

The tavern keeper eyed the coin with distaste, but clunked a tankard in front of Arnault and turned to fetch an earthen jug of ale.

"You'll have been away for a while, then," he said as he filled the tankard. "That will cover the cost of your drink— just." He jutted his chin at the coin. "But if you want food, even a chunk of bread and cheese, it will cost you another of those."

"Indeed," Arnault said, producing another coin. "Prices do seem to have risen since I last traveled in this part of the world."

The tavern keeper gave a mirthless laugh and scooped both coins into a pouch at his waist, though his tone became more genial, now that he knew his patron had money. "Well, if you've come from abroad, sir—though by your accent, I take you for a Breton—my advice is to go back there. Around here, your money soon won't be worth anything— thanks to yesterday's royal decree."

Further converse revealed that King Philip was devaluing the currency of the realm to increase his revenues—not the first time he had tampered with the coinage to ease fiscal embarrassment in the royal treasury. Recent rumor had it that he was fretting increasingly about his indebtedness to the Jews, who were always a good target for resentment when finances got tight. Given that the Templars served as the king's bank and were among his principal creditors, even more than the Jews, Arnault found himself wondering uneasily what measures Philip might be considering to rid himself of these obligations.

Taking bread and cheese with him as well as information, Arnault rejoined Grigor and resumed his journey—and continued to pick up local gossip that suggested disturbing changes since his last trip back to France. By the time the barge passed the meeting of the Oise with the Seine, two days later, he had come to suspect that matters here were nearly as dire as in Scotland, if for different reasons.

He stood with Grigor in the bow of the barge when the Abbey of St. Denis at last hove into view, knowing that it marked nearly the end of their journey. The river was running high from the recent storm, and everywhere men could be seen laboring to repair damage to the dikes and embankments. Grigor had never been to Paris, and declared himself unimpressed, though he craned his neck to gaze upward as they passed before the spires of the abbey church.

"We ha' better in Scotland," he grumbled. "Ye should see th' cathedral in Elgin. Tha's where I was born. 'Tis sae fine, they call it the Lantern o' the North."

"I've seen it—and it *is* fine," Arnault conceded. "But this is also beautiful, I think."

Grigor considered, then shook his grizzled head. "Nah. Elgin is better."

Controlling a wry smile, Arnault decided that any further attempt to convert Grigor to an appreciation of French culture and artistry was likely to be so much wasted energy, regardless of the fact that St. Denis marked the focus of much of the sacred tradition of France. Made a royal mausoleum by the present king's grandfather, the saintly Louis IX, the venerable abbey church housed holy relics and effigies and tombs of past monarchs dating back to Carolingian times.

Perhaps its most precious relic was the sacred chrism kept in an ampulla shaped like a dove, said to have been delivered directly from heaven, without which no king of France might be validly anointed and crowned. But since Scottish kings had not yet won the right to be anointed at their coronation—a privilege that must be granted by the pope—Arnault supposed that Grigor had every reason not to be impressed by that distinction of St. Denis.

Nonetheless, he gazed up at its spires as they passed it by, considering its past, and found himself reflecting that every age had its battles to fight. Where the paladins of Charlemagne had waged war against ignorance and barbarism to lay the foundations of Christendom, their successors, the

Templars, were facing an equally hard battle to preserve that spiritual inheritance. It helped to put things into perspective, as he returned to his roots after his sojourn in Scotland.

Following two more bends of the river, their barge at last came within sight of the towers and bridges of Paris itself. Grigor merely scowled and hunched down in his mantle, hugging the leather satchel he had been charged to deliver, looking more uneasy by the minute. For different reasons, both of them were more than ready to go ashore—and did so, as soon as their barge had skirted the point of the Île de la Cité and swung into a toll station in the lee of the Grand Pont. Shouldering the modest weight of their packs, and with Grigor also carrying his satchel, the pair left the barge captain disputing with the customs agents of the *marchands de l'eau* and made their way up the embankment to the thronging streets above, where Arnault motioned them into the shadow of the church of St. Germain, so he could take his bearings. Bewildered, Grigor stood close to his side, satchel now hidden under his white mantle, looking around uneasily.

"It isn't very far from here—less than two miles," Arnault said, gesturing in the direction they needed to go. "The Paris Temple is just outside the city walls—that way. It will do us good to stretch our legs, after so many days on the river."

"If you say so," Grigor murmured, though his tone made it clear that, like most knights, he did not regard foot travel as a proper chivalric pursuit. No sooner had they set off along the Grand Rue, however, when a voice on a note of query called Arnault's name from behind.

"Arnault? Arnault de Saint Clair?"

Hand on the hilt of his sword, Arnault turned to see a mounted party of Templars approaching over the bridge: four white-clad knight-brothers shouldering their horses through the crowd, accompanied by an equal number of ser-jeants, the latter in their customary brown mantles ensigned with the red Templar cross. The knight in the lead was a proud, erect figure with a silvery beard and a backswept mane of silver hair, who raised a gloved hand and grinned as Arnault turned.

"Now, *there's* a bit of luck!" Arnault said to Grigor.

He, too, raised a hand both in greeting and salute as the party continued toward him, for their leader was the very man Arnault had come to see: Gaspar des Macquelines, one of the senior members of *le Cercle,* and a close friend as well. He saw the flick of Gaspar's gaze toward Brother Grigor as he worked his horse through the crowd, and knew that both of them would needs be circumspect until they could find some privacy.

"It *is* you!" Gaspar exclaimed, dismounting to come and greet Arnault with a fraternal kiss of peace. "What on earth are you doing in Paris, and on foot? If you'd let us know you were coming, we'd have sent a proper escort to meet you."

"To make sure I didn't get lost along the way?" Arnault said with a chuckle. "I know it's been a while since my last visit, but I can still find my way home. This is Frère Grigor Murray, bringing responsions from some of the Scottish commanderies. His French is not so good, but he's been welcome company on the journey."

"Indeed. Welcome, Frère Grigor," Gaspar said in Latin. "My English is not so good, either," he continued in that language, at Grigor's look of mystification, "but I fancy we'll limp along somehow. I am Gaspar des Macquelines. You are most welcome."

With Grigor, too, he exchanged a stiff kiss of peace, returning his attention then to Arnault.

"It is good to see you, old friend. And look there," he added, flinging a hand in the direction of the three other knights. "You don't seem to have noticed that your young cousin is fair bursting to speak to you."

He beckoned forward a dark-eyed young knight on a tall gray, who immediately swung down, grinning, and came to present himself before the newcomer.

"Jauffre?" Arnault exclaimed. "Sweet Jesu, you've quite caught me off my guard. My apologies. You are quite the grown man! Rome obviously agreed with you!"

The warmth of his salutation dispelled any diffidence in the younger man, and the two embraced enthusiastically. "I'm delighted that you noticed," Jauffre said, still grinning. "It's good to see you again."

Gaspar clapped their young colleague on the shoulder. "You should be proud of him, Arnault. If he hadn't elected to join the Order, he would have made a gifted scholar. I don't know which is stronger: his grasp of philosophy or his affinity for medicine."

Jauffre had the grace to look abashed, but Arnault recalled that even as a boy, his young cousin had displayed a rare sensitivity to things unseen by most. If early signs were any indication of things to come, Jauffre would one day be a potent addition to *le Cercle*. As he turned to glance expectantly at Grigor, Arnault made the introductions.

"Grigor, this is another of my cousins: Frère Jauffre de Saint Clair. Jauffre, Frère Grigor Murray, from Balantrodoch."

"Well, you can only be bound for the Temple," Gaspar said, switching to English again for Grigor's benefit, "so why not let us bear you company? Especially if Brother Grigor is carrying responsions. The streets of Paris are full of footpads and cutpurses."

"We would welcome that," Arnault replied, "but I fear we're afoot, as you can see."

"Well, that's easily enough remedied," laughed Gaspar, with a glance back at the serjeants. "Etienne, Jean-Louis, would you be so good as to give our brothers the use of your mounts? Viose, you and Michel can take them up double behind you, and remind us of our origins."

Soon mounted, amid good-natured banter as horses were reallocated, Arnault fell in beside Gaspar as the Templars set out along the boulevard, Grigor riding with Jauffre and the others, who dropped back to a discreet distance.

"Did you have any difficulty getting out of Scotland?" Gaspar asked as they rode, continuing to speak in English, for the sake of possible overhearing.

Arnault grimaced. "No more than I expected. Edward of England is poised to mount a new invasion, which means everything is in a state of upheaval. But no one questioned our political affinities. As far as the English are concerned, the Temple is still regarded as a neutral observer."

"I'm relieved to hear that," Gaspar said. "It's important that the Order should maintain an appearance of neutrality with regard to Robert Bruce."

"Oh?" Something in Gaspar's tone made Arnault glance at him sharply. "Why? What's wrong?"

Gaspar squared his shoulders and took a deep breath, though he kept his voice low. "The Holy Father has been persuaded to declare Bruce excommunicate."

"Surely that isn't possible!" Arnault murmured, feeling slightly sick to his stomach. "On what grounds?"

"For shedding the blood of John Comyn on sacred ground."

"But he confessed it!" Arnault blurted, though he kept his voice low. "Bishop Wishart gave him absolution, within days of it happening. Torquil was there!"

"It doesn't matter," Gaspar replied. "The Holy Father either doesn't know or doesn't care. So far as he's concerned, Bruce is guilty of sacrilegious murder."

"Comyn was possessed by a demon," Arnault said stubbornly. "If Bruce hadn't killed him, I would have—or Torquil would have. I wish we had."

"So do I," Gaspar said, "at least for Bruce's sake. But you didn't, and he did—and he's the king. The fact remains that he has lost the official support of the Church, because of his action. And anyone who aids him will fall under the same sentence."

Arnault fell silent for a long moment as they negotiated a crowded portion of the street, gravely troubled by what he was hearing. The excommunication could not reflect any honest, prayerful assessment of the true circumstances—not that the pope could be told the true circumstances—but surely, word from Wishart would have reached the pontiff by now. The act opened an ugly rift between the heavenly Jerusalem and the Papal See of Rome. It remained to be seen whether even the building of the Fifth Temple could heal the breach.

"It's specious, of course, but the Holy Father has spoken," Gaspar said, when they had cleared the crowd. "How will Bruce react, when he hears the news? You've told us he's devout, if open to notions beyond orthodoxy. Will an excommunication undermine his confidence?"

Arnault briefly considered. "I don't think so. If anything, it could even strengthen his resolve. Whatever else may befall, Bruce and his people still have the support of the Celtic Church—which counts for a lot. It has long been his aim to restore a Celtic monarchy, working to reclaim the Celtic sovereignty of the land in partnership with a Celtic Christian church. After spending some time amongst the Columban brethren, I think I understand why. I suspect you do, as well."

"Indeed," Gaspar murmured.

Indeed, both of them understood, for they both had worked with Columban monks to renew the mystic powers of the Stone of Destiny for Bruce before and during his enthronement. Following in the footsteps of their founder, Saint Columba, his followers took their spiritual inspiration from Saint John the Evangelist, rather than from Saint Peter. Mystical and tolerant in its outlook, their church was not Rome's rival, but rather its complement. With their affinity for the land itself, the Columbans had proved invaluable allies in the struggle to assert Scotland's independence. Very soon during his time spent among them, Arnault had come to hope that their harmonizing influence would one day assert itself to the benefit of Christianity at large.

"Tell me," Gaspar said, keeping his voice low, "is the Stone still safe?"

"For the moment, it is," Arnault replied. "Physically, it's been made as secure as possible, given the times; our Columban friends have cast over it their strongest charms of warding. But I've counseled Luc and Torquil to remain vigilant. The war with England will be entering a new stage, now that Bruce is crowned, and for all we know, there may be other hostile powers at work beyond those exerted by the Comyns."

"How well you echo my own worst fears," Gaspar murmured. "Oh, there's trouble at this end, as well," he continued at Arnault's look of inquiry. "You knew, of course, that there has been talk of amalgamating the two military orders. It's the king's idea, because he wants to be the head of the combined order that would be created—the *Rex Bellator*, or some such thing—but now His Holiness seems to be going along with the notion. He has summoned the Masters of both the Temple and the Hospital to meet with him in Avignon."

"Are you serious?" Arnault asked, dumbfounded.

"I wish I were not," Gaspar replied. "We received our summons only a few days ago, to forward to Cyprus. The Visitor is preparing his own letter to accompany it. He's strongly counseling that the Master *not* return, that he make up some excuse; but you know how stubborn de Molay can be."

Arnault did, indeed. Though his own interactions with the present Grand Master had never been other than routine, he well remembered the grumbling speculations at the time of de Molay's election, nearly fifteen years before. In fact, the expected choice had been Hugues de Paraud, then the treasurer of the Order and now the Visitor: a consummate politician who had developed a good working relationship with Philip of France.

De Molay, by contrast, was primarily a military disciplinarian, rigidly conservative and nearly illiterate, devoid of imagination—which was one of the many reasons he had never been told of the existence of *le Cercle*. Though he had learned something of administration during a stint as Master of the English Templars, his immediate posting before his election as Grand Master had been as Grand Marshal, the supreme military leader of the Order. In neither post had he particularly excelled; yet he still had managed to get himself elected. According to some, the voting had been so contentious that the Master of the Hospitallers had been asked to arbitrate. Arnault wondered whether Foulques de Villaret intended to obey the papal summons

"Will the Master of the Hospital obey the summons?" he asked.

"He'd be best advised not to," Gaspar said. "He's presently involved in an important campaign on Malta, so he has a perfect excuse *not* to come. But de Molay wants another crusade; he'll come—and if he does, I strongly suspect that Pope Clement may intend to turn this conference into an inquiry."

"An inquiry over what?"

Gaspar hunched down in his saddle, obviously choosing his words with care.

"An inquiry over *us*," he murmured. "Hostility against the Order is on the rise. We have always had our detractors, of course, but the accusations we've been hearing lately are increasingly scandalous. It's entirely possible that many of the common folk are starting to believe that these lies must be true—and it isn't just the usual resentment of our success. If de Molay finds himself obliged to defend the Order against charges of sorcery and perversion, I worry what the outcome will be."

The prospect caused Arnault to glance at Gaspar sharply,

but mindful of their exposed location, riding down a public street in Paris, he kept his response very general.

"I don't suppose you've been able to track down the source of any of these rumors?"

"No," Gaspar said, "and that, too, gives me cause for grave concern. We're on trial without having seen the faces of our accusers."

They were approaching the market quarter of Les Halles. Though the streets were crowded, missing was the usual congenial uproar of city commerce. Instead, everywhere Arnault looked, he read sullen expressions of discontent and unrest—though the mood seemed not to have anything to do with their presence, riding through the streets in Templar habit.

"Is this a reflection of the economic climate?" he asked, jutting his chin at a group of sour-looking merchants. "We heard about the latest tampering with the currency, on the way here. The good citizens of Paris don't appear any happier about it than their provincial cousins."

"And who can blame them?" Gaspar said. "When it comes to matters of money, the king's greed has no bounds. But there is a price to be paid for such dealings."

The sullen rumble of a discontented crowd had been growing as they approached the next corner, and both Templars instinctively reined in to listen, their escort closing ranks.

"I don't think I like the sound of that," Arnault said, with a glance at Gaspar.

"Nor do I."

The hubbub was coming from the direction of the marketplace. As they rode closer to investigate, one loud, angry voice rose above the din.

"How much more must we endure? This king of ours cares for nothing but his own luxury! In his eyes we are merely sheep to be fleeced for his profit. And he will continue to fleece us as long as we behave like sheep!"

This fierce assertion drew an answering roar. Off to the side, Arnault noted other townspeople converging toward the square in twos and threes.

"Unless I'm greatly mistaken, this has all the earmarks of a riot in the making," he said to Gaspar.

"Aye, and it wouldn't be the first time. We'd better see if we can't calm things down. If violence breaks out, it will end in bloodshed, and these folk will have infinitely more to grieve about."

At a hand signal from Gaspar, the Templar party closed ranks and moved forward in a body, hands on sword hilts. The marketplace ahead was a jostling sea of humanity, though it parted reluctantly before the Templar phalanx pushing through it, along with a murmur of resentment. Toward the center of the crowd, just visible above it, a squat, squint-eyed man in threadbare clerical garb was haranguing the throng from the back of a produce wagon.

"What is it to the king if your children are crying from hunger, as long as he can still cram his belly with dainties?" he shouted hoarsely, waving his fists in the air. "What does he care if we are cold, as long as he still sleeps warm in his silks and furs? This is no true shepherd, as the blessed Saint Louis his grandfather was. This is a wolf in shepherd's clothing, and we are fools to endure him!"

This declaration produced a swelling roar of agreement, punctuated then by a single voice that rose above the others like a clarion call.

"The king! The king himself is heading this way from the Place du Siège!"

"Do you hear?" the preacher shouted from the wagon. "God has delivered him into our hands! Let us not lose this chance to cast down the tyrant in his pride!"

Another ragged cheer answered this declaration as the crowd surged toward the south side of the square like a mighty wave. Just preparing to enter at the western edge, Gaspar and Arnault exchanged dismayed glances.

"I think we'd better see that this doesn't get out of hand," Gaspar said, sharply signaling the troop to follow as he kneed his horse around to the right.

In good order, the company clattered along an alternate route toward the Place du Siège. The crowd got there ahead of them, however, and already had the royal party backed up against a building on the east side of the square, hemmed in on three sides, with only a single line of royal men-at-arms holding them at bay with shields and spears at the ready.

Drawing rein, hand on the hilt of his sword, Arnault made a quick assessment of the odds, counting perhaps twenty men in the royal livery—all on foot, and clearly intended only as a guard of honor—and several hundred in a crowd that was starting to get ugly. Conspicuous in the scant clear space behind the royal line was a richly painted but somewhat ungainly-looking conveyance on wheels, drawn by a single white horse with sumptuous caparisons. The shutters on the windows were drawn tight.

"*Here's* a salute to His Majesty!" a raucous voice skirled from the midst of the throng.

With that, an overripe melon came sailing out of the crowd and struck the door of the conveyance, obliterating the royal crest under a smear of pulp. The carriage gave a lurch as the horse tried to bolt, and the king's bodyguard tightened their ranks, glancing anxiously at the carriage they were meant to protect. As more produce took flight, the driver leapt to the ground to try to calm the increasingly frightened horse. Jeering, the crowd began to close in.

"I think this has gone about far enough," Gaspar muttered, drawing his sword as Arnault did the same. Behind them, the others followed suit.

The roar of abuse grew louder as the crowd began flinging stones and garbage. Hefting their shields, the soldiers struggled to maintain their position as the townsfolk pressed closer still.

"To the king!" Gaspar ordered, signaling with his sword.

At once the Templar party started briskly forward, fanning into an arrowhead formation by the time the first of them began bulling into the crowd. Startled by the suddenness of the attack, and now caught between royal guards and mounted Templars, the crowd began to give ground, their taunts giving way to cries of alarm and occasional yelps of pain as the Templars began laying about with the flats of their swords.

Leaving the others to break up the rioters and disperse them, Gaspar and Arnault pushed through to the king's conveyance. The driver was clinging desperately to the wildeyed horse's headstall to keep it from bolting. Edging his own mount alongside, Arnault seized the animal's reins with a firm hand while Gaspar directed the driver to reclaim his seat.

"And you!" Gaspar said to the captain of the royal escort. "Stand your ground and cover the king's withdrawal!"

At that, one of the shutters of the conveyance popped open, and a lean, scholarly face appeared, taut with fury.

"What is the meaning of this?" a waspish voice demanded. "By what right do you presume to give orders to the king's own troops?"

Arnault caught only a glimpse of the speaker, but the imperious tone and Gaspar's taut expression suggested that it might be the king's chief minister, Guillaume de Nogaret. And the elder Templar's stiff bow confirmed that the other occupant of the carriage was, indeed, the king.

"A thousand pardons, Sire," he said smoothly. "Please allow my men and me to conduct you to safety."

"And just where do you propose taking me?" a second voice demanded.

"To the Paris Temple," Gaspar called above the din of combat. "Your Majesty will be safe there."

Chapter Six

June, 1306

A CHUNK OF PAVING RUBBLE STRUCK THE DOOR OF THE king's carriage with a splintering crack, and both its occupants retreated behind a rapidly closing shutter. Quickly the king's foot soldiers regrouped around the royal carriage, while the mounted Templars took up flanking positions on either side and ahead and behind. Several of them were sporting cuts and bruises from stones and other flying debris.

Arnault was still gentling the carriage horse. He swung up onto its back as the two extra serjeants clambered onto the carriage roof to fend off anyone who got past the riders and the men on foot. Seeing what Arnault had done, Gaspar motioned one of the serjeants down onto the extra horse before kneeing his own mount to the head of the new procession, to ride beside Arnault—who flashed a sour look at the carriage behind him as they started moving forward.

"I have a feeling we'll regret this," he said to Gaspar in a low voice. "Those aren't exactly friends of the Order."

"What else can we do?" Gaspar countered. "It's too far to the Louvre. We dare not risk it."

He stood briefly in his stirrups to gaze ahead, where the

knights in the vanguard were using their horses to force a path through the jostling crowd. The more belligerent continued to jeer and occasionally throw things, but they kept their distance, still muttering.

By dint of steady persistence, the whole company retired from the square in good order, followed in their wake by a goodly proportion of the rioters, who, unable to get at the king, vented their anger on their surroundings, smashing shutters and wrecking shop fronts. Behind them, Arnault caught glimpses of smoke pluming up among the tangled rooftops.

"This could still get ugly," he said aside to Gaspar.

"Aye, that mob is looking for a scapegoat. We'll just have to hope they won't find one. For now, however, our first concern is to get the king to safety."

They managed to do just that. At length, the tangled streets gave way to the turreted battlements of the Paris Temple, whose gates parted immediately to admit them, a dozen more mounted Templars streaming out through the gatehouse arch to cover their arrival. The men on foot broke into a jog as they surged through, the sortie party holding back as a buffer against the mob until king, carriage, and official bodyguards had passed inside. When the last horse had clattered through the entryway, the gates closed behind them with a sonorous clang, shutting the angry mob outside.

The king's party halted in the center of the courtyard, looking uncertain, and Arnault sprang down from the carriage horse to hold its head as the mounted sortie party continued on toward the stables in good order. One of the king's men hastened to open a carriage door and fold down a footstep, but it was the black-clad Guillaume de Nogaret who alighted first from the carriage, turning then to assist his royal master, who leaned a gloved hand on his minister's offered forearm and stepped down daintily.

"I trust you have sustained no injury, Sire," Gaspar said, swinging down from his horse.

Philip twitched at a trailing sleeve and glared down his long nose as if he found the question offensive. He was tall and fair, with a heavy jaw and a peevish expression.

"I do not require any solicitude from you, Templar," he said coldly. "Sieur Nogaret, I shall expect you to make certain that this outrage does not go unpunished."

"Consider it done, Sire," Nogaret replied, inclining his head to the king.

During this exchange, servants and grooms had come running from all directions to take charge of the horses and see to the injured members of the king's escort. As this continued, Arnault joined Gaspar, taking the opportunity to study Nogaret covertly.

Seen at close range, the king's chief minister appeared singularly undistinguished, other than for the richness of his dress. Wiry and slight of build, with deceptively mild pale eyes, he had an elusive quality of containment about him that belied his submissive appearance. Glancing from Nogaret to the king and back again, Arnault found himself wondering who the real master was.

But he was given no time to refine this first impression, for almost immediately, a delegation of senior Templars emerged into the yard to give official welcome to their royal guest, led by Hugues de Paraud, the Visitor of France and the Temple in the West, who was second only to the Grand Master in the hierarchy of the Order. Among the others, and only recognized at second glance, was Frère Christoph de Clairvaux, one of the most senior members of *le Cercle,* tonsured and clean-shaven since Arnault last had seen him, having put aside his sword to answer a calling as a priest. Christoph's presence was reassuring, for Arnault could think of few men more capable of dealing with the awkward situation that had just been thrust upon them all.

"Sire," Paraud said to the king, making him a spare bow, "I am very sorry to hear of your distressing experience. While the incident is, of course, deplorable, we are honored to have you and Monsieur de Nogaret as our guests. If you will be pleased to accompany me, I will show you to apartments where you can rest and refresh yourselves after your ordeal. I fear it may be necessary for you to remain here for some time. The city is very unsettled."

With a sour glance at Nogaret, Philip suffered himself to be led away without comment, his minister and several guards following, along with Christoph and several other senior Templars. Watching them depart, Arnault glanced at Gaspar with growing misgivings.

"The king was hardly effusive with his gratitude, was he?" he noted quietly. "One might almost conclude that he is nearly as angry at us, for witnessing his discomfiture, as he is at the citizens of Paris for daring to vent their displeasure."

"I daresay you may be right," Gaspar agreed, though he kept his voice down. "I don't envy Hugues the task of soothing the king's ruffled feelings."

Once their unwelcome visitors had been installed in the Temple's best guest accommodation—and Brother Grigor had been dispatched to the refectory for a meal, his satchel entrusted to Gaspar for deposit in the treasury vaults—Christoph quietly summoned those members of *le Cercle* presently in residence at the Paris Temple. Several key members of that elite fraternity were currently on missions in Cyprus or in Scotland, but those who remained were acutely aware that the presence of the king and Nogaret within the walls of the Paris Temple was likely to prove awkward, at best.

"I fear we've bought ourselves nothing but trouble by letting the king and that beady-eyed Nogaret inside our defenses," said Oliver de Penne, Christoph's closest associate within *le Cercle*. They were meeting in a tiny mural chamber adjoining Gaspar's office, huddled around a small table lit by a single candle: only five of them, to make decisions that possibly could determine the future safety of the Order.

"Philip already owes the Order substantial sums of money, thanks to the expense of his wars in Flanders. We've saved his skin yet again, but he'll see this as simply another debt he owes us. You could see the resentment and hatred in his eyes."

"He did look less than happy," Christoph agreed, "but frankly, I'm just as worried about public opinion. There's been a lot of muttering in the streets, even before this incident. It will not much help our reputation in the eyes of the people when it becomes known that we gave sanctuary to the king who has so often trampled on their rights. Those who hate us will hate us all the more. And even our friends will have trouble justifying our actions. I wish he were not here!"

"So do we all," Gaspar replied, "but what else would you have had us do? Leave him to the mob?"

Christoph shook his head. "Of course not. No one is faulting your decision. But you must admit that he and that toad Nogaret could hardly have picked a worse time to intrude on our affairs."

"From what I hear," Arnault said, "any time would have been a bad time."

All eyes turned his way as Oliver said, "You've heard correctly. And I gather, from your unannounced presence, that the news from Scotland may be no better. Perhaps you'd better bring us up to date."

In as few words as possible, Arnault reviewed the circumstances by which Robert the Bruce had come to his throne, and the dangers that now confronted Scotland and its new-crowned king.

"He wears the crown," he said, "but now he must earn the right to keep it, and to exercise its authority as a true king. The odds he can do that are not at all good—and getting worse by the day."

"I take it," said Hugues de Curzon, "that King Edward knows what he's done?"

"Aye, he's preparing for another invasion," Arnault replied. "While I was in Berwick, waiting for clearance to leave, I had a good opportunity to observe the preparations in progress. If numbers are any indication, Bruce is going to be at a serious disadvantage."

"But you saw him properly enthroned on the Stone of Destiny," Gaspar said. "You and Torquil and Luc."

"We did," Arnault agreed. "And all the signs suggest that it has enhanced all the personal qualities he needs to wage this war: strength, courage, and discernment. But those gifts may not be enough to enable him to win it without some additional assistance from us."

"What kind of help did you have in mind?" Oliver asked.

"Anything that might give him an edge," Arnault said. "At the very least, he could do with some protection beyond his own prowess at arms. Remember that his success ensures that Scotland can provide a foundation for the Fifth Temple. We owe him all the help we can give him—for our own sakes, as much as his own."

"Nothing would please me more than to lay the full fighting strength of the Order at his disposal," Christoph replied, with crooked regret. "Sadly, this is neither the time nor the place. Nor does this lie within our power." He sighed. "This request of yours will bear some thinking, Arnault. All I can promise you now is that we shall do all we can."

"It's doubtful we can do much of anything while the king and Nogaret are in our midst," Hughes warned. "Philip probably already suspects us of a multitude of crimes—fed, no doubt, by Nogaret's poisonous tongue. We mustn't do anything that might lend credence to their suspicions—or to whatever fabrications Nogaret may be concocting."

"That's what worries me about this summons from the Holy Father," Gaspar said darkly. "It wouldn't surprise me to learn that Philip—or Nogaret, even more likely—was the one who persuaded His Holiness to summon the Grand Master back to France."

"Aye, and despite all advice to the contrary, de Molay almost certainly will come," Christoph replied. "He's convinced the Holy Father will protect us."

Oliver shook his head. "I'll be very surprised if he *doesn't* come—but he can be one of the most pigheaded men I've ever met."

"Don't we have an advisor with him?" Arnault asked.

"Oh, yes, two full initiates: Father Anselmo and Armand Breville. It hasn't done much good."

"Well, they ought to come with him," Gaspar said. "And they should be advised of the changing circumstances before they leave Cyprus—though it isn't anything I particularly want to entrust to writing."

"We could place someone trustworthy among the members of the escort sent to bring him," Oliver said. "Perhaps one of the younger knights being groomed for eventual initiation, someone who isn't known to de Molay."

"How about young Saint Clair?" Gaspar said thoughtfully. "He handled himself very well today—I've been pleased with his progress—and he can certainly deliver a firsthand account of what happened."

"Whoever we send will also need to carry news of the situation in Scotland, some of which is sensitive," Hugues pointed out. "Jauffre is still a probationer."

"Which is precisely why I suggested him," Gaspar replied, with a speaking glance at Arnault. "We can give him a report that carries meaning on several levels. Breville and Father Anselmo will understand."

Arnault smiled. "Jauffre probably will understand as well."

"My point, exactly," Hugues replied. "And if he understands it, he could betray it."

"If he understands it, it means he's *ready* to understand it," Arnault pointed out. "And he's strong enough not to betray it. Unless you believe there are traitors in our midst, in the Grand Master's immediate counsel, the question isn't likely to arise—and it will be a good test for Jauffre. Or is there a danger of which I'm not aware?" he asked, turning his gaze to Christoph and Gaspar.

Both men shook their heads.

"Not that we're aware," Christoph said. "But I'm afraid that these are questions we must begin to ask." He sighed. "I agree, however, that young Jauffre is a good choice. I'll make certain that he's with the delegation sent to Cyprus to serve as the Master's escort. Arnault, I'll leave it to you to brief him about Scotland."

While the resident members of *le Cercle* were secretly discussing the future of the Order, King Philip was pacing the floor of his chamber in the Templar guesthouse.

"This is a damnable state of affairs!" he complained forcefully. "It is intolerable!"

Guillaume de Nogaret affected a solicitude he was far from feeling.

"Is the accommodation not to your liking, Sire? If you wish, I shall demand that our hosts find you a different apartment."

"The accommodation is excellent," Philip snapped. "That's exactly the point." He waved a hand around the room. "Glass in the windows, silk velvet hangings for the bed, furnishings of ivory and rare woods! I am more graciously housed here than I would be in my own palace. No religious establishment should be so luxuriously appointed."

Nogaret forbore to remind the king that this was the best chamber in the guest wing of the commandery, not the brothers' own quarters. Instead, he nodded his head sagely.

"You are entirely right, Sire. Such opulence is most unseemly among monks supposedly sworn to poverty, chastity, and obedience."

"Unseemly? It's positively scandalous!" Philip retorted. Moodily he flung himself into a heavy carved chair laden with fat feather pillows. "These Templars have brought me here to taunt me with their superior wealth. They serve me wine in a golden cup," he continued, picking up a stemmed goblet, "and food on silver plates! And then they have the audacity to reproach me with unpaid debts!"

No mention, in fact, had been made of the large sum of gold that Philip had borrowed from the Templar Order five years earlier, or the like amount advanced to pay the dowry of the king's daughter in bride-price to the Lord Edward of England. But once again Nogaret refrained from issuing a reminder.

"The money they loaned me was the merest trifle," the king continued on a note of petulance. "They could easily afford it. By rights, they ought to have made me a present of it! Instead, they choose to heap scorn upon my head. Oh, one day they shall pay for their arrogance, their insults."

"A reckoning is long overdue," Nogaret agreed, as Philip drank deeply. "But thus far, no one has had the courage to demand it."

"It is not for want of courage," Philip pointed out through clenched teeth. He held the emptied cup to be refilled by Nogaret. "They are answerable only to the pope—and he's as corrupt as they are!"

"Too true, I fear, Sire," said Nogaret, and added, "Perhaps bringing the Templars to justice is an undertaking reserved for a king."

Philip's eyes kindled at the suggestion, nostrils flaring, and after a moment he said, "You may be right." He paused. "Go now. I must think on this." He waved a hand in dismissal.

Nogaret departed with only a silent bow, well satisfied with his work. Inciting a riot to gain entry to the Temple had been more than a little risky, but it had paid off. Not only had it enhanced his standing with the king, but it had finally given Nogaret access to the Temple—and not just for an hour.

Mentally commending the industry of those responsible

for rousing the mob—most of the Decuria, if the truth be known—he made his way to his own accommodation and, locking himself in, prepared to embark upon an even more dangerous gambit. He had been seeking such an opportunity for months.

Focused and intent, he took from the sleeve pocket of his robe a small leather bag containing a stoppered vial of holy chrism oil mixed with bone ash. The ashes were not those of a saint. Working quickly, he used this mixture to smudge symbols of warding about the room with his thumb, finally tracing an inverted pentagram of oil and ash in the center of a table in the middle of the room. He cleaned his thumb carefully before putting away the vial. Then he took the ruby ring from its chain about his neck and placed it at the heart of the pentagram.

"Now . . ." he whispered under his breath as he stepped back a pace from the table.

Crossing his arms over his chest with a muttered incantation, he thrice repeated the ancient phrases, with varying pitch and intensity. At the end of the last recitation, he uncrossed his arms and flung out both hands in a commanding gesture of summoning, both palms upheld and turned toward the focus of his intent.

The ring at the heart of the pentagram quivered and began to spin, rattling against the wooden tabletop. Very soon, a thin plume of crimson smoke began curling upward from the center of the circlet, slowly taking the form of a crimson-skinned miniature homunculus the size of a child, with yellow eyes like a goat's, fangs overhanging its full lower lip, and muscular arms folded above genitalia of obscene proportions.

It could and would come in any shape he desired—and for its former master, the despised Pope Boniface, had often come in female form, of astonishing beauty, compliance, and sexual appetite; but the price for that came high. Noga-

ret preferred not to press his luck. This was its true form—
or as true as could be manifested on any physical plane.

"*Ialdabaeoth issss here, Massster,*" it hissed in a whis-
pery, sibilant voice. "*How may he ssserve?*"

Nogaret smiled thinly, regarding the apparition through
narrowed eyes. "Well come, Ialdabaeoth. I have some work
for you to do. Do you know where we are?"

The imp's yellow eyes swiveled this way and that, and it
spat in disgust.

"*Thiss isss a sssacred place.*"

"It is not so holy as that," Nogaret said dismissively. "We
are in the heart of the Paris Temple. It is not only a commandery of monks, but also a treasure house. I wish you to
descend into the treasury vaults and show me their contents."

"*Pleassse, Massster,*" the imp begged, on a thin whine of
protest. "*There isss much holinesss. It painsss Ialdabaeoth.*"

"Nevertheless, you will do as I command," Nogaret said
firmly. "Now go, before you rouse my displeasure."

With a silent, sulking grumble, the demonic image dis-
solved, fading away like mist until only a faint shimmer remained to show that its essence still was anchored to the
ring. Nogaret extended his left hand over the ring where it
lay on the tabletop, not shrinking from the scorching sensation in his palm that marked the point of communion between the demon's essence and his own. As he closed his
eyes, he at once found himself drawn along a trail of images.

The demon's flight whisked him down stairways and
around corners. Corridors flew past in a dizzying series of
twists and turns. Clinging to the ceiling, the demon flashed
past over the heads of two lay servants engaged in scrubbing
a floor and flitted onward like a bat, until at last it entered a
dimly lit passageway lined with doors along one side.

Probing at the first keyhole, Ialdabaeoth registered a
quiver of excitement at the smell of gold and gems—and
squirted through into the chamber beyond. Following the

demon, Nogaret feasted his gaze on a profusion of chests and coffers. The adjoining vault housed maps and documents, some of them richly illuminated with powdered jewels and gold leaf. Further explorations revealed more treasure: armor and weaponry chased with gold and silver, bales of furs and rich fabrics, and troves of reliquaries from which the demon shied away with hissing revulsion.

Then, to the rear of the final vault, they came upon a concealed doorway leading to another chamber beyond. Here Ialdabaeoth came to a shuddering halt, for the hidden door was wreathed in mystical symbols, invisible to human eyes but agonizingly bright to the demon's gaze. The very air crackled with emanations of power that made the little demon bristle and spit, but its reaction was almost certain confirmation that Nogaret at last had found at least a part of what he was looking for: the *sanctum sanctorum* of the Templars' treasury.

But all at once he became aware that Ialdabaeoth was shrieking in silent agony. The backlash of the demon's pain struck him with the force of an explosion, and for a moment the whole of creation seemed to career round them. By sheer effort of will, Nogaret brought the world back into focus and bade the demon return, as did he himself.

Once back in the confines of his chamber, he severed the connection and allowed his demon servant to return to the ring. Oblivious to the residual pain that throbbed in his hand, he carefully erased all traces of the work he had done, then closed the ring in his hand, its cool metal easing the ache he now began to feel. Finally, he lay down with closed eyes, to recover his strength and savor his discovery.

Even without the evidence of the sacred inscriptions, there was no mistaking the aura of divine power radiating from the secret vault, strong enough to manifest through the surrounding shielding of masonry and the seals guarding the door. Without more direct examination, he had no way to be certain precisely what relics and magical talismans might lie within that *sanctum* the demon had been unable to broach, but he thought he might have located the particular one he had long been seeking.

"So," he muttered aloud to himself, opening his eyes to gaze at the vaulted ceiling above. "*This* is where the High Priest's Breastplate resides. And the Templars are its keepers."

The discovery suggested a further measure he might employ to ascertain more precisely the extent of the Temple's mystical treasures. He was smiling faintly as he slowly sat up.

Among the belongings brought in from the king's carriage was a dispatch case containing several deeds of royal property and a costly string of pearls intended as a gift for Philip's current favorite among the ladies of the court. This the guards had deposited in Nogaret's room for safekeeping.

With the case in hand and the ring back on its chain inside his clothing, Nogaret left his room and went in search of a suitable guide. From the outer door of the guesthouse, he spotted two young Templar brothers making their way across the courtyard, and accosted them with a wave of his hand.

"I have valuables belonging to the king in this satchel," he informed them officiously. "Since it appears we may be here for some time, I wish to place the satchel in a secure vault."

"Of course, my lord."

The pair conducted him to one of the brother treasurer's deputies. Once down in the crypt, Nogaret made a show of inspecting the locks on the treasury room doors.

"You're certain this will be secure?" he said as he handed the satchel to the deputy, whose curly beard reached nearly to his waist.

"Quite sure, my lord," the man replied, before disappearing inside.

Seizing this opportunity, while his attendant's notice was

otherwise occupied, Nogaret planted the demon ring in a cranny behind a wall sconce, which commanded a view of the corridor.

"Very well, then," he said when the man had emerged from the vault. "I shall require a receipt for the item—and I shall hold you personally accountable."

"I assure you, there can be no question of its safety, my lord," came the answer.

Nogaret merely gave the man a curt nod, waiting while the receipt was prepared. Later, back in his room, he once again invoked the demon Ialdabaeoth, calling upon the link that would remain until his death.

"You will watch the passageway day and night, noting who comes and who goes," he instructed. "And if anyone should appear bearing a relic of the One you do not name, I charge you to show me his face."

Chapter Seven

June, 1306

"DAMN THAT TRAITOR BRUCE!" EXCLAIMED AYMER DE Valence, Earl of Pembroke. "And damn his audacity! How dare he parade his rebel troops before the town, in contempt of our presence?"

This rant was addressed to a gathering of the highest-ranking officers of the English army under his command, presently quartered in the town of Perth, on the River Tay. Pembroke and his senior advisors had taken over the town's guildhall as their headquarters, where they were now assembled to discuss matters of strategy.

During their march north, the English had captured several Scottish lordlings and three of Bruce's staunchest adherents among the Scottish clergy: the bishops of Glasgow and St. Andrews, Wishart and Lamberton, and Abbot Henry of Scone. The laymen had been hanged; the clergy had been sent south in chains, bound for captivity in English castles. Bruce's own whereabouts, however, had remained a mystery—until that very afternoon, when the Scottish rebel army had suddenly materialized out of the hills and Bruce himself had challenged Pembroke to come out and fight.

"We should punish this upstart's presumption as it deserves!" cried Sir William Latimer, a senior banneret of the king's household. "Our strength exceeds his by at least fifteen hundred men. I say we form up our followings and attack!"

His proposal met with an outburst of approval from all sides. Only Bartholeme de Challon remained unmoved.

"That is something that only a fool would do," he observed.

His voice cut through the din, eliciting a bristling silence. Pembroke gave him an icy stare.

"Perhaps you ought to explain yourself, Lord Bartholeme," he said.

"Willingly." Bartholeme swept the company with a look of mild scorn. "Is it not obvious that Bruce is trying to provoke you? Why else should he do this? If he can goad you into launching an ill-planned attack in the heat of the moment, the advantage is all his. He knows this area, as you do not. Doubtless, he has already picked his ground. If you go after him, the fight will be fought on his terms—and you will be the losers."

Grudging murmurs here and there acknowledged that he had made his point with some members of the gathering, but others remained unconvinced. Pembroke himself scowled darkly.

"Let me remind you that we've been hunting Bruce for days, with nothing but midge bites to show for our efforts," he said. "Now that he's suddenly popped up under our noses, are you suggesting we should let him vanish into the hills again without making some effort to engage him?"

"Not in the least," Bartholeme said. "I merely point out that there are more ways than one to flay a cat."

"Meaning what?" said Sir Geoffrey Segrave, another of the king's bannerets.

"Meaning that if you are prepared to exercise a little patience, you can get the better of Bruce without exposing your own troops to any great danger," Bartholeme replied.

"You are here not to wage honorable warfare, but to exterminate a race of treacherous vermin. For such a task, guile is the best recourse."

"Very well," Pembroke said cautiously. "I'm listening."

Bartholeme raised his voice for the benefit of the whole room. "Ignore this challenge for the moment. Hold your position within the town walls and wait until the summer twilight settles. Those few hours of darkness will suffice to mask our movements. When the Scots least expect it—that's when we strike."

"Easier said than done," Segrave said with a snort.

"No, easier than you think," Bartholeme countered. "The Scots are an undisciplined rabble, ill accustomed to maintaining order in camp. In the absence of any obvious danger, they will break up into small groups to forage for food, once nightfall comes. And once they disperse, we shall be able to round them up and cut them down like so many stray sheep."

"So you say now," said a knight called Sir Thomas Grey. "But you yourself have pointed out that Bruce and his following know the forest better than we do. If we leave the town in force, even under cover of darkness, how can we hope to surprise the enemy without giving ourselves away?"

Bartholeme's smile had a wolfish edge.

"Leave that to me," he said.

When the English declined to offer battle, the Scots' reaction was largely one of contempt.

"What do we have to do to make these cowards come out and face us?" one wag grumbled. "Dress ourselves up as women and pretend to be whores?"

"They're probably even afraid of our women!" someone else scoffed, to an answering ripple of laughter.

"Aye, maybe they've finally figured out what we've known for years," came the scornful rejoinder. "That one Scot in a fight is worth a dozen Englishmen!"

While such remarks were being bandied about the Scottish camp, a few miles northwest of Perth, Bruce drew apart with his advisors, among them Torquil Lennox and Aubrey Saint Clair.

"Well, simply offering a challenge to our enemies has failed," he said somewhat perplexedly. "Pembroke, quite rightly, is too astute to order an uphill charge against a Scottish spear force. We're going to have to come up with some other ploy to make the English come and fight."

"We could set fire to the fields and farms round about," young James Douglas offered, somewhat doubtfully.

Bruce shook his head. "Not this time. Many of the people of Perth are in sympathy with our cause. I don't want to inflict the hardship of a ruined harvest on them, unless there's no other way."

"If the English won't attack *us,* we may have to attack *them,*" Christopher Seton said.

"Bad strategy," said Gilbert de la Haye, Scotland's High Constable. "That amounts to laying siege to the town, and we don't have enough men, let alone time, to pursue a course like that."

"Especially when we know that there's a second English army out there, that could descend on us at any time," Torquil pointed out. "We know Percy's on his way."

"So, how long can we afford to remain here?" asked Neil Bruce, the king's favorite brother.

"Not long," Bruce said bluntly. "Supplies are our biggest problem. If we can't bring Pembroke to battle within the next two days, we'll have to withdraw."

A delegation of sergeants was approaching. The most senior of them put himself forward with a respectful salute.

"Yer Grace, we'd like permission for the men tae go foraging," he announced gruffly.

Bruce's gaze flicked among his advisors, and he grimaced.

"Bide a moment, will you?" he said to the sergeant. "I have one or two matters to settle here first."

He waited until the sergeant and his companions retired out of earshot before turning back to his companions.

"Well, gentlemen, what do you think?"

His brother Thomas shrugged. "You've just admitted that we're low on supplies. As well to let them go. If the men can find food for themselves, that will help stretch the resources we have, and buy us more time to come up with a workable battle plan."

"That may be practical, but I'm not sure it's wise," Torquil warned. "If you let the army disperse, even for a few hours, you court the risk of the enemy catching us off guard and picking us off piecemeal."

"But how likely is that?" Seton argued. "The English don't know the local area as well as we do. If Pembroke wouldn't commit his troops to fight us on an open field in broad daylight, he certainly won't be eager to send them into unknown territory under cover of night."

"That depends on who's advising him," Torquil reminded Seton. "Pembroke has a significant number of Scots in his following. Some of the Balliol men, and the Comyns, too, were out with Wallace in the early years. They know that a Scottish army is accustomed to living off the land, and may urge Pembroke to exploit the fact."

"That's a chance we may have to take," James Douglas said. "One way or another, our men have got to eat. And the sooner we send them out, the quicker they'll be back."

Bruce pondered the matter a moment longer, but finally shook his head.

"I certainly don't relish the idea of allowing our forces to split up," he said, "but I also don't like the idea of depleting our supplies before we've had a chance to engage the enemy. In the balance, I think I'm going to have to authorize forage parties. Unless there's something I've overlooked?"

No one spoke, but no one looked terribly happy about the

proposition, either. Afterward, when the meeting broke up and Seton went to relay the orders, young Aubrey drew Torquil aside. They had not known one another well before Aubrey joined Bruce's band, but the past weeks had forged a bond of easy camaraderie between the two, despite a generation of age difference.

"Torquil," Aubrey murmured, "is it just my inexperience and natural skepticism, or is this a really bad idea?"

Torquil shook his head. "I only wish I knew. I don't like it any more than you do. I know it's the Scottish way, to forage off the land—the men do have to eat—but I keep getting this twitchy feeling that something is watching every move we make, and poised to pounce. Let's hope it's only a figment of my own suspicious nature."

With the summer solstice less than a week away, the Scottish sunset lingered late over the Perthshire hills. As the sky slowly darkened, Pembroke's forces began assembling for action. John Macdougall of Lorn and Sir Alexander Abernethy, together with their followings, were in the vanguard. They were waiting to move out when they received a message instructing them to rendezvous with Bartholeme de Challon at an abandoned bothy just outside the town.

The bothy stood on a rocky hillock backed by a stand of windblown trees. Ordering their men to keep under cover, Lorn and Abernethy drew their swords before approaching the low stone cottage. Pale light from a flickering cruse lamp showed through the open doorway.

"You won't need your weapons just yet," Bartholeme's voice advised from the room beyond.

Muttering a curse under his breath, Lorn led the way across the threshold. There they found Bartholeme seated at a crooked table, poring over a set of parchments. The dwarf Mercurius was with him, wearing a miniature copy of his master's leather battle harness and mail, stubby hands thrust into his belt.

"All right, we're here," said Abernethy, as he and Lorn sheathed their swords. "Now what do you want?"

"To set you on the right path to seizing Bruce," Bartholeme replied.

Both men drew themselves up straighter. "We're listening."

"A short while ago I did some spying. Bruce's troops are camped near Methven, as you know. His personal encampment lies in a hollow about a quarter mile north of the main force. I've prepared a map."

He passed the topmost sheet of vellum to Lorn, who tilted it closer to the lamplight as Abernethy peered over his shoulder.

"We are here, and Methven is there," Bartholeme said, a well-manicured fingertip tracing the distance between them. "Heading northerly, follow the line of this burn. Bruce's force is scattered through these woods, but his personal encampment lies here."

The two Scottish lords stared at him with mouths agape. "How do you know this?" Lorn demanded.

"Suffice it to say that I have my sources," Bartholeme replied, toying with the swan signet on his hand. "Now get moving. And do try to take him alive," he added, as the two started to leave. "King Edward will derive great satisfaction from watching him writhe and scream under the hands of the executioners."

Midnight approached, and it was full dark at last, but Torquil found himself growing more and more uneasy as the night went on. Too restless to sleep, and still in his harness, he eventually threw off his blanket and got up, buckling on his weapons. The fire had died back to embers. He made his way quietly to the edge of the campsite and stood staring out into the darkness with his nerve ends bristling. Aubrey joined him not long after.

"Still stalking shadows?" the younger man inquired.

Torquil made a disgruntled noise in the back of his throat, noting that Aubrey, too, was fully dressed and armed. "I'd be a lot happier if all our forage parties were back."

"Aye, that's been worrying me, too," Aubrey said. "Do you think we ought to take a turn around the outer perimeter?"

"Might as well. We aren't sleeping anyway."

A tour of the neighboring campsites, however, only reinforced their misgivings. Most of the camp slept, and the guards were vigilant, but many of the foragers were still abroad, their movements unaccounted for.

"I don't like this," Torquil muttered, as he and Aubrey started back toward the king's encampment. "It will be light soon, and too many of our troops are still scattered. If Pembroke attacked us now, he'd have us at his mercy."

They paused to trade watchwords with one of the perimeter guards before moving on.

"At least our sentries are alert," Aubrey remarked.

"I suppose that's some comfort," Torquil agreed, albeit grudgingly. "I still don't like it. Let's check on the horse lines—"

A choked outcry rang out from behind them, and both Templars reached instinctively for their swords as they whirled.

"The sentry!" Aubrey cried.

"Get back to Bruce and stay with him!" Torquil barked, catching Aubrey's arm and spinning him back around. "Raise the alarm, and leave this to me!"

As Aubrey set off on the run, shouting "Alarm, alarm!" Torquil drew his sword and raced back toward the sound of the disturbance. Bursting through the undergrowth, he almost tripped over the body of the sentry, dead with an arrow through his heart.

Torquil's own alarm rang out even as a score of armed figures burst from the trees and more arrows whispered from the darkness, one whining right past his ear. He ducked and ran, zigzagging through the woods and bracken but making for the king's encampment as fast as he could go.

He could hear the enemy contingent crashing after him, in full pursuit—and the alarm spreading. The king's camp loomed ahead through the trees. Putting on a burst of speed, Torquil raced to join the ring of defense forming up with Bruce at its center—who was also dressed and fully armed, pulling on his helmet with the gold circlet round it.

Torches flared red on the high ground as more enemy troops poured out of the trees and down the slope, accompanied by hoarse battle yells. The Scots met the charge with a tumultuous clangor of meeting blades, and then it was every man for himself.

Fighting his way through to Aubrey and the king, Torquil cut down one snarling opponent, only to have two more burst from the darkness to take his place. Out of the corner of his eye he was aware of Bruce himself engaged in furious swordplay, but holding his own. Sir Alexander Scrymgeour, the king's hereditary standard-bearer, was fighting at their back, not far from James Douglas and Christopher Seton. From all around them in the Scottish encampment came screams and clashes of weaponry. The surrounding woods seethed with the sounds of combat.

Here and there, stray torches had set fire to the bracken. The smoky glare showed more English reinforcements arriving. Bruce and his companions were giving a mortal account of themselves, but it seemed clear that the English had the advantage of surprise.

Shaking his head, Torquil bulled his way closer to Bruce, working his way into the king's line of vision as he continued to hew at new attackers. Bruce had lost his helmet, and was sporting a bloody scuff across one cheekbone, but appeared to be otherwise unharmed, thus far.

"We can't hold this!" Torquil shouted to Bruce above the din. "We're too widely scattered. *You* have to get away, no matter what happens to us! Make for the horses—*now!*"

The king's face showed angry resistance, but he reluctantly nodded his assent and disengaged. Edward Bruce and James Douglas also broke, and hustled him toward the horse lines as Torquil and Aubrey closed ranks with several other defenders to cover their retreat.

Bruce's younger brothers fought through to him, reinforcing his defense as they continued to fall back. Meanwhile, the two Templar Knights formed the center of the rear guard, gradually forced to yield ground, but buying Bruce the time he needed to get to the horses.

There were English there, too, but somehow Douglas managed to get the king mounted. An English knight grabbed the reins, trying to unhorse him, but Christopher Seton bashed him in the face with a fist and sent Bruce on his way—into the midst of another knot of English knights, who caught at the horse's bridle and brought the animal down, spilling Bruce onto the ground.

Frantic for the king's safety, Torquil and Aubrey tried to fight their way through to him, but somehow Bruce managed to elude his would-be captors and scramble back into the saddle, desperately spurring free and now flanked by Douglas and Gilbert de la Haye, themselves finally mounted. Only when he was safely on his way did Torquil and the others of the rear guard break off to make their own escape.

"Go!—go!—go!" Torquil yelled to his companions. "It's our turn now!"

A final vicious sortie bought them the chance to make a sprint for the horses. There was no time to be selective. Seizing mounts at random, throwing themselves astride bareback, they eluded the last of their immediate attackers and galloped off after the king.

Their initial flight was desperate, but they knew the terrain better than their pursuers, and soon caught sight of Bruce and some others ahead. Gradually the sounds of combat and even pursuit fell away behind them as they plunged into the sanctuary of a dense forest, the drum of their horses' hooves muffled by the carpet of leaves.

Only exhaustion finally obliged them to slacken their pace and close up ranks—but a handful of them, in this immediate company—and stop to rest the horses. Seton and Scrymgeour were conspicuous by their absence; Aubrey had seen Seton taken or killed. At Bruce's side, his brother Edward breathed out in an audible sigh of dejection.

"It may take weeks to discover whether we have an army left."

"I know that!" Bruce said sharply, stiff-backed and with head held high, looking stricken in the moonlight. "God forgive me, it was my decision to let the men forage, and divide our strength. This was no one's mistake but my own."

"You could not know, Sire," James Douglas murmured.

"No, I *must* know! I am the king!"

Bruce drew a deep breath and let it out, shaking his head and bracing himself. "This night surely has been the death of many of our dearest friends," he said softly, bowing his head. "If it would undo the error, I would willingly hand myself over to the torturers. But that cannot be, so I must bear the penance of living with my grief."

He lifted a closed and trembling fist nearly to his mouth, then made himself relax it with an effort of will as he raised his head again.

"Whatever comes, I must not falter," he said. "From this moment forward, there can be no thought of surrender. Too many brave hearts have suffered and died to serve this cause—and there will be more. Those lives must not have been wasted. No, we must fight on—and fight harder. For the only true way to redeem this night's tragedy is to dedicate ourselves to victory."

Chapter Eight

July, 1306

NEARLY A FORTNIGHT PASSED BEFORE EVEN SKETCHY RE-
ports of the Methven disaster reached Paris.

"The Earl of Pembroke has won a significant victory over
the Scots, near Perth," the Visitor of France announced
grimly, tossing an unfolded sheet of parchment before the
select council he had summoned.

Present in his private conference chamber in the Paris
Temple were nearly a dozen of the Order's most trusted senior knights, all of them with reason to have keen interest in
the situation in Scotland. A goodly percentage of them, including Arnault de Saint Clair, were also members of *le
Cercle*.

"Somehow the English got wind of Bruce's position," the
Visitor went on, "and attacked under cover of night, before
he could marshal his forces. The Scottish rebel army has
been scattered, many men killed. This news comes from
Walter de Clifton, the Master of Scotland. Whether Bruce
himself is alive or dead, no one seems to know. Frère Walter does not mention the fate of our brethren advising Bruce,
so presumably he does not know that, either."

Guarded glances were exchanged among the other men seated at the table. Gaspar was first to speak.

"This is grave news, indeed," he said. "Brother Arnault, you know the situation in Scotland better than any of the rest of us. How could such a thing have happened?"

"I only wish I had an answer," Arnault answered. "When I left the king, soon after his inauguration, he had mustered a significant following. Of our own, Brothers Torquil and Aubrey are with him, both of them Scots. We did know that Pembroke was marching north with a new invasion force, to meet a second force led by Sir Henry Percy. I believe it was Bruce's intention to attack the one before the two could join forces. Clearly, something went badly awry."

A lengthy pause followed. Oliver de Penne had been reading the missive for himself, and at length lifted his head.

"It says here that Pembroke had a significant advantage in numbers. Maybe Bruce was simply outflanked and overwhelmed."

Arnault was unconvinced. He pointed out that this would have required the speedy deployment of mounted troops.

"The English certainly have numerical superiority in heavy cavalry, but the terrain in that part of Perthshire is hilly and densely forested—too rough for their effective use," he said. "Bruce could rely on the ground to protect him from the threat of a heavy cavalry charge. I can't see him allowing himself to be outmaneuvered."

"Maybe he counted too much on having the advantage of terrain," Christoph suggested. "Maybe he got overconfident, failed to set an adequate guard."

Arnault shook his head. "Bruce wouldn't omit an obvious precaution like that—especially not with two Templar advisors on hand to weigh up the tactical possibilities."

"And we have heard nothing from our brothers?" Father Bertrand asked.

The Visitor, Hugues de Paraud, shook his head. "Not that has come to my notice."

"Perhaps we should consider that they may have been among the many who lost their lives in the engagement," Oliver said.

"Highly unlikely," Arnault stated flatly, certain in his heart that he would have known, at least regarding Torquil.

"Then why haven't they contrived to send us word by now?" Oliver replied.

"I would guess that Torquil considers it too dangerous," Arnault said. "Written messages can be intercepted. Signs can be read by eyes other than those for whom they were intended."

Hugues de Paraud cocked his head at Arnault, obviously choosing his words with care. Though not of the Inner Circle, he knew that certain of those present had access to sources of information he did not question. "Have you reason to suspect some unnatural agency at work, which is hostile to our cause?"

"I would not discount the possibility."

"But you and the Scottish Templars did flush out the cult that was assisting the Comyns," Gaspar pointed out.

"We destroyed the sanctuary and broke that particular alliance with evil," Arnault said. "Nonetheless, the Comyn family remains a strong and unknown factor. There may be those among them still who hate the Christian faith enough to strike a bargain with some other power of Darkness."

"Then it seems," said Christoph, "that much now depends on Bruce himself. If he has survived, then all things are yet possible, and the Order may find a safe refuge in Scotland. Without him, I very much fear that the Order may be doomed."

They waited anxiously for further news. Arnault chafed at the bit, eager to return to Bruce's side. However, the next two weeks brought no news of where the king might be; only grisly tales of King Edward's vengeance toward his captured foes.

Many of Bruce's staunchest friends and kinsmen had been taken at Methven and were hanged, drawn, and quartered like William Wallace before them. Christopher Seton, the king's brother-in-law, had suffered this fate devised particularly for traitors, and also Alexander Scrymgeour, Scotland's hereditary standard-bearer. The carnage was so great that even the Earl of Pembroke at last had been moved to beg for clemency on behalf of the survivors.

Edward's only concession was to pardon the landless and untitled members of Bruce's army, whom he contemptuously termed "the middling folk." Otherwise, he remained brutally true to his intent in raising the red dragon war banner.

Then, at long last, a ciphered message arrived from Luc de Brabant, giving the members of *le Cercle* the news they had almost stopped daring to hope for: Robert Bruce had escaped alive from Methven, along with his Templar guardians.

"This is welcome news, indeed!" Christoph proclaimed, reading over the message Gaspar had received. "But it appears that the danger is not yet past."

By Luc's account, King Edward's forces were scouring the hills, forests, and villages along both banks of the River Tay, in a concerted effort to locate the remnants of the Scottish rebel army. So far, neither bribery nor intimidation had brought them any news of Bruce's whereabouts, but that was no guarantee of safety. Significantly, Luc had refrained from supplying any further details, even though his message was intended for friendly eyes.

"He is right not to be too specific," Gaspar said, "but I wish we knew more. For now, I fear that our prayers are the only thing we can offer by way of assistance."

"Prayers are good," Arnault agreed, "but I'd feel better if we were able to offer something a bit more tangible—and perhaps we are. . . ."

"You have something in mind?" Father Bertrand asked.

"Aye." Arnault drew breath and let it out with an explosive sigh, for while they waited for news, he had been troubled increasingly with a sense of impending peril that had to do with a threat far greater than any physical pursuit by King Edward's men.

"I cannot yet be as specific as I would like," he said slowly, "but I feel that we ought to consider protection of a more spiritual nature for Bruce—and I've thought of a way to provide it."

He had their attention, little though he wanted it, and reluctantly continued when no one spoke.

"I've been giving this a great deal of thought, while we waited for news," he said. "Wherever he is, wherever he goes, Bruce is spiritually linked with the Stone of Destiny—and that, in turn, is mystically attuned to a powerful artifact in our possession: the Breastplate of the High Priests of Israel. If we utilize the affinity between the two, we should be able to direct our intent through that link to send additional protection to Bruce via the Stone, even if we ourselves remain ignorant of his physical location."

Gaspar looked dubious, but Christoph was nodding thoughtfully.

"It *is* just a theory," he agreed, "but admirably reasoned. Putting it into practice, however, could be dangerous."

"In what way?" Oliver asked.

"In mystical terms," Christoph said, "to do what Arnault proposes would be akin to setting off an explosion—or at least lighting a signal beacon on a high hill. The resonances of power would be palpably discernible on the metaphysical plane, not only to our friends, but also to our foes. In other words," he finished, "by calling up any significant degree of power on Bruce's behalf, we risk exposing him—and us— to hostile discovery."

"The fact that we exist—yes," Arnault agreed. "But sometimes it's useful to make a show of force, to warn off any would-be predators. If there is still a cadre of Comyn strength attempting to engage dark powers against Bruce, perhaps they'll think again."

There was a long pause, but no one ventured a differing opinion. Christoph exchanged a glance with Gaspar, received his reluctant nod, then polled each of the others in turn, from each receiving silent assent.

"Very well," he said finally. "Today is the feast of the desert saint, Armenius. Like him, then, let us venture boldly into the wilderness, trusting in God to see us through the trials that lie ahead."

And so it was agreed.

Later that night, following the conclusion of Vespers, the members of *le Cercle* made their way by separate routes down to the lower levels of the treasury wing, each bearing a lamp to light his way. Arnault was the last to arrive—and had a sudden sensation of being watched, as he traversed the passageway giving access to the treasure chambers—but it was gone as quickly as he noted it.

He cast an involuntary look over his shoulder, but could sense nothing more. None the wiser, he shrugged the sensation aside and joined his companions in the antechamber, passing then into the secret inner strong room where the Order's choicest treasures lay hidden.

As always, his pulse quickened as he stepped across the threshold. The very air of the inner chamber seemed rarefied yet invigorating, and he inhaled deeply, tasting the indefinable savor of purity and power. The others had set their lamps on a narrow ledge that ran at eye level around the circular chamber, the positions marking out the room's four quarters. Christoph took Arnault's lamp to a bracket suspended above a square central altar-table of white marble. Several brass-bound coffers and a large oaken chest occupied space on the floor nearby.

Arnault set his back against the door to compose himself as the others continued preparing the room with quiet efficiency. While Gaspar and Hugues de Curzon did what was necessary to ward the room, Christoph and Oliver de Penne began removing items from the oaken chest: first an altar cloth of pure white linen, and then a collection of ceremonial items including a pair of seven-branched candlesticks cast from bronze. When these had been properly arranged, Christoph beckoned Arnault to his side as he took out a stack of folded vestments.

"You can work without these, I know," he said, as he helped Arnault don the checkered linen tunic, "but it isn't always that we have the luxury of full ceremonial preparation." He laid the white silk stole around Arnault's shoulders, with its fringe of golden tassels. "It's been a while, hasn't it?"

Arnault smiled faintly as he pulled the ends of the stole under the linen cincture Christoph tied around his waist.

"Yes. Thank you," Arnault murmured.

In fact, he had not worn these vestments since a night some fifteen years ago in Cyprus, when he had received the revelations that had impelled *le Cercle* to abandon Outremer as a site for the Fifth Temple and transfer their focus to Scotland. He had been involved in far more arduous and dangerous workings since then, but he had no doubt that appropriate ceremonial accoutrements could do a great deal to enhance the desired spiritual focus—and tonight, he wanted all the help he could get. As he again donned the mantle of purple silk, with its border of golden bells and pomegranates, he could only hope that the Providence that had brought them so far would sustain them to their journey's end.

Meanwhile, unlocking another of the treasure caskets, Oliver removed a silver reliquary box inscribed with Hebrew characters and placed it on the altar between the candlesticks. Then, from inside, he lifted out a silk-wrapped bundle the size of a small book. Even before Christoph folded back the wrappings, Arnault felt a stirring in the depths of his very soul, for power radiated from the High Priest's Breastplate like an invisible corona of glory reflecting from the throne of Heaven itself.

"*Baruch ateh Adonai, Elohenu melech ha-olam* . . ." Arnault murmured, moved to prayer in the language of the object's origins, for its visible splendor was no less arresting. *Blessed art Thou, O Lord our God, King of the Universe* . . .

His touch was reverent as he laid his hand briefly over the twelve large jewels adorning the face of the Breastplate, set in bezels of pure gold and arranged in three rows of four. Stitched to a backing square of stiffened linen, they shimmered in the light of the lamps with a more than earthly luster. On each of the stones was engraved the name of one of the Twelve Tribes of ancient Israel.

These, on their own, were a wondrous treasure, but the true glory of the Breastplate was vested in a less obvious component known as the *Urim* and *Thummin,* the Lights and Perfections. The very name attempted to embrace not a physical object so much as a concept, though the spiritual attributes of the *Urim* and *Thummin* were presently embodied in a pair of flat, coin-shaped stones, one black and one white, which resided in a double linen pocket stitched to the back of the Breastplate. Said to be of celestial origin, their siting on the back of the Breastplate ensured that, when the Breastplate was worn, the *Urim* and *Thummin* rested over the wearer's heart—for it was from the heart's truth that the wearer drew his inspiration, when invoking their power.

Placing the Breastplate there now, and holding it over his heart while Christoph secured it with fine golden chains fastened to the corners, Arnault could feel both the physical substance and an inward shiver of anticipation, calling to him. Oliver lit fresh candles on the altar, and Hugues ignited a cone of incense set in a silver dish. As the fragrance of frankincense and myrrh wound gently upward on the still air, Christoph summoned the rest of them to gather at the altar, where, after commending themselves and their work to

God with the sign of the cross, he offered up an opening invocation.

"Find your strength in the Lord, in His mighty power," Christoph murmured, paraphrasing Saint Paul. "Put on all the armor that God provides, so that you may be able to stand firm against the devices of the Devil . . ."

His words hung on the silence of the little chamber. As Arnault started to add an invocation of his own, according to usage long familiar in Roman rite, he was suddenly reminded how, when empowering the Stone for Bruce's sacring, they had used more ancient Celtic prayers—and he reached deep into memory for more fitting words.

"Thou Michael the victorious,
I make my circuit under thy shield.
Thou Michael of the white steed,
And of the bright brilliant blades,
Conqueror of the dragon,
Be thou at my back.
Thou ranger of the heavens,
Thou warrior of the King of All,
O Michael the victorious,
My pride and my guide,
O Michael the victorious,
The glory of mine eye. . . ."

As Arnault spoke, resting his hands on the altar and closing his eyes to the material world, the air began to tingle with invisible energies. Welcoming it, he flung open the gates of his soul and let himself fall into the angelic Presence drawing near.

In that instant, in a dizzying burst of inner illumination, he felt himself transported in spirit to a realm of supernal light: a sanctuary not made by hands, where stood a glorious Presence robed in living flame and holding a blazing sword at rest beneath powerful hands. Joyful recognition pierced

Arnault to the heart, and he knew that he knelt in body and in spirit before the Archangel Michael, whose great wings trailed flames and the many iridescent eyes of peacock feathers, and gently stirred the breath of incense that gusted through the celestial vault.

"Be the cowl of Michael militant around me," he murmured, enwrapped in wonder.

Fearlessly he opened his heart to the Other, offering up the needs of the Order and his own fears for the life of Robert Bruce as a single oblation.

The moment of mutual understanding was ravishing: brighter than the sun, more terrible than the lightning, more beautiful than all the stars of the western sky. As the great Archangel touched a fiery fingertip to the Breastplate adorning Arnault's chest, energy sang around him like music as the twelve gems came to life with scintillating radiance— and kindled the throbbing, pulsing power of the *Urim* and *Thummin* against his heart.

Trembling, physical sight half-blinded by joyful tears, Arnault lifted his hands in supplication and called to mind the image of the Stone of Destiny as he last had seen it, in a crypt beneath Dunkeld Cathedral. As he did so, an old scar in his right palm began to tingle, self-inflicted to establish a blood bond with William Wallace.

That bond had allowed Arnault to mediate between the Stone and Wallace at the moment of his sacrificial death, channeling Wallace's life force to reinvigorate the Stone. The Breastplate had been part of the focus for that working. Now, as Arnault laid his scarred hand upon it, he again reached out through its power to make of himself a living bridge—for Bruce, too, had made the blood bond with the Stone.

He could feel it happen: a glowing warmth tingling and pulsing under his hand as the connection leapt between Breastplate and Stone. In that same instant, Arnault became keenly aware, as he had been at the moment of Bruce's mystical enthronement, of how vitally Bruce and the Stone were linked. Unbidden, the ancient words of a Psalm whispered from his lips.

> *"God will cover you with His pinions,*
>   *and you shall find safety beneath His wings;*
> *you shall not fear the hunters' trap by night*
>   *or the arrow that flies by day.*
> *A thousand may fall at your side,*
>   *ten thousand close at hand,*
> *but you it shall not touch.*
> *For He has charged His angels*
>   *to guard you wherever you go. . . ."*

In his mind's eye Arnault suddenly saw Bruce sleeping rough on a bed of bracken, wrapped in a tattered tartan—and a golden radiance enveloping the sleeping king like water pouring from a spring, leaving Bruce himself bathed in radiant energy.

"Be the helmet of salvation about thy head," he whispered, again reverting to words of Celtic blessing.

> *"Be the corselet of the covenant about thy throat,*
> *Be the Breastplate of the priest upon thy breast,*
> *To shield thee in the battle and the combat of*
>   *thine enemies. . . ."*

When Arnault opened his eyes again, he was lying on his back in his own cell. Gaspar was sitting beside him, quietly reading by the light of a tiny oil lamp, but he closed his book with a crooked smile when he saw Arnault was awake.

"Welcome back."

Arnault knuckled his eyes. He felt drowsy, but more at peace than for a very long time.

"How long have I been asleep?"

"Nearly five hours. It's almost dawn." After blowing out

his lamp—for morning light was starting to stain the high, narrow window—Gaspar added, on a lower note, "Just off-hand, I would say that you made a powerful connection."

Arnault slowly nodded. "I would have to agree. I only hope it will be enough."

He sat up, rubbing both hands across his face, then glanced again at the older Templar.

"I should be with him, Gaspar."

"Alas, we cannot be two places at once. You are needed here. He is in good hands with Brother Torquil."

Arnault sighed and said nothing.

"You know I am right," Gaspar said. "You have done what you can for Bruce. No man could do more. Besides that, he soon will be going to ground for the winter—and his enemies will also mostly go to ground. Torquil will keep him safe.

"As for us," he concluded, "I think we must concentrate on holding our ground here in France."

Chapter Nine

July, 1306

As if to underscore the growing precariousness of the Order's position, a message arrived a few days later from Jauffre de Saint Clair, en route to Cyprus to deliver the pope's summons to the Grand Master. Since the delegation sent to escort him would sail from Marseilles, they had instructions to pass through Avignon, some fifty miles short of the busy Mediterranean port, there to deliver an account of the Paris riots to the pope's representative. In addition, Jauffre had additional orders of a more confidential nature: to observe the tenor of the papal court and relay his observations to his mentors within *le Cercle*.

Following the daily chapter meeting in the Paris Temple, Gaspar summoned the resident members of *le Cercle* to a private chamber in the treasury wing. Here he capsulized the contents of Jauffre's letter.

"On the Scottish front," Gaspar began, "he says that the Holy See has received a strong letter of complaint from Edward of England, condemning the bishops of Scotland for their support of Bruce. However, a bout of illness has delayed His Holiness from taking any action as yet. But he did receive our delegation in a private audience and reiterated that the Grand Master should attend him as soon as possible."

"I wonder how serious this illness is," Hugues said.

"Jauffre doesn't know," Gaspar replied. "Apparently the Holy Father is feeling pressure from King Philip; his agents are everywhere, making no secret of their presence. One must wonder whether fear may, perhaps, be contributing to this decline in the pope's health."

Oliver gave a snort of agreement. "Clement has cause to be nervous. The king's agents are run by Nogaret—who may be excommunicate, but that means that the Holy See has little left with which to threaten him. This pope will not have forgotten that Nogaret incurred his excommunication by assaulting a previous pope."

Nor did the excommunication seem to concern Nogaret himself, though the king kept pressing for it to be lifted. Arnault, after watching Nogaret during his time spent at the Paris Temple, did not believe the king's first minister had any particular wish to be reconciled with the Church.

"Nogaret is no friend of ours *or* the Holy Father's," Arnault said. "On the day he and the king became our guests, it was as if a cloud had descended on the Paris Temple."

"Aye, *that's* the truth," Christoph agreed. "I fear that we have yet to see the full repercussions from what began that day."

And it had gotten worse before it got better. For three days following the riot, the Paris mob had besieged the Paris Temple, demanding to see the king. When Philip declined to appear, the crowd had turned their wrath on a wealthy citizen whom rumor accused of having acted as the king's advisor. The man's property had been ransacked, and the man himself had been hanged.

Eventually, soldiers from the Louvre had descended on the mob to restore order. Many people had been killed, and many more arrested with scant regard for justice. A month later, the city was like a lean and hungry beast that grew angrier and more restless with each passing day.

"Hmmm, here's a reminder that the world is wider than our own besetting concerns," Gaspar remarked, returning to Jauffre's letter. "He says that an embassage from Ethiopia has arrived in Avignon requesting a papal audience. Some members of the delegation are fluent in the Latin tongue, and have presented His Holiness with many gifts, including an ivory triptych depicting scenes from the life of King Solomon. They apparently made quite an impression."

He reverted to their young informant's own words.

The central panel of the triptych features the building of the Temple. A delegate named Iskander informs me that Emperor Wedem Ara'ad chose this motif himself. I am given to understand that the emperor wishes to erect an alliance between Ethiopia and the princes of Christendom against the Muslim hordes now occupying Egypt and Syria.

"That would make a great deal of sense," Hugues said. "The rulers of Ethiopia have been Christian for centuries— and even their subjects who still adhere to Judaism have equal reason to fear the might of their Muslim neighbors."

"True enough," Oliver agreed. "It's the kind of alliance that might just swing the balance for a new crusade."

"That doesn't mean it's a good idea," Christoph said. "I fear the time of crusades may be past. We'll not win back Jerusalem while the princes of the West snap and bite at one another."

Arnault, however, was remembering a tale he had heard some years before, in the Holy Land—how an exiled Ethiopian prince named Lalibela had come to Jerusalem in search of sanctuary, more than a century before. For twenty years he had remained there, making friends and becoming acquainted with the ways of the Franks—and when, at last, he returned home to claim his kingship, a contingent of Templar Knights had been among the members of his escort.

Arnault had never been able to discover what became of

those knights. Of a certainty, no record could be found in the archives of the Temple.

"Does Jauffre feel that the pope might be receptive to such an alliance?" Oliver asked, snapping Arnault back to the discussion at hand. "We know that the *king* wants another crusade—not that he can afford it."

"He doesn't say," Gaspar replied. "He's simply reporting what he's heard. The delegation was to sail for Cyprus the next day—but my heart tells me that the survival of the Order will not depend upon any battle in Outremer."

The remainder of the day passed uneventfully, but Jauffre's letter continued to nag at Arnault's mind. The suggestion of a possible alliance between Ethiopia and the princes of the West, with the renewed possibility of a new crusade, had reminded him of the expense of same, and the penurious state of King Philip's exchequer, and the source of his indebtedness.

As evening wore on, Arnault fell prey to a nagging sense of uneasiness. When he retired, after evening prayer, he lay awake for a long time, listening to the darkness; and when he finally slept, he dreamed.

There was a demon prowling in the city. In one taloned hand it carried a ram's skull filled with blood, in the other, a wooden wand frayed at the end like a brush. Robed in darkness, the monster crept from street to street, seeking out certain neighborhoods, leaving others alone. Wherever it stopped, it painted bloody sigils above the lintels of each door, like the symbols painted above the doorways of the Israelites to ward off the Angel of Death—except that this *was* Death, marking its own. Coming at last to a halt, it dashed the ram's skull to the cobbled pavements, to shatter into a thousand shards.

The shards gave birth to a seething mass of giant rats with eyes like live coals and razor-sharp fangs. At the demon's command, the horde dispersed throughout the city, sniffing out the dwellings marked with the blood-sign and swarming through doors and windows. Screams rent the night as the rats ripped and tore at the occupants inside.

Inside the fastness of the Paris Temple, Arnault heard the cries. Snatching up his sword, still dreaming, he rushed out through the gates to set off after the rats. In a cobbled cul-de-sac near the Porte St. Denis, he found a teeming mat of them swarming up the doorstep of a modest house. But before he could turn them back, the sheer weight of the rats burst the door's hinges and they poured inside, screeching and chittering for blood.

Arnault charged in after them, crushing some under his boots, flaying about him with his sword—but there were always more. Fighting his way up a narrow stair, he came face-to-face with a frail old man with a patriarchal beard, his lined face contorted in a rictus of horror. Askew on his hoary head, only noted at second glance, was a peaked yellow cap that marked him as a Jew.

And behind the old man, the hell-rats had already savaged his family. In the room beyond, Arnault saw a woman, a man, and two young boys lying dead in their own blood. The rats were swarming over the body of the woman, stripping the flesh from the bones. And before Arnault's horrified eyes, the rats' bodies melded and merged into new flesh that rose up in grotesque mockery of human form—a lean, wiry man with lank, dark hair and pale eyes.

Guillaume de Nogaret!

The shock of recognition jolted Arnault from sleep, to find himself standing barefoot in the Temple's cobbled outer courtyard, clad only in his shirt and sheepskin trews, right hand knotted around the hilt of his sword and with no clear recollection of how he came to be there. The sky to the east showed the pale glimmer of dawn, and as he swayed on his feet, trying to collect his bearings, he became aware of rough voices and running feet converging on the Temple gate from outside—a sound he had heard all too recently: the ugly snarl of a mob in pursuit of its prey.

An alarm rang out from the main gatehouse. Other knight-brothers and lay servants were already pouring into the yard, swords in hand, as a frantic hammering broke out from the postern gate in the south wall. Already in motion, Arnault set out across the yard with scant regard for his un-shod state, collecting several other knights along the way.

The watch had already opened the postern gate when he got there, and two brothers of the watch were bending over a limp form crumpled before the opening: an old man in tattered garments, his silver hair matted with blood from an ugly head wound. When Arnault bent down to turn the old man's face to the light, he was shocked to see the elderly Jewish man of his dream.

Meanwhile, there came a fresh burst of noise from outside, as a motley crowd of townsmen erupted from the shadows of an adjoining street, brandishing clubs and fleshers' knives and other crude weapons. Their leader was a burly, blond-bearded man in a blacksmith's leather apron, who let out a hoarse whoop of elation as he saw the old man being dragged through the postern gate.

"There he is, lads!" he shouted, pointing. "Don't let them take him!"

The mob surged forward. Letting the men of the watch drag the old man inside, Arnault directed several better-armed knights into the doorway around him and lifted his sword to sight down the blade at the old man's pursuers.

"That's far enough!" he said sharply. "You have no business here."

The mob came to a stumbling halt. Their leader hefted a wicked-looking hammer in beefy hands and planted his feet defiantly. "Oh, yes, we do. We're here to carry out the king's orders."

"And which orders would those be?" Arnault inquired on a note of dangerous calm.

"The king has ordered all Jews expelled from the kingdom," came the defiant reply. "The sooner we rid ourselves of these soulless child-killers, the better for all!"

Arnault raked the mob leader with an icy glare, and the knights to either side of him took half a step forward, weapons at the ready. Recent months had seen a resurgence of the old, old fiction that the Jews were sorcerers who kidnapped and murdered Christian children to serve their impious blood rites. In a flash, it came to him that Philip was after the wealth of the Jews, and had spread the lies to justify taking it. And if he was brazen enough to seize the Jews' gold, the Temple's wealth might well be next.

"Whatever the king's orders may be," he said evenly, "you and your companions have no mandate to act as executioners. Now, be off with you, while you still have time to repent of your folly."

An angry flush suffused the blond man's face.

"You don't frighten me, Templar!" he blustered. "We'll not let you or anyone else stand in the way of the king's justice!"

He hefted his hammer again and started forward, several companions in his wake. Arnault let him come within arm's reach, then dealt him a stunning blow with the flat of his sword. The blond man went down like a felled ox, and the others skittered back.

"Now, get you gone," Arnault ordered, "and take him with you—before my brothers and I forget we are sworn not to shed Christian blood!"

The remaining members of the mob recoiled before his anger, though two of them dared to dart in and seize their felled leader; but the sight of a dozen more armed knights pouring through the gate to fan out before it quelled any lingering bravado. Sullenly the crowd retreated into the shadows, muttering darkly amongst themselves. As soon as they had disappeared from sight, Arnault summoned the sortie party back inside and singled out two of his subordinates.

"Find Father Christoph and Brother Gaspar and tell them

what has happened," he instructed them. "They have friends and acquaintances among the city's Jewish community who may be in need of assistance. And inform the Visitor."

Directing the remaining knights to secure the gate and keep close watch, Arnault crouched down beside the old Jew. As he laid aside his sword, glancing at the lay brother examining the old man's wounds, the patient stirred.

His eyelids fluttered open, and his wandering gaze lighted on Arnault's face. One eye was nearly swollen shut, but the other widened as he reached out to clutch at Arnault's sleeve, a low groan escaping from between battered lips.

"No, don't try to speak, friend," Arnault murmured, clasping the old man's hand. "Rest easy. You're out of danger now."

The old man gave an agitated shake of his head. "No. . . . No safety here. . . . Fire and the sword—"

A shudder racked his battered frame, cutting off his utterance, and the lay brother slid an arm under his shoulders to raise him up.

"Give me some help here," he instructed. "We need to get this man to the infirmary."

Arnault bent to comply, gathering his arms under the injured man's legs; but before they could lift him, the old Jew gave another shiver and opened his eyes wide, with a quivering forefinger sweeping across all the Templars present.

"The Law will be your death!" he cried in a loud, harsh voice. "And the Law will set you free!"

Startled, Arnault stared at him, but before he could muster a question, the old man gave a bubbling cough. As dark blood trickled from between his broken lips, the dark eyes went glassy and he slumped back lifeless against the supporting brother's arm.

Chapter Ten

July, 1306

$\mathcal{F}$AR IN THE WEST OF SCOTLAND, A FEW WEEKS LATER, YET another summer storm scoured at the slated roofs and stone walls of Dunollie Castle. The winds that swept in off the Bay of Lorn invaded every corner of the keep, sending cold drafts whisking up and down its narrow corridors like invisible rats. The sullen fire tucked into a corner fireplace of one of the guest chambers did little to dispel the cold or to banish the smell of damp, and the stone walls wept with a bloom of condensation.

"Master, I have seen better-appointed cow byres than this hovel the lord of Lorn is pleased to call his family honor," Mercurius grumbled, huddling closer to the chimney breast. "How much longer must we languish here?"

"Long enough to ensure Bruce's capture," Bartholeme replied. "And I want to be around, when it happens." He was sitting near the room's single window, gazing out at the rain while he honed a dagger on a whetstone. "I don't want him killed before I can question him about the whereabouts of the Stone of Destiny."

It had been nearly six weeks since the engagement at Methven. Failing to apprehend Bruce on the battlefield, the

Earl of Pembroke had dispersed his forces with orders to hunt down the royal fugitive. His allies among the Scottish lords had been sent home to patrol their own ancestral territories, spurred on by the promise of rich rewards for the man who could take Bruce alive. The rebel king was still at large, but Bartholeme was determined that this state of affairs would soon end.

Mercurius, tossing more wood on the meager fire, was not so confident, and recoiled cursing when a gust of wind down the chimney sent a cloud of smoke and soot billowing into the room. He was coughing and slapping ash from his clothing as he retreated nearer to Bartholeme and the window.

"Master, what makes you so certain that Bruce must come this way?" he asked.

Bartholeme tried the edge of his blade against his thumb, then resumed his slow, steady sweep against the whetstone. "It's the only avenue still open to him," he said, not looking up. "The Borders are effectively closed, and Pembroke has secured all the east coast ports from Berwick to Banff. Meanwhile, the Comyn earls of Badenoch and Buchan have tightened their hold on the North—and Bruce will know this. I suspect that he is far too canny to attempt slipping past them for an escape to Norway.

"No," he continued, "his sole remaining hope for sanctuary and support lies with his wife's father, the Earl of Ulster. The safest route to Ireland is by way of the Mull of Kintyre, which lies but a day or two from here. Sooner or later, Bruce will be forced to turn south—and when he does, we will be on hand to seize him."

Mercurius cocked an ear toward the door as footsteps approached.

"Someone's coming, Master."

Bartholeme was already rising, his dagger sliding into a boot-top sheath as the footsteps halted just outside the door. A peremptory knock heralded the precipitous entrance of

John Macdougall of Lorn, the castle's owner. Clenched in one fist was a crumpled sheet of parchment bearing fragments of a broken seal. Mercurius retired discreetly to the shadows of the chimney corner.

"So much for our plans to let Bruce come to *us*!" Lorn blurted, brandishing the parchment. "A messenger just delivered this. It's an order from the Earl of Pembroke to gather my following and return immediately to Perth."

It cost Bartholeme an effort to mask his annoyance at this threatened upset of his plans. "I assume," he said, "that Pembroke gives some reason for the urgency of the summons?"

Lorn emitted a rumble of disgust. "The Prince of Wales has come north from Carlisle, bringing substantial reinforcements. All who have sworn fealty to the English crown are ordered to Perth straightway to attend a council of war."

"Where is the Lord Edward at present?"

"Dumfriesshire, according to this," Lorn replied. "He turned aside just north of the Borders to receive the surrender of Lochmaben Castle—which at least closes another door on Bruce! He'll remain there long enough to dispense justice. Then he'll be on his way again. We're all expected to be waiting in Perth when he arrives."

Bartholeme pinched his lip thoughtfully. "Inconvenient timing—but it still gives us a few days to hunt Bruce down."

"We've been doing that for weeks—and look where it's got us. He could be anywhere!"

"No, he is *some*where," Bartholeme said, his voice trailing on a note of speculation. "Leave me to think, and I'll let you know what I come up with."

Lorn bristled resentfully, but a look at the Frenchman's face caused him to swallow his arguments and retire from the room. When the door had closed behind him, Bartholeme cast a pointed gaze toward the shadows of the chimney corner.

"Mercurius," he drawled, "I fancy a game of chess. Be so good as to fetch the pieces."

The dwarf gave him a knowing grin and, while Bartholeme secured the door, went to the traveling chest set under the window and dragged it into the center of the room. There he took from a compartment at its bottom a checkered game board and a flat, brass-bound box containing a set of chess pieces, half carved from ivory and half from jet.

Cushioning the pieces was a folded square of black silk, which he shook out and spread over the chest before laying out the checkered board, careful to align the corners according to the cardinal points of the compass. He then brought a pair of stools to flank the chest, straddling one and beginning to lay out the game pieces—not to begin a new game of mere diversion, but to establish the positions in a more deadly game already in progress.

Bartholeme, meanwhile, prepared the room itself, unsheathing his dagger to anoint its tip with a mixture of spittle and adder's venom taken from a vial he removed from the medicine chest beside his bed. Then, invoking the powers of darkness with a muttered incantation, he used the dagger's envenomed point to sketch a large pentagram on the floor, its center encompassing the chessboard and the two stools. He sealed the pentagram with a tracery of power, then cleaned the blade, sheathed it, and claimed the stool opposite Mercurius.

The dwarf was seated on the side of the board dominated by the black pieces. From behind the ranks of white pieces, Bartholeme surveyed the state of play.

"*Bon,*" he declared, "but the balance of the game has shifted since Methven. We must begin by removing the pieces that are no longer in play." He plucked the two white bishops from the board. "These are Lamberton of St. Andrews and Wishart of Glasgow, both now bound for imprisonment in England. Better, had they been executed like the others, but they can do little harm where they are going." He dropped the two white bishops into the box with a clatter of ivory against wood. "May they live to see the extinction of their hopes.

"These pawns I likewise declare forfeit," he continued, plucking more white pieces from the board as he spoke the names. "Simon Fraser . . . Alexander Scrymgeour . . . Christopher Seton . . . William Gourlay. . . . May their death agonies feed and strengthen the power of their foes!"

More ivory pieces clattered into the box, whereupon he reached for the two rooks.

"Here are the castles of Lochmaben and Dumfries, which the fortunes of war have delivered into English hands. May the Scottish loss of these citadels be a sign of things to come!"

Only seven white pieces remained on the board: the ivory king, the queen, three pawns, and two knights. Bartholeme cast them into shadow as he passed his hands over them in a gesture of conjuration.

"Here is Bruce," he declared. "And here is his queen, with her attendants following. Here are the Knights Templar, their would-be protectors. The maledictions of the Lords Infernal be upon them, waking or sleeping! From this moment onward, let the forces of destruction shadow their every move!"

For an instant, all the light in the room seemed to falter, though a hint of firelight reflecting on the remaining white pieces somehow cast a faint glow over Bartholeme's face, giving it a skeletal aspect.

"Now for the work of the night," he breathed. "Mercurius, are you ready?"

"Yes, Master," came the eager answer.

Faintly smirking, Bartholeme slipped the black swan signet from his finger and took from his sleeve a skein of dried catgut. This he threaded through the circle of the ring, tying the ends together with an intricate knot whose peculiarities bound and harnessed dark arcane energies. As he let the ring dangle over the game board, grasping the length of gut by its knot, the dwarf settled in anticipation, stubby hands braced on his knees, fixing his gaze on the ring as Bartholeme set it gently swinging like a pendulum.

"The swan is a symbol of perfection," Bartholeme whispered in a sibilant, singsong tone. "Perfection is the key to wholeness. Be one in spirit with the swan, and embrace the wisdom of Hermes. . . . Surrender your will to the great Darkness which is the *krater* of transformation. . . ."

Mercurius's eyelids drooped as he watched the pendulum swing above the board, the long lashes fluttering and finally closing over the beautiful eyes as he exhaled softly, coarse features relaxing. As he sank deeper into trance, Bartholeme slipped the loop of catgut over the dwarf's head and around his neck. Then, keeping hold of the ring, he invoked by name the spirit of his ancestral familiar.

"Hear me, ye gates of Hell," he whispered. "I summon to this time and place Thierry de Challon, who once was Magister of Shadows and now is thrall to the Dark Lords. In the name of Lucifer Prince of Darkness, I call you forth, Thierry de Challon, from the womb of infernal night! Be present *here,* in this living vessel who waits to receive you, and speak through his mouth!"

A noise like rushing wind invaded the room. In that instant, the dwarf gasped and his misshapen body went rigid, stubby hands reaching out to brace against the edge of the trunk. The beautiful eyes snapped open, unseeing, but now lit by an eerie gleam betokening intelligence of a far different magnitude than that of the dwarf known as Mercurius. As the fleshy lips parted to speak, there issued a deep, harsh voice wholly unlike his own.

"I hear and attend," came the whispered response. "Ask what you will."

Bartholeme's eyes narrowed, taking on a predatory gleam. "I seek Robert Bruce, the One chosen by Many. Cast your vision over the land and tell me where he is to be found in this present moment."

"I hear and obey. . . ."

Eyes unseeing, moving his arms with the stiff, jerky motion of a marionette controlled by invisible strings, Mercurius began rearranging the chess pieces on the board between them, placing the white king and queen, the white knights, and the remaining white pawns in a beleaguered cluster at the center of the board. Around them his stumpy hands positioned the black pieces, their array growing ever more threatening as the entity possessing him related its vision.

"I see a village beside a great waterfall . . . and a ragged column of men marching westward along the bank of a wide river." The voice gained in strength and volume as it continued—and was not that of Mercurius. "In their midst rides the White King, with the White Queen at his side, and four other women. . . ."

Bartholeme's smile held a sly satisfaction, for the whereabouts of Bruce's wife, Elizabeth de Burgh, and the other female members of Bruce's family had been previously unknown.

"Excellent! We will capture the king and queen together, in a single move. If Bruce declines to trade the Stone of Destiny for his own life, most assuredly he will yield it up for the life of his consort."

"First you must overcome their guardian knights," the alien voice warned.

"It will take more than two Templars to deny me this prize!" Bartholeme retorted. "Where will Bruce be tomorrow?"

"He follows the river's course west, then north," came the reply. "Before him lies the gateway to an open valley—"

The voice abruptly ceased, and Bartholeme leaned forward with a scowl.

"Continue."

The dwarf's face contorted in a grimace of pain, but his lips parted again, the voice of Thierry de Challon taking on a harsher note.

"The valley bears the name of a Christian saint," came the strained reply. "Those who dwell in the sight of the Prince of Darkness are forbidden to speak it."

"The name I can learn for myself," Bartholeme said impatiently. "Will Bruce enter this valley?"

"He will."

"Where will he go from there?"

"I cannot tell. The saint's influence clouds my sight."

When Bartholeme attempted to press the matter, the dwarf's body began to manifest signs of stress. Eventually, Bartholeme gave Thierry's spirit leave to depart and brought Mercurius back to his senses, instructing his exhausted servant to pull the pallet from beneath the bed and sleep off the aftereffects of his trance. After erasing all trace of their recent working, he then went in search of Macdougall of Lorn.

"Is there a valley near here which takes its name from a local saint?" he asked, forestalling any questions from the Scots lord.

Lorn ceased pacing the floor of his private solar and thought a moment. "There's a place called Strathfillan, about a day's ride from here. It's said that an Irish missionary named Fillan preached his first sermon and made his first converts there."

"That has to be the place," Bartholeme decided. He rounded briskly on Lorn. "Assemble your men and make ready to ride out. If you can reach Strathfillan before nightfall tomorrow, you may be confident of capturing not only Bruce himself, but also his queen and his Templar bodyguards."

Chapter Eleven

July, 1306

THE VALE OF STRATHFILLAN LAY OPEN TO THE NORTHWEST. A chill wind swept along the valley floor, flattening the reeds along the riverbank that marked the route Bruce and his men had been following for several days. They had seen no sign of human habitation since passing through Killin, a remote village overlooking a sweep of cataracts known as the Falls of Dochart. But despite the apparent emptiness of the vale ahead, Brother Torquil Lennox remained on alert, unwilling to relax his guard as long as the company were on the march.

There were hardly two hundred of them, strung out along the riverbank, some mounted, but most on foot—all that remained of the Scottish rebel force routed at Methven. At Torquil's side, Bruce rode bareheaded; he had lost his golden circlet of kingship when he lost his helm at Methven. Now, save for a fine brooch clasping the faded plaid about his shoulders, there remained little to distinguish him from the others, save his proud carriage in the saddle and a gleam of utter determination in the light eyes.

But all of them were distinctly the worse for wear, after nearly six weeks on the run—and several of Bruce's staunchest supporters were conspicuous by their absence. Some of the missing might have escaped in other directions, melting into the Highlands and perhaps taking refuge in one of the few strongholds still held by forces friendly to Bruce, but many more would have died where they fell; and only ignoble death awaited those who had been captured at Methven.

In particular, Torquil knew that Bruce was fretting over the missing Christopher Seton, who perhaps had been his closest friend, as well as being his brother-in-law. They had seen him taken as he fought to cover their dash toward the horse lines—and his valor and loyalty surely had helped to ensure their escape; but unless he somehow had managed to win free, Seton's fate was likely to be grim.

Twitching his own threadbare cloak back on his shoulders, Torquil stood briefly in his stirrups to gaze backward, where he could see the survivors toiling along the tussocky ridge with bent backs and gaunt, careworn faces. All of them had shared the stress of living like hunted animals, being constantly on the move, scavenging what they could. Yet despite hardship and privation and fear for those they had left behind, their loyalty to Bruce showed no signs of faltering.

The women in the party were bearing up no less heroically than the men. There were five of them: Bruce's wife Elizabeth, his daughter Marjorie, his sisters Mary and Christian—the latter sick with worry for the missing Seton, her husband—and the redoubtable Isabel, Countess of Buchan, who had defied her husband to ride to Scone and place a royal circlet on Bruce's head, on that fateful Palm Sunday that officially marked the beginning of his reign.

Shortly before Methven, the king had installed the women at the nearby manor of Weem, where Sir Alexander Menzies had vowed to keep them safe; but following Methven, when it became clear that the rebel forces were on the run, Bruce had returned to move the women elsewhere, judging them safest in his own company. The monks of Inchaffray had assisted in the escape, diverting Pembroke's pursuit by misdirection. Before leaving Inchaffray, Bruce had also paused to seek absolution again for what he had done at Dumfries, kneeling before the abbot at the ancient shrine of the Celtic Saint Fillian—this time with his men as witnesses, for he wanted it known to them beyond any doubt just how seriously he regarded his responsibilities as king.

Since then, the hunt had never been far behind, as the fleeing Scots drove ever deeper into the mountainous protection of Argyll. After several narrow escapes, however, the king was rethinking his decision to take the women with him, and had decided to entrust them to the protection of his wife's father, the Earl of Ulster—or failing that, to send them northward, across the sea to Norway, where another of his sisters was queen.

But the route to Ireland was by no means unguarded, skirting the hostile territory of Macdougall of Lorn to the west; and the route north was hardly safer. Bruce himself would strike out for Macdonald country, in the Western Isles, where he hoped to obtain assistance from the Lord of the Isles.

Torquil had just returned from scouting into a side glen when Neil Bruce came galloping back from far ahead, Aubrey at his side.

"We must be very close to the head of Strathfillan," Neil reported, as he reined in and turned to ride knee to knee with his brother. "I can see the pass at Dail Righ. From there, we can head in several different directions. You're sure you want me to take the women on to Ireland?"

"I don't *want* that," Bruce replied, "but they'll be safer there than with me." He glanced at Torquil, then at James Douglas. "Let's have a closer look. Jamie, you're in charge."

With Aubrey leading the way, the king and Torquil galloped back up the valley, making for the dark line of trees that Aubrey pointed out ahead and to their left. Glancing upward at a flash of movement, just before they gained the shelter of the trees, Torquil noticed the lone, dark shape of a corbie circling high above the entrance to the adjoining valley. The bird's presence in an otherwise empty sky reminded him yet again of how exposed the whole company was. But he thought little more of it as he followed Bruce and Aubrey into the narrowing at the end of the glen and they drew rein in the shelter of the trees, branched over like the arched aisle of a leafy cathedral.

Only a subdued twitter of birdsong mingled with the small sounds of horses' breathing and harness softly creaking—but that, in itself, suggested that no one else was close by. They were turning to go back when Bruce suddenly gave a little gasp and stiffened, reining up sharply, gaze unfocused as one hand groped for balance against the front of his saddle and the other lifted in a gesture for silence. As his head cocked back toward the head of the glen in a listening attitude, the gray eyes held an odd, fey gleam.

"Fifty paces back and to our right . . ." he finally muttered, in a flat tone Torquil had never heard him use before. "There's a hidden ravine. Armed men are waiting to ambush us when we start down the glen—several hundred of them—men of Lorn."

Aubrey registered a blink, and Torquil laid a staying hand on his sleeve, looking at Bruce askance. John Macdougall of Lorn was cousin to the slain Red Comyn.

"I know what I'm talking about," Bruce insisted. "I can *see* them."

And Torquil had no reason to suppose that Bruce could not, or to question that it was not with his eyes that Bruce saw. The king had never shown any visionary powers before, but Torquil's own experience had taught him that such abilities could lie dormant for years—an entire lifetime—until a moment of crisis unlocked their potential. Whether this revelation was a gift of the Stone of Destiny or the bequest of some other benevolent power, Torquil had no idea; but he also had no doubt but that the vision was true.

"That's good enough for me, Sire," he murmured, warning Aubrey to silence with a look. "Let's get back and warn the others."

Swiftly and silently they retraced their path, doubly cautious now that they knew an enemy was nearby. Upon rejoining the others, Bruce summoned his close advisors for a hurried consultation.

"How in God's name could they have found out we were coming?" Neil Bruce exclaimed, casting a nervous glance in the direction of the waiting ambush.

"Aye, you'd almost think it was sorcery," Gilbert de la Haye muttered.

The notion had already occurred to Aubrey, but it chilled him to know that Gilbert also had thought of it. Nor would this be the first time that Bruce's adversaries had struck a bargain with the powers of Darkness.

"Well, we daren't turn back," the king said, dismissing the possibility of avoiding an engagement. "There's precious little concealment to our rear. If we simply turn tail and run, they could harry us all the way back to Killin, without ever losing sight of us."

"So, what are we to do?" Alexander Lindsay asked.

"Make a stand here—but on our terms," Bruce replied.

Briefly he explained what he had in mind. His proposal was audacious enough to draw a chuckle of grim appreciation from James Stewart, the aging Earl of Atholl.

"It sounds sae daft, it just might work," he said under his breath.

Bruce turned to his brother Neil. "They haven't any horses. How many have we got?"

"About thirty, not counting your own," Neil replied.

"Then, *count* mine," Bruce said crisply, as he swung down from his mount and handed the reins to his brother, also beckoning Alexander Lindsay and Stephen Boyd to join them.

"I'm putting all the horses at your disposal," he told them, though his focus made it clear that Neil Bruce was in command. "Make up a mounted escort party for the queen and the other women, and mount as many more men as you have horses, for a decoy. When the ambushers break cover to give chase, and we've engaged them, be ready to ride like the Devil himself is after you. We'll do our best to cover your escape."

The rebel band split up at the intersection of the two streams. As the decoy party got into position, and the rest of Bruce's men faded into the trees, he exchanged brief farewells with his wife and daughter, his sisters, and his friends.

"God keep you!" he bade them, when he had outlined his plan. "Whatever befalls us from this moment on, I promise you, as God is my witness, we shall meet again in triumph!"

Elizabeth de Burgh pressed her hand to her husband's cheek, her dark eyes troubled, faintly rebellious. "I like this not, my lord. I pray God to guard you as well." She grimaced, shaking her head. "Sometimes it seems to me that we are as children playing at a summer game of kings and queens. . . ."

Bruce said nothing, but pressed his lips to her hand a final time before passing on to embrace his daughter. His sister Mary was bending to take her leave of her husband, Neil Campbell.

"You'd better go now," Bruce said to his brother, who sat waiting on his own mount. "Ride north into Aberdeenshire. Make for the safety of Kildrummy Castle—and failing that, press on to Orkney, and thence to Norway. Our sister Isabella will give you sanctuary."

Most of Bruce's following had now dispersed into the trees, fanning out in preparation to deal with the waiting ambush. Torquil and Aubrey, like the rest of Bruce's following, had given up their horses and waited on foot with Edward Bruce and several others.

"Give us until the count of three hundred," Bruce said to

his brother, clapping a hand to his stirruped boot in farewell. "Then ride like the wind!"

He watched them go, then turned to rejoin his brother Edward and James Douglas. Torquil and Aubrey fell in to flank them as they headed into the trees with the others, where Bruce selected a coppice of young elms and hunkered down in the midst of them. Drawing their weapons, the two Templars dug themselves in amid the bracken close by.

Spears bristled in the shadows among the low-hanging boughs, and an expectant hush gathered, broken only by the gurgle of the stream in its stony bed. Then, abruptly, the air was riven by a shout of alarm, followed by a brief but convincing flurry of confusion, both on the trail and in the woods all around them. Even as startled exclamations rang out from the hidden ranks of the ambush party ahead, hoofbeats thundered off at the gallop, rapidly receding.

"After them, you fools!" an authoritative voice roared above the rest. "They're getting away!"

The men of Lorn burst from cover, shouting and brandishing weapons as they poured down from the neighboring ridge. Bruce's hidden forces held their ground until the attackers were well onto the forest floor before rising up to confront them with a shout that set the vale ringing.

The two parties collided head-on. Above the harsh clang of weaponry, battle cries turned to screams of pain. Torquil cut down one man armed with a battle-axe, then wheeled to take on another. Off to his right, Aubrey rushed three attackers at once, driving them back in their tracks with great, scything two-handed sweeps of his sword, though he was somewhat hampered by the trees.

More of the men of Lorn came rushing up from the rear. For several seconds, Torquil had his hands full, just staying alive; and by the time he fended them off, he had lost sight of the king. Alarmed, he looked around for Bruce—and had to take on another assailant. At the same time, he spotted Bruce off to his left, locked in hand-to-hand struggle with a hulking behemoth in a leather jerkin. The king was ably holding his own, but at that moment more men of Lorn burst from the shadowed wood, swords and axes and spears in hand, yelling and shouting as they came. The silver glint of a heavy shoulder brooch set apart one of the men, taller than the rest—quite possibly John Macdougall himself.

"Back-stabbing coward!" the man snarled, hurling himself at the king. "I'll gut you like a herring and feed your liver to the gorcrows! You murdered my cousin!"

He launched into a savage exchange of attacks and parries that put Bruce on the defensive. Before Torquil or Aubrey could go to his aid, they were cut off by more of Lorn's henchmen.

Bruce and Lorn traded a flurry of clashing sword blows, amid a whirlwind shower of sparks that glittered in the twilight. Lorn was good, and fresh—and Bruce was tiring. As the deadly battle continued, the king's responses began to flag—and suddenly his blade went spinning from his hand.

Bruce staggered backward, scrambling for balance amid the tree trunks and drawing his dirk, looking desperately for his sword. With a triumphant grin, Lorn stalked toward his now vastly underarmed foe, sighting down his sword with murderous intent.

Both Torquil and Aubrey were locked in heated combat with other assailants, as were Edward Bruce and Neil Campbell and every other Bruce man in sight. With a twist and a desperate lunge that nearly got him skewered for his trouble, Torquil finished his own attacker and broke free, but in that same instant, he caught movement in his side vision and whirled to look up.

Blotting out the sky above him was a huge black bird with a serpentine neck and a bright, predatory beak, folding powerful wings to settle like some great vulture on the stout branch of a nearby tree. As it cocked its head at Torquil, eyes like twin rubies fixed him with their baleful gaze, and a sudden weakness seized him in the knees, dragging him to a standstill.

His instinctive sketching of a sign of protection seemed to have little, if any, effect. Appalled, Torquil could feel the weakness rising up his legs, sapping his strength and threatening to topple him.

Powerless to take another step, he cocked his arm and hurled his sword at Macdougall of Lorn. The effort also sent him staggering to his knees. The weapon spun as it flew through the air, but the flat of its blade glanced off Lorn's shoulder hard enough to knock the sword from his grasp. Lorn tried to recover, fumbled, and knocked the weapon farther out of reach, then abandoned it with a curse and made a bare-handed lunge for Bruce's throat.

Both men fell heavily to the ground, grunting and straining as they tumbled. Torquil was struggling to get back to his feet, even to crawl to Bruce's aid. Lorn's throttling fingers locked in the folds of Bruce's cloak as they grappled nose to nose, twisting at the fabric to choke him. One of the henchmen joined the struggle, leaping onto Bruce's back and clinging like a limpet—too close to use his sword—but the king managed to twist his dirk around and stab behind, at the same time bucking to throw that assailant clear.

At that, the weatherworn fabric in Lorn's hands gave way and Bruce wrenched free, leaving the torn garment in his enemy's hands. As the king scrambled to his feet, Lorn rolled and fetched up hard against the trunk of the tree where the bird had perched, sending it beating airborne with a raucous screech.

In that instant, Torquil felt the life return to his legs. Shouting to Aubrey and Jamie Douglas to help Bruce, he made a scrambling dive to recover his sword. A shadow passed over him, and something heavy struck him hard between the shoulder blades and sent him tumbling—the wheeling bird, he saw as he rolled, glaring down at him with hatred in its eyes!

He got his hand around his sword hilt just as the bird wheeled around for another pass, but this time he was ready. With a scream of rage, it sheered aside from the sweep of his blade and soared upward, powerful wings beating at the air, screeching a final cry of defiance and challenge as it headed off.

Breathing hard, and well aware that this had been no ordinary bird, Torquil picked himself up and flung a look around. Bruce had recovered his sword and was flanked by Aubrey and James Douglas, who were seeing off several Lorn men, but Lorn himself had disappeared. Even as this fact registered, a dissonant horn blast rent the forest air, at which sound the remaining men of Lorn immediately disengaged and melted back into the forest shadows and the high ground.

"They may only be pausing to regroup!" Neil Campbell said, panting. "But it may be our chance to get out of here!"

Bruce had turned to look in the direction where his brother and Argyll and the women had disappeared, catching his breath and fingering his throat, looking a little dazed.

"The women—did they get away?" he managed to rasp.

"They're well on their way," Torquil assured him, seizing his shoulder. "Come *on*! We've done all we can here. Now it's our turn to be going."

A single piercing whistle signaled the rebels to disperse— Edward Bruce, rallying what remained of the shattered rebel force. Taking their wounded with them, the Scots faded swiftly and silently into the trees, their flight carrying them ever deeper into the densely forested heart of the glen. The men of Lorn attempted to give chase, but they were no match for Bruce's men in the woods. As the long summer twilight deepened and the survivors pressed on, it gradually became apparent that their pursuers finally had been obliged to abandon the chase.

Torquil and Aubrey were among the handful of followers still attached directly to the king himself, along with his

brother Edward and James Douglas and a few others of
Bruce's closest companions, when Bruce at last signaled a
halt in a small forest clearing, beside a rocky pool. The darkness was settling in earnest and would soon be full upon
them.

"I think we've come far enough," the king announced,
looking around. "We should be able to rest here in safety—
at least for a few hours."

Around him, his men flung themselves down wearily on
the mossy ground, a few tending to wounds, some of them
beginning to forage in haversacks for supper. Some collapsed beside the pool to slake their thirst, or merely sat
there gasping for breath. A few were already rolling up in
their plaids to snatch what sleep they could. After arranging
the order of watch, Torquil settled wearily beside the king.

"You seem to know this countryside," he said. "Dare we
risk a fire?"

Smiling crookedly, and gnawing on a bannock Neil
Campbell had given him, Bruce shook his head.

"I fear not—though I'll share my bannock. Mind you, it's
stale." He lifted the bannock with a grin. "At least 'tis still
summer—nearly Lammas. We can make do for a while.
Still, the nights are chill. I don't doubt that I shall miss that
tattered old plaid of mine, far more than the brooch that
clasped it, though that was a pretty piece."

A prickle of uneasiness stirred the fine hairs at the back of
Torquil's neck as it registered that Bruce's plaid was, indeed,
gone, along with the brooch—and in whose hands both now
must be.

"Lorn has the brooch?" he asked.

"Aye, he got it off me in the scuffle," Bruce said, and
shrugged. "Heigh-ho, it was a small enough price to pay for
escape. Do have one of Neil's bannocks. They're hard as
rocks, but they're all we've got, for now."

Torquil only nodded his vague thanks as Campbell
handed over another bannock—burnt on one edge—for he

was trying to picture the missing brooch. There had been a large, domed crystal mounted at its center, as he recalled, surrounded by pearls. The pearls were of no concern, but the crystal was—for such a stone was capable of absorbing psychic impressions from its wearer.

He nearly dropped his bannock as that registered, for now an even more insidious danger suddenly became clear. He had been worrying about the giant black bird since leaving Dail Righ, and had been in no doubt of the creature's evil origins. To conjure such an entity into the material world would have required the skills of someone with formidable arcane abilities—who now had access to Bruce's brooch, which might well be used as a link to work mischief against him.

Shivering, Torquil glanced off into the darkness gradually deepening around their impromptu camp, more than ever regretting the absence of Arnault, his mentor as well as his companion-at-arms. Arnault would have known what to do—and might even have anticipated the magical attack. For all Torquil knew, the demon-bird might still be nearby, shadowing their every move. If it attacked again—or brought reinforcements!—Torquil was by no means certain that he would have the resources to fend it off a second time. Aubrey was a good man, and one day would be accomplished, but right now he lacked experience.

There was only one place Torquil could think of where the king might find safe refuge, while they sorted things out. But first he had to convince Bruce of the enormity of the danger, and without tipping his hand to the others.

"Sire," he said, after a moment's further reflection, "where do you plan to go from here?"

Bruce gave him a shrewd look. "Where would you suggest we go?"

Torquil drew a deep breath. "If you will be counseled by me, Sire, I would say the Isle of Iona. Not all of us—for there are things that must be done, messages that must be sent, contacts to be made. Winter will be coming, and your allies must use that time for preparations."

Bruce nodded, chewing on a mouthful of bannock.

"Iona," he said. "That would be risky—for the holy brothers, as well as for me, if King Edward's spies were to learn of my presence there."

"I think they would not shrink from that danger," Torquil replied. "And you should not underestimate the resources of the Columban brothers. Against certain forms of danger, their defenses are formidable." He glanced up as Aubrey and Gilbert de la Haye joined them. "By chance, did you get a close look at that black bird that came in Lorn's wake?"

"Black bird?" Bruce repeated blankly.

"Never mind," Torquil murmured, choosing his next words with care. "You'll not have forgotten the kinds of things that happened after you killed the Red Comyn . . . ?"

Bruce's gaze narrowed, remembering precisely what had been brought into play, both for good and for ill—but also reminded of the others' presence, as Torquil had intended.

"Are you telling me I have something greater to fear than King Edward's malice?"

Torquil drew a deep breath. "I am telling you that your life, your land, and possibly your soul are in danger, so long as these unknown enemies are seeking you," he said, declining to be more specific. "And those enemies may well hound you to your death, if you do not seek the sanctuary that only Iona can provide."

Bruce hung his head, saying nothing for a long moment.

"If I go into hiding as you suggest," he finally whispered, "what is to become of the rebellion? How can I justify leaving my family and my friends to face King Edward's wrath without me?"

"The fate of the rebellion stands or falls by you," Torquil replied. "If you do not put yourself out of harm's way while we try to regroup, all that has been sacrificed so far will have been in vain." He leaned closer to Bruce.

"Do you think I don't know what it is to make a hard choice?" he asked softly. "During the final defense of Acre, some of us were obliged to abandon the city and our brethren, in order to carry to safety the treasures that the Order holds in trust. To remain faithful to our duty, we had to live when we would more gladly have died. Now you are being asked to do the same."

Bruce's face was a mask of warring emotions.

"Very well," he said at last, with obvious reluctance. "I will retire to Iona—but only for as long as it takes to seek out the source of this evil and devise a means to combat it."

Torquil nodded his assent, more relieved than he could say. A chill breeze stirred the surrounding foliage, and he saw the king's shoulders brace against the nip in the air.

"Will you take my cloak, Sire?" he offered.

Bruce smiled crookedly, but shook his head.

"I think not, my friend, though I thank you for that generous offer. I wouldn't sleep easy, knowing you were cold."

"Then, perhaps you'll be guided by the example of the good Saint Martin," Torquil replied, removing his cloak anyway. "We can divide the use of it between us for the watches of the night. I'll take the first watch—so it's your turn to sleep first, with the cloak."

Shaking his head in resignation, too tired to argue, Bruce let Torquil lay the cloak around his shoulders, hugging it around his knees and resting his chin on his folded arms. He was fast asleep when Torquil came back to check on him a few minutes later.

Chapter Twelve

September, 1306

"I WANT TO KNOW WHERE YOUR BROTHER IS," THE EARL OF Pembroke demanded of the battered figure who stood before him in chains. "Has he fled with the women?"

The prisoner lifted his chin defiantly. One eye was swollen half-shut, and his face and limbs were purpled with bruises incurred during capture, but Neil Bruce was unbowed.

"If your own spies can't sniff him out, that's your loss," he said. "Treachery may have got you Kildrummy, but that's all you'll get from me."

After fleeing Dail Righ, he had led Bruce's queen and her escort to Kildrummy Castle unchallenged. Shortly thereafter, however, the garrison received word that an English army was approaching under the joint command of Pembroke and the Prince of Wales. Desperate, Neil Bruce had sent his sister-in-law and the other royal women off to sanctuary at the shrine of Saint Duthac at Tain, on the extreme north coast of Scotland, under the protection of the Earl of Atholl. The king's brother and the remaining members of the garrison had then set about strengthening the keep's defenses, hoping to occupy the enemy's attentions while the queen's party escaped to safety.

But that plan had been undermined by treachery. Two weeks into the siege that followed, one of the castle's treasonous inmates had set fire to the grain stores. The blaze had raged unchecked through the castle vaults, filling the air with choking clouds of smoke. Threatened with mass suffocation, Neil Bruce and his fellow rebels had been forced to surrender.

The Prince of Wales had left it to Pembroke to interrogate the prisoners—most particularly, the young brother of the upstart Robert Bruce. To assist him, the earl had called upon the skills of several of his subordinates, including Bartholeme de Challon. Pembroke did not like the handsome Frenchman, but he was prepared to waive his personal antipathy because of the man's usefulness. In addition to being a shrewd tactician on the battlefield, de Challon possessed a formidable aptitude for intimidation. His dwarf, it was said, surpassed even de Challon himself, when it came to subtleties of torture and ways to prolong the agonies of execution. Thus far, however, very little information had been extracted from Bruce's brother.

"I warn you, Neil Bruce," Pembroke said sternly, "I have been given leave to use every means at my disposal to bring your upstart brother to justice. *Every* means," he repeated for emphasis. "You will be spared nothing if you refuse to cooperate. I draw your recollection to the fate of William Wallace."

Neil Bruce's jaw tightened, but he favored his questioners with a defiant glare and a shake of his head. "You can threaten me with whatever you wish, but I can't tell you what I don't know."

Pembroke wheeled away with a snort of disgust. Bartholeme, observing coolly, folded his arms across his chest and strolled closer to the earl.

"He may well be telling the truth, my lord," Bartholeme

offered. "The other prisoners we've questioned attest that Robert Bruce did not accompany his wife here. As far as I can determine, there has been no communication between them since they parted company at Dail Righ."

"Then where are the women now?" Pembroke demanded. "He must know *that*! He knows where he *told* them to go. Did they leave here intending to meet up with Bruce at some designated rendezvous point? Or are they attempting to flee the country?"

"There are strong intimations that they set out north," Bartholeme said. "But that is all I have been able to gather so far."

With a snort of disgust, Pembroke signaled his guards to remove the prisoner. As they hustled Neil Bruce from the hall, the earl's secretary entered from a side door.

"The last of the fire has been completely extinguished, my lord," he reported. "Sir Henry Percy advises that it is now safe for you to inspect the premises."

Still muttering, Pembroke led his entourage outside. Percy was waiting for them in the courtyard, where the reek of burning still hung heavy in the air as he conducted the party on a tour of the battlements and outbuildings. As they came abreast of the stables, a burly figure in a leather apron stepped out of the shadows of a stable arch, cap in hand.

"A word, m'lord."

Pembroke eyed the man coolly.

"Who are you?"

"I'm Osborne the blacksmith, yer lordship," the big man announced, a trifle belligerently. "I'll be claiming my reward now."

"Reward?" Pembroke repeated. "What reward?"

"This is the man who claims to have set fire to the granaries," Sir Henry Percy supplied in an undertone.

"I was told that the man wha' delivered the castle into yer hands would be handsomely paid in gold," the blacksmith said.

Sir William Latimer, Pembroke's lieutenant, eyed the man with fastidious distaste. "Thirty pieces of silver, I should say, would be a more fitting recompense for your services."

The blacksmith's mouth hardened in his scraggly brown beard. "The offer was for as much gold as a man could carry," he insisted.

"I would be more open to persuasion," Pembroke replied, "had we captured something more valuable than a set of stone walls. As it is, the real prize has eluded us."

"By your leave, my lord," Bartholeme interposed smoothly. "It is true that Bruce temporarily has eluded us. However, he is not the only prize to be had."

Before the blacksmith could jerk back, the Frenchman's hand shot out to snag the cord of what proved to be a small leather bag around the big man's neck, hitherto hidden under his shirt. When the blacksmith tried to snatch it back, the bag gave off a metallic clink. Bartholeme gave it a sharp yank, breaking the cord, then upended it over his palm, tumbling out a glittering tangle of earrings and brooches.

"A great lady seems to have made you a present of her jewelry," he noted with a chilly smile. "Or perhaps it was intended as a queen's ransom," he added, capturing the smith's gaze as he extended the handful of gold for Pembroke's perusal.

As the blacksmith's mouth opened and closed several times, his eyes round, Pembroke probed at the tangle of items with a gloved forefinger and turned over an egg-sized gold pendant engraved with a heraldic achievement.

"Interesting," he said coldly. "These would be, I believe, de Burgo arms—the arms of the earls of Ulster."

"Precisely." Bartholeme kept his gaze fixed on the gaping blacksmith, weighing the gold in his hand. "One ventures to speculate that the lady in question might have been the present Earl of Ulster's daughter, the Lady Elizabeth, who is wife to the traitor Bruce. What of it, blacksmith? You must have done her a valuable service. Perhaps you even acted as her guide on the first stage of her journey. . . ."

The blacksmith's beefy face had gone as pale as suet. "No, m'lord, I—I *never*— She left them behind! I—I found the wee baubles in th' stables, after they'd gone."

"Did you, indeed?" Pembroke said mildly. The blacksmith now was visibly quaking, twisting his cap into an unrecognizable wad. "Tell me where the Lady Elizabeth was bound, and perhaps I'll let you keep your miserable skin."

"I dinna ken!" the blacksmith blurted. "She didna say. Nae one said." Seeing Pembroke's face harden, he fell to his knees.

"Please, m'lord, hae mercy," he begged. "Dinna forget that if it werena for me, you wouldna now be here, inside this castle!"

"True enough," Pembroke said, "—and your greed sickens me. You are like a carrion crow hovering over a battlefield, eager to pick the bones on both sides!"

"No, m'lord! It isna true! I hae always been loyal—"

"You have a miser's heart and a liar's tongue," Pembroke retorted, "and for that, you shall have ample recompense." His expression did not change as he glanced at Bartholeme. "My lord, be so good as to arrange for those trinkets to be melted down in the smith's own forge. Then see that this wretch receives all the gold he can carry—by swallowing it!"

"No!" the man shrieked, as guardsmen seized him from either side and the enormity of his fate registered. "No, ye cannae . . . !"

Closing his hand over the fistful of gold and smiling faintly, Bartholeme merely bowed in acknowledgment of the order as the guards dragged the blacksmith away, howling and struggling, and Pembroke and his party departed. Before going to inspect the castle forge, Bartholeme sent a servant to fetch Mercurius.

"Stoke the fire in the forge," he ordered when the dwarf

arrived, handing over all except the pendant. "But before we deal with yon greedy blacksmith, I want to see if there's more to be learned from these morsels of gold than the identity of their previous owner."

"Aye, Master," the dwarf murmured, hefting the handful of jewelry. "The English earl devised this fate for the blacksmith?" His grin broadened at Bartholeme's curt nod. "Then he is learning well."

As he turned away to tend the forge, chuckling gleefully, Bartholeme retired to a corner of the smithy, fingering the pendant, and seated himself on an upturned bucket. He cupped the pendant between his palms and closed his eyes as he quickly shielded himself with a charm of warding, then focused his perceptions on the pendant, concentrating on making himself at one with the woman he was seeking.

Very shortly, he opened his eyes to find Mercurius standing over him, stripped to the waist and dripping with sweat.

"The forge is ready, Master," the dwarf announced. "The gold is beginning to liquefy."

Smiling grimly, Bartholeme rose and handed over the pendant.

"Add this, then. It has served its purpose."

It took six strong men to hold the blacksmith while a seventh—the dwarf—poured the draught of molten gold down his throat. Somewhat surprisingly, they discovered that the receptacle held far less gold than expected; and retrieving it proved decidedly distasteful. But Bartholeme stayed until all was quiet again and the corpse had been removed, only then going to Pembroke to report.

"The deed is done, my lord," he informed the earl, "and I've had an inspired thought. It occurs to me that the Bruce women might well be making for Orkney. One of his sisters is queen in Norway, which is but a short distance from there—and she would give them sanctuary."

"Quite true," Pembroke agreed, after considering. "I confess, that would be *my* choice. But we'll have to move quickly, if we're to overtake them."

"They will have gone by way of Inverness, I think," Bartholeme offered, knowing that they had. "Then north along the Firth of Cromarty toward Tain and beyond. In fact, they might well seek sanctuary there at Tain."

"You know our geography well, my lord," Pembroke said. "Those are the domains of William, Earl of Ross. I confess I've had doubts, of late, about his enthusiasm for our cause—but this presents an excellent opportunity for him to prove his good faith. If he can run Bruce's vixens to earth, we can use them as hostages to bring their lord to heel."

"The women won't lead you to the Stone of Destiny," Mercurius observed later, when the victors had dispersed to consolidate their gains.

"No," Bartholeme agreed, "but Bruce will. The Lady Elizabeth's pendant was useful, on several counts, but we also have something belonging to Bruce himself. Or rather, Lorn has it."

"The brooch Bruce lost at Dail Righ?" Mercurius guessed, then shook his head. "He won't want to give it up. He regards it as a personal trophy."

"We only require the loan of it," Bartholeme said. "Do you know where he is, at present?"

"Out on patrol, helping round up any stray rebels who might have slipped through the net."

"Then perhaps we'll ride out and join him," Bartholeme replied. "This castle is far too busy for what I have in mind. Have horses saddled, and I'll join you shortly."

A swath of burnt fields and razed cottages marked the path Lorn and his retinue had taken through the surrounding countryside. Bartholeme and his servant came upon them in the act of dismantling a water mill on the outskirts of an abandoned village. As they had hoped, Lorn was wearing the brooch ripped from Bruce's shoulder at Dail Righ. A handspan across, with large pearls studded around a large central boss of polished crystal, it seemed to glow in the sunlight.

"A word, when you're finished," Bartholeme told him, with a meaningful glance.

He and Mercurius withdrew to the burnt-out ruins of the village chapel, where Lorn soon joined them. The Scot greeted Bartholeme's proposal with wolfish interest, the while fingering Bruce's brooch.

"You can have the loan of it, then," he said. "But only if I can be present."

Bartholeme sized him up with a long look. By the fastidious standards of the French court, John Macdougall of Lorn was uncouth and unpolished, but he had exhibited enthusiasm and inventiveness in the months since his initial introduction to the black arts. It would do no harm to test his obedience—and his nerve.

"Very well," he agreed. "You may assist me. On our way here, we passed a herd of pigs running loose in the woods. Among them was a yearling boar. I want you to find it and kill it. Then drain its blood and bring that to me, along with the creature's head."

Lorn gave him a lazy, hard-eyed grin, then turned on his heel and strode briskly from the chapel.

Dusk was lowering when Lorn returned. Bartholeme met him at the door, stepping aside with a silent nod when Lorn held up two leather sacks, one of which was taut with fluid.

Certain preparations had been made in his absence. After clearing the altar with a sweep of his mailed arm, Bartholeme had instructed his dwarf to assemble various accoutrements. Torches now burned at the four corners of the chapel's sanctuary, and a sibilant resonance of words better left unspoken seemed to linger on the close air, along with the stench of urine and ashes. The crucifix on the wall behind the altar had been reversed. Lorn saw it, and his nostrils twitched as he handed over what he had brought, but he said nothing.

"Were you seen?" Bartholeme asked.

"No."

"Good. These will enable us to complete our preparations. Use the blood to wash down the altar—if, that is, you still are willing to assist me."

"And if I were not willing?" Lorn said, resuming his hard-eyed smile.

"At this point, if you were not willing," Bartholeme said mildly, his smile matching Lorn's, "Mercurius already would have put his throwing knife into your heart." He jutted his chin toward the shadowed doorway of the former sacristy, where torchlight glinted from a bright blade in the hand of the dwarf, who was lowering an arm cocked to throw. Smiling an almost-disappointed smile of his own, Mercurius returned the clipped bow given him by Lorn and made the dagger disappear.

He and his master watched without comment as Lorn briskly mounted the three steps to the altar and poured the bag of blood over it, at Bartholeme's direction using the empty bag to smear the blood evenly over the surface. Throughout, the lips of both Frenchmen whispered in mute invocation, which became audible as Bartholeme gestured for both his acolytes to flank him.

From the second sack, Bartholeme himself then took the bloody boar's head and lifted it high, turning widdershins to present it first to the north and then to each of the remaining quarters in turn. His chant was low and sibilant, and ended with a barbaric cry as he set it on the bloody altar in offering.

"*Terribilis est locus iste!*" he declared, shifting into Latin. "*Altaris Luciferi est, Princeps Tenebrae. . . .*" Terrible is this place. It is the altar of Lucifer, Prince of Darkness, whose presence we now invoke to aid us. . . .

Eyes agleam in the torchlight, Bartholeme turned to Lorn

and outthrust his bloody left hand, palm up, with a speaking glance at Bruce's brooch. Lorn's fingers trembled only slightly as he unpinned it from his shoulder and set it in the Frenchman's hand.

Smiling faintly, Bartholeme folded back the barb of the clasp and jabbed it hard into the fleshy pad of his right index finger. In the torchlight, as he smeared his bloody finger over the center stone, it took on the sickly opacity of an eye occluded by cataract.

"Hear me, Lucifer, Light-Bearer!" he declared, casting his glance at the boar's head. "I seek Robert Bruce, whom some call the Chosen One, heir to the Stone of Jacob. Through this sacrifice of my blood as an oblation, let the eyes of my mind be opened to the presence of him whom I seek. Let his spirit be revealed to me, wherever it may be!"

Swiftly, chillingly, the shadows seemed to close around the sanctuary as Bartholeme thrust the brooch briefly toward the boar's head in offering, as a priest lifts the paten at the moment of consecration, then licked the blood away with a sweep of his tongue. As he did so, his senses kindled to the scent of his prey: the heady perfume of blood, bone, and spirit.

He bent his gaze to the crystal, peering into its murky depths. His breath quickened, and he caught his balance on the edge of the desecrated altar, no longer seeing with mere vision. Like a panting hound, he turned unseeing eyes this way and that, straining to pick up his quarry's elusive trail. The ghostly scent drew him out of himself as, leaving his body behind, he hurled his spirit into the hunt.

Whole landscapes opened before him. The lure drew him racing through the mountains of Atholl, weaving in and out of moon-silvered glens where rushing cataracts tumbled through the rocks and red deer trembled at the howling of wolves. The trail he followed led him south—east—north—west. Then abruptly it vanished.

Snarling frustration, Bartholeme cast round him, trying to

recover the scent, but all in vain. The trail of Bruce had suddenly vanished into thin air, with no slightest trace of his essence lingering to suggest where the rebel king might have gone to ground.

Only reluctantly did he abandon the chase and allow his perceptions to return to normal, slowly straightening from his bent stance before the desecrated altar. He opened his eyes to find Lorn and Mercurius gazing at him expectantly.

"Did you find him?" Lorn dared to ask.

Curtly, Bartholeme shook his head.

"What does this mean?" Lorn demanded, looking to Mercurius for enlightenment. But the answer came from Bartholeme.

"It means," he said, "that someone has contrived to place Bruce in sanctuary. My suspicion would be the Templars who are said to ride in his company. I cannot even guess where that sanctuary might be, but as long as he remains there, he is beyond my reach.

"But this sword cuts both ways," he continued, handing the brooch back to Lorn, eyes agleam in the dying torchlight. "While Bruce remains in hiding, he is as lost to his followers and his cause as he is to us. Sooner or later, however, he will have to emerge—or abandon forever his claim to the Scottish throne. It may well be that fears for his wife will lure him out, if nothing else does.

"And when that happens, we will have him."

Chapter Thirteen

Early February, 1307

"I GIVE UP," AUBREY SAID ON A NOTE OF EXASPERATION. HE drew up the hood of his mantle and braced against the wintry wind as he mounted the top of a knoll. "How can a sheep just vanish?"

"Well, she can't have strayed far," Torquil said from farther downhill. "This island isn't that big."

"Aye, and there aren't any wolves," Bruce added, with attempted good humor. "It's probably just as well that none of us plan to be herdsmen the rest of our lives."

His tone was lighthearted, but Torquil knew that the easy banter covered an inner restlessness that had cost the king many wakeful nights since their arrival on Iona four months before. Not for the first time, he found himself wishing that Bruce could find some relief from the growing burden of grief and frustration he carried in his heart.

News had reached them early in the winter of the betrayal of Kildrummy Castle—and crueler still had been the reported death of Bruce's brother Neil, subjected to all the horrors of a traitor's death: hanged, drawn, and quartered like William Wallace.

Since then, they had heard nothing more, and the absence of information weighed as heavily on the king as any chain.

"In the days of our Celtic forebears," old Abbot Fingon had reminded them, as no further news came, "this time following Epiphany was called Imbolc. It was and is a time of waiting, the season when the sap returns to the roots, when seeds lie dormant under the ground. The whole earth sleeps, gathering strength to bear fruit in the coming year. So must it be with you."

But as the long nights stretched on, taking that counsel to heart was becoming more and more difficult for all of them—here, sequestered away from family and friends. And Bruce was finding it harder still to reconcile the royal necessity to preserve his own life with his fierce desire to confront the enemy who had so destroyed Scotland's sovereign peace. The very isolation upon which his safety depended chafed him like a hair shirt. For hours each day, he prowled the narrow confines of the island like a prisoner in a cell, as though seeking by an act of will to enlarge its boundaries.

More than a month had passed since the king and his two Templar companions had observed the gentle solemnities of Christmas with the little Columban community. It now was nearing Candlemas, the Christian name for the ancient time of Imbolc, when the new candles were blessed for the service of light in the coming year.

With the gradual lengthening of days, Torquil believed and hoped in his heart that their fortunes would likewise lighten; but so far, the prospects for their future and that of Scotland seemed as bleak as the dark clouds massing over the neighboring Isle of Mull, heavy with the promise of snow. It was the prospect of yet another storm that had prompted Abbot Fingon to send them out looking for the sheep that had strayed.

"Ho! Hello, up there!"

A voice faintly hailed them from farther down the slope: the fourth member of their party, in the white robes and mantle of a Columban monk, pointing excitedly to another patch of white at his feet.

"There's Ninian waving to us," Bruce said, peering in that direction. "Looks like he's found that ewe."

As the three of them made their way quickly back down the hillside, Ninian briefly bent out of sight and reappeared with something white cradled in his arms.

"Look what Cushla has given us!" he exclaimed, displaying a tiny lamb. "It's *very* early for lambing—and a good thing we found her, with a storm coming on." He glanced at the mother, who was somewhat anxiously nuzzling at his knees. "Can the three of you bring her along?"

"Of course," Torquil said.

Somewhat inexpertly, the three of them began chivvying the ewe back in the direction of the abbey, though the animal was happy enough to dog Ninian's heels without prompting, since he carried her newborn lamb. Reckoned now as one of the more venerable members of the Columban community, Brother Ninian had lost nothing of the serene humility that Torquil remembered from the earlier days of their acquaintance, more than a decade before, embodying all the gentleness and grace he had learned to associate with the followers of Saint Columba.

"I do believe we've found them not a moment too soon," Ninian said, as a bank of darker-looking clouds passed in front of the wan patch of brightness where the sun would have been, further dimming the pallid daylight. "The storm will soon be upon us."

Aubrey glanced at the clouds and ducked deeper into the cowl of his white mantle—Columban habit, here among the brethren, very like Templar robes, though he and Torquil would resume the leathers and tweeds of the Highlands when they eventually left the island. Bruce alone wore secular attire.

"Brother Torquil says that you and your brothers can affect the weather," he observed. "If that's so, why don't you ask the winds to hold the snow at bay? Or better still, send the clouds away to heap it on the heads of the English?"

Smiling, Ninian paused and bent down to let the anxious ewe sniff her lamb. "It is as well not to beg a favor from a friend unless you truly need it," he said. "If we were forever petitioning the saints to change the weather, they would soon lose patience and turn a deaf ear when we pray for truly important things."

Aubrey looked nonplussed, clearly uncertain whether he was meant to take these remarks seriously, and Bruce looked faintly dubious. Torquil might have shared their skepticism if, on a previous visit to Iona, he had not seen Brother Ninian call upon Saint Columba to shift a contrary wind in their favor. (That time, it had been an important thing.) The relationship between the Columbans and their spiritual patrons was uniquely intimate—with results that would astonish the uninformed. In time, both Aubrey and Bruce might witness a measure of the Columbans' spiritual alignment for themselves, and would look back on this time among the brothers with new vision.

The temperature was definitely falling; the warmth of the fire in the abbey refectory would be most welcome after several hours in the cold. They were still a furlong away from the abbey gate when they heard the pealing of the community bell.

"It can't be time for the evening office," Torquil said, with a glance at Ninian, though it was growing very dark. "Does that mean there's trouble?"

"Possibly," Ninian allowed.

They crested the last hill and started down, with the steel-gray chop of the sound of Iona stretched out before them under a shroud of lowering cloud and the beginning flurries of snow. As they did so, a ship materialized out of the mist, making for the beach: not the flat-bottomed raft that served the community as a ferry, nor a local fishing coracle, either, but a graceful, high-prowed galley of twenty oars. Standing apart from the men who manned the oars were four passengers, muffled for warmth in mantles and sheepskins. Before Torquil could caution Bruce to draw back out of sight, the king gave a joyous cry of recognition.

"It's my brothers!" he exclaimed, pointing. "Look! It's Thomas and Alexander!"

Straining to pierce the gloom, Torquil confirmed it.

"So it is."

"Is that Robert Boyd with them?" Aubrey said.

"God be praised, it *is*!" Bruce replied.

"And Alexander Lindsay," Torquil supplied, his own excitement kindling. The revelation brought immediate relief for all of them, for the younger Bruce brothers had been unaccounted for since Methven. And neither Boyd nor Lindsay had been heard from since Dail Righ, when Bruce had charged them with escorting the royal women to safety.

"Now we'll have news at last!" Bruce cried, his gray eyes alight with long-suppressed relief.

Careening recklessly down the slope, he set off impetuously toward the knot of Columban brothers gathering on the shingled beach. Torquil left Ninian and Aubrey to shepherd the ewe into the shieling and hurried after the king, occasionally slipping on loose shale. Ominously, he found his own emotions vacillating between curiosity, hope, and foreboding; he prayed the latter was mere anxiety. Hungrily intent as a hawk on its prey, Bruce had not taken his eyes from the incoming vessel.

Most of the community now had gathered on the shore. With a final sweep of the oars, the galley's crew sent it coasting into the shallows toward the beach. Kilting up their habits, several of the younger brethren braved the icy water to wade out and help tow the vessel up onto the shingle. Bruce rushed to greet his brothers and his friends as they disembarked, flinging his arms around them in wolfish affection.

"Alexander! Thomas—all of you! To see you alive and

well is worth more than all the gold in England!" he cried. "Now, as you love me, tell me what brings you here, and how our cause is faring."

Before any of the newcomers could answer, Abbot Fingon pushed through the gathering knot from the shore behind them, arms outstretched in a shepherding motion to draw them away from the shore.

"Come in first!" he said, with a glance at the lowering sky. "The snow is nearly upon us. Time enough for news, once everyone is safely indoors. Come, come. . . ."

Fat, wet snowflakes were starting to fall, sporadically set awhirl by gusts of wind. Leaving the galley crew to secure their vessel, the newcomers followed Bruce and the aging abbot up the stony slope toward the monastery. Brother Fionn, the community's acting guest master, was waiting to hurry them into the cloister court. By then, visibility had fallen dramatically, along with the temperature.

"The chapter room is at your disposal, Sire," Abbot Fingon said, leading them across the yard. "There's a fire lit, and hot broth to warm you. You'll not be disturbed. I know you will have much to discuss."

Inside, the king and his companions crowded close around the blazing hearth while a young brother dispensed steaming cups of broth and then departed. Aubrey soon joined them. By then, Bruce's initial elation had subsided to guarded sobriety, for none of the newcomers had volunteered any news.

"I feared you slain at Methven," he told his brothers, sitting as he cupped cold hands around a warm cup. "What took you so long to seek me out?"

Thomas Bruce gave a snort. "We were in hiding ourselves, for much of the time."

"Thomas was wounded in the fighting," Alexander offered. "Not badly, but too much for serious hill-stalking. Crofters helped us tend his wound and hid us until he was well enough to move on. By then, Dail Righ had happened, and you were nowhere to be found. The only reason we didn't give you up for dead was that the English are still out looking for you."

"Then—how did you know to come here?" Bruce asked.

"We paid a call at Balantrodoch," Thomas replied. "Which took some doing, since the English are all around that area, but we managed a word with Brother Luc. We figured that if you were still alive, you'd be with Brother Torquil and Brother Aubrey—and the Templars would know where they were. Brother Luc didn't know for certain where you'd ended up, but suggested that they might have brought you here for refuge—or at least that the good brethren of Iona might know your whereabouts. So here we are."

Smiling, Bruce shifted his attention to Boyd and Lindsay, who as yet had spoken not a word. His expression sobered as he searched their faces.

"I am glad of it," he said, "but I had hoped for fair tidings. Your expressions speak otherwise. Tell me the grimmer news. Whatever our losses, I must know what they are."

Boyd nodded reluctant acceptance, glancing uncomfortably at Lindsay.

"You will have known to expect some of the deaths— Seton, Scrymgeour—probably most who were taken at Methven. We saw men wade into the water in their armor to drown, rather than face capture and execution by the English."

Torquil recoiled, glancing at the king to gauge his reaction. A coldness had stolen over Bruce's countenance, leaving his features hard as granite as he set aside his now-forgotten cup.

"Continue," he said quietly.

"Simon Fraser was captured at Caerlaverock," Lindsay said. "His head now adorns a pike on London Bridge, side by side with that of William Wallace."

Bruce stiffened. Fraser had been one of his closest friends. All of the dead had been men of courage and conviction. That they had been willing to die for Scotland's cause did not make it any easier to contemplate the manner of their deaths.

"He abides in good company," the king said softly, haunted eyes focused on something only he could see. "There is more, I think. . . ?"

"Aye, fourteen others have been hanged at Newcastle," Boyd admitted. "More, I fear, will soon follow."

"What of my wife and the other women?" Bruce asked, after a beat. "Do you know if they reached Orkney safely?"

Mutely Lindsay shook his head.

"They were captured at Tain—taken from sanctuary at the church of Saint Duthac," Boyd said. "The Earl of Ross seized them before the very altar, despite old Atholl's efforts to protect them. They are now in English custody. Atholl . . . has since been hanged, and his body beheaded and burned."

Bruce looked like a man just kicked in the stomach.

"Dear God, no!" he whispered. "What about Neil?"

"No one knows," Lindsay said quietly, "but we must assume the English have him as well. Kildrummy was betrayed from within. Pembroke holds it now."

Bruce had clasped his hands together in front of him in a parody of prayer, fingers white at the knuckles, as though he clutched an enemy by the throat, but he forced himself to flex the fingers and relax them, breathing out with a heavy sigh.

"At least the women are still alive," he muttered after a moment. "Where are they being held?"

"Your wife is under house arrest at a manor house down in Holderness," Boyd said. "We believe that your sister Christian and your daughter Marjorie have both been sent to nunneries."

Bruce briefly closed his eyes, breathing a faint sigh. "They might have fared worse. And Mary and Isabel?"

No one spoke.

"Tell me."

"Edward—has ordered them put into cages."

"What?"

"They say that Mary has been taken to Roxburgh Castle, and Lady Isabel to Berwick," Thomas said miserably. "The cages are suspended outside the walls—in this weather! On display like so many wild beasts in a menagerie!"

Torquil's shock was mirrored in the king's stunned expression. For a moment no one said anything. Then Bruce got blindly to his feet.

"Scripture says that all the kingdoms of the earth are the Devil's, to dispose of as he wills," he said dazedly, his gaze vaguely turned toward the fire. "Have we been guilty of the basest folly, in seeking to claim this kingdom for our own? Has God, in truth, abandoned us? If so, what hope have we of withstanding the powers of Darkness, if we are left to stand alone?"

"Robert—" his brother Alexander began.

"No, make me no excuses!" Bruce said hotly. "For four months I have played the monk to no good purpose, while Edward visits on my family and friends the vengeance he would like to vent on me. Perhaps the only attribute bestowed on me by the Stone of Destiny was the pride of self-delusion. Perhaps the power to shape our country's future rests in hands other than mine. I owe it to those who have died, no less than to those yet unborn, to confront the truth."

With these bitter words, he snatched up his cloak and made for the door.

"Robert, wait!" Thomas called after him. "Where are you going?"

"To wrestle, like Jacob, with the angel of the Lord!" Bruce shouted back fiercely. "Now leave me to it!"

There came the sound of swiftly receding footsteps, followed by the bang of the outer door. Resolutely, Torquil seized his own cloak and headed after the king.

"The rest of you stay here!" he ordered over his shoulder. "I'll be certain he does himself no harm."

Chapter Fourteen

February, 1307

Outside, THE SNOW WAS FALLING THICK AND FAST, AND AN early twilight had set in. A dark line of footprints pointed the way to the garden gate, but they were fast filling with snow.

Throwing his cloak around his shoulders and pulling up the hood, Torquil followed the footprints through the gateway and down the slope in the direction of the shore. Out in front of him, barely visible in the white blizzard gloom, he caught a glimpse of the dark blur of Bruce's receding figure.

Torquil charged after him, calling his name. Deaf to his shouts, Bruce plunged into the storm with the determination of a man possessed. Torquil quickened his pace, casting caution to the winds as he floundered through the deepening drifts, fighting to keep the king in sight.

There followed a blind, headlong chase with many zigzags and doublings. Bruce moved as though he were at one with the storm itself, and Torquil toiled along behind him, with the wind and snow whipping about him in freezing sheets. As he trailed the king down a slope made more treacherous by snow muffling hidden rocks and holes, Bruce suddenly disappeared before his very eyes.

Torquil continued in that direction, calling for Bruce, but

could see no trace of him. He yelled into the wind, but to no avail. It was as if the earth had swallowed Bruce up.

Now concerned that the king had suffered some fall or injury, Torquil plunged ahead even faster—and tripped and stumbled, to slide down the remainder of the slope in the grip of a minor avalanche, arms and legs flailing.

He came to rest with a bone-bruising jolt, lying atop a sharp stone that was digging into his side. As he spat out a mouthful of frozen grit and levered himself painfully onto his elbow, testing for broken bones, he realized he was lying next to a rough cairn of stones, its outlines all but buried in the snow.

Still a little shaken, he struggled to his knees and then to his feet, casting for his bearings in the driving snow, which was worsening by the second. Feeling his way toward the lee of the cairn, he guessed it marked one of three makeshift shelters on the island that the monks occupied during lambing season. Face averted from the stinging drive of the snow, he probed his way into an opening—and came abruptly face-to-face with Bruce.

"Damn it, Torquil, is there no getting away from you?" the king demanded, as the two men recoiled onto their haunches and stared at one another.

Torquil's ribs hurt, and he was still short of breath, so he mutely shook his head.

"Well, since you're here, you might as well come in," the king said testily. "I've already got enough on my conscience, without leaving you outside to freeze in the storm."

Torquil scrambled the rest of the way inside without need for further invitation, shaking the snow from his cloak and hood as he eyed what he could see of their refuge. The space was cramped and ripely redolent of sheep droppings, with an underscent of old campfires—hardly wider than the span of a man's outstretched arms—but it was refuge from the storm, and almost warm compared to outside. Its walls were freestone, with moss stuffed into the chinks, and its low-hanging roof was fashioned of stone slabs overlaid with turf. As Torquil wrapped his cloak around him and hunkered into a cross-legged position, he wiped the snowmelt from his face and beard and drew a deep breath.

"I was worried for your safety, Sire. It's lucky you managed to find shelter."

"Luck had nothing to do with it," Bruce said tartly.

"You *meant* to come here?"

"I've come to know every inch of this island. I could find my way here blindfolded, in the dark of a moonless night."

Something in his tone warned Torquil not to answer. After a long silence, punctuated only by their breathing and the howl of the storm outside, Bruce said, "I felt the need to be alone with my own thoughts. I told you not to follow. Whatever possessed you to disobey?"

"It goes against higher orders, Sire, to let you risk losing yourself in a blizzard."

"I only wish I could see my own duty as plainly," Bruce said. He cocked his head to listen to the gale outside, howling around the cairn like a banshee. "At least I'm not apt to have any more well-meaning intruders—and I won't send you back out into that. We'll be safe enough here. We can even build a fire." At Torquil's grunt of question, he gestured farther into the shelter.

"There's a hearth here somewhere, and turf and dry kindling stored farther back. The brothers leave these shielings stocked for emergencies. I have tinder and flint in my pouch."

Torquil's questing hands soon located a hollowed-out hearthstone, where he and Bruce quickly built a small turf fire. The peat was slow to kindle, but eventually its smoldering ember glow suffused the little shelter's interior with much-needed warmth and light along with the distinctive aroma of the burning turf.

The pair of them settled into companionable silence, broken only by the wailing of the storm outside. Wisely, Torquil did not attempt further conversation, well aware that he was there on sufferance. For a time, both men merely huddled close before the fire, cold hands outsplayed to catch the rising heat. Then, all unexpectedly, a chuckle bubbled up from Bruce.

"Hullo, what's this?"

"Sire?"

"It seems we are not the only tenants of this humble abode."

Bruce directed Torquil's gaze toward a shadowed cranny near a corner of the roof. Craning closer, Torquil was surprised to see a small gray spider suspended from the midst of a half-finished web. Even as he looked, she anchored the strand to part of the web, then scuttled busily to another, spinning another strand to add to her creation.

"It always amazes me that such tiny creatures manage to survive in so harsh a place and season as this," Bruce murmured. "I suppose the sheep drop mites and ticks and such—but she's building a web."

"Maybe she catches midges in the web," Torquil said doubtfully.

Bruce made no response, only picking up a piece of burning kindling and holding it up to light the spider better, though not so close that it threatened her web. Continuing her weaving, the spider moved back and forth like a living shuttle, reinforcing the web with each new filament, until suddenly one of the supporting threads gave way, and the web collapsed.

"A pity, to see so much labor wasted," Torquil commented, as the spider swung free by a thread and disappeared into a crevice.

"Aye." Bruce sighed and retracted his lit stick. "Even amongst such small creatures as these, the way of the world tends all too often to ruin."

The storm gusted a flurry of snow and cold air through the doorway opening, causing the embers in the hearth to gutter and flare. Torquil went back to tending the fire. Bruce started to do likewise, then held up his lit stick again.

"Here's our eight-legged friend back," he said in some surprise. "She's trying it again. Let's see if her next attempt fares better than the first."

Wrapping his cloak more tightly around his shoulders, he settled himself to watch. Torquil cast a glance at king and spider, then resumed nursing their meager fire.

The light from outside faded from storm glow to pitch-darkness, but the storm did not abate. As the shadows deepened, Torquil's eyelids grew heavy. Resigning himself to a long night on an empty stomach, he huddled closer to the fire and hugged his mantle around his knees, setting his chin on his forearms to doze.

Howling night set in around them. From time to time, Torquil roused himself to feed the fire with another chunk of peat—or Bruce did—but neither of them spoke. As midnight came and went, the king continued his curious vigil while his Templar guardian drifted in and out of uneasy slumber. It was not yet dawn when Torquil was startled into wakefulness by a sudden outcry.

"At last!"

Robert Bruce sounded jubilant, not alarmed. Squinting against the firelight, Torquil hauled himself into full consciousness. "What is it, Sire?"

"Come and see!" Bruce said, beckoning.

Bleary-eyed, Torquil scrambled to his knees to peer along the king's pointing finger, where a finished spider web hung perfectly formed among the eaves.

"Do you recall how often I have wished for a sign?" Bruce said with an exhausted grin. "Now see how God, in His mercy, has answered me!" He sighed as he sank back on his hunkers, but there was a new light in his eyes, which seemed to have driven the previous day's shadows from his mind and heart.

"Yon wee ettercop has been trying all night to fashion that

web," Bruce said with a nod toward the spider and her web. "I've never seen any creature, great or small, work so hard in defiance of all adversity! Six times she got her net half-woven, only to have a thread break or a random draft come along and tear the thing to pieces. But she never gave up try-ing—and this seventh and last attempt has seen the fulfill-ment of all her labors."

"You watched the whole night through?" Torquil asked in surprise.

"I couldn't tear myself away," Bruce said. "Such persis-tence seemed to merit a witness, even in so lowly a creature as a spider. But I see now that the true miracle of revelation was meant for me. Having beheld what a spider's persever-ance can achieve, I realize that it would be a shame and a sin for a man to strive any less, when he has so much more to gain."

Torquil slowly nodded as the king went on.

"The spider and I each have a purpose ordained for us," Bruce said. "To complete our appointed tasks, however great or small, requires our unstinting labors. It is not for us to know how or when Providence will crown our efforts with success. We must labor on in hope, trusting that, with God, nothing is impossible.

"Yes, I see my way clearly now," he concluded, chucking his kindling stick back into what was left of their fire. "The time has come for us to return to the fray, fearing nothing but fear itself. I *know* that the God who ordained me king is mightier than the mightiest of our enemies. My sword must not rest in its sheath until I have set my kingdom free!"

"Amen, and God grant that it be so!" Torquil breathed; and a little later, dared to lay an arm around the king's shoul-ders and offer a shoulder for the royal head when Bruce at last let himself doze in the final predawn hours.

With the breaking of first light, the two men emerged from their shelter to find that the storm had cleared. Snow lay in heavy drifts that concealed hazards to footing and made their going slow, but they pressed on to the abbey yard, where a search party was just preparing to leave.

"Robert!" Alexander cried, as he and Thomas raced to embrace their brother.

"You'll have found shelter in one of the shielings," Brother Ninian said, eyeing them as he motioned the others back inside. Aubrey was with them, and looked greatly relieved. "We spent the night in prayer for your safety."

"I'm sorry you felt obliged to go to such trouble," Bruce replied, nodding to Abbot Fingon, standing in the background. "I kept my own somewhat different vigil, as Brother Torquil can attest—though he slept through most of it." He grinned almost boyishly. "Still, your intercessions may have helped secure me the revelation I was seeking. If you can spare us something to eat, I'll tell you the tale in full."

Over bowls of salted porridge oats rich with butter and cream, Bruce shared his observations of the spider, to the amazement of his brothers, Boyd, Lindsay, Aubrey, and the senior Columbans. When he then declared his intention to leave Iona on the morrow, not even Abbot Fingon made any attempt to dissuade him. Surprised, Torquil later drew Brother Ninian aside.

"Are you sure this is the right time?" he asked.

"Whether *I* feel sure," said Ninian, "matters far less than whether the king feels sure. By virtue of the Stone of Destiny, Robert Bruce is heir to Solomon and Columba alike: the Appointed One, who is both ruler and prophet. There will be times when he is able to discern a clear path where others see only thorns and scorpions."

"But he's still only human," Torquil protested. "He's still capable of making mistakes. Surely our own duty demands that we question any action we regard as dangerous."

"I am not advocating the abandonment of conscience or caution," Ninian said. "I merely point out that Bruce has the final word. He is king. The action of the Holy Spirit reveals Itself as and when It wills, making even our errors an occasion for redemption. It apparently has spoken to Bruce through the spider. If his mind and heart are set on this venture, we are bound to abide by his decision. But that isn't what is really bothering you," he added.

Taken aback, Torquil realized that Ninian was right.

"No, it isn't," he replied, and drew a breath to gather his thoughts. "It isn't something I dared mention in front of the others, but it's been bothering me all winter."

"Yes?"

"I told you about that attack by the giant black bird at Dail Righ."

"Go on."

"We never decided who might have been responsible, but somehow it didn't really matter, so long as we were under your protection, here on Iona."

"I still have no more insights on that matter than you do, Torquil," Ninian said gently.

"No—and I didn't expect that you would," Torquil replied. "But there's another aspect of Dail Righ that we never really addressed—and that's the brooch that Bruce lost there. Macdougall of Lorn took it—and I don't know that he necessarily has the means to do anything with it— but he *is* the Red Comyn's cousin."

"And you worry that he may share his cousin's taste for dark alliances," Ninian said.

Torquil flashed him a sickly smile. "Not necessarily. I'm trying not to let my imagination run rampant. But the brooch could be used as a sorcerous link to get at Bruce, if it fell into the wrong hands—and *someone* sent that black bird to Dail Righ."

"True enough."

"We've been safe enough here," Torquil went on, "but once we leave, I fear the worst."

Ninian was slowly nodding, his face gone still and sober. "Let me refer the matter to Abbot Fingon," he said. "I understand what you're saying. Perhaps he will be able to suggest some means for severing the link between this object and the king."

"I would be very grateful," Torquil said. "If I have to fight the king's enemies, I need a weapon."

A little later, to accompany their midday meal, the king convened a council of war.

"Edward believes he will win by taking away everything we have to lose," Bruce began. "He is wrong. The only way he can defeat us is to take away our will to fight—and that he will never succeed in doing, as long as I live."

"Indeed, he will not!" Thomas Bruce assured his brother. "We never had a chance to convey our other news. Your friends in the north and west remain true, Sire. Christiana MacRuiaridh of the Isles has pledged both men and galleys to serve your cause. Angus Og MacDonald of Kintyre has done likewise. And there are many more scattered throughout the Mounth who are ready to support you against the English."

"With the Lady Elizabeth taken captive, I wager you'll find not a few swords in Ulster ready to stand by you, as well," Alexander put in eagerly. "Robert, with your permission, Thomas and I will journey to Antrim and plead your case before her father."

"A useful notion," Bruce agreed. "But before we are free to engage the English on all fronts, we must first get the better of Galloway." He tapped that section of the map with one hand. "Our opening blow must be struck there."

"Let us have the honor," Thomas offered eagerly. "The lands of Lorn need cleansing of the Macdougalls and all their ilk!"

After some further discussion, it was agreed that Thomas and Alexander Bruce should pay a recruiting visit to Ireland, leaving Bruce himself to rally the support of his northern allies.

"We'll bring you Irish troops," Thomas declared. "Where and when shall we meet up thereafter?"

Bruce indicated an area off the coast of Antrim.

"Rathlin Island. It lies too far off our coast for English ships to pay it much heed. We'll rendezvous there in a month's time to firm up our strategy. Right now, I'd like to make certain our ship is seaworthy, before we lose the light."

Torquil had intended to go with them, but Ninian beckoned him aside, taking him to the abbot's small scriptorium.

"Brother Ninian has told me of your concerns," Fingon said, when Torquil had taken a seat before the room's tiny fire. "I well understand them. One reason that scripture advises us not to store up treasure for ourselves on earth is that a man can be bound by his possessions—and in ways that most people never consider. Even when one is free from the vices of cupidity, he invariably sets the stamp of his personality on objects he has worn or used. As you have rightly conjectured, that link can be exploited by the man's enemies, and the object itself can be made to betray its owner. Unless the connection can be severed."

"You're speaking of the king's brooch," Torquil said, nodding. "How is that to be achieved?—the severing of the link."

"By a principle of analogy," Fingon replied. "The act of cutting something away is the same in mystical terms as it is in physical terms. The key is to find the right corollary."

On the table at the abbot's elbow lay a longish, silk-bundled object the size and shape of a man's forearm. This he handed to Torquil to unwrap. Inside was a sheathed dirk with silver mountings and a hilt carved of blackthorn, in a design of Celtic interlace. Surmounting the pommel was a fine blue jewel the size of a pigeon's egg.

"A weapon fit for a king," Torquil said, closing his hands around hilt and sheath and drawing the blade. "But how can such a weapon serve against the creations of sorcery?"

"A dagger or dirk is merely the point of the sword. The sword itself represents the will of the wielder." Fingon lightly touched Torquil's fist where it grasped the weapon's hilt.

"Each of us stands at the center of a pattern," he went on. "The pattern is made up of different threads, interwoven and all radiating outward, much like Robert's spider's web. These strands, both dark and bright, bind and anchor us to the world around us. And within this binding lies the source of the danger you fear.

"As long as the pattern of life is undisturbed, it will be hard to discern the single thread which spells ruin—and impossible for anyone to follow one of these threads back to its source without detection. So you must be like the spider, patiently awaiting her prey. If a hostile hand should shake the web from afar, you will know in that instant which thread to cut." He glanced at the dirk. "And you now have the means to do so."

Slowly Torquil nodded, casting his gaze along the length of the blade.

"I understand," he said, "and I will be watching." He fitted the tip of the dirk's blade to the opening of the sheath. "And when I strike," he added, shoving the blade home, "it will be with all my strength."

Chapter Fifteen

Late February, 1307

A FORTNIGHT LATER, AFTER A BITTER WEEK OF FROST AND snow, the February day dawned winsomely mild in distant Paris. The sun glared in a clear blue sky, transforming the snowcapped towers of the city into shimmering confections like icing sugar, with string-courses of icicles scintillating like prisms in the new-minted light. By noon, the hard-packed crust of ice in the streets had given way to a malodorous slush, redolent with the reek of manure.

Undaunted, the city's citizens cast aside some of their winter layers and sallied forth in their stoutest boots, ready to make the best of this ameliorating turn in the weather. Among those abroad was the king's principal minister, Guillaume de Nogaret—though any pleasure he might expect to derive from the day's outing came not from the fine weather, but from the business shortly to be conducted. The modest horse-drawn conveyance with its anonymous markings and drawn shutters was not his accustomed mode of travel within the city; but nor were his two companions men with whom he willingly would have associated, save through professional necessity.

He kept his antipathy carefully masked as his transport

lurched along the mud-clogged street, idly studying the pair seated across from him. The smaller and possibly brighter of the two, called Esquin de Floyran, was slender as a weasel, with pinched features and fine blond hair, who sat nervously plucking at the ends of a sparse moustache with fingers as slim and deft as a woman's. The other, one Arnolfo Deghi, was squat and squint-eyed, with a florid, coarse-featured face and greasy black curls. His dingy robe strained across his slack belly as he sprawled in his seat and dislodged shreds of food from his strong yellow teeth with a dirty thumbnail.

Two very different men: the core of the case Nogaret was building against the Templars. But though physically at odds with one another, the pair shared in common the shifty, calculating demeanor of the paid informant. Backing them, Nogaret had recruited ten additional spies from the gaols and the streets: forgers and swindlers, perjurers and thieves, sending them to infiltrate selected Templar preceptories throughout King Philip's domain.

There, fortified with promises and bribes and curbed by threats, their work of the past several months had been both to gather information and to construct an elaborate network of lies. Now it was time to invoke the aid of the king. By no means satisfied with the wealth he had ravished from the Jews, Philip remained covetous of the property of the Templars. All he lacked was an adequate pretext for seizing it. And that, Nogaret's two hired accomplices were about to give him.

"I trust I need not remind you," Nogaret said, instantly engaging the attention of both men, "that any deviation from your agreed instructions will have serious consequences. You know what the king desires to hear. Have you any doubts regarding what you are to say?"

His two associates exchanged wary glances and shook their heads in unison.

"None, Messire," the blond, weaselly man said with obsequious eagerness.

"I feel obliged to point out that your attempts to enlist the suspicions of the King of Aragon were somewhat less than convincing," Nogaret said blandly. "I hope you're prepared to make a better case this time. You wouldn't want to disappoint me."

The blond man paled a little, and he ducked his head submissively.

"No, Messire," he muttered.

Smiling faintly, without a trace of humor, Nogaret turned his unwavering gaze on the second man.

"What about you? You're certain your Templar superiors suspected nothing?"

"Nothing, Messire," the dark informant said at once. "The hints I've let drop will amply support the rumors we've been circulating. I've drawn up a list of those who are prepared to offer testimony, given the right price."

The wheel rumble of their conveyance changed, and Nogaret briefly drew aside one of the shutters to confirm that they had passed onto the Grand Pont, lined on either side by the colorful booths of the money changers. Emerging onto the Île de la Cité, they skirted the chapel of Saint Bartholeme and approached the gates of the Palais Royal, where Nogaret's driver was recognized at once and the rig allowed to pass.

The king's chief minister and his companions alighted from their conveyance in the palace forecourt, where Nogaret instructed the driver to remain in readiness. He then led the way through an inner court to the main entrance of the palace itself, where they were met by a steward whose fawning respect paid tribute to Nogaret's influence. Inside, the man ushered them past several interior guard posts to the privy chamber of the king himself.

Philip was already present, pacing the floor with petulant impatience.

"You are late, monsieur," he snapped. "You know I dislike being made to wait."

Nogaret bowed with suave self-confidence. "A thousand pardons, Sire. We set out in good time, but traffic in the streets detained us." Without giving Philip time to rebut, he presented his two companions. "Sire, these are the men I told you about. I believe you will find their testimony enlightening, to say the least."

The king waved the explanation aside irritably and flounced into a chair, subjecting the two men to a hard-eyed glare.

"These are the witnesses who have come forward, ready to give evidence against the Templars?"

Nogaret inclined his head. "They are, Sire." He first beckoned his blond hireling forward. "This is Esquin de Floyran, once a subprior of the preceptory of Monfaucon. And this man," he went on, indicating the darker man, "is Arnolfo Deghi, a Florentine lay brother, previously sworn to the preceptory of Richerenches. Both of them are moved to come forward and expose the perfidy that lurks beneath the mask of sanctity presented to the world by the Order of the Temple."

Philip looked from one to the other, then singled out Esquin, who had doffed his cap before entering the presence chamber and was fingering it nervously.

"Your name seems familiar to us," he noted with a scowl. "We seem to recall having had a letter from you."

Esquin made a simpering obeisance.

"I had the honor to write to Your Majesty some six months ago, Sire, warning of certain dangers the Templars pose to all decent men whilst professing themselves to be warriors of God. They proclaim themselves dedicated to the service of Christ, but in fact they are dedicated to nothing but their own iniquitous vices."

When he did not go on, Philip impatiently made a rolling motion with one hand.

"And? And?" he prompted. "We would hear the details of what you have witnessed. Tell all that you have seen, and have no fear; We will protect you from the Templars."

Esquin flashed an oblique glance at Nogaret, who returned a curt nod by way of encouragement.

"Yes, Sire," he began on a note of wheedling humility. "I am but a poor clerk, as Your Majesty can plainly see. I joined the Order out of a sincere desire to do good, little guessing what would be my fate once I was professed. These many years, I have held my tongue in dread of reprisals. But seeing that the authority of the blessed Saint Louis lives once again in Your Grace, I will make so bold as to speak freely, for I can bear my silent shame no longer."

The king accepted this piece of flattery as his due, inclining his head in acknowledgment. "Proceed."

Esquin lifted his eyes piously to the ceiling, managing to look somewhat embarrassed.

"When I was a youth of barely eighteen," he began, "I was approached by the head of the local preceptory. The knight asked me if I would like to become a member of the Order of the Temple. Most respectfully I told him that I should like it very much, only I had no property to hand over by way of a gift. The knight smiled at me in a speaking manner and said, 'A handsome young man like you need bring no gift other than his presence, to be welcome to our brotherhood.'"

"And how did you respond?" the king asked.

Esquin assumed an air of blushing hesitation. "I thanked him for correcting the error of my assumptions, and said I was glad to think that rumor had lied in claiming that the Knights of the Temple loved only wealth. I told him if my poverty was no impediment, that I would be most eager to join, whereupon he offered to act as my sponsor. Thinking no ill, I accepted, counting myself most fortunate to have found so kind a patron."

King Philip frowned. "I see nothing of substance in this."

"Nor did I, Sire—to my lasting shame," Esquin said, modestly dropping his gaze. "Initially, all seemed innocent. Under my patron's auspices, I was enrolled amongst the postulants at the preceptory of Monfaucon. There followed a period of instruction, during which I learned to practice what I assumed was to be my rule of life. It was not until the day of my formal reception that I discovered the dreadful truth lurking beneath my patron's fair speech and benevolent treatment."

Philip had sat forward, and now was hanging on Esquin's every word.

"What truth is that?" he demanded.

Esquin feigned mortification. "A terrible truth, Sire. That night, after we had all taken our vows, my sponsor came to me in my cell. Ordering me to arise, he led me to another part of the preceptory, to a richly furnished chamber I had never visited before. Reminding me of my vow of obedience to my superiors, he then astonished me beyond measure by ordering me to remove my garments. When I would have protested, he said to me, "Have you so soon forgotten the words of our Rule? *Do as you are bidden with full compliance or it shall go ill with you. You are now ours to command, body and soul.*'

"What he meant, I could not imagine," he continued, "but his manner struck fear in my heart. I did as he commanded and stripped myself naked, blushing to find myself the object of his gaze. Ordering me to leave my garments where they lay, he led me down a secret mural stair to an underground chamber appointed like a heathen temple. There I was shocked to see the senior members of our community assembled round an altar, arrayed like pagan priests in robes of purple and gold.

"My sponsor led me closer, and the senior among his companions addressed me in these words.

"*'The Temple which we serve is the body. The body is a temple of delight. He who would serve the Temple serves his*

*brothers by giving them his body. Thus do we keep ourselves
undefiled by women, whilst gratifying our bodies' natural
appetites.'"*

The king's face had gone very still as he listened to this
recitation, and he hung on Esquin's every word as the narrative continued.

"As it came upon me what he meant, I was seized by
many hands and forced to kneel before him," Esquin said.
Now thoroughly captivated by his own fancy, he wove his
lie with lurid zest. "While they held me thus helpless, my
sponsor bent and kissed me on the mouth. It was—not the
chaste kiss by which oaths are sealed."

He had the grace to pause as if in discomfiture, swallowing nervously, but went on before the king could speak.

"There was—more," he said. "After that, at his instigation, I was taken to the altar and bent face down across it,
compelled to accept a second kiss in a more obscene manner. And then they—used me as a stallion uses a mare . . .
and did not desist until each one had taken his pleasure of
me."

At this, the king could contain himself no more.

"Can this really be true?" he demanded. Beneath the note
of incredulity was an undercurrent of hopeful glee.

"As God is my witness, Sire," Esquin assured him. "I can
hardly bear to speak of it, for shame. After my ordeal, I was
told that I now belonged to Satan, who would come for me
and consume me with fire if ever I spoke of what had tran-
spired." He hung his head most convincingly.

"Thereafter, terror sealed my lips and chained me to a life
of degradation—until Monsieur de Nogaret found me. He
persuaded me that, by casting myself on your mercy and
speaking out against my slave masters, I would find the
safety and redemption I had long craved."

"You have richly earned both!" King Philip declared, and
turned to Nogaret. "This is a bitter thing, a lamentable thing.
It is horrible to contemplate, terrible to hear!"

"An execrable evil," Nogaret agreed. "And the tale is only half-told yet."

He directed a look at Arnolfo Deghi, who took his cue with well-oiled ease.

"Sire, I regret that what I must say to you is, if anything, even more shocking than the testimony rendered by my counterpart," he began in a smooth voice that belied his coarse appearance. "The Templars are wolves who have put on the appearance of sheep, the better to serve their master the Devil. By day, they make an outward show of piety and prayer; but dead of night finds them in the guise of the vilest blasphemers ever to walk the earth since Judas Iscariot."

Philip's bright, pale eyes were bulging with excitement. "Speak on," he ordered.

"Yes, Sire. I will spare Your Majesty an account of my own reception into the ranks of the Templar Order. Suffice it to say that my experiences bear a close and painful resemblance to those endured by Monsieur de Floyran. What I am about to disclose would be grossly horrible for any Christian to hear, much less a Christian king.

"Nevertheless, the facts must be told," he went on, at Philip's warning look, "for only you, Sire, have sufficient weight of power and authority to wipe out the evils that I have witnessed and of which I am about to speak."

"Out with it, man!"

"Yes, Sire. The preceptory at Richerenches, like the one at Monfaucon, has a secret and accursed chapel dedicated to the Prince of Darkness. By day, it is dressed as a house of God, but by night, it is a theater for incorrigible iniquities. You have already heard how the Templars, in their secret sanctuaries, regularly engage in acts of bestial fornication. But you have not yet heard how the name and likeness of Our Lord are ritually desecrated in honor of the Prince of Darkness."

"Surely this cannot be true!" Philip blurted.

"I fear that it is," Arnolfo went on. "The Templars have

their priests to celebrate the Mass," he went on, "but this, Sire, is for outward appearances only. They do not speak the words of Consecration; and during their secret initiation ceremonies, each new knight or brother is required, on pain of death, to deny Christ three times in the hearing of the assembly. With each denial, he is obliged to spit on the cross, or upon the likeness of Our Lord—or to urinate upon them. Then he is compelled to sacrifice a black cat or a black cockerel on the altar in honor of Satan, who appears to them in the likeness of a disembodied head to be worshiped and adored."

Throughout Arnolfo's narrative, Nogaret had kept a close eye on the king. He was pleased to note that Philip was drinking it all in with horrified fascination and a thirsty eagerness. This last piece of invention caused the king to strike his fist against his palm with an exclamation of triumph.

"I knew it!" he cried. "This is an abominable work! A detestable disgrace! A thing almost inhuman! This evil shall be seized and plucked out by its roots! I swear it, by the head of my grandfather Saint Louis!"

Controlling a smile, Nogaret signaled his henchmen to withdraw. When they had departed, the king turned to his chief minister, beaming with profound satisfaction.

"Monsieur Nogaret, I congratulate you!" he declared. "It is even worse than you led me to believe. The witness of these men will serve as a lever to force wide the doors on every Templar preceptory in France."

Chapter Sixteen

Spring, 1307

Arnault had just returned with Oliver de Penne from an inspection of the Order's major preceptory at Gréoux when Christoph convened an informal meeting of *le Cercle:* only the three of them, plus Gaspar.

"De Molay has arrived in France," Christoph announced. "He sailed into Marseilles three days ago, with six galleys and a retinue that would have done credit to a Byzantine prince."

Gaspar sighed and rolled his eyes, for the Grand Master had been instructed by the pope to travel with a minimum of fanfare, even incognito.

"What *can* he have been thinking?"

"Obviously, it wasn't about following orders," Christoph said sourly. "Apparently he's brought an escort of sixty knights, plus their lay servants. His baggage train, I'm informed, includes twelve packhorses laden with plate and jewels. They are making their way north at a leisurely pace, with a show of pomp that could scarcely be more ostentatious, or more calculated to arouse public hostility."

"Whatever could have possessed him to indulge in such a display?" Arnault muttered, half to himself.

"Our esteemed Grand Master is ever zealous to uphold the dignity of the Order," Oliver said. "He probably considers it only right and proper that he should present himself as a visiting head of state. Unfortunately, by defying the Holy Father's orders, he's apt to alienate our single staunchest champion."

"Aye, and it lends credence to the claims of our detractors," Gaspar agreed. "Sometimes, I do despair of the man! When he shows his face in Avignon, I have no doubt that the Holy Father will have a few well-chosen words for him!"

No one raised any demur. Already subject to intimidation by the French crown, Clement V was only too likely to feel doubly threatened by this flexing of power by another rival dignitary—a dignitary, moreover, who was technically subject to papal authority, but independently possessed of very significant financial and military might. It occurred to Arnault that the higher echelons of the Church, like those of the Templar Order itself, were being subjected to powerful external pressures. The damage was insidious, and was only getting worse.

Was there a common agency at work, he wondered, trying to maneuver the Church and the Order into fighting one another? If so, the consequences could be disastrous for both.

A week later, the Grand Master's advance party arrived in Paris to prepare the way for his arrival. Among them were Father Bertrand and two members of *le Cercle* not normally resident at the Paris Temple: Father Anselmo, a Templar priest whom Arnault had known for many years, and a senior knight called Breville, known to Arnault by name and reputation but whom he had met in person only once or twice. Whatever Breville's particular talents might be, Arnault could only speculate; but he liked the look of the wiry, intense little man who came into Gaspar's office with Oliver de Penne and Father Anselmo. Father Bertrand was already there, along with Christoph and Gaspar himself.

"Fortunately, I think that one vault will do," Breville was saying to Oliver, as they followed Anselmo into the room. "I won't say that he brought *all* of the treasure of the East, but it's certainly more than I'd hoped. I wish I could have persuaded him to heed the Holy Father's instructions."

"So do I." Oliver gestured toward chairs around the conference table, where Gaspar and the others had risen at their arrival. Behind them, Oliver closed the door and locked it, standing then with his back against it as the others took seats.

"Our brother informs me that the Grand Master has brought treasure to the value of more than 150,000 golden ducats," he said to the room at large. His voice was low, clipped. "Gold, plate, specie . . ."

"Indeed," Gaspar said. "And where does this hoard come from? And why?"

"It comes from our treasuries at Limassol, Famagusta, and Nicosia," Anselmo replied. "I fear he cleaned them out—practically everything, down to the last silver *gros.*"

"That explains where," Gaspar said. "And the 'Why'?"

"He's convinced he can persuade the pope to declare a new crusade," Anselmo said. "If so, the assets will be more secure here in France than they would be on Cyprus. It would be the Order's contribution to the war effort."

Gaspar was shaking his head. Christoph looked troubled.

"The king would like that," Gaspar said, "but the prospect will get little support from the common folk. I expect you'll have heard about the riots here in Paris. Any trouble on the road from Marseilles?"

"Nothing serious," Anselmo replied, "but it's obvious that our popularity has declined drastically since my last visit. Villagers give us black looks, and townspeople jeer as we go past. In one village, they even threw stones. All the individual episodes were trivial enough, on their own, but the change in public attitude gives me cause for concern."

"Aye, if we plan to move our spiritual focus out of France," said Breville, "I'd say we'd best do it sooner rather than later."

Father Anselmo glanced at Arnault. "That would be your cue, I think, Brother Arnault. I mean no criticism, but the rumors we've been hearing about Scotland are not encouraging. The gossip on the road is that Scotland's war of independence is over, and Edward of England's victory secure. Is it?"

"Certainly not!" Arnault said indignantly. "I'll concede that Scotland's fortunes are somewhat in eclipse—and it's true that the rebel forces have been defeated and dispersed. It's even true that, for the present, Edward's lieutenants hold sway over the countryside. But don't believe for an instant that Scotland's hopes for freedom are dashed, so long as Robert Bruce still lives!"

"Then, Bruce is alive?"

"Aye, he was at last report—and I think I would know if he were not. Brother Torquil is with him, along with one of our probationers: Brother Aubrey Saint Clair, a distant cousin of mine. I gather from Brother Luc's reports that they took Bruce into hiding on Iona for the winter, under the protection of the brethren of Saint Columba. During that time, his supporters hopefully will have been marshaling the support to launch another campaign."

"*Can* they launch another campaign?" Anselmo asked.

"Physically—yes, I believe so," Arnault replied. "But when I said Bruce was under the protection of the Columban brothers, I was referring to spiritual as well as physical dangers." Both newcomers looked at him sharply.

"Whatever you may have heard about the Scots, make no mistake," he said. "The reverses Bruce has suffered weren't owing to poor strategy or even bad luck. Torquil believes that someone, probably in the English camp, has been attempting to get at Bruce by means of sorcery."

"Merciful Lord!" Anselmo exclaimed, as Bertrand silently shook his head. Breville's face had gone very still.

"Explain," he said softly. Something in Breville's tone made Arnault pause to moisten his lips before answering.

"You'll have been told about the trouble with the Comyns, several years ago." Breville nodded. "This was different. Torquil smuggled a report to us, a few months after it happened. There was a skirmish with the English at a place called Dail Righ. At the height of the fighting, while Torquil was trying to defend Bruce, something supernatural came hurtling out of the sky. Its glance stopped him in his tracks—drained the strength from his legs—but he was able to drive the monster away. He avers it was no beast of nature, but a fiend in the form of a huge black bird."

Breville's eyes narrowed. "A black bird?"

"That was how Torquil described it, yes. He said it was nearly the size of a pony, with a long serpentine neck and a toothed bill—something like a cross between a serpent and a great black swan."

"*Nom de Dieu!*" Breville's eyes briefly closed as he whispered the expletive, and the others looked at him askance.

"You know something of this apparition?" Gaspar asked.

"Or one like it," Breville replied. "I wish I did not. In Spain, there is an accursed brotherhood known as *los Caballeros del Cisne Negro*—the Knights of the Black Swan. Such a creature is the physical manifestation of a demon that serves them. They have secret strongholds scattered throughout Spain and the Mediterranean. I did not think it possible that they had sown their polluted seed so far afield."

Gaspar exchanged a glance with Arnault, then said, "Brother Luc wrote to us last summer, relaying a report from the Master of England. It seems that the English king produced a pair of sculpted ebony swans at the feast following the knighting of his heir, and swore upon those swans, not to rest until he had won his war against the Scots—as did nearly very other knight present."

"*Madre de Dios,*" Breville murmured, gone ashen. "You do not think . . ."

"That King Edward is a black magician?" Christoph shook his head. "No. In any case, he is dying, so it would make little difference if he were. Last summer, when he left London, his strength was only sufficient to take him as far north as Carlisle. Luc expects news of his death within a matter of weeks. Besides, the swans may be mere coincidence. On the other hand, it is possible that someone close to him . . . But, tell us more of these Spanish knights."

Breville nodded. "They are followers of a cult who claim to have inherited the secret lore of an Egyptian adept called Zosimos of Panopolis, but what they practice is a perversion even of that. They are led by a council of masters calling themselves the Decuria, and believe that alchemy offers man eternal life without recourse to God. They contend that men can attain physical perfection, and therefore immortality, through the transforming influence of the philosophers' stone."

"Salvation without sacrifice," Father Anselmo said, nodding.

"As I said, they are a perversion, a blasphemy," Breville agreed. "Their teachings and practices are rooted in the pride of Lucifer, whom they take as their patron. They predate us by several decades, but also arose in the Holy Land. They perceive us as a threat to their ascendancy. More than once, they have attempted to undermine the integrity of the Order from within. Mine was the task of foiling one of those attempts, many years ago, when one of the Decuria infiltrated the Order and brought the *caput propheticus* back to Jerusalem as a trophy of war."

Oliver exhaled through his teeth with a hissing sound, and Arnault pursed his lips. Even before his initiation into the ranks of *le Cercle,* he had heard whispered rumors concerning a strange head-shaped relic said to have been recovered from an accursed city somewhere in the Arabian desert.

Some tales identified it as the skull of one of the Nephilim, a strange race of beings alluded to in the Book of Genesis. Others claimed the relic was actually the mummified head of John the Baptist, perversely made into an idol of veneration. But all the versions agreed that destructive affinities associated with this "head" had begun immediately to exert their influence over the Order, with the loss of Jerusalem mere months after the head's acquisition.

The tales surrounding the *caput* had been linked to other rumors as well, suggesting the existence of a renegade assassin sect calling itself the Brethren of the Cygnet—or of the Signet, for they were said to wear a ring inscribed with a swan on the seal.

Could it be, Arnault wondered, that the Brethren of the Signet and Breville's Decuria shared a common allegiance with the forces of Darkness? It was not inconceivable that such a sect might have attracted recruits from the West. And if they had divined the importance of an independent Scotland as the site of the Fifth Temple, they would have ample reason to see this thwarted.

By Gaspar's next comment, he had been following a very similar line of reasoning.

"This tale suggests a worrisome possible connection," he said. "Robert Bruce bears upon his shoulders not only the fate of Scottish sovereignty, but also the fate of the Temple. Whether it is Knights of the Black Swan or the Brethren of the Cygnet or your Decuria makes little difference. What matters is that, somehow, forces of Darkness have become aware of our interest in Scotland, and are attempting to thwart us."

"The signs are clear enough," Breville said. "I have little doubt we are dealing with the Decuria—and if so, no one in *le Cercle* knows better than I, what we are up against. Let me attend to this, Christoph. I have dealt with these vile sorcerers off and on for the better part of fifteen years. Whatever guise they may have adopted, they won't be able to hide from me."

"And let *me* go back to Bruce!" Arnault added. "Torquil needs to know about this, and he shouldn't have to deal with it alone."

Christoph shook his head. "I cannot spare you both. There remain a great many questions regarding the Grand Master's plans—and the Holy Father's intentions, and the king's. No, for now you must stay with us here in Paris, Arnault. I need your counsel and your skills." He turned his gaze on Breville. "But you I give leave to take whatever assistance you require, and endeavor to discover the identity of our enemy. We must know what and whom we are fighting."

Breville gave a curt nod, a predatory gleam already kindling behind his dark eyes. "Consider it settled. I will take my leave as soon as the necessary arrangements can be made."

"What are we to do in the meantime?" Oliver asked. "We have the greatest Treasures of the Order housed here in Paris. Can we not invoke their powers for our own protection?"

Christoph shook his head regretfully. "The Treasures aren't meant to be used as weapons. To use them thus would be an abuse of the trust vested in us. No, whatever is to become of the Order, our first priority must be to safeguard the Treasures for the sake of future generations. Nor can we justify taking any action that might cause harm to the ignorant and the innocent."

"Then, *protect* the ignorant and the innocent," Arnault said. "Protect Bruce! Without him, and the refuge of the Fifth Temple, I don't see how we *can* guard the Treasures for the sake of future generations!"

Christoph sighed. "I understand what you're saying—and believe me, I want to find a way to do what you ask. But let us never forget that we are sworn to the service of God, in a war that will never end until the world itself ceases to be. We have always been ready to give our lives in our Master's cause. Henceforth we may be asked to sacrifice our very identity in a greater cause." He allowed himself a faint, ironic smile. "Believe me, I have no more wish to die than the next man. Give me time to think and pray about this, Arnault. Let us all pray about it."

A reflective silence followed. Arnault was the first to break it.

"If you will not let me go, then we must find a way to apprise Luc and Torquil regarding the Knights of the Black Swan," he said. "Perhaps it will help them put a name and a face to the enemy that has been pursuing them."

"The warning must be subtle," Breville said. "The Decuria will have many resources at their disposal. Whatever form your warning takes, be aware that if it falls into the wrong hands, it could assist them in their dark work."

"Then, we dare not commit any word to writing," Christoph said. "No cipher would suffice to baffle our foes. Nor can we trust to word of mouth. There are ways to sift a man's knowledge, with or without his consent. No," he concluded, "we must devise something new."

Chapter Seventeen

Spring, 1307

A NARROW SEA STRAIT SEPARATES RATHLIN ISLAND FROM the northern coast of Ireland. Allied to the earldom of Ulster, the island's population of farmers and fishermen were accustomed to minding their own business. But they were not oblivious to the plight of their Scottish neighbors, nor were they resigned to English ships encroaching on their fishing waters. Thus they raised no objections when, early in the spring of 1307, their island became the mustering point for Scottish rebels poised to renew their country's bid for freedom.

In the dawn of a morning late in February, keen winds buffeted the north shore of the island, frothing up cascades of foam with each incoming wave. Standing on the shingle, Robert Bruce narrowed his gaze against the morning light as he surveyed the array of galleys riding at anchor beyond the shore break.

"They make a brave sight, don't they?" he remarked to Torquil Lennox.

"Aye, they do," Torquil agreed. "Your friends have exerted themselves nobly."

"It remains for us to seek a fitting victory that will crown their efforts," Bruce replied. "But the ultimate prize will be to see the full restoration of Scotland's sovereignty."

The fleet already had begun to muster when Bruce arrived a few days before. The contacts pursued by his brothers over the winter months had reaped a swift and generous response, not only from his staunch supporters in Scotland, but also from Ireland, on behalf of Bruce's Irish-born wife.

The single strongest contingent had been furnished by Christiana MacRuiaridh of Mar, hailed by her own clan folk as "Lady of the Isles." The MacDonalds of Argyll likewise had sent both men and ships, as had Malcolm MacQuillan, the lord of Kintyre. As a result, Bruce now had thirty-three galleys at his disposal and enough seasoned fighting men to renew the campaign that had foundered so close to extinction at Dail Righ.

The moment of departure was rapidly approaching. In the fields adjoining the seafront, the men were breaking camp. Most of the army's weapons and supplies had already been loaded aboard the waiting galleys. The ships' masters and their crews were standing by, ready to raise anchor and sail at the king's command.

The timing could hardly be better. Edward Plantagenet was lying bedridden at Lanercost Priory, a sick man dependent on letters to acquaint him with what was going on north of the Border. The Earl of Pembroke might have taken up at least some of the resulting slack, but his efficiency was being hampered by the Prince of Wales, attached to his command, whose love of tournaments had taught him little of actual warfare. Not for the first time, Torquil found himself thinking how matters would fare far easier with the Scots, once a new king was on the English throne—and wishing for that day. God willing, it would not be long in coming.

Crunching footsteps on the shingle behind them put an end to Torquil's musings.

"Sire," Aubrey announced, "they're saying that we have about two hours' grace before the tide turns."

"Well enough," the king replied. "Call our captains together. I want a final word with them before we embark."

The conference took place on the beach before the king's tent. Bruce wasted no time getting down to business.

"Gentlemen, today marks a new beginning," he began without preamble. "Today we set out in earnest to recover the freedom which Edward of England has stolen.

"The English are masters of war," he went on, scanning the keen faces. "To them it is a time-honored game—and no one knows better how to exploit the rules. If we try to fight them on their own terms, we are doomed to lose. So we are going to play the game a new way, by rules of our own making."

A stir rippled through the crowd. Even Bruce's veterans craned forward, battle-worn faces lighting with new interest.

"So, how are we to wage war our way?" the king asked in ringing tones. "To begin with, we must renounce the empty vanities of chivalry that the English nobility hold so dear. Let the Prince of Wales and his lisping favorites sport their banners and parade their horses, and vie with one another for pride of place. We, for our part, will not be ashamed to adopt tactics more common to brigands—tricks, sleights, and diversions. Only by these means can we hope to achieve our ends."

A rumble of tentative agreement answered him. Bruce waited for it to die down.

"We lack the numbers to fight a pitched set battle," he stated flatly. "We always have. So what I propose to do instead is to divide our forces into three separate raiding parties. Our first objective will be to harass and confuse the enemy. If these operations are successful, we can expect greater gains to follow."

He went on to outline the plan in greater detail. Torquil was already familiar with its features, having helped Bruce formulate his strategy. An advance guard was to go ashore on the Mull of Kintyre, and from there make inroads into

Arran, taking every opportunity to gather supplies and information along the way. Stephen Boyd would command this party, assisted by the talented and loyal James Douglas.

A larger raiding party of eighteen galleys was to be commanded jointly by the king's two brothers, Thomas and Alexander. Their objective was to make for Galloway, there to engage and subdue the MacDoualls and McCans.

The largest landing force, led by the king himself, would sail for Carrick, formerly the territorial demesne of the Bruce family. If all went well, the three companies would rendezvous at Turnberry Point.

The plan met with hopeful approval, and the captains dispersed to their ships. Soon sails were being raised to catch the wind, and oars were trimmed to plow the waves. Shouts of farewells rang out over the water as the three fleets dispersed like migratory birds, unerringly homeward bound.

Far to the east, an overnight change in the weather cast a pall of cloud over the Scottish lowlands. Snow was falling lightly as a well-armed party of horsemen approached the gates of English-occupied Berwick Castle. A sentry on duty at the main gate came to attention as the party's obvious leader drew rein before the interwoven bars of the heavy iron yett that secured the outer barbican.

"I am Bartholeme de Challon," the rider announced. "I have permission of King Edward to question a prisoner in your charge."

From the pouch at his belt, Bartholeme produced a folded square of parchment secured with a lozenge of sealing wax. Recognizing the imprint of the royal privy seal, the sentry handed it to an officer, who likewise glanced at the seal, then signaled his men to unbar the port.

"Sorry to delay you, m'lord."

Bartholeme merely nodded acceptance of his due, reclaiming his document and riding through the barbican arch with the air of a man who has every right to the deference the seal had produced. Amid the party that followed him, the sight of Mercurius riding pillion behind one of his retainers, wearing a miniature replica of his master's fighting harness, drew glances of good-natured amusement from the guards posted on the adjoining parapets.

"Be so good as to inform your superior that I must speak with him at once," Bartholeme said to the guard who came to take his horse, as he swung down from the saddle.

Sir John Botetourt was in his private apartment, morosely nursing a cold and something hot in a cup between his two hands. Heat from a pair of charcoal braziers, added to the glow from the hearthfire, gave the room the air of a glassblower's forge. Sir John looked up as Bartholeme entered, Mercurius tagging at his heels, and stifled a sneeze. One bandaged leg was propped up on a stool, and there was a walking stick leaned against the raised hearth.

"This damnable climate!" he complained through a soggy linen handkerchief. "The Scots are welcome to it, so far as I'm concerned! Which prisoner did you wish to see?"

"Isabel, Countess of Buchan," Bartholeme replied.

Sir John registered a rheumy blink. "You must know that she is being held under terms of—significant duress. No one is allowed to communicate with her save myself and the two women who look after her needs."

"You will find that an exception has been made," Bartholeme said mildly.

Smiling faintly, as if in apology, he presented his document for the other man's inspection. Sir John permitted himself a noncommittal grunt, but set his cup aside and broke the seal, dabbing at his nose while he read the order. His eyebrows rose.

"So it has," he observed on a note of mild envy. "You evidently occupy a high place in the king's esteem. Very well, my lord." He laid the document aside and picked up his stick. "Give me a moment to make ready, and I will take you to see her."

A short delay ensued while Sir John retired to don additional layers of clothing. In his absence, Mercurius did little to disguise his impatience.

"Master, I hope we haven't come all this way for nothing," he grumbled under his breath.

"If the woman knows anything," Bartholeme said crisply, "we'll have it out of her. If not—" He shrugged. "Perhaps she will at least provide us with a bit of sport."

Sir John rejoined them, heavily muffled in a fleece-lined mantle, knitted gloves, and a fur cap. Accompanied by two guards, he led them limping along the length of an adjoining passage and up a spiraling mural stair. A stout oak guard port at the top gave access to the citadel's rooftop battlement. An icy blast of wind greeted the party as they emerged into the open air.

Suspended in a salient angle of the northwest tower wall, just at the level of the crenellated parapet, was a large cage made of latticed timber and iron, its top fashioned in the shape of an iron crown. In one corner of the cage, tightly huddled under some skins and what appeared to be a heavy blanket, Bartholeme could just make out a figure that looked scarcely human, let alone female.

He smiled as he saw her: Isabel of Buchan, estranged wife of John Comyn, Earl of Buchan. She had dared to place a crown on the head of Robert Bruce—and Bartholeme thought what delicious irony it was, that Edward should have seen fit to have her cage surmounted by a mocking replica of that crown.

Seeing her miserable state, it also occurred to him to wonder whether her husband shared any of the proclivities of his cousin, the John Comyn slain by Bruce—though that would do *her* little good. A curious family, the Comyns, though Red John had been inept, in the end. But the once-fair Isabel—if she knew anything—perhaps could redeem the failure of her husband's kinsman, whether or not she willed it.

Snuffling into his handkerchief, Sir John approached the cage and rattled his stick between the iron bars.

"Wake up in there!" he ordered.

The face that slowly lifted to look at them from wind-reddened eyes was pinched with cold, and looked like that of an old woman. Dingy blond hair streamed down her back in matted elf locks, and her clothes were those she had been wearing at the time of her capture several months before, now grossly stained with travel and hard usage. The blanket she drew closer around her shoulders to supplement the meager warmth of a tattered traveling cloak had once been worn by a horse.

"Ah, you *are* home," Sir John said mockingly. "Here's someone come to talk to you, my fine lady."

Isabel lifted her chin and glared back at him, managing to look defiant.

"He may talk as long and as freely as he pleases," she said hoarsely, shivering, "but I have nothing to say in return."

"You would be well advised to keep a civil tongue," Sir John warned her.

"Or what?" came the spirited response. "Will you deprive me of my maintenance? Now, that would, *indeed*, be a serious threat, seeing the luxury in which I am kept by the gracious indulgence of Edward Longshanks."

Bartholeme, meanwhile, had amused himself by inspecting the cage and its appurtenances. The enclosure was perhaps eight feet on a side, roofed with hides, but the open sides were merely barred. A tiny, partially screened cubicle in one corner gave off the stench of a privy. The only other meager concessions to human need were a very small charcoal brazier and a wooden bench to serve as either bed or seat.

"She is a tiresome hag, as you can see," Sir John said, turning to Bartholeme with a sniffle. "Shall I call my men to secure her?"

"I think there will be no need," Bartholeme said lightly.

"Nor would I dream of imposing further, by asking you to remain out of doors at the risk of your health. I'm sure the lady and I will have a very agreeable visit."

Sir John gave a mocking snort, but showed no disposition to linger.

"As you wish. I shall leave guards posted at the bottom of the stair, should you require assistance. They will show you back to my chambers when you are finished."

With these parting words, he retired indoors. Mercurius took up a station against the door that closed behind him. Only when Bartholeme had satisfied himself that there was no one else but the dwarf within earshot did he address himself to the wary prisoner.

"I am here to trade information," he informed her.

"I have nothing to exchange," she said.

"That may or may not be true," Bartholeme allowed. "It has been some months since you were taken into custody. I should think you must be starved for news. Are you not the least bit curious to know the current state of Scottish affairs?"

"I have no interest in listening to a pack of lies."

"You may judge what I am about to say for yourself," Bartholeme said. "Perhaps this will serve as a token of truth."

Slipping his right hand into the breast of his doublet, he produced the brooch taken by John of Lorn. Isabel went pale at the sight of it.

"Perhaps you have seen this ornament somewhere before?" he inquired. "Do feel free to take a closer look."

Clasping her horse blanket more tightly around her shoulders, Isabel reluctantly drew nearer and bent her gaze to his outstretched palm. As she did so, Bartholeme's free hand whisked from under his cloak and darted between the bars, gloved fingers crushing a tiny glass vial mere inches from her face.

She recoiled with a gasp as a plume of black steam filled

her eyes and nose. Her gaunt features went blank, and her eyes glazed, the pupils going wide. The blanket slipped unheeded from her shoulders, to fall in an angular heap at her feet.

Confident that she had gotten a full dose of the drug, Bartholeme dropped the remains of the vial to the stone floor and ground it to powder under his boot, then executed a compelling gesture of command before her dilated eyes, binding her will even as he captured her gaze.

"You will listen and obey me," he murmured, with a sidelong glance at Mercurius. "Nod to show me that you understand."

Isabel's disheveled head slowly bobbed up and down. He could sense a part of her will struggling to break free, but he knew it was fruitless.

"Give me your hands," he ordered.

Isabel complied with the stiffness of a puppet, not flinching as Bartholeme raked the barb of the brooch across her right palm and drew blood, then smeared the blood across the crystal in the center. Smiling thinly, he then placed the bloodied brooch in her wounded hand and closed her fingers over it.

"Name the man to whom this ornament belongs," he commanded. His grasp exerted cruel pressure on hers, where it enclosed the brooch.

Isabel drew a shuddering breath, her lips moving in a rasping whisper.

"King Robert Bruce."

"What cause have you to call him king?"

"I witnessed his investiture."

"Describe this investiture. Describe your part in it."

"I conducted him to his enthronement seat, as is my family's right. I placed the crown upon his head."

A feral gleam kindled in Bartholeme's eyes. "This enthronement seat—describe it to me."

The countess responded slowly, like a dull-witted child.

"It was a wooden chair with a high back. It was draped and canopied with crimson velvet."

"Was this chair not designed to provide a setting for the Stone of Destiny?"

A frown of perplexity creased the countess's brow. "I do not know."

"There was no stone in it?" Bartholeme asked. "Something brought out of hiding?"

"No stone," she mumbled.

Bartholeme traded glances with Mercurius.

"Where is it, then?" he demanded. "Where is the Stone?"

A look of desolation flickered across her face. "Away down in London," she whispered. "Longshanks stole it, years ago."

Mercurius uttered a muffled exclamation of disgust, but Bartholeme silenced him with a gesture.

"Come, Lady Isabel, I'm sure you can give me a better answer than that," he chided.

The woman's white lips twitched uncertainly, but she did not speak. Smiling pitilessly, Bartholeme increased his pressure on her hand, so that the sharp angles of the brooch dug into her flesh. A breathless whimper of pain whispered from between Isabel's chapped lips.

"I suggest that you think again," Bartholeme said softly.

Tears were welling in her eyes, starting to runnel down her dirty face, but she said nothing. At increasing pressure on her trapped hand, she moaned and swayed, but still failed to find her tongue. With a hiss of contempt, Bartholeme relaxed his grip on her hand, but did not release her.

"So much for nothing, Master," Mercurius said. "Let's be off."

"I'm not finished yet," Bartholeme replied. "Were she not in this cage, I might inflict more traditional assaults upon her virtue, but I have a far more effective weapon." He drew her closer to the bars of the cage. "She may not know it, but she played the role of high priestess when she placed the crown on Bruce's head. Perhaps she can penetrate the veil that shields him from our sight."

With his teeth he pulled the glove from his left hand, exposing his black swan ring. With almost caressing precision he touched its onyx seal between the woman's eyebrows, keeping its demon in check, but letting her know the terror of its presence.

"Listen and heed me, Isabel," he whispered softly, seductively. "You hold in your hand the king's token. It knows him . . . and you know him. Your blood can bridge the distance that separates you, washing away the barriers of space and time. . . .

"Yield to it, Isabel. Yield, and do my bidding. Be one with him . . . and see with his eyes. . . ."

Her surrender came almost immediately. Her drooping frame slowly stiffened, and her head lifted. Jerkily at first, she turned her ensorceled face this way and that, like a hound seeking an elusive scent. Then, abruptly, her gaze sharpened to a distant image, and her expression grew keen.

"Good. . . . You have found him," Bartholeme observed, nodding. "Tell me what you see, Isabel."

Isabel drew a short breath. Words tumbled disjointedly from her lips.

". . . ship heaves and tosses . . . the shore draws near . . . my family's ancient seat . . . I will not be denied. . . ."

"Where are you?" Bartholeme prompted.

"Turn—Turnberry . . ." came the whispered response. Then abruptly her tone stiffened.

"I have returned to fight! I will not be driven into hiding again!"

With this she gave a little cry and started to go limp, her grip on the brooch relaxing. As Bartholeme fumbled to keep the ornament from falling from her hand and possibly through the barred floor of the cage, his control slipping, she crumpled unconscious at his feet. With a grimace of frustration, he retrieved the brooch and returned it to his belt pouch, turning to glance at Mercurius.

"We'll get no more from her," he said, with a disdainful glance back at the unconscious Isabel. "But at least we now know that Bruce has come out of hiding at last. And where else would he go, but Carrick—the homeland of his birth?" Smiling, he stroked his signet ring, calming the demon within. "I should say that this revelation amply repays the trouble we went through to get it!"

Chapter Eighteen

Spring, 1307

BARTHOLEME DECIDED NOT TO LEAVE BERWICK THAT night, for his newfound information suggested several good measures to which he might apply it. The most ambitious of them required privacy as well as certain preparations, though he had no doubt that the former could be procured through the offices of the good Sir John. And it would be expedient to send immediate word to King Edward—though if his own plans succeeded, that precaution would have been rendered irrelevant.

Before leaving the tower roof, he carefully wiped every trace of blood from the Lady Isabel's hand with a square of linen. He then took a knife from his boot and cut off a lock of her hair, folding this carefully in the linen square before tucking both items into his belt pouch, along with the brooch.

"Now to arrange for a place to work," he said to Mercurius, as they started down the turnepike stair.

An hour later, he had secured accommodations for the night, penned a missive to King Edward, and enlisted the services of a reliable messenger on Sir John's fastest horse to deliver it. Controlling a smile, he watched from a window

overlooking the castle yard as the courier clattered out the
barbican gate, already at speed.

Mercurius, standing beside him, murmured, "You know,
of course, Master, that by the time King Edward's troops arrive in the area, Bruce will have moved on."

"That need not concern us," Bartholeme said with a thin
smile. "The important point is that he finally has ventured
out from wherever he had gone to ground, these past few
months. Before tomorrow's dawn, our Templar friends will
deeply repent having allowed him to do so."

They had retired to the quarters allotted them. Sir John
had dutifully extended an invitation to join him at table, but
had evidenced no sign of disappointment when his guest declined, pleading fatigue; the state of his cold made it likely
that he was more than grateful for the chance of an early
night. Mercurius barred the door behind them before turning
to his master, for it was clear that Bartholeme had other intentions than recovery from his "fatigue."

"What is your will, Messire?" he asked.

Bartholeme's eyes shone like burnished steel as he turned
from the window, twisting the swan signet on his finger.

"Fetch me my case," he said softly. "Tonight we summon
up the *Cygnus Hermetis*. I intend to send it to Bruce, to rip
his living heart from his breast. In the moment of his death,
his very soul will be laid bare to me—before I offer it up to
the Lords of Darkness—and I will know all he knows, from
the name of his favorite hound to the whereabouts of the
Stone of Destiny."

A malevolent grin creased the dwarf's goblin face, but he
said nothing as he fetched the small traveling chest containing his master's alchemical paraphernalia. He watched with
keen interest as Bartholeme carefully selected several items
from the chest's contents.

By way of preparation, Bartholeme traced an alchemical
sigil on the mantel above the fire, with a drawing stick of tallow and ashes. Directing Mercurius to build up the fire, he

then made a measured circuit of the room, sketching further symbols of warding on each of the four walls. A low-voiced incantation activated the wards, sealing the room from the inside. A deft series of mystical gestures sent flames roaring up the chimney.

Satisfied that his preparations were adequate, Bartholeme returned to the fireside and rapidly stripped to the waist, exposing a dark, zoomorphic tattoo at the base of his breastbone. Then, signaling Mercurius to stand clear, he muttered a further invocation and flung the drawing stick into the fire.

The blaze leapt higher, with an accompanying billow of heat into the room. Bathed in its sorcerous glare, Bartholeme plucked up a parchment packet of alchemical salts and cast that into the flames. As it burned, flaring up in hues of emerald, violet, and indigo, he added the severed lock of Isabel's hair—though not its linen wrap—which the fire consumed in a hungry flash and the sickening stench of burning hair.

The heart of the ritual was approaching. Kneeling, Bartholeme used a second tallow stick to sketch an inverted pentagram on the floor in front of the hearth, its points as wide as the span of a man's arms. In its center he laid out the bloodied linen from Isabel's hand, and placed thereon the brooch of Lorn and his own swan signet ring. Around these, encompassing the five points of the pentagram, he sprinkled a circular trail of coarse black powder—and then sat well back.

At his gesture of command, a spark from the fire ignited the powder with a bang, defining a circle of fire and sending acrid gray smoke roiling into the room. Drawing a deep breath of the smoke-laden air, Bartholeme lifted his hands in a suppliant's posture and whispered the final words of an ancient rite of summoning.

A spot of darkness appeared within the ring of fire. A mere speck at first, the darkness quickly blossomed into the hulking shape of a great, long-necked bird with wings of shadow. Man-tall, it glared around the room with ruby-glowing eyes, its saw-toothed bill gnashing hungrily. The slow surge of its pinions caused the flames to gutter.

"Hail, *Cygnus Hermetis,* bird of infernal night!" Bartholeme whispered, abasing himself before the creature. "Hail, Hawk of Lucifer, Harrier of Shadows! Behold my oblation, an offering of blood and ash. Feed and be glutted!"

As he opened his hands toward the blood-streaked linen at the center of the pentagram, the creature cocked a baleful eye, then lowered its great head. The linen vanished with a searing crackle and a hint of blood-stench, leaving the brooch and the ring behind. With a harsh laugh, Bartholeme scuttled forward on his knees, fearless now, and picked up the brooch, cupping it in both hands to cradle it against the tattoo on his chest.

"Hail, Swan of Darkness, I give you him who owned this object: Robert Bruce, so-called King of Scots!" he declared. "You have tasted the body and blood of his priestess. Now find the king himself, and feast upon his heart!"

Blinking its ruby eyes, the Cygnus spread its shadow-wings and, with a great beat of its pinions, shot up the chimney in a gale of sulfurous ash. The flames roared after it, changing briefly from phosphorescent green to deepest blood-crimson.

Midnight and a rime of sleety mist blanketed the southern Ayrshire coast, where Torquil Lennox watched on the forecastle of the king's galley. It was one of a fleet of fourteen vessels drawn up in the shelter of the Isle of Arran's southernmost tip. Off to the left, the broad sweep of the Clyde estuary stretched northward toward Glasgow town, dark under the stars as far as the eye could see. To the east, but a few miles away, lay Turnberry Point and the castle guarding it, backed by the shadowy mass of the hills of Carrick. The castle once had belonged to Bruce's mother, but was now in the hands of Edward's man, Sir Henry Percy.

Knuckling at his eyes, weary after his long watch, Torquil returned his gaze to sweeping that distant shore, his leather jack creaking as he shifted position. The only faint lights showing aboard the galley came from covered lanterns strung fore and aft. Most of the men were taking their rest, either sprawled between the oar benches or curled up in the cargo space astern. The only sounds were the distant murmur of gentle surf and the closer sounds of wavelets lapping against wooden hulls, the occasional muted creak from a ship's cable. Presently a familiar muffled figure joined Torquil at the forward railing.

"No sign yet?" the king asked.

Torquil shook his head. "No, nothing."

"Well, it's early yet," Bruce breathed, adding wryly, "Nothing's come easy on this venture so far, has it? But the balance of luck is turning in our favor."

That much, Torquil reckoned, certainly seemed to be true. Though their crossing from Rathlin Island, off the Ulster coast, had been hampered by late-winter storms, most of the fleet had survived the voyage with only minor damage. One galley had gone afoul of rocks off the Mull of Kintyre, but the men aboard her sister ships had managed to rescue the crew before she broke up, with no lives lost.

Their biggest recent piece of luck had come two days before. Whilst reconnoitering on the Isle of Arran, Robert Boyd and an advance force had surprised and captured a number of supply boats arriving at Brodick Bay to reinforce an English garrison at Brodick Castle, thereby gaining a valuable haul of food and weapons. Encouraged by this success, the rebels were now contemplating a more ambitious prize: Turnberry Castle itself.

It was a chancy undertaking, but worth some risk if they succeeded. Four hours earlier, young Aubrey and a man called Cuthbert, one of Bruce's retainers from the local area, had gone ashore to spy out the English positions in the castle's vicinity. It had been agreed that if conditions were favorable, they would light a signal fire on the beach at Maidens, out of sight and just to the north of the castle. The two had been gone long enough that the signal could come at any time, but Torquil had to keep reminding himself that a proper assessment of the situation could take longer than expected. Still, he could not shake off a nagging sense of uneasiness.

The waning moon, a quarter past full, came out from behind cold-looking clouds, its pale radiance highlighting a range of snow-powdered hills to the east. Sighing, Bruce surveyed the scene with a crooked smile, half-pained and half-reminiscent.

"My brothers and I used to hunt in those hills," he recalled. "Neil once—" He broke off, shaking his head, for Neil was dead; but he quickly resumed.

"I promise you, Torquil, these are still my lands, and the folk are still my people," he said steadily, "whatever Edward Longshanks says to the contrary. It would take more than any edict by an English king to turn their hearts and minds against me—and more than the death of a brother to make *me* give up the fight!"

As he spoke, a ruby spark like a dragon's eye flared from the dark stretch of beach at Maidens, swiftly blossoming into a bright amber bloom. With a little gasp, Bruce started up, his eyes alight with excitement.

"That's it!" he murmured. "All right, men, it's time," he called more loudly, as his men began to stir.

Swiftly, the galleys unshipped their oars and made for the distant shore, beaching only long enough to off-load their landing parties. When the men had regrouped, just at the edge of a sprawling fir wood, they began moving southward, skirting the base of Turnberry Point. They were deep among the trees when the forward scouts slipped back to report a second armed party coming the other way.

Silently the order was passed for everyone in the vanguard to take cover. Fading back with Bruce and Boyd behind a screen of mature trees, Torquil strained every part of his body to listen. Gradually, through the breeze-rustle of the surrounding forest, he began to make out the muted scrunch of many booted feet advancing along the trail, trying to be quiet.

Waving Bruce and Boyd to better cover behind another tree, not far away, Torquil set his hand firmly on the hilt of his dirk and waited. The stealthy footsteps drew nearer, then stopped, to be replaced by a bristling silence. Straining to pierce the darkness, Torquil caught a glimpse of a single tall shadow detaching itself from the surrounding trees, gliding soundlessly from tree to tree in a zigzag pattern.

Not daring to breathe, he eased his dirk from its sheath, waiting until the other was almost abreast of him before he sprang. The newcomer wheeled aside with a startled grunt, evading the arm that would have muffled any outcry, but gave no alarm, though steel flashed briefly in the tree-filtered moonlight. In the course of their quick but silent tussle, Torquil's grasping hands fumbled against a stout leather scabbard slung across his opponent's back—sword harness that was entirely distinctive.

"Aubrey?" he breathed, though he did not loose his grip.

Instantly his opponent's struggling ceased, and a breathy sigh of relief escaped the other's lips.

"*Jesu*, Torquil, what are you doing here?" Aubrey exclaimed. "Why did you land? And where's the king?"

As they helped one another to their feet, several other shadows separated themselves from the undergrowth.

"I'm right here," Bruce said in a low voice. "We saw your beacon—that's why."

"We lit no beacon!" Aubrey protested.

"Well, someone did."

As he spoke, there came a crackling in the undergrowth behind them. Instinctively Bruce and his companions reached for swords and dirks as a swarm of armed men materialized from the darkness, but Aubrey's lack of alarm confirmed that the men were allies, not foes. In their vanguard, the missing Cuthbert escorted a handsome young woman dressed in breeches like a boy, who unshielded a horn lantern and thrust it before her.

"Robert, it isn't safe," she said. "I don't know whether you've been betrayed, but you mustn't attack."

Torquil would have interposed, but the king checked him with a hand on his shoulder.

"It's all right," he said. "I know this fair champion. 'Tis Christian of Carrick, a kinswoman of mine." And a former mistress, according to what Bruce once had told Torquil.

Christian seized the king's arm with urgent familiarity, her other hand holding the lantern so he could see her face.

"You must away from here at once," she warned. "Sir Henry Percy commands the castle. He has over three hundred men billeted there and in the village. An attack on the castle would be sheer folly."

The village was less than half a mile away. As Torquil exchanged glances with Aubrey, he felt a queasy pang to think how narrowly they had escaped walking into disaster.

"Were they expecting us?" Boyd murmured.

"Maybe. I don't know. It may be that—"

Christian stopped short, biting at her lip in distress, and Bruce laid a hand on her shoulder.

"What is it?"

Mutely she shook her head.

"Christian, if there's ill news to come, speak out and we'll bear it. It may be that—what? I have to know the worst of what I'm up against."

Christian closed her eyes briefly and took a deep breath. "Your brothers Thomas and Alexander have come to grief in Galloway, at the hands of Dungal Macdouall."

Stunned, Bruce merely stared at her for several heartbeats before whispering, "Killed?"

"Not—there."

"Dear God. . . ."

"I didn't intend to tell you until this was over," she went on dully. "They were captured almost as soon as they went ashore, together with their following. The reports we've had are garbled, but this much is clear: Macdouall killed some of the others on the spot, then sent your brothers to Lanercost as a gift to King Edward—dragged at the tails of horses."

An appalled silence met this declaration. No one present had any illusions about the fate reserved for anyone so closely connected with the rebel cause—especially Bruce's own brothers. Neil Bruce had already suffered a traitor's death at Edward's orders.

"Both of them are dead, then," he whispered dully.

"Aye, Robert. I am so sorry."

The king turned abruptly away, burying his face in one hand as he stifled a sob. But as Torquil made to move the others back, to afford the king a moment of privacy for his grief, Bruce drew himself erect and turned back to face them, unashamed to let them see the tears glittering in his eyes.

"The English will pay for this," he vowed quietly. "One day, there will be a reckoning."

"That's why I've come," Christian said. "Here are forty volunteers from my household, ready to serve you, if you'll have them."

As she gestured behind her, at the ranks of her followers, Bruce ran his gaze over them gratefully, recovering his equilibrium.

"You know that I can offer you nothing at present but hardship and danger," he told them. "That, and the chance to strike a blow against our enemies."

"We ask no more than that, Sire," one of them replied.

A bleak smile transfigured the king's countenance. "Then, swear it on your blades," he told them, "and vow loyalty not to me, but to this realm of Scotland!"

"So do we swear!" they replied, amid the slither and hiss of steel being bared as, to the man, they gave him their troth.

On the heels of this new development, Bruce and his

chief advisors fell back briefly to reconsider their strategy. They now had forty men added to their strength. What was more, they still held the element of surprise.

"If Percy's got three hundred men garrisoned in and around Turnberry," Gilbert de la Haye pointed out, "it isn't likely we can successfully attack and take the castle itself."

"No, but we still might make him regret this night," Cuthbert said coldly. "We could go for the garrison itself, fall on them while they sleep. It isn't pretty warfare, but it worked for William Wallace."

Bruce's expression hardened, though ordering such an attack would be at odds with the ethics of his training as a knight. But desperate times called for desperate measures—and his Highlanders were bred to such silent cut-and-thrust work. And then, there were three dead Bruce brothers to avenge. . . .

"Organize it," Bruce said to de la Haye.

They attacked a short time later, silent and deadly, falling on the sleeping town like wolves, slaughtering the English soldiers where they slept. There were a few pockets of resistance, quickly overcome, but the element of surprise helped Bruce's men carry the night.

In the company of Torquil and Aubrey, the king was helping clean out one such pocket, his dirk reddened by English blood, when all at once a serious counterattack came—and from a totally unexpected direction. As they emerged from a foray down a lane near the edge of the village, a sudden shadow passed across the face of the moon. Torquil's startled glance upward caught a brief impression of dark wings and a toothed avian bill as, in that instant, the thing dropped out of the sky like a thunderbolt.

Only a handful of others were anywhere near the king; Aubrey was closest. At Torquil's warning cry, the younger Templar simultaneously glanced up and grabbed a handful of Bruce's sleeve to yank him out of the creature's path as it swooped to kill, flinging himself bodily between the king and almost certain death. One black wing buffeted him aside with stunning force, tumbling him into the undergrowth, but its target clearly was Bruce, who rolled clear as talons of darkness snatched at empty air.

Hissing with frustration, the creature instead seized one of Bruce's men in its toothed beak and carried him, struggling and screaming, out over the water, where it let him fall on the jagged rocks below. Horrified, Bruce started to pull himself up, but Torquil could see the monster veering about on the wing.

"It's coming back!" he cried. "Robert, stay down!"

"No!" Bruce shouted back, shifting his dirk to his off-hand and drawing his sword. "It wants *me*! The rest of you, scatter!"

It was no time to argue. The shadow was almost upon them again, beating wings briefly splayed against the moon. Torquil started toward Bruce, sword in hand, but his legs seemed to be wading through cold treacle, and he knew he could never get there in time. Words of desperate petition welled from his heart, taught him by the Columbans.

> *"I wrap me in the mantle*
> *of the grace of the Chief of chiefs!*
> *Michael's shield is over me,*
> *Christ's shelter is over me,*
> *The fine-wrought breastplate of Columba*
>   *preserves me—*
> *from these wings of Darkness!"*

The creature was stooping in a new attack, seconds away from contact, but the faith behind Torquil's prayer yielded a clarion flash of revelation. All at once, he knew the focus of the creature's power: a glittering point of murky brightness in the center of its chest that pulsed like a living heart—discernible, as the creature hurtled toward them, as the ghostly image of a bright-glinting object the size of a man's fist, that looked very much like a cluster of jewels.

Somehow, Torquil did manage to reach the king before the monster struck, interposing himself between them to fling Bruce to the ground and stand astride him, sword raised to repel the attack.

"Daystar of battles, be our shield!" he cried. *"Christ before me, Christ behind me—"*

Miraculously, the monster recoiled just short of him and wheeled to beat skyward again, casting its demonic glare back on this human who had dared to challenge it. Screaming defiance, it opened its bill and spat as it once again plummeted toward him, vomiting forth a scalding shower of venom.

Torquil ducked his face partway behind one arm to shield his eyes, at the same time swiping at the creature with his sword, but the blade sang as it passed harmlessly through the creature's shadowy body, causing no injury and leaving no mark behind.

No substance! a part of Torquil's mind screamed. And in the next instant, an explosion of winged turbulence knocked the sword from his hand.

It was hovering a few feet above his head, and spat at him again—more stinking breath than venom, this time—and the blast staggered Torquil off his feet, to sprawl akimbo over Bruce, shielding him with his body but also pinning one arm beneath him. He struggled to wiggle free as the bird again beat for altitude and came around for another pass—and suddenly felt the raking pressure against his hand of the rough setting that clasped the pommel jewel of the dirk Fingon had given him.

Hope stirred in his breast along with his gasping breaths—and Bruce's—as his fingers closed around the hilt of the weapon and drew it out in a blaze of cool blue light. The jewel shed gentle radiance like sunlight seen through water, enfolding and protecting him like a mantle of mercy.

It was the moment for which Fingon had given him the

weapon. As the serpent-bird plummeted toward him, nearly upon them, Torquil suddenly could discern the web of power that sustained the creature—and at its heart, its focus and its anchor point, what he now could see was the unmistakable image of Bruce's brooch, with filaments joining it simultaneously to Bruce and to the creature's summoner.

In that instant, he knew the creature's vulnerability—and that of its summoner. Almost of its own volition, his hand thrust the dirk skyward between himself and the hurtling bird, at the same time launching a final, desperate prayer:

"Saint Columba, guide my hand!"

His blade and his clenched fist met resistance with a jolt and an explosion of black feathers, in a sensation like punching through rotting flesh. A rending scream rang in his ears, and the dark headland winked out of existence. Suddenly it seemed to Torquil that he stood in a firelit room, his dirk half-buried in the cluster of jewels that a wide-eyed man was trying to claw from his bare chest.

Instinctively Torquil shielded his own eyes with his free hand and gave another thrust and a twist to his dirk, repeating the prayer he had murmured in another time, another place—and was answered with a rending scream as the man staggered desperately backward, pulling free of the dirk but clutching at his chest in a blind rictus of pain and shock. Just as the web of power snapped, Torquil had a fleeting impression of blood welling from a strange birdlike tattoo beneath the other's breastbone.

The next instant, he was back in the darkness beneath the stars of Ayr, piled atop Bruce, who was struggling to sit up.

"Christ, get off me! I can't breathe!" Bruce demanded. "What happened? Are you all right?"

Dazedly, his breath coming hard, Torquil let himself be shifted onto the ground and to a sitting position. The dirk was still in his hand, its blade bent out of true and even fractured near the hilt, but of the demon-bird there appeared to be no sign.

"Where did it go?" Bruce murmured, using one of Torquil's shoulders to lever himself upright. "Did you kill it? Christ, what's that on your hand? Is it blood?"

Still a little dazed, Torquil took a closer look at his hands. There was, indeed, blood from the earlier battle. But what besmeared them and the dirk was no ordinary blood, and almost seemed to glow in the darkness. He had done the creature hurt—or its sender.

"It isn't mine," he said, getting to his feet and then helping Bruce to his. "But we must be away from here."

"You don't think it will come back, do you?"

"No, but Percy may, when he learns what we've done to his garrison."

"You're right." With a nod, the king beckoned to James Douglas, who was approaching on the run with Gilbert de la Haye.

"Have the men scavenge what armor and weapons they can carry, and be quick about it," he ordered.

Torquil's hands had started to shake in afterreaction, but he made himself clean his hands and the dirk on a fold of a dead man's plaid before sheathing the blade—or trying to sheath it. The blade was bent too far to fit the scabbard, and snapped off when he tried to straighten it, so he fit the broken pieces together as best he could and thrust the damaged weapon back into his belt. He hoped he would not need to use it again before it could be repaired—*if* it could be repaired. His sword he found a few feet away and sheathed that as well.

"I wonder who sent that thing," Bruce said to him, as their thwarted invasion force headed off into the Carrick hills. "Any ideas?"

Torquil shook his head.

"None," he said flatly. "But I hurt him. And I do know that if I were to meet up with him again, I'd recognize him instantly."

Chapter Nineteen

May, 1307

HAVING RAIDED TURNBERRY SUCCESSFULLY, IF NOT ACcording to original plan, and even having snatched survival from the jaws of apparent disaster, Bruce and his forces melted back into the hills of Carrick to regroup, never sleeping two nights in the same place, reverting to the hit-and-run tactics that had served him so well in the weeks immediately after his enthronement.

But he had enemies all around him. Macdouall of Galloway and Robert Clifford were in the south; Pembroke himself was to the west. In the north was Macdougall of Lorn, possibly with an ally who had access to even darker allies who had sent the black bird to Turnberry. Eastward lay more English supporters in Nithsdale. But Bruce kept always one step ahead of his English pursuers, in a running succession of minor sorties and unexpected victories.

Reports of various English setbacks found their way to Berwick-on-Tweed, where a onetime advisor to Edward of England lay still abed with injuries suffered in the exchange that had begun the turn of English fortunes. When two French knights arrived at Berwick Castle late in May, asking to see the Sieur Bartholeme de Challon, the castle's governor had them taken immediately to the tower suite occupied by the French lord and his servant for the past three months. The dwarf Mercurius admitted the two Frenchmen without comment, though he closed the door on the English lord.

"Sieur Rodolphe . . . and Sieur Thibault," the dwarf acknowledged, with a bow that somehow conveyed as much mockery as respect. "My master will be pleased that you have finally come."

The pair removed gloves and caps and deposited them on a side table as they surveyed the room.

"Mercurius," the senior of the newcomers said by way of greeting, accompanying the name with a curt nod. "How fares your master?"

"Admirably well," the dwarf drawled, "considering how close he came to being impaled through the heart."

The other man, Thibault de Montreville, bridled at his tone. "You keep a civil tongue, dwarf, unless you want a thrashing."

"Peace!" Rodolphe interposed smoothly. "Let us not forget that we are here on a mission of goodwill." He bent his gaze neutrally to the glowering dwarf. "Lord Bartholeme requested our presence—"

"Some weeks ago!" the dwarf interposed boldly.

"We came as quickly as we dared," Rodolphe replied, ignoring the reproach. "Will you take us to him, or must we find our own way?"

With a surly grunt, Mercurius beckoned the pair to follow, preceding them up a narrow turnepike stair to the room above. The heat from a blazing log fire on the hearth was such that the newcomers immediately shed their heavy riding mantles.

A large canopied bed, hung with curtains of purple damask, dominated the room. The curtains hung partially open toward the fire, revealing a wasted figure lying supine under a pile of furs and quilts. Swaddled in bandages from waist to neck, the figure looked as gaunt and pale as a tomb effigy.

"Visitors, my lord," Mercurius piped.

Even from across the room, the newcomers could see evidence of a narrow brush with death. Pain and fever had reduced Bartholeme's already-lean face to a mask of bones under several months' growth of dense black beard. His closed eyes were deeply sunken in their sockets. The sinewy hands lying open on the counterpane might have been those of a skeleton.

"Visitors, my lord," Mercurius prompted again, in a louder voice.

Bartholeme's bluish eyelids flickered open, the ghost of an ironic smile plucking at his cracked lips when his gaze lighted on the newcomers,

"Rodolphe? Thibault? I am deeply gratified."

"And so you should be," the former replied, advancing from the threshold. "In coming here, Thibault and I are committing a serious breach of protocol."

Bartholeme's bandaged chest swelled and deflated in a resigned sigh. "So I am given to understand. I am informed that I have fallen from grace in the eyes of the Decuria."

"You came to Scotland promising to thwart Bruce and retrieve the Stone of Destiny," Rodolphe summarized baldly. "You have failed to achieve either of these objectives. It is Magister Nogaret's assessment that you have willfully squandered the resources that were placed at your disposal. By his decree, you are to be deprived of your rank as a member of the Decuria and relegated to the lower orders of our fraternity, until such time as you prove yourself worthy of—"

"Do not speak to him that way!" Mercurius blurted. "Magister Nogaret can go to the devil! If it hadn't been for my master, the Templars already would have steered Bruce and his rebel followers to victory!"

Ordinarily, such an outburst from an underling would have merited a savage rebuke, but none followed—a point that was not lost on Bartholeme. Indeed, the pair merely exchanged bland, if troubled, glances. To Bartholeme, it seemed a hopeful sign that his visitors might be less than committed to Nog-

aret's way of thinking. Rodolphe's next words strengthened
that impression.

"Magister Nogaret sets no store by partial achievements,"
he observed neutrally. "Final results are his sole concern."

"I trust," Bartholeme countered, "that he will bear that principle in mind with regard to his own endeavors. I must point
out that I have not heard of any particular Templar setbacks in
France."

"Some might construe such words as a challenge," Thibault
replied, after a beat, though his tone remained neutral.

"Make of them what you will," Bartholeme said. Twin
patches of hectic color had risen to his ashen cheeks, and one
almost-skeletal hand plucked distractedly at the bedclothes as
his gaze wandered, slightly fevered.

"For my own part, I confess to having made two mistakes,"
he went on, after a moment. "On the one hand, I underestimated how much power the Templars were prepared to squander, to protect their puppet-king, Robert Bruce. And on the
other," he concluded bleakly, "I failed to realize just how much
Magister Nogaret feared me as a rival . . . until now."

Again the two visitors exchanged speaking glances. This
time, when they exchanged guarded looks with him as well,
Bartholeme curtly signaled Mercurius to withdraw, also motioning his visitors to be seated. When they had done so,
pulling stools closer to the bed, he asked, "Is it permitted to tell
me who has been appointed to succeed me in Scotland?"

After a beat, Thibault said, "No one. Magister Nogaret has
been focusing on a prospect closer to home. He has determined a surer way to destroy the Order, as Hercules killed the
legendary hydra—by lopping off all its heads at a single
stroke."

"Has he, indeed?" Bartholeme murmured, a touch of scorn
to his tone. "And just how does he propose to do that? Invade
the council chambers of king or pope and put them all to the
sword?"

"Nothing so crude," Thibault said blandly. "Nogaret is master of the Law. And he has determined that the Law will serve us better in this instance than any army of paid assassins."

Bartholeme attempted to raise himself up, only to fall back with an involuntary grunt of pain. His visitors exchanged glances, but it was a moment before he recovered enough to speak.

"Nogaret has completely misread the situation," he stated flatly.

"Has he indeed?" Rodolphe replied, lifting an eyebrow. "Perhaps it may interest you to know that he has discovered the existence of a secret vault in the bowels of the Paris Temple. Among the treasures they keep in this vault will be the Breastplate of Aaron. Close watch is being kept on the brothers who have access to the vault. Mass arrests are being planned. When the raids begin, Nogaret intends to arrive at the Temple ahead of the royal baillies and seize the Breastplate on behalf of the Decuria."

"If it's still there," Bartholeme muttered.

"Why wouldn't it be?"

"For any one of a number of reasons. A breach of secrecy, for instance. The Templars aren't fools, Rodolphe. Don't you think they have their spies, as we have ours? If they get so much as a hint of what Nogaret has in mind, they'll move Heaven and earth to put their treasures beyond his reach."

"And take them where? Not to Scotland, surely."

"What's to stop them, now that my presence here has been compromised?" Bartholeme countered.

He took a deep breath to steady himself. "I tell you, the Templars will stop at nothing to secure Scotland's independence. I have not yet learned why, but somehow, that independence is vital to their own existence. Do I not carry the proof upon my body?"

He indicated the heavy pad of bandaging at the center of his chest, going on even more fiercely when his visitors were slow to respond.

"What must I do to persuade you?" he demanded. "If you

doubt the scope of my talents—if you doubt either my intelligence or my fortitude—I invite you to examine this wound. It will bear ample witness to the powers arrayed against us. Why do you think I begged for one of you to come here? I cannot do this by myself!"

Rodolphe lifted an eyebrow. "You do know what you are asking?" he said on a tentative note.

"Do you take me for some weakling child?" Bartholeme retorted. "Of course I know! And I also know that only this ordeal will enable the wound to heal. I have endured far worse to serve lesser causes. I invoke the test of blood and blade."

A facial muscle ticked at one side of Rodolphe's mouth, but then he gave a formal nod and rose.

"As you will, then."

Thibault summoned Mercurius back. At Bartholeme's command, the dwarf brought a pair of tallow candles set in iron and a shallow brass salver with the image of the *Cygnus Hermetis* engraved across its face. He made a second trip to fetch a flask of ink, an open crock of rock salt, and a flint-bladed dagger with a zoomorphic overlay of openwork silver binding the hilt. These objects he arranged on a table adjacent to the bed, before withdrawing once again to the outer room.

Bracing himself for what he had invited, Bartholeme submitted to having his wrists and ankles secured to the bedstead. While Thibault warded the room, Rodolphe deftly cut away the bandages swathing the injured man's torso. Removal of the final layer exposed an ugly cicatrix, like a burn crater, over Bartholeme's breastbone, crusted at the edges and with a softly weeping scab at the center, though of infection there was no sign. Still, Bartholeme flinched as Rodolphe ran his fingers experimentally over the skin surrounding the wound, probing at its edges.

"You're certain you want to go through with this?" Rodolphe asked.

Swallowing with an effort, Bartholeme nodded his head.

"We must know," was all he whispered.

"Very well."

Eyes narrowing thoughtfully, Rodolphe picked up the dagger, briefly fondling it as though it were a live thing, then plunged it to the hilt into the crock of salt. Thibault, meanwhile, had lit a wax spill from the fire and used this to light the two tallow candles. After relegating the spill to the fire, he set the brass salver between the candles and filled it with ink.

"Darkness is the womb of all knowledge," he declared, bowing to the other two men. "I embrace the Darkness, that I might See."

Closing the dagger's hilt in his left hand, Rodolphe murmured a charm of empowerment under his breath, at the same time withdrawing the blade from the salt. After that, he sketched an occult symbol above Bartholeme's chest with the weapon, touched the flat of the blade briefly to his own forehead, then lowered the point to the wound.

Bartholeme's eyes closed and a cold sweat broke out on his haggard face, sheening his neck and chest, as Rodolphe then began to probe at the wound. His breath hissed from between clenched teeth, but he did not cry out as Rodolphe proceeded to explore the wounded flesh with the dagger's crude point. His body twitched convulsively as Rodolphe continued to probe, arching and recoiling in its bonds as his tormentor suddenly made a surgical jab to the center of the wound, pressing to the bone, briefly pinning his subject with agony that was mirrored in his own face.

The point of the dagger came away red—far redder than justified by the depth of the jab. Muttering a further invocation, Rodolphe plunged the point of the dagger into the salver of ink.

Ink and blood merged with a sibilant hiss that exuded steam or mist across the dark surface, imparting a rainbow sheen that pulsed like a heartbeat. Bartholeme's eyelids flickered and opened, but the images he saw, mirrored on the surface of the ink for Rodolphe's perusal, were coming to him through some agency besides mortal vision.

The pictures presented themselves in reverse order of time. Watching with bated breath, Rodolphe beheld Bartholeme lying in this very bed, burning with fever . . . Bartholeme lying stricken before the fire in the room below, half-delirious, bidding Mercurius prise the brooch of Lorn from his stiff and bloody fingers, aghast at the smoking wound disfiguring the flesh on his chest . . . .

Concentrating, his fist locked tight around the hilt of the flint-edged dagger, Rodolphe willed himself to visualize the weapon that had inflicted the wound. Before his eyes there formed the image of a handsome, silver-mounted dirk, its carved black hilt surmounted by a clear blue stone the size of a pigeon's egg.

The gemstone scintillated with power—power with a pure, crystalline savor, like the light from a polar star, so unsullied that all of them recoiled as from a live coal. That puissance was celestial in nature, divine in origin, with a resonance emanating from ancient Israel. But the intensity of that disclosure brought with it the staggering, almost stupefying realization that its ultimate source was the same as that which empowered the Stone of Destiny.

Breathing heavily, for his own ordeal was becoming hardly less than Bartholeme's, Rodolphe willed the focus of his questing to shift to the wielder of the weapon. The intent required a further infusion of Bartholeme's blood, drawn by a second probing of his wound, but the image of the dirk slowly yielded to the face of a bearded man of middle years, with fading red hair and green eyes that seemed to gaze into eternity. Lean and powerfully built, he had the aspect of a seasoned warrior, but more significantly, he bore about him the unmistakable aura of a Knight of the Temple, as palpable as any visible white mantle.

Bartholeme saw it, too, straining upward in his bonds, his hollowed eyes fixed with burning intensity on the mirror of vision.

"I see him—the man who struck me down!" he gasped.

"And I will remember him! I will have my retribution! When we meet again, I will give his heart's blood to Lucifer as a victory tribute!"

He fell back panting, a white froth of pain and rage gathering at the corners of his mouth. As he did so, the images faded from the ink in the salver of brass, releasing Rodolphe to a pounding headache behind his eyes and Bartholeme to a fainting swoon.

Spying a flagon of restorative cordial beside the bed, Thibault seized it and tipped a measure between Bartholeme's livid lips, then passed it to Rodolphe for a like draught before himself drinking deeply of the flagon's contents. He then set about releasing the bonds binding Bartholeme to his bed, while Rodolphe briefly bowed his head in the vee of thumb and fingers to make his own recovery.

After a moment, Rodolphe lifted his head to exchange a troubled glance with his companion. Together they examined the brooch that Mercurius reluctantly produced for their inspection, though it was now totally empty of any psychic trace that might have connected it to its former owner. When Bartholeme's breathing finally eased, and his eyes fluttered open, Rodolphe addressed him in measured tones.

"Your suppositions regarding Scotland would appear to be correct," he admitted. "The Stone of Destiny represents an artifact of exceptional power. It is no wonder that the Templars are devoting all their energies toward acquiring it. But Magister Nogaret's plan, if it succeeds, will eliminate them before they can claim their coveted prize."

"And if Nogaret's plan fails?" Bartholeme rasped.

No emotion showed on the face of either of his visitors, but Rodolphe's tone, as he replied, was chillingly precise.

"If it should fail," he said, with a side glance at Thibault, "we would be justified in looking for a new leader."

Chapter Twenty

August, 1307

BARTHOLEME'S RECOVERY, WHILE NOT IMMEDIATE, WAS NO less remarkable than his injury had been, though by the time he was well enough to leave Berwick, a few weeks later, the fortunes of war in Scotland had shifted dramatically.

For Edward of England died early in July at Burgh-by-Sands, just north of Carlisle, finally defeated by illness. His successor, Edward of Caernarvon, had little of the mettle of his father, and retreated to London within the month, where he soon concerned himself with his own pleasures and the advancement of his favorites. These distractions gave the rebel King of Scots a welcome reprieve, and the opportunity to take advantage of English uncertainty.

Thus it was that, late in August, Brothers Torquil Lennox and Aubrey Saint Clair found themselves riding with a small escort of Bruce's Highlanders north of the Firth of Clyde, bound for a secret rendezvous that would greatly benefit Robert Bruce and his cause. Bruce himself was consolidating his forces farther south—safe enough, for now, from magical attack, since Torquil had severed the link with his brooch—and hoped for their return sometime later in September. For the two Templars, the mission had an aspect of welcome diversion from the previous months on the run with Bruce.

"Brother Torquil," Aubrey said good-naturedly, swatting at a cloud of midges, "kindly remind me again why our good friend Brother Flannan felt obliged to make us meet him all the way out here. If it isn't the rain and the midges, it's the *heat* and the midges! If there might be a less hospitable part of Scotland, I canna think where it is right now."

Riding just ahead of Aubrey, Torquil chuckled despite his own equally miserable state as he fanned absently at a midge-cloud.

"Aside from the fact that it's close to the coast—"

"*And* the midges!" Aubrey interjected.

"Aye, and the midges," Torquil agreed. "It's also remote enough that we aren't likely to meet up with anyone other than the folk we're meant to meet."

"Apart from maybe a few wild goats," Aubrey said with a snort.

The man riding behind Aubrey chuckled: one of six, likewise mounted on sturdy Highland ponies, each leading a pack pony, though these were unladen. To their left, the gorse and broom fell away steeply toward the steely waters of Loch Fyne. Ahead, the sun was slipping behind the rugged hills that rose from Knapdale to the west. Ponies and men were strung out along the rocky track, parts of the line sometimes disappearing briefly as they negotiated the awkward dips and hummocks.

Aubrey glanced down at the gray wavelets lapping against the humped rocks below. With the coming dusk, and its clouds of midges, a clammy haze was creeping in off the sea, already hinting at a chill night to come. He peered ahead, half-standing in his stirrups, but the jagged contours of the coast made it impossible to see beyond the next headland.

"How much farther to this bothy of Flannan's?" he asked.

"Anytime now, I think," Torquil answered. "I've been seeing landmarks that look familiar."

"I hope you're right," Aubrey said with a grimace. "There can't be much more than an hour of daylight left."

"Aye. Thank God for long summer twilights."

They had parted company from Bruce's main force nearly a week before, near Loch Linnhe. Having harried his local enemies into submission, the king planned to push north into the Highlands, there to assault the last of the Comyn strongholds and make himself master of Scotland in more than just name.

The rendezvous for their present mission had been arranged by means of a coded letter passed from hand to hand by a series of trusted messengers who had brought it all the way from Luc, at Balantrodoch. Before that, it had come from Paris, so the source was good. But despite his outward show of confidence, Torquil was only too well aware of how many things might have gone wrong since the plans were set, at least a month before.

"I just hope they're there," Aubrey said, voicing Torquil's unspoken concerns. "The gold they're bringing can certainly be put to good use—because the English *will* finally recover their wits."

"Aye, they will," Torquil agreed. "But Flannan's a good man—and like us, as a Scot, he has a personal stake in this war. If it's humanly possible, he'll be there."

He spoke from long friendship with Flannan Fraser, who was slightly older than he but somewhat junior within *le Cercle*. Torquil had found him to be fearless and unflappable under any kind of pressure. In recent months, their superiors in Paris had been turning Flannan's talents to smuggling, helping to slip consignments of Templar treasure out of the Paris treasury and into temporary hiding places outside the reach of the French crown. Some of the treasures were of an esoteric nature; some were quite ordinary gold.

It was a consignment of the latter being sent to Bruce's aid—whose survival, in turn, would permit fulfillment of the Temple's longer-term objective: to erect the Fifth Temple here on Scottish soil. In the past year, as Torquil had bent all his en-

ergies toward merely keeping Bruce's skin intact, he sometimes had begun to lose sight of their ultimate goal.

He slapped at another midge bite and gave his pony a bit of
heel, urging it up a gentle incline, for the hill line ahead was
definitely beginning to look familiar. But as he topped the rise,
he found a broad rift yawning before him, where the trail
sheered away to a gravelly streambed below. The stream itself
was running shallow at this time of year—easily fordable—
but getting down to it safely was likely to be difficult, with the
light failing.

Signaling the rest of the company to halt, Torquil kneed his
mount closer to the edge to look for a way down—and a way
back up the other side. The slope was clogged with rocks,
brambles, and nasty-looking patches of mud, but there seemed
to be a very narrow game trail snaking its way downward and
then back up.

"It looks like we can go that way," Aubrey said from beside
him, as he swung a leg over his saddle and slipped to the
ground—not far, because his feet hung well below the pony's
belly.

"Aye, but we'd better take it on foot," Torquil said, also dismounting. "If we weren't losing the light, it'd be no problem."

He looped an arm through a stirrup leather and pointed his
pony down the canting path, giving it its head and letting his
heels dig in as brakes as they started down. Given a choice,
one wanted to be *beside* a horse headed down a steep hill, or
even behind it—not in front, in danger of being over-run; and
his added weight at stirrup level would help the pony keep its
balance.

Aubrey followed a few pony lengths behind him. The footing proved better than they had feared, and they soon had
started scrambling up the other side, this time with Torquil
hanging onto his pony's tail. They were still a dozen horse
lengths short of the summit when Torquil's sharp hearing
caught the sound of voices ahead.

Signaling a halt, and also for silence, he scrambled to the

pony's head and clamped a hand over its nostrils as he listened intently. He couldn't make out words, but the tone was aggressive. Behind him, the ungainly chain of men and animals had come to a halt at his warning gesture. Motioning them to hold their positions, Torquil summoned Aubrey to his side.

"I don't like the sound of that," he whispered, gesturing ahead with his chin as he continued to keep his pony quiet. "I think we'd better have a look, before we go charging over the hill."

Leaving their ponies in the keeping of the next man behind Aubrey, the two Templars made their way silently to the top of the rise, keeping low in the undergrowth. Some fifty paces down the other side of the hill face they had just climbed stood the abandoned crofter cottage Torquil had been looking for. The cottage itself looked long derelict, with chinks in the walls and gaping holes where the thatched roof had fallen in; but they were not the first to arrive.

More than a dozen armed men were ranged before it: a motley and uncouth band, dressed in ragged shirts and weather-worn plaids. Though a few carried only cudgels, most had swords or axes, and bore round leather bucklers on their arms, studded with brass nail heads in different patterns. Simple helmets of steel or boiled leather crowned most of the shaggy heads, but a few merely sported sewn bonnets of rough wool cloth, with sprigs of wilted greenery stuck into the bands.

"Macdoualls?" Aubrey mouthed silently to Torquil, barely breathing the name.

Torquil gave him a cautious nod, not taking his eyes from the band. It was the Macdoualls who had captured the king's two brothers and handed them over to a terrible death at the hands of the English. He wondered if one of the Bruces or their men might have talked, alerting the Macdouall chief to post a coast watch, in hopes of preventing any aid from reaching Bruce from Ulster.

"Ye canna win free, ye feartie basterts!" yelled the leader of the Macdoualls, brandishing his axe in the direction of the bothy. "Gi'e it up, an' we'll mebbe let ye live."

His men seconded his utterance with their own threats and jeers.

"I dinna think I like the terms," came the defiant rejoinder from inside. "If ye want us, I think ye'll have to come and get us!"

Both Templars recognized the voice only too well.

"Jesus, it's Flannan!" Aubrey whispered to Torquil, indignation in his soft undertone.

"Aye, bring up the rest of the men and have them prepare to attack."

Aubrey slipped back down the slope to execute his orders. Meanwhile, the Macdouall leader appeared to have reached the end of his patience.

"Ha' done wi' ye, then!" he cried. "Lads, gi'e us some wuid! We'll build a wee banefire and smoke 'em out."

Hoarse cheers and whoops of approval greeted this proposal, and his men set to work with a will, snatching up armloads of gorse and dry brushwood and starting to pile it around the bothy's crumbling walls.

"Will ye no hustle yersel', Sorley?" one quipped. "I'm cravin' smokit chookie fer supper tonight."

Coarse laughter and the mocking cackle of chicken sounds rang out as the Macdoualls continued their fire-building preparations, but the activity was giving Aubrey and the others time to get into position. Torquil glanced pointedly to left and right at the nearest of them and gave a nod, sliding sword and dirk from their sheaths as he began easing his way forward through the bracken. The dirk was one he had taken in a raid since Turnberry, to replace the broken one that now traveled in his saddlebag. Aubrey and the rest advanced with equal stealth, using their long experience of ambush. Intent on building their bonfire, the Macdoualls carried on with their crude banter.

"I'm thinkin' this'll make a bonnie wee oven," one man declared.

"Aye," another agreed, laughing. "Did I not tell ye that Angus was a braw guid cook?"

Keeping their heads well down, the Templar company started forward. The leader of the Macdoualls crouched down beside the kindling and brought out tinder and flint. But before he could strike the first spark, Torquil bounded up from cover with a hoarse shout.

"Non nobis, Domine!"

The famous Templar battle cry stopped the Macdoualls for just a second, frozen with shock. But even as they dove for weapons, their attackers were upon them. The shout had also brought an immediate response from inside the bothy, as the door flew open and Flannan Fraser dashed out with two other men behind him, all of them with bared steel.

The clangor of combat shattered the stillness of the deepening twilight. One broad-chested Macdouall went down before he could strike a single blow, spitted on Flannan's blade. Another fell to one of Torquil's men, screaming as blood gushed down his leg from a pumping wound to the groin.

Some of the Macdoualls gave a better account of themselves. One dealt a vicious thigh wound to one of Torquil's Highlanders that sent him to his knees—though the attacker, in turn, was dispatched by Aubrey, who took up a stance athwart the wounded man and dealt death to several more Macdoualls who tried to finish both of them. Their Highlanders accounted for several more Macdoualls.

Meanwhile, the leader of the Macdoualls was laying about him with a long-handled axe, exhorting his dwindling band with a volley of obscene oaths. Torquil made for him, killing another Macdouall man on the way and then engaging the leader, blocking the haft of the axe on the quillons of his sword and forcing the weapon aside while his dirk drove home in the other man's belly. As he wrenched the blade free, his opponent's wild eyes were already glazing as he crumpled to the ground in a pool of blood.

He looked around to see the remaining Macdoualls—only

three of them—taking to their heels, flinging down shields and weapons to bolt for the trees that flanked the croft on its landward side. Torquil's Highlanders took off after them, brandishing their weapons and howling like demons.

"Christ, they'll only lose them in the dark!" Torquil muttered. "Aubrey, see if you can call them back. And you"—he nodded toward one of Flannan's men—"see to that wounded man, and check the dead."

Only then did he spare a relieved greeting for Flannan, who had already started prodding with his sword at some of the corpses crumpled nearby.

"Brother Flannan, I do believe they were ready to make a meal of you," he quipped, as he bent to clean his blades on the edge of a dead man's plaid.

"Aye, and I'm verra glad you came along to spoil the banquet," Flannan said with a grin, cleaning his own weapons and sheathing them. "We might've fought our way clear, but we hardly could've left our baggage."

He inclined his head in the direction of the bothy, where his remaining companion had taken up a guard position outside the ramshackle doorway, sword still in hand. By the man's bearing, Torquil guessed he was probably a Templar serjeant, though he did not look familiar. Within the shadows beyond, he thought he could see the outline of several small chests.

"You've brought the gold?" he asked, sheathing his own weapons as he approached to peer inside.

"It's all there, as promised," Flannan assured him. "And something specifically for Bruce."

He stepped inside and knelt beside the nearest of the chests, opening it to unwrap something bundled in heavy silks. Inside was a golden circlet of kingship, similar to the one Bruce had lost at Methven, with open lilies set around the band.

"Luc sent word that Bruce had lost the one we gave him at Scone," Flannan said. "Mebbe it's been replaced by now, but Arnault had this one made in Paris." He glanced at the serjeant still standing in the doorway beside Torquil and nodded to him. "Jules, you can go help Dalmont with that wounded man. We're secure here."

As the man nodded and headed off, sheathing his sword, Torquil came to crouch beside Flannan, briefly picking up the circlet to hold it to the failing light.

"I would've thought you'd bring more men," he said, laying it back in its wrappings. "Is it really just the three of you?"

Flannan re-wrapped the crown and closed the chest.

"I didn't want to attract undue attention, once we'd got the cargo ashore. I knew ye'd be bringing men. As it happens, a few more would've been useful, on my part."

A brief cry, sharply cut off, drew their attention outside, where one of the serjeants had just given the *coup de grâce* to one of the "corpses." The other serjeant was bandaging the leg of Torquil's wounded Highlander.

"That's part of the danger in a country at war," Torquil observed. "When the people are fighting amongst themselves, a foe can come from any direction. This is proof."

"Aye. D'ye think there are any more Macdoualls in the area?"

Torquil shook his head. "I shouldn't think so—but then, I didn't expect that *these* would be here."

"At least I think we probably got them all, if your lads caught up with those last three."

"I'll be surprised if they didn't," Torquil replied. "But we'll do a tally when they get back, compare numbers from everybody's head count. I made it thirteen."

"Aye, so did I." Flannan sat down wearily on one of the chests. "How fares Bruce?"

"Much better, of late," Torquil answered. He smiled faintly and sank down beside Flannan. "When news of King Edward's death came north of the border, there couldn't have been greater rejoicing if the Devil himself had been announced dead."

"I know *I* gave a whoop, when I heard," Flannan said, grinning. "Still, I might half expect a man like Edward to tighten his grip on his foes e'en from the grave—the way a dead man's fingers will lock round his sword in his death rigor."

Torquil snorted. "In a way, he did just that. They say that on his deathbed, he ordered that his flesh should be boiled from his bones and buried, but he wanted the bones themselves borne before the army as they marched into Scotland. Small wonder that they called him the 'Hammer of the Scots.' "

Flannan's shock was enough to drive him briefly from his mostly educated accents.

"He wanted his mait seethed frae his bones? Bluidy hell! Dinnae tell me they *did* it?"

"Far from it," Torquil said with a chuckle, as Aubrey and then their five Highlanders emerged from the trees. Three of the men carried bulky shapes over their shoulders, and another raised a fist in triumph as he saw Torquil stand to look at them.

"Three for three," Torquil murmured, raising a hand in acknowledgment. "Unless we've both miscounted, that's all of them. As for this new Edward, however," he resumed, as Flannan joined him, "alas for the father, Plantagenet passion has not bred true in the son. The new king hurried home to London and buried the old man at Westminster, flesh and bones together. With his departure from Scotland, the planned invasion has melted away."

"But, have the English troops melted away?" Flannan replied. "There were English ships off the Western Isles, I can tell ye!"

"No, the English still hold many key positions," Torquil agreed, "but there again, the new king has served Bruce's interests better than he knows. He's relieved Pembroke of his post as lieutenant of Scotland, and has given it instead to one of his own favorites—someone called John of Brittany."

The Highlanders had reached the bothy, and without ceremony dumped the bodies they carried beside the ones already there.

"We haven't time to bury those," Torquil said to Aubrey. "Does everyone agree on how many there were?"

"Thirteen," Aubrey said.

"That's what we counted," Torquil replied. "Have the men bring the ponies around, so we can get the chests loaded. I want to be out of here by moonrise."

As they dispersed to carry out his orders, Flannan asked, "What next, then?—besides getting out of here. What will Bruce do next?"

"He's on his way north. Unfortunately, Scotland is still home to many who would rather sell themselves to England than see him on the throne. Until he has brought the likes of the Comyns, the Balliols, and the Macdoualls to heel, he is not truly ruler of this land. That's why he needs the gold you've brought: to support his army in the field until he's in a position to collect the royal revenues due to him."

"God grant it may be soon!" Flannan said fervently. He sighed and gnawed his lip, casting a glance around the darkening clearing before the bothy. Even though only dead men were nearby, he kept his voice low.

"I canna lie to ye, Torquil. The news from Paris isn't good. We need victory here—and swiftly. The troubles we envisaged two years ago are gaining momentum, and every day brings a fresh threat to the Order. Without a secure base, all that we have striven for will be lost."

"What of the mystical Treasures?" Torquil asked concernedly. "Are they safe?"

"Some are," Flannan said, "but it has been slow work, lest we arouse suspicions. One by one—along with more ordinary treasures, like the gold"—he glanced toward the doorway behind him—"we have been smuggling them out of France by various routes, using different ports up and down the French coast. But we daren't move too much, too quickly, lest we draw the attention of our enemies. And not all our repositories are as secure as we could wish. The Treasures won't be truly safe until we've managed to erect the Fifth Temple."

"How much does the Grand Master know of this?" Torquil asked.

Flannan shook his head. "Nothing. We daren't tell him. He arrived in the spring, as I think ye know, and has had several meetings with the king and with the Holy Father, but he refuses to see any danger. He did convene a Chapter General last month, but little came of it beyond the usual business of the Order."

He paused, then added, "Something's in the wind, though. Just before I left, I even heard Hugues de Paraud say that any Templar with reason to leave the Order should do so quickly, because a terrible calamity is imminent."

"He said *that*?"

"Aye."

Torquil shook his head. "This is ill news, indeed. What do you think is going to happen? What does Arnault say?"

"Later," Flannan murmured, for the men were returning with the ponies. "This is something Aubrey should hear, too. But first, we need to get this gold moving."

As hoped, they had the gold loaded by moonrise, and were soon under way, back the way they had come. Not until just before dawn, when they stopped for a few hours' sleep in the shelter of a point with vision for miles around, did Flannan share with his fellow knights what Brother Armand Breville had told *le Cercle* of the Knights of the Black Swan, and the danger they posed. Only in that moment did he understand, for the first time, the true nature of the demon-bird he had fought at Turnberry Point.

"Sweet Jesus, and I've left Bruce all unguarded," he murmured, turning a sick gaze on Flannan and Aubrey.

Flannan shook his head. "From what you've told me, you severed the link. You mebbe even killed whoever sent the creature."

"But he may have associates," Aubrey pointed out. "And they may have other weapons."

"We can only do what we can do," Flannan said. "For now, we can make the rendezvous with Bruce as quickly as possible. But first, both of you should get some sleep."

Chapter Twenty-one

August–October, 1307

IN PARIS, THOUGH ARNAULT DE SAINT CLAIR KNEW ABOUT the gold sent to aid Bruce's cause, he and the rest of *le Cercle* had been obliged to focus all of their energy of the past several months pushing the boundaries of the Temple's intelligence network, in an effort to discover the true intentions of king and pope—and attempting to minimize the consequences of the Grand Master's apparent blindness to the signs that calamity was approaching.

De Molay had, indeed, convened a General Chapter late in July, as Flannan Fraser had reported. In addition to the general convent, attended by all members of the Order, the Grand Master had held several private meetings with various of his senior officers. Oliver de Penne had been in attendance at several of these, as part of the staff of Hugues de Paraud, the Visitor of the Order. He, in turn, had relayed details of these meetings to *le Cercle*.

"The king apparently said nothing to indicate that anything is wrong, in that one meeting he had with de Molay," Oliver said, "but the Holy Father got his information from somewhere—and who but God and the king has the power to put fear into the heart of a pope? Apparently, Clement gave the Grand Master an astonishing assortment of alleged 'irregularities' within the Order, and asked if any of them were true."

Oliver had then proceeded to enumerate a catalog of supposed offenses, ranging from simple infractions of the Rule to sodomy, blasphemy, and outright heresy.

"It's clear that the Grand Master doesn't understand the implications," Oliver said. "Since the question has been raised, the Holy Father *must* investigate—and apparently, de Molay has welcomed the chance to defend the Order. What worries me is that I've been getting whispers of rumors about charges being drafted by the king—that this will become a civil matter. If it does, I'm not sure the pope can protect us."

Oliver's influence with Hugues de Paraud had been partially instrumental in persuading the Grand Master to issue a directive reminding all brethren to be mindful of the section of their Rule that forbade discussion of the Order's internal rites and disciplines with any outsider. De Molay had also ordered the burning of certain written documents that, in the wrong hands, might have been used against the Order. Arnault's young cousin Jauffre had been among those charged with collecting and disposing of said documents.

Meanwhile, *le Cercle* took measures to protect the Temple's more esoteric interests, though they were hampered by the delays in establishing Robert Bruce in a secure Celtic monarchy. Gaspar des Macquelines, in his capacity as an assistant treasurer of the Paris Temple, had begun late in the summer to divert consignments of the Temple's wealth to safer havens—and since only *le Cercle* knew the true extent of what the Temple held in the way of less conventional treasure, he was able to send many of these out of the country.

By the end of September, he had persuaded certain senior officers to consider a more official removal of Templar treasure beyond the reach of the French crown, for it was believed that King Philip was developing an active but thus far secret plan to appropriate the Temple's wealth in much the way that he had seized the wealth of the Jews.

Meanwhile, *le Cercle* continued putting out its intelligence feelers, and prayed for a favorable turn in the fortunes of Robert Bruce. For Arnault, the waiting grew more and more intolerable, for he longed to be at Bruce's side. Yet he knew that, for now, *le Cercle* needed him where he was—and knew that, if disaster came, he was obliged to flee Paris at once, abandoning his fellow knights—and fly straightaway to Bruce, in hopes that, in time, another change of fortune might make it possible, after all, to establish that vital Fifth Temple in another land.

And the others would have their tasks as well. For hidden deep in the bowels of this physical Temple was a carefully hoarded collection of mystical artifacts amassed by the long-ago founders of the Temple and their spiritual successors, of diverse origins, that were bridges between the earthly and heavenly Temples: precious hallows that the Inner Temple guarded, sacred to many faiths.

One of them, the High Priest's Breastplate, Arnault knew well—and was, in fact, more skilled than any other in *le Cercle* at focusing its virtues in the service of the Light. There were others that he had never actually seen—and one, most precious, by far—so sacred that its name was never spoken save in the matrix of a ritual of initiation, when oaths were sworn upon it. Sometimes, during those tight-wound days of late summer, helpless to make any meaningful impact on what was brewing for the Order at large, Arnault retreated to the secret chapel where it resided, known only to the Temple's inner order, to take comfort from merely being in its presence.

That hallow was in Christoph's charge; and often Arnault found him there before him, kneeling in rapture before the altar where it lay. The long, shallow box that housed it was clad in gold and studded with gems along its edge; but what lay inside, behind a golden grille, was the true Treasure—the image of a face imprinted on a yellowed cloth.

Arnault did not know whether it really *was* the sacred Shroud, folded to show the face of the crucified Christ; but Christoph believed that it was; and Arnault had no doubt that the ancient relic was imbued with a powerful imprint of the Holy—so he was content to accept that it was what Christoph believed. If the time came when it must be removed to safety, Christoph had asked for Jauffre to accompany him—though Jauffre did not yet know this. Arnault feared for his young cousin, if that came to pass; but he knew that Jauffre would not shrink from this charge, whatever the cost might be.

But as the days passed, and neither king nor pope made any move, Arnault began to hope that their fears had been exaggerated. He kept calling in his sources of information, in conjunction with Oliver and Gaspar and the others, and shared their frustration that no further details were forthcoming.

Early October brought with it the first lessening of the summer's heat—and also the death of the king's sister-in-law, who was married to Charles of Valois. The funerals of the highborn always occasioned great interest in the capital, and never more than when the deceased was royal. The impending obsequies of the Princess Catherine became an occasion for significant preparations, focusing the attention of all the court on the spectacle of the coming state funeral. The date selected was the twelfth of October.

As was traditional, the place appointed for her entombment was the Abbey of St. Denis, where the kings and queens of France, together with the members of their families, had been laid to rest for centuries. Accordingly, the coffined body of the Princess Catherine was duly conveyed to the abbey church, there to lie in state while a host of great lords and prelates assembled from near and far to pay their final respects.

Among those worthies invited to serve as pallbearers was the Grand Master of the Temple, Frère Jacques de Molay. It was a signal honor, which he eagerly accepted as a right and proper tribute to the Order's importance and high prestige; but those of *le Cercle* viewed the gesture with rather more suspicion, and wondered what ulterior motive might have prompted the king's apparent generosity of spirit.

The day of the funeral dawned fair, though with more than a hint of frost in the October air. As the morning light broadened, a flotilla of state barges festooned in funereal black embarked from the quays along the Île de la Cité to head downriver toward the abbey. The vessel bearing de Molay and the senior officers of the Paris Temple occupied a place of eminence toward the front of the procession. Many of the preceptors from other Templar provinces were also present, some of them having lingered after the summer's General Chapter.

At the recommendation of Oliver de Penne, who stood with Hugues de Paraud in the Grand Master's immediate entourage, Arnault de Saint Clair had been included among the dozen knights of the Grand Master's personal guard of honor—one of several components of the team placed by *le Cercle* in hope of gleaning some inkling of the king's true intentions. Also in the Grand Master's party, and for similar reasons, were Frère Christoph and Father Anselmo—and, as its most junior member, Arnault's cousin Jauffre.

But for the duration of the journey downriver, until they were actually in the king's proximity, Arnault had little to do save to take his turn attending on the Grand Master—a matter of standing solemnly behind de Molay's chair, in full habit and mantle, and looking inscrutable. His thoughts, however, were fully occupied. The vistas along the river were scarcely altered since his arrival in Paris almost a year ago, but beneath the seemingly innocuous ebb and flow of ordinary city life, even subdued by the day's funereal atmosphere, he sensed the imminence of some great upheaval.

Though the sun shone brightly, welcome warmth against the autumn chill, the day itself seemed haunted by intimations of darkness. Every landing stage along the riverfront, like every barge in the procession, was decked out with black mourning draperies.

As the vessels approached the last bend in the river, however, with the spires of St. Denis looming against the skyline a little back from the river, a brisker breeze out of the north snatched at the funeral banners and set them flapping like great black wings. In that instant, it occurred to Arnault that, with their high prows and rounded bows, the barges looked like nothing so much as a flock of black swans a-glide on the water.

Even as the comparison suggested itself, Arnault became aware of an uneasy prickling at the base of his skull. Instinctively he turned to cast an appraising glance around him, singling out the procession of royal barges approaching up-river from the direction of Versailles—and at once found himself scanning the vessel carrying the king and his brother, with a cluster of attendants. Immediately conspicuous in the midst of the latter—though bedecked in black like all the rest, yet somehow apart from them all—stood Guillaume de Nogaret, the king's chief minister.

By no means that he could specify, Arnault knew at once that this was the likely source of his uneasiness. Nogaret was standing by the starboard railing, head lifted to contemplate the approaching landing stage at St. Denis, but the merest hint of a smile played about his thin lips, as if in response to some inner contentment. The man's pale gaze held a disturbing glitter as he, in turn, cast his glance over the Templar barge now bumping against the landing stage. He seemed coolly interested in de Molay and the other senior officers rather than Arnault and the other ordinary knights, but he looked—too much for Arnault's peace of mind—like a man privately anticipating a moment of triumph.

Recalled to his duty as the Templar party made ready to

disembark, Arnault fell into formation and followed them ashore. The Abbot of St. Denis and a gathering of canons gave perfunctory greeting to the Templars, one of the latter leading them on toward the abbey church as the abbot turned his attention to the royal barge taking the place of the one the Templars had just vacated. Disembarking in their turn, the king and his brother were met by the waiting prelates to join the solemn procession into the church, preceded by a choir of monks chanting the entrance antiphon.

Inside, the brightness of the long nave belied the solemnity of the day, flooded with jewel-hued sunlight from the wide expanse of glass at the end of either transept. The wash of light—and the white mantles of the Templars—made the funereal dressing of the great church all the more a contrast as Arnault moved down the center aisle with his brother knights.

The coffin containing the body of the dead princess lay before the high altar on a bier draped with sumptuous black brocade, the pall likewise of a stygian richness. The double line of knights paused to bow by pairs before passing into the place reserved for them in the north transept, with a clear view of the sanctuary. Massive silver candlesticks stood three to either side along the bier, each with a lit candle as thick as a man's arm, ornamented with placards bearing the coat of arms of the House of Valois.

To the hauntingly beautiful chanting of the choir monks, the mourners shuffled into their places, the king and his brother joining other members of the royal family gathered to one side. Kneeling briefly in prayer with his brother knights, as the presiding clergy took their places, Arnault spared a moment's admiration and thanksgiving for the long-dead Abbé Suger, whose vision had shaped every aspect of the building to be a Bible in stone. Each detail, from the intricate wealth of carvings to the interplay of light slanting through the stained-glass windows, was designed to enlighten the hearts of all who entered. But for once, as

Arnault brought his formal prayers to a close, his spirit remained earthbound, unable to cast off its burden of apprehension.

With the commencement of the Mass, he tried once again to lose himself in prayer, but neither the sweet savor of incense nor the ascendant voices of the choristers could lift him out of himself. At the Consecration, even gazing upon the beauty of Abbot Suger's own chalice could not impinge upon his mood. The vessel was no less exquisite than its setting—a cup wrought from sardonyx set in gold, so thin as to be almost translucent, and adorned with filigree, pearls, and precious gems—yet Arnault was acutely aware that this whole church and all it contained, however rich and rare, could not rival the inestimable value of even one of the Treasures in the keeping of *le Cercle*.

Briefly contemplating those Treasures, Arnault knew that it was only a matter of time before he and his companions would be compelled to risk all, and move the rest of the Treasures to safer quarters. Plans had been fixed for that final dispersal, but no amount of preparation could wholly eliminate the risks. Watching the king and his family and ministers receive Communion—without Nogaret, who still lay under formal excommunication, and had remained outside the church—Arnault fancied he could feel an enormous weight pressing upon the Temple, smothering and heavy like a funeral pall.

After Communion, eight burly knights took up the actual weight of the princess's coffin to conduct it to its final resting place. The Grand Master joined the other worthies chosen as honorary pallbearers, each of them taking up one of the silk cords forming a symbolic cradle beneath the coffin as the little procession made its silent way to the open grave in the church ambulatory. There the Bishop of Paris offered up the final prayers.

A choral amen brought the funeral to a close, after which the Grand Master rejoined his fellow Templars for their recessional from the church. Arnault dutifully followed as part of the rear guard, glad to be leaving the place, thinking of nothing much at all, only vaguely watching on ahead. But then, as de Molay and the others neared the western doors, a sudden blaze of sun glare seemed to billow upward like an eruption of flame, blinding-bright against snow-white mantles—or was it merely a reflection from the polished brasswork on the heavy church doors?

The same fiery radiance spilled hungrily down the ranks of the rest of the Grand Master's train, including young Jauffre but not quite reaching Arnault. For a terrible instant, every one of them appeared to be engulfed in consuming fire.

The illusion so startled Arnault that, without thinking, he reached out to seize a handful of young Jauffre's mantle and drag him back a step, out of the sun-fire—which immediately subsided to mere sunlight. Jauffre, himself startled, flashed his elder cousin a look of blank inquiry as Arnault recovered himself and let go of the mantle, though he had the wit to keep his expression neutral and to continue walking, watching his kinsman sidelong.

Put an overmastering dread sealed Arnault's lips. And as he, too, emerged into the light, it was merely that: sunlight. Between one step and the next, the terrible glory had evaporated, the vision ended, leaving him feeling weak at the knees, as if in the aftermath of a griping pain.

"It's all right," he managed to murmur to Jauffre, smiling faintly. "The sunlight dazzled my eyes, and then I misstepped."

Satisfied, Jauffre moved on. A moment later they descended the abbey steps, now in more normal sunlight, and Arnault drew a deep breath, glad to be out in the free air. He put the incident firmly from mind as he made his way down to the landing where the Templar barge stood waiting.

Later that night, however, he received another prompting, this time in his dreams, and even more insistent than the first. The dream commenced with a knocking at the gate. He knew he was in his bed in the Paris Temple, but somehow he could hear the knocking all the way at the outer ward.

The knocking went unanswered until Arnault rose up in his dream to answer the summons. Standing on the other side of the threshold, separated from him by the iron grid, stood a shadowy figure in bloodstained garments. As the figure set its hands on the bars of the gate, Arnault took a closer look and recognized the elderly Jew who had died in his arms over a year ago. Leaning closer, the old man addressed him with fierce intensity.

The hell-hounds are set to slip their chains! he warned. *The hunt begins at morning light. Save the Treasures! Get you gone!*

Arnault woke abruptly, in a cold sweat. The whole preceptory was quiet as the grave, but he knew he dared not ignore the warning. Throwing on his outer garments, he hastened next door to rouse Gaspar, who was already up and dressing as well.

"I gather you had a dream, too," Gaspar whispered, flinging his mantle around his shoulders.

Arnault nodded. "Aye. It's time to go."

They set out at once for the arranged meeting place—and met Father Anselmo and Hugues de Curzon on the way, both with dreams to relate. Christoph and Oliver were already waiting in Gaspar's office above the treasury; Father Bertrand arrived shortly thereafter.

"We dare not regard these dreams as anything but a warning sent by God," Christoph said quietly, when he had polled them all. "And He has spoken to each of us. If daybreak finds us still here, under this roof, we are all dead men—and the Order is dead, as well."

The rest of them exchanged sober glances, bleak concurrence in every pair of eyes.

"He's right," Gaspar agreed. "We dare not question the authority or the validity of these warnings. Faith has ever been our guiding force—and never more than now. We've come too far along this road to let doubt turn us back. If faith cannot lead us home, then nothing can."

Resigned nods of agreement supported this declaration.

"You all have your orders, then," Christoph said briskly. "You know what is at stake. Our first priority is to get the Treasures to safety—and, if we can, to save ourselves to continue the fight in another time and place. Summon the men you've chosen to accompany you, and gather at once at the appointed place."

Only Arnault went directly to the designated vault in the heart of the Temple, where clothes and other necessities for a journey had been stored in readiness. He had already changed his Templar habit for the well-worn tunic and leather jack of a common mercenary by the time Oliver and then Father Bertrand joined him.

More of them arrived as Arnault buckled on his sword and then threw on a somewhat threadbare mantle of faded tartan, legacy of his years with Bruce. While the others dressed in silence, he moved among them with a word of farewell for each man, his hand briefly lingering on young Jauffre's shoulder before moving on to where Gaspar was distributing pouches prepared for each of them, each with money and travel documents appropriate to the man's assumed guise. Arnault received a pilgrim's scrip and a very well worn saddlebag, with a hefty weight to it.

"There's gold there, for Bruce's cause," Gaspar whispered, as the two briefly embraced. "I've also given you King Solomon's Seal. It was the smallest and lightest of the Treasures that need taking to safety.

"Go now, and Godspeed. Guard Bruce, and build the Fifth Temple. God willing, some of us will join you in a few weeks' time. Go!" he repeated, as Arnault hesitated. "Go. Your horse is waiting."

Chapter Twenty-two

October 13, 1307

IN THOSE SMALL HOURS BEFORE DAWN, IN A PRIVATE SUITE in the bowels of the palace of the Louvre, the senior Knights of the Black Swan resident in Paris were also astir.

"The men you've selected for your own escort are all assembled in the outer court," Valentin de Vesey reported to Nogaret. "We're ready to ride at your command."

Sitting before the fire, Nogaret lifted a cup of wine to gaze into its depths, where the firelight reflected from the polished inside of the vessel. The wine was a hearty claret, the color of blood.

"Excellent," he said, looking up. "We are on the brink of an historic moment, gentlemen. Sit, Valentin, and have some wine. In only a few hours, the Templars will have ceased to be an obstacle in our path."

These remarks were addressed to several other members of the Decuria, seconded to join the party Nogaret would lead personally to make arrests at the Paris Temple. Only Count Rodolphe dared to voice uncertainty.

"Much could still go wrong."

"What could possibly go wrong?" said Peret Auvergnais. "Nothing has been left to chance. The orders are in place, there's been no leak, and men are standing ready to execute them. By nightfall, every Templar in France will be in royal custody—and the keys to all their treasuries will be in our hands."

He raised his cup to salute their coming endeavor—and their leader's role in conceiving it—and the others followed suit, with varying degrees of enthusiasm. Nogaret, assessing their mood, set about soothing any lingering misgivings with small talk, though the preparations appeared to be flawless. He was holding his cup for a refill when his inner composure was jarred by a silent shriek, and then the urgent alarm of the demon Ialdabaeoth.

Massster! Massster! the demon shrilled anxiously. *Templarsss have come to the treasssury! They are opening the vault of Ssssecretsss!*

Nogaret started up from his chair, almost spilling his cup. "What is it?" Baudoin demanded.

Gesturing sharply for silence, Nogaret put down his cup and closed his eyes, setting fingertips to his temples. After a moment's concentration, his perceptions merged with those of his demon familiar and images took shape before him, accompanied by murmuring voices.

He could not make out words, but through Ialdabaeoth's eyes he beheld a handful of men in the guise of common mercenaries gathering before the vault beside the one the demon guarded—Templars, all, and a few of them even known to Nogaret by name, from his sojourn in the Temple with the king. As one of them opened the door, glory blazed forth with an intensity that caused Ialdabaeoth to recoil in howling anguish. Only Nogaret's strength of will compelled the demon to stand its ground.

But as the men entered and closed the door, Nogaret knew that at last he had discovered the hiding place of the Temple's choicest Treasures, for which he was prepared to gamble so much. Nothing else could account for the holiness the place exuded—and far more than could be explained if it were merely a chapel where the Sacrament resided.

Furthermore, the fact that these Templars had put aside their habits suggested that they were about to bolt—that they somehow had gotten wind of the orders, now only hours from execution, that would have netted all the Temple's treasures—and were preparing to take away the ones Nogaret most wanted.

Releasing the demon to its sentinel duties, Nogaret broke contact, already getting to his feet as he opened his eyes.

"Something has alerted the Templars' Inner Circle," he said, reaching for his cloak. "Some of them are preparing to flee the Paris Temple, dressed as ordinary soldiers—and I have no doubt that they will take the choicest Treasures with them. We must stop them!"

The sound of the cavalcade clattering through the streets of Paris brought fearful citizens to windows and doors, only to shrink back in fear. It was still dark as the company converged on the Temple gates, where Nogaret himself leaned down to hammer on the outer port.

"Open at once, in the name of the king!" he demanded.

A porter's face appeared at the wicket gate, but immediately turned to confer with a companion, clearly uncertain what to do.

"Open up, I say, or it will be infinitely the worse for you!" Nogaret repeated.

"A moment, my lord," came a hesitant response. "We have standing orders never to open the gate before dawn, save on higher authority."

"I *am* higher authority!" Nogaret retorted. "Open at once!"

The gate did not open, but after a brief interval the Grand Master himself appeared at the wicket, looking sleepy and affronted. Nogaret heard him give the order to unbar the gate, and signaled his own men to be ready. When the port swung open, the riders surged inside and promptly occupied the courtyard beyond. Most of them rode with drawn swords, and a few braced cocked crossbows at their hips.

"What is the meaning of this?" de Molay demanded furiously, from the midst of a growing contingent of his officers and serjeants, though few of them were armed at this hour of the night, and most were at least twice the age of any man in Nogaret's armed escort.

"This Order's evil heresy has come to light at last," Nogaret proclaimed coldly, for the benefit of the uninitiated—his own men and those of the Temple. "You are being called to book for your crimes." He pulled from his belt a folded document heavy with pendant seals. "I have here a warrant under the king's own authority, ordering the arrest of every occupant of this place."

"The king has no authority over us, save by leave of the Holy Father," de Molay said boldly. "Your order has no force."

"My order," Nogaret said, thrusting the document under the Grand Master's nose, "bears the king's own seal. If you are innocent, will you force us to shed your innocent blood to enforce the lawful order of our sovereign liege? *You* may not be bound by the king's command, but we are."

De Molay opened and closed his mouth several times, clearly at a loss for words, then turned to murmur something inaudible to one of his subordinates. Nogaret only nodded toward two of his sergeants with a faint, cold smile.

"Take these men into custody," he said mildly, "along with every other man in this place."

De Molay recoiled, spluttering with outrage, but neither he nor any of his officers made any serious resistance— though it could not be said that any went willingly into captivity. Leaving the royal troops to make a sweep through the compound, rounding up the other Templars in residence, Nogaret dismounted and made his way swiftly down to the treasury level, trailed by the four other members of the Decuria. The vault where he had left his ring was empty, as were the chambers adjacent to it; the one from which Ialda-baeoth had recoiled appeared to be but an ordinary chapel, though further investigation might prove otherwise.

Sending the others to check the rest of the vaults, Noga-ret hung back to retrieve his ring from its hiding place. As he closed it in his hand, he re-engaged the connection with the demon that resided therein.

"Ialdabaeoth," he called softly.

Yesss, Masster?

"Where have they gone?"

Ialdabaeoth doesss not know, Massster.

"Did they take the Treasures?" Nogaret asked.

Yesss, Massster. Many Ssssecretsss.

"Show me," Nogaret ordered, closing his eyes.

At once, images began to pass before his vision: the dis-guised Templars slipping from the chapel vault by ones and twos, most with an accompanying aura of formidable power benignly contained—surely, the esoteric Treasures of the Temple.

All sources of such power were potentially of interest, of course, for the ways their potency could be corrupted to his use, but suddenly Nogaret's attention was sharply diverted to one of the older knights, among the last to leave the vault, who was drawing his robe closed over what appeared to be bandages closely wrapped around his chest. The taste of power that emanated from the man—or what he carried—was of a subtle difference from the others, and might well be the very item Nogaret most sought.

What is it he carries? Nogaret demanded of the demon.

A Ssssecret, Massster!

What secret? Is it the Breastplate?

Ialdabaeoth doesss not know . . . ooooh, do not punish Ialdabaeoth, Massster!

Indeed, the little demon had tried to get a closer look at the man, as he closed and secured the door of the empty vault and then headed off in the direction the others had gone; but the power radiating from whatever the man carried, bound to his person, was too potent for Ialdabaeoth to endure.

But not too potent for Nogaret. Closing his hand more tightly around the ring where the demon lived, the king's chancellor let himself breathe out in a sigh, his thumb caressing the stone with malicious pleasure as he opened his eyes—for he knew what the man carried, even if Ialdabaeoth did not. It was, indeed, the long-sought Breastplate of the High Priests of Israel.

"Ialdabaeoth?" he said softly.

Yesss, Massster?

"That last Templar—you have the scent of what he took from this place, bound close to his body," Nogaret said. "Follow it, and direct me where the trail leads."

Yesss, Massster!

He was turning to go, threading the ring back onto the heavy chain around his neck, when the tramp of heavy footsteps announced the return of Count Rodolphe, along with Peret Auvernais and Valentin de Vesey.

"Magister, the men are in the process of forcing the doors on the rest of the treasure chambers," Rodolphe reported "but so far, they're all empty."

"Of course they're empty! I told you they were taking the treasures!"

"No, they're *empty*," Rodolphe repeated, his face impassive. "There's no gold. No jewels or furs or anything else of worth. Not even a silver penny."

"What?"

When Rodolphe merely gazed at him, not flinching from his stare, Nogaret stormed past him to fling open door after door, where his men had been. Every treasure vault had, indeed, been stripped.

"They knew," Nogaret whispered. "*They knew!*"

"Perhaps it's only happened here, in Paris," Peret said uncomfortably.

"Yes, and perhaps fish can fly!" Nogaret snapped.

"In that case," Rodolphe said, "I suggest that we dispatch riders immediately to warn the officers at all the major ports. That may stop some of the fish from slipping through the net."

"Aye, and some of the treasure, too," Valentin de Vesey chimed in. "They can't have moved the entire treasury out of here without attracting local notice. We *know* what riches were here, only a few months ago."

Nogaret only nodded vaguely, his head cocking briefly in a listening attitude. Then, with a glance at Rodolphe, he said, "See to it. I have a mission of my own. Peret and Valentin, you're with me. We are going hunting for a pigeon that has flown."

"And what am I to do?" Rodolphe said sharply.

"I leave you in charge," Nogaret said over his shoulder. "You will secure this place, and all its prisoners. Follow up all clear leads. When I return, we'll carry out more subtle investigations. They may have emptied the vaults, but there will still be clues to signify what they have taken with them. If you like, you may begin on that, as well."

With the two younger members of the Decuria dogging his heels, Nogaret made his way briskly back to the yard, where the rest of his personal escort stood waiting.

"One of the particular men I want has flown—but only with a modest start on us," he told them, as they all mounted up. "With luck, however, we will have him in our hands before the ending of the day."

He returned his attention to Ialdabaeoth as they rode out the gate. The little demon was snuffing the air and gabbling discontentedly to itself.

"Which way?" Nogaret demanded under his breath, addressing the ring where the demon dwelt.

North. . . . came the response. *He followsss the water.*

With Ialdabaeoth directing, they set out in pursuit, tracking their quarry westward across Paris and into the countryside, traveling with the dawn.

"He'll be making for the coast," Valentin said, as they careened into a turn at a fork in the road. "If he reaches a port—"

"He'll never get that far," Nogaret said flatly. "He is already a dead man."

They rode on at speed for another hour, passing through a succession of sleepy villages and across rolling farmlands. They had just crested a rise when, just ahead, Nogaret's gimlet eyes spotted a well-mounted horseman bending to exchange words with a woman at a crossroad ahead. In the same instant, there came a shrill squeal from Ialdabaeoth.

There he isss, Massster! The keeper of the Treasssure!

Nogaret was already spurring forward, his men a-clatter behind him, but Valentin de Vesey soon took the lead, bent low over his horse's neck. The thunder of their approach drew the alarmed glance of the rider ahead, who immediately clapped heels to his horse's flanks and took flight.

"Get him!" Nogaret shouted.

Valentin de Vesey continued to lead the pursuit, through another village and past a tiny churchyard at reckless speed. A flock of grazing geese scattered before their quarry in a storm of white wings, but he stayed with his startled mount, pushing the beast, making far better time than the animal's appearance would have suggested. Ahead, as the road veered northward, Nogaret spied the arrow-straight line of an ancient Roman bridge spanning a river far below. Beyond lay the densely wooded slope of a forest that stretched for miles.

"Don't let him reach the bridge!" Nogaret shouted. "If he crosses it, you'll lose him in the trees!"

Their quarry, however, was already approaching the bridgehead, though his horse checked as the road met the bridge, reluctant to gallop hell-bent along the high, narrow span. Through much desperate spurring and urging with hands and legs, the rider managed to keep moving onto the bridge, but his pursuers were closing fast. As the first of them reached the bridgehead, Nogaret gave a shrill whistle and a hand signal, causing several men to rein short and pull crossbows from behind their saddles.

The Templar had nearly reached the midpoint of the bridge when a whispering flight of crossbow bolts overtook him from behind—though only one came close to hitting him, fouled harmlessly in his mantle. His horse, however, fared far less well, stumbling with a shrill whinny as two quarrels smacked into its hindquarters with meaty thunks. As it recovered its footing and bravely continued forward, another bolt caught it behind one shoulder, causing the beast to rear up in pain, twisting as it pawed the sky and fell, spilling its rider heavily to the ground.

The Templar rolled clear and scrambled to his feet, one leg clearly injured, dragging his sword from its scabbard as he peered back dazedly at his pursuers. He had lost his cap in the fall, and his hair gleamed silver in the early-morning light. Dismounting in a more leisurely fashion, half a dozen of Nogaret's men began venturing onto the bridge, drawing their swords, while the crossbowmen nocked new bolts to their weapons.

"Surrender, Templar, and I may allow you to live," Nogaret called from horseback, walking his mount just behind them.

For answer, the fugitive shook his gray head and began backing off, deftly avoiding the flailing hooves of his mount. The animal could not get up, and clearly had been crippled by the fall, so he gave it the *coup de grâce* before taking wary cover behind its body, continuing to back away. Watching him, Nogaret was able to put a name to the noble, silver-bearded face: Gaspar des Macquelines, one of the deputy treasurers of the Paris Temple.

Massster, he hasss a Treasssure, came Ialdabaeoth's seductive whisper.

Nogaret only smiled, his gloved hand on the ring around his neck, caressing its stone with a thumb as his men advanced.

The bridge being narrow, they could not attack him save one or two at a time, by climbing over the dying horse. Valentin de Vesey closed first, cautiously—and with good reason, for the Templar parried the younger man's attack with a fury worthy of a man half his age. The clangor of their exchange echoed from the high bridge span as he yielded ground—and retreated farther along the bridge, toward possible escape.

Valentin fell back, to be replaced by Peret Auvernais. With him the Templar exchanged another intense flurry of sword blows, but neither did the other harm, even when the latter was joined by another swordsman, and then another, in rapid succession. Two of the crossbowmen came beside Nogaret, weapons cocked and ready, but he shook his head; he did not want damaged what the Templar carried next to his body.

The Templar fought with a strength and speed born of desperation, but he was one aging man against an almost endless series of younger, fresher men than he, and his endurance could not last forever. When he finally began showing definite signs of fatigue, Valentin de Vesey reentered the fray and, when the Templar's blade briefly faltered, darted his blade past the other man's guard and up under the rib cage, taking him through a lung.

The Templar uttered not a sound, but clearly, his wound was mortal. Yet, with blood starting to bubble from his lips, Gaspar des Macquelines somehow managed to resume a formidable defense, the flash of his blade belatedly taking up its deadly pattern, nearly wounding Valentin, all the while glancing around him like a man with all the time in the world.

After a few more exchanges, as if his hands moved of their own accord, he suddenly reversed the sword end for end and launched it in an arching throw that sang past Valentin and very nearly struck Nogaret himself, sitting on his horse. As part of the same move, as the horse shied and the sword fell to the ground with a clang, Gaspar wheeled about and staggered to the guard wall to pitch himself over, his right hand perhaps moving in self-blessing as he fell toward the river far below.

His body struck the water with a heavy splash, dead or dying, limbs all akimbo. Nogaret's men rushed to look over the parapet, where his body briefly surfaced in a spreading patch of crimson and then was dragged under in a swirling eddy, to reappear periodically as it bumped along on its way toward a millrace, facedown and limbs vaguely moving. Peret started to summon the crossbowmen with orders to shoot, but Nogaret restrained them.

"Don't waste your bolts," he said scornfully, kneeing his horse close enough to the parapet to gaze down into the water. "He's already dead—or will be, by the time anyone can get to him. Some of you get down to the millrace; don't let the body slip past you. I want it."

Valentin set a closed fist against the guard wall and cursed, rubbing at a pulled muscle in his sword arm.

"He *jumped*! Damn him, he *jumped*!"

"Indeed," Nogaret agreed thinly. "For all the good it will have done him."

He called after the soldiers starting to head downriver. "Do not search the body, when you recover it!" he ordered. "Bring it straightaway to me."

Chapter Twenty-three

October 13, 1307

FIRST LIGHT WAS STILL AN HOUR AWAY WHEN ARNAULT DE Saint Clair presented himself at one of the south ports of the city, wrapped in a swath of faded tartan and mounted on an ugly, rough-coated dun. The animal had the plodding temperament and conformation of a plow horse, but he knew it also had speed when needed, and the stolid endurance to last, if he had to make a run for it. The gate warden emerged yawning from the guardroom, thrusting a horn lantern aloft for a better look at the pair.

"You're taking to the road early," the warden remarked, idly noting the rider's disheveled appearance and the pilgrim badges of Notre Dame and Santiago de Compostella on his weather-beaten cap. "Got a jealous husband after you?"

"Not this time," Arnault said with a grin, accenting his French with the Scottish burr that had become so familiar on Torquil's lips, over the years. "I've a long day's ride ahead of me, that's all."

He opened his scrip and produced a letter of credence identifying him as a Scottish knight on pilgrimage to visit the sacred shrines of France. The seal and signature were genuine, having been issued by Bishop Crambeth of

Dunkeld, a supporter of Robert Bruce and an ally of the Templar cause. The gate warden handed the letter back with another yawn, unimpressed.

"Scottish, eh? Where are you bound?"

"Vézelay," Arnault replied. "The shrine of Saint Marie Madeleine." And in fact, that was the general direction he intended to go, at least for the first few miles. "If I hope to arrive in time for the feast of Saint Luke, I need to press on. This nag of mine has more strength than speed to him," he added, sourly lifting the reins of his steed.

"Aye, he'll never win a race for you," the warden agreed, and gave the dun a starting smack on the rump. "Get on with you, then."

As soon as he was out of sight of the guard post, Arnault left the road and set off across the fields in a more southwesterly direction. It was still too dark to go very quickly, for fear of rabbit holes, but a thin, autumnal mist hovered low over the ground and would give him cover. A distant cockcrow pierced the predawn hush, sounding strangely doom-laden.

The feeling stayed with him as he carried on across country into definite dawning. By the time he reached a dense wood, a few miles outside the city, there was just enough light to make his careful way into it; the sun was just rising clear of the horizon as he emerged on the crest of a low hill, with a muddy and rutted road below him.

A farmer was driving a small herd of milch cows along the left-hand embankment, a wiry, sharp-tongued sheep dog nipping at their heels. Arnault waited in the trees until the farmer disappeared around the bend, then descended onto the road and turned the dun's head in the opposite direction, which would take him toward the cathedral city of Chartres.

He encountered only country folk for the first hour or so—herdsmen and plowmen going about their business. But as the sun rose higher, he began to overtake and meet a greater variety of fellow travelers. Merchants in lumbering oxcarts and the occasional horse-drawn conveyance rumbled slowly along the rutted road amid a strolling array of tinkers and vendors and an accompanying cloud of dust. A goodwife with a gaggle of children and a basket of eggs made her way toward market; a farmer goaded a string of pack mules, their panniers loaded with fresh produce, and two young girls chivvied several geese. Interspersed among them walked an assortment of brown-robed friars, students, and the occasional pilgrim such as Arnault purported to be.

Intent on their own affairs, none of Arnault's fellow travelers spared much more than a passing glance for the stoop-shouldered rider in faded clothes, plodding along the roadside on his heavy-boned nag. It was a function, if not a specific role, to which he was well accustomed, for his work for the Order often had called for him to travel inconspicuously and incognito. In the Holy Land, he had even passed for Muslim. None of his fellow wayfarers was likely to suspect that the battered saddlebag at his knee contained anything more valuable than a spare shirt and perhaps a packet of journey rations. As long as he could sustain his humble disguise, what he carried was safe enough; and the sword at his side would discourage interference.

It was midmorning before he encountered the first sign of trouble, in the form of a pair of royal messengers. Mounted on well-bred steeds, they galloped past in a thunder of flying hooves, scattering other travelers before them like barnyard fowl—and, fortunately, paying Arnault absolutely no regard.

"What's that all about?" a pimply young cleric wondered, peering after them from the shelter of a roadside tree.

"Maybe the king's thought of a new tax to levy," the leader of a troupe of players said with a grimace.

"Maybe war's broken out again in Brittany," another traveler said. "Or maybe there's fresh rioting in the provinces."

Arnault found himself confronted by a rubicund cloth merchant.

"You have the look of a fighting man," he noted in a bluff voice. "Have you heard any rumors? *Is* there another war on?"

Arnault shrugged—and made certain his French carried a definite Scottish accent. "I wouldn't know. I'm only a pilgrim. You'll have to find your answers elsewhere."

Later in the afternoon, as he stopped at a village green to water his horse, he found half a dozen local men talking among themselves as they brought their herd of cattle to drink at the millpond.

"—would have thought that the king would order such a thing?" he heard one man saying to another.

"It must be true," another one replied. "Pierre heard it from Jean Paul, who heard it from Father Gaetan. Apparently, they're being rounded up all over France."

Arnault turned his focus on the conversation, straining to hear more without appearing to eavesdrop.

"Templars!" another man growled, and spat in the dust. "I've always said they were sorcerers! It's about time somebody did something to curb their arrogance and pride."

"I wonder what will happen to them," a younger man murmured.

"From what I hear, they'll be brought to trial, made to answer for their heresies."

Sick at heart, his horse watered, Arnault hurriedly checked his girth and mounted up to set out again. The news he had been dreading apparently had spread with alacrity. At every place he passed thereafter, the rumors grew more extravagant and ugly. Toward dusk, as weary from emotion as from physical exhaustion, he drew aside for a body of troops on the march, coming the opposite way—and stared, along with everyone else, as they passed by.

In their midst, under close guard, a nicely matched pair of draft horses pulled a wagon piled high with household goods. Two elderly men in Templar white sat on the wagon's tail, heavily shackled and fettered and with rope halters around their necks, both with eyes downcast. Plodding behind the wagon, chained together like felons, came several brown-robed lay brothers. All of the prisoners looked dazed and exhausted, totally bewildered by their fate.

Dismayed and chilled, Arnault dared a closer look at the nearer of the knights, for he thought he recognized the man. And he did—though, thankfully, the old man did not look up. Having served with distinction in the Holy Land, when Arnault first had taken his vows and gone to war, the old knight had been living in honorable retirement on a small farm belonging to the Order—and now had come to this! Appalled, Arnault averted his face to keep from being recognized in turn. The necessity turned him sick at heart, but he had no other choice.

As he rode on, he heard the comments of some of the villagers, many of whom had turned out to witness the spectacle. Several jeered and sniggered, but many looked as bewildered as the prisoners. One man, more intrepid than his fellows, boldly accosted one of the soldiers bringing up the rear, tugging at his stirrup.

"What have they done?" he demanded. "This can't be right. These holy brothers have lived amongst us for a good few years, and I've never known any harm in them."

One of his neighbors chimed in with a snort.

"That's as may be, but what about their superiors? We don't know! Remember what they say about fire always being where there's smoke. . . ."

The soldier shot a warning glance at the man beside his stirrup, who backed off with alacrity.

"This doesn't concern you," he said. "They'll get their chance to plead their case. If they're innocent, they'll be freed. Right now, we have our orders."

As he sped up slightly to draw even with the rest of the troop, a wiry, rat-faced laborer shouldered his way to the fore.

"Sorcerers!"—he shouted after the Templars. "Magicians! Why don't you do a magic trick and set yourselves free?"

Jaw clenched, Arnault forced himself to ride on, keeping his eyes averted. For several hundred more yards, he kept hearing other mutters.

"Wonder what'll become of all the treasure they've stashed away."

"It's probably cursed. Whoever gets his hands on it will live to regret it."

"I'd be willing to take that chance."

"So will the king, I daresay. . . ."

Arnault slept rough that night in a wood. The next morning he cut his beard as closely as he could, using only a dagger, and pressed on for Chartres. Arriving before sunset, he sought out an unassuming hostel in the vicinity of the cathedral. There he stabled his weary horse and bespoke a bed for the night.

The adjoining tavern was crowded, and news of the Templars' arrest was still fresh. The innkeeper confided his opinion as he served Arnault a tankard of ale and a wooden trencher of bread and cheese.

"Maybe what they're saying is true. Maybe the Templars had it coming," he said with a shake of his head. "Maybe they *do* traffic in black magic. If you ask me, though, the root of all their trouble is all the wealth they've accumulated over the years—and power. Wealth and power always breed envy. And envy breeds enemies like flies on a dung heap."

He paused to give the tabletop a wipe with the corner of his apron. "If they had no riches worth the taking, I daresay, the Templars would still be walking around free."

Arnault found the innkeeper's surmises disconcertingly shrewd, but he thought it best to divert the conversation away from the subject of treasure. His saddlebag, with the riches *he* carried, lay on the floor between his feet, for he dared not trust it to the dubious safety of the room he would share with several others tonight.

"Then you don't believe they're guilty of the charges everyone is talking about?" he asked, again careful to speak with a strong Scottish accent.

The innkeeper shrugged. "What I believe doesn't matter, does it? The king means to have his way. And no one on earth, not even the pope, is in a position to stop him.

"But that's fickle fortune for you, making sport amongst the great men of the world. Those she raises up today, she casts down in the dust tomorrow." He sighed gustily and gave Arnault's table a final swipe. "I suppose we should be glad we're only common folk. Whatever becomes of the Templars, it's hardly going to matter to the likes of us."

As the man turned away in summons by another patron, Arnault reflected that the innkeeper could hardly be blamed for taking this view. How were ordinary men to know of the Temple's secret mission—or the secret war being waged between the Templars and their bitter enemies, the Knights of the Black Swan?

As he took a long pull of his ale, he found himself wondering if King Philip himself might be an initiate of the Black Swan. It seemed unlikely, given the king's shallow nature—for magic, whether black or white, required a focus and dedication almost certainly lacking in the king.

But Nogaret had such a focus and dedication—Guillaume de Nogaret, the king's excommunicate first minister, whose parents had been burned at the stake as heretics, who had not scrupled to lay violent hands on a pope, and whose rise to power coincided very closely with the rise in hostility toward the Temple. And only the previous year, he had been inside the Paris Temple long enough to take a good look around—and to make plans to take what he wanted.

Even more compelling, from Arnault's point of view, was the appearance of Nogaret in his dreams. Though the evidence was circumstantial, the weight of circumstance was bitterly convincing.

A bell began ringing out the Angelus nearby, intruding on

his speculations, and he looked up, leaning back then to peer out the open door toward the cathedral.

"There's evening prayer after Angelus," the innkeeper said to him, noticing his interest. "Since you're on pilgrimage, you'll maybe be wanting to attend. If you do, you might spare me a prayer."

Arnault thanked the man and gulped down the rest of his ale, tucking his bread and cheese into his saddlebag before slinging it over his shoulder and heading for the cathedral. In fact, he had been there often, for this greatest of all churches honoring the Blessed Virgin had been built with the help of Templar architects and engineers, starting nearly a century and a half before, and embodied many facets of sacred geometry and symbolism. During his training for service in *le Cercle,* he had spent many an hour studying some of it, and knew it well. He had always derived comfort within its walls—and, sometimes, inspiration.

Passing through the Royal Portal, which lay between the two great western towers, he skirted the eleven-ringed labyrinth inlaid in the floor of the graceful nave crossing and found a quiet place in one of the side chapels, in the shadow of a pillar, seeking more private reflection than the formal prayers being chanted by the monks in the choir. Candles at the front of the chapel signified the Divine Presence, as embodied in the Reserved Sacrament that was kept in a gothic tabernacle on the altar.

He had drawn his mantle more closely around him and had bowed his head in one hand, floating in the healing grace of that Presence, when he became aware of a dark silhouette pausing in the chapel's entry archway. A sidelong glance in that direction suggested that it was but another worshipper, but after a moment, the newcomer entered, passing so close that his dark robes brushed Arnault's shoulder as he sank to his knees hardly an arm's length away. The stranger's hooded outer garment was cut in the style of a desert *djellaba,* though he wore Western-style mail and leather beneath it. The man himself was dark-skinned and dark-eyed, quick and supple in his movements as he traced a cross upon his breast—though he signed himself as was done in the East, from right to left. He favored Arnault with a slight nod as their eyes met.

"You are a pilgrim, I see," the stranger observed. "Tell me, brother, have you ventured so far as Jerusalem?"

His voice was resonant and low, with a curiously lilting intonation. By his appearance, Arnault had thought he might be Castilian, but the accent was neither Spanish, nor Arabic, nor anything else in Arnault's experience.

But why had he spoken? Though it occurred to Arnault that the man might be an agent of the Crown, sent to arrest him, he found himself curiously unconcerned that this might actually be true.

"Not so far as Jerusalem," he said neutrally.

"Then perhaps you have not ventured far enough," came the cool answer.

Arnault was taken aback by the other man's tone, for it hinted at subtle power, closely guarded, and purposes as yet undisclosed—but, quite possibly, alliances in harmony with his own.

"The roads to the Holy Land have never been more perilous than now," he said tentatively, daringly.

"The roads in France are more perilous still," the stranger amended quietly. "Especially to a man of your stamp."

Startled, though he did not let himself show it, Arnault glanced around them, to be certain no one could overhear.

"What kind of man do you take me for?" he whispered uneasily.

"A man with a task to perform, a mission to fulfill," came the cryptic response. "A man with a secret burden weighing on his shoulders. A man who fears the law—and with good reason."

Arnault recoiled inwardly, gripped by a prescience of

dread, but he could not seem to pull away from the stranger's dark gaze.

"The Law will destroy you," the man stated distinctly. "The Law will set you free."

This time, Arnault could not repress a start. *"What did you say?"*

The stranger eyed him steadily. "You know the words. You have heard them before."

"Yes, but how—?" Arnault stopped.

"Eli ben Ezra lived and died a seer," said the stranger. "He spoke with a prophet's tongue concerning days and times to come. He and I have drunk from the same sacred well. That is how I know you are of the brotherhood for whom my message is intended."

"Who *are* you?" Arnault blurted, though he knew instinctively to keep his voice down. "Where do you come from, and who sent you?"

"My name is Iskander," said the stranger. "More than that I may not tell you at this time, save at the risk of imperiling us both."

The name struck a curiously familiar chord, but before Arnault could recall where he had heard it before, Iskander continued.

"If we meet again hereafter, there will be every reason to speak freely. For now, suffice it to say that I am a friend who wishes to see you and your companions succeed in your mission."

He paused to sketch a sign in the air—a Templar recognition signal, though one out of use for decades.

"Speak on," Arnault whispered cautiously.

Iskander's dark eyes took on a fey, faraway look, as if he gazed far beyond the chapel walls.

"Wings of darkness overshadow the land. Talons of envy grasp at a sacred prize. Unnatural birds of prey seek to devour, and the weal of future generations hangs between darkness and light. Darkness threatens to sweep away the Temple. . . ."

Arnault shivered to a sudden thrill of premonition. The images clearly referred to the tide of recent events.

"Do you know how this will end?" he asked.

"With the death of many," came the grim response, "but some may survive. There is hope for redemption, but only at a price."

"How?"

"The answer lies in Jerusalem."

"Jerusalem?"

Before Arnault could say more, Iskander continued in the same prophetic tone.

"Before the Temple, there was the Ark of the Covenant. And before the Ark, there was the Covenant itself. The voice of God spoke, and the Tablets of the Law received the sacred Word. And the power of the Word will abide forever, though the Tablets themselves crumble into dust."

He leveled his keen gaze at Arnault with an air of expectation, but Arnault was shaking his head.

"I—hear," he whispered, "but I do not understand. . . ."

"You will," Iskander assured him with a glinting look.

He raised the hood of his *djellaba* and rose, moving toward the nave. Arnault tried to follow him, only to discover that he could not clearly pick out Iskander's form from the surrounding shadows. Even as he strained to penetrate the meaning behind Iskander's words, a voice whispered in his mind or in his ear, so soft that he could not be certain which.

"The First Temple was raised in accordance with the Word. In the place where the Temple was raised, you will find the answers that you seek. Hope dwells for all eternity in the City of God."

"Wait! I don't understand," Arnault whispered urgently. "What does this mean?"

But Iskander had gone, leaving no trace.

Chapter Twenty-four

February, 1308

THE CASTLE GUARDING THE NARROW VALLEY WAS NO longer known by any name. Stark and forbidding, it squatted above the valley's mouth like a basilisk guarding its lair. Especially in winter, the surrounding foothills of the Rouerge represented one of the most forbidding regions of southern France. Farther into the valley, the unsightly refuse of an abandoned stone quarry littered the snow-covered ground like the picked bones of a carcass.

The castle's outward appearance of neglect, however, was mere camouflage, instigated by Nogaret. Having acquired the shell of an ancestral ruin, he had since transformed it into a secret citadel of power. Inside, every room in the castle had been scoured and refurbished, from the deepest cellars to the topmost chamber of the highest tower.

The resident garrison was small, its numbers limited to those who could readily be housed within the castle's outer baillie. The handful of servants who maintained the place had been carefully chosen for reasons that had nothing to do with providing hospitality. Visitors, apart from Nogaret himself, were unheard of. When he summoned three other members of the Decuria there for a secret meeting, the occasion was virtually without precedent.

Baudoin de Champiere edged his chair closer toward the fire and rubbed his cold hands briskly to warm them.

"Sensible of what an honor it is for me to be here," he observed sourly, "I can hardly deem the experience a pleasure. You would think these loutish servants would know enough at least to bring us refreshments. I'm perishing for a cup of wine!"

He helped himself to a sugared rose leaf from the jeweled comfit box he habitually carried in one of his silken sleeve pockets.

"Magister Nogaret's servants take their tone from their master," Peret Auvergnais said with an offhand shrug. "If they didn't have their uses, he wouldn't keep them."

"Our peerless leader has the appetites of an anchorite," Baudoin said with a snort. "He is incapable of enjoying the finer things life has to offer—though he does have that demon in his ring. . . ."

"Guard your tongue," Peret advised. "Nogaret's churls may lack manners, but I daresay they have ears."

Hitherto silent, Valentin de Vesey turned restlessly away from the window, where he had been contemplating an ice-rimed view of a long-dead orchard.

"This is as joyless a retreat as I can imagine," he said. "Is it true that this castle was once a Cathar stronghold?"

"So I understand," Baudoin said around another sugared petal, though without any great interest. "It's said that his parents were Cathars, you know: condemned as heretics and burned at the stake, when he was but a lad."

"I'd heard that," Valentin replied. "And that the Church took great pains to educate him, in hopes that it might keep him from following in their footsteps."

"Well, he didn't follow in the footsteps of his parents *or* the Church fathers, did he?" Baudoin said slyly, sucking the stickiness from his fingers. "You don't suppose this is where his parents were burned, do you?"

Both his companions gave him warning looks, which Baudoin shrugged off as he leaned forward to pitch another chunk of wood on the fire.

The appearance of a servant at the door brought all three visitors to their feet.

"Magister Nogaret is ready to receive you now," the man informed them. "You will come with me."

He led them to the topmost room in the east tower. As they approached the door, Valentin detected a lurking tingle of power in the air. It was not sufficient to prepare him for the scene that met his eyes when they entered the room beyond.

The chamber itself was circular, its stone walls perforated by four deep lancet windows. But the windows had been blocked and then covered over with screens of silk, embroidered with traceries of Hebrew writing. In the absence of daylight, the room was illuminated by four bronze lamps placed at the four cardinal points of the compass, whose amber glow picked out an assortment of chests and bookshelves ranged about the chamber's perimeter.

Dominating the center of the room, upon a raised dais paved with alternating squares of black and white, was an altar draped with a rich cloth of creamy silk, beneath a silken canopy. A seven-branched candelabrum guarded one end of the altar; at the other, a bronze lectern supported a large leather-bound volume of Hebrew *arcana,* held shut by a pair of jeweled clasps. It was, Valentin realized, quite a passable imitation of a Jewish sanctuary.

More astonishing still was the sight of Guillaume de Nogaret standing in the shadows behind the altar, arrayed in a purple tunic embroidered with scarlet and gold and wearing the priestly ephod upon his breast. Draped over his shoulders was a rich mantle, also of violet silk, and on his head he wore a turban secured with a jeweled brooch—the complete raiment of a Jewish High Priest, save for the Breastplate.

Peret and Baudoin both were gaping. Belatedly Valentin discovered he was doing likewise. Nogaret smiled thinly at their astonishment.

"What you see should come as no surprise," he said mildly. "Perhaps *this* will speak more eloquently than mere words concerning my motives and intentions."

From the folds of his mantle he produced what he had taken from the body of Gaspar des Macquelines some months before. It was the shape and the size of a small book, and swathed in muffling layers of crisp white linen. Power emanated from it in palpable waves, like the fluctuations of the tide. At the very sight of it, an expression of greedy concupiscence transfigured Baudoin's large features. Valentin's expression was more one of concern.

"It wasn't damaged by its immersion, was it?"

"No, it was sealed in wrappings of waxed cloth."

"Then, it *is* the High Priest's Breastplate!" Baudoin breathed. "I was beginning to wonder whether you would ever allow the rest of us to catch a glimpse of the prize."

Nogaret whisked the packet out of sight again.

"This is not some vulgar piece of strumpet's finery," he warned sharply. "This is a sacred standard, a weapon, a key to powers that brought the very cosmos to birth! Its natural affinities are entirely inimical to our own. Anyone attempting to unlock its secrets must armor himself in appropriate ritual, or else court annihilation."

"Hence these gaudy affectations of a primitive Judaic priesthood," Baudoin said scornfully, waving a hand around the room.

"You may live to be grateful for the thoroughness of my preparations," Nogaret said tightly. "Tonight we are going to awaken the powers of the Breastplate—and bend them to our will."

Glances of varying degrees of alarm flew among his three subordinates.

"Ah, Magister . . ." Valentin ventured, "would it not be wiser if *all* the members of the Decuria were present for a ceremony of such importance?"

"By no means," Nogaret replied. "There are some upon whose confidence I cannot rely as I can on yours."

"Eventually, they *will* learn what we have done," Baudoin pointed out. "They'll demand to know why they were excluded."

"And I shall tell them it was for their own protection," Nogaret said icily. "Or do some of *you* wish to be excluded?"

Smiling sardonically, Peret said, "I believe I speak for all of us when I declare that ten thousand devils could not drive me from this room."

"I trust," Nogaret said coldly, "that you will not have occasion to try the accuracy of that statement." He gestured toward three stacks of folded garments atop a trunk to one side of the room. "Pray, vest yourselves appropriately, from the skin out."

Somewhat sobered, the three newcomers traded their travel attire for ceremonial vestments similar to Nogaret's. Nogaret himself undertook to cleanse and ward the room, setting candles and incense alight to the accompaniment of a complex sequence of cabalistic signs and prayers and a keening Hebraic chant. By the time he had finished, the other three were ready to join him at the altar.

"Now," Nogaret said, carefully positioning the linen-wrapped packet at the base of the lectern. His habitually pallid face was flushed with excitement as he folded back several layers of linen and then silk, beneath which lay the long-awaited prize.

A collective sigh breathed from the lips of his three colleagues at the sight of it, the twelve large jewels set in three rows of four and stitched to a backing of stiffened linen, each stone engraved with a sigil of one of the Twelve Tribes of Israel. The stones were held in bezels of polished gold—topaz and sapphire, emerald, diamond, and other gems—glinting in the slanting light, each stone remarkable in its size and purity. Nogaret's pale, protuberant eyes glowed with excitement, reflecting the jewels as a tiny pair of multicolored constellations.

"Behold the Breastplate of Aaron, perhaps the greatest treasure of Solomon's Temple," he murmured. "Each jewel is a storehouse of mystical energy. Their arrangement forms a matrix for containing the harmonization of those energies. But the source of the power itself resides here, in these two stones secreted at the back of the Breastplate."

He turned it over to show them two slightly bulging pockets stitched to the back of the linen, carefully opening the mouths of both so that they could see what lay within: two more stones of similar size to those stitched to the front of the Breastplate, one black and one white.

"Behold, the legendary *Urim* and *Thummin*—the Lights and Perfections," he said, as they bent to peer into the pockets. "They have divinatory properties on their own, but harnessed to the jewels of the Breastplate, they can generate such force as has not been seen on the earth since the destruction of Gomorrah."

"Strange, that they should appear as dark and lusterless as river stones," Baudoin remarked, starting to prod at one of the pockets with a forefinger.

"Do not touch them!" Nogaret warned, slapping Baudoin's hand away. "They can kill if mishandled!" He let out a deep breath. "If we succeed in attuning them to the Breastplate, the power at our command will enable us to reshape the material world."

With due respect, if not reverence, Peret and Valentin helped Nogaret fix the Breastplate to the priestly ephod, fastening the golden chains to the shoulders and waist. Thereafter, now meticulously obedient to their superior's directions, the three acolytes dispersed to the eastern, western, and southern quarters of the chamber and assumed attitudes of abject supplication, even Baudoin at last sobered by the seriousness of the work about to commence.

Himself standing before the altar, Nogaret opened the book to a page covered in Hebrew writing and raised his hands to begin chanting. The words were familiar at first, but quickly shifted into language that was beyond the knowledge of the others to interpret. After the first few phrases, they recognized only an occasional mystical term as he lightly touched each of the gems in turn, some with the right hand and some with the left. When all had been thus invoked, he placed a finger to his brow and another over his heart, eyes closed in rapt concentration.

A deep hush settled in their midst, centered on Nogaret. His lips twitched and trembled, mouthing soundless syllables of supplication. His acolytes watched anxiously for some glimmer of life from the gems adorning the Breastplate, or from the Lights and Perfections. But the only lights visible were reflected glimmers from the neighboring candles.

Peret stirred restlessly. After a time, Nogaret abandoned his silent pleading in favor of more imperious cadences of bidding and then command. Beads of sweat broke out on his taut brow, beginning to run into his eyes, but the Breastplate remained unresponsive.

After what seemed an eternity, Nogaret suddenly wrenched himself from his concentration with an explosive curse and half turned away, causing his three companions to start back.

"What is it? What's wrong?" Baudoin demanded.

Nogaret indicated the Breastplate with a savage stab of his hand. "See for yourselves!"

Peret raised an eyebrow. "There's nothing to see."

"Precisely! Because *nothing* has happened!"

Nogaret struck the altar a frustrated blow with his fist. "I performed the ritual in *perfect* accordance with the ancient injunctions! Every detail is correct—and yet the Breastplate remains inert."

Spurning assistance, he stripped off the Breastplate and the ephod and flung them down on the altar. Flipping the Breastplate over, he fumbled with the fastenings securing the pockets at the back of it. Before any of his subordinates could restrain him, he reached inside and pulled out the *Urim* and *Thummin*.

Valentin recoiled with a gasp, then realized Nogaret was perfectly unharmed. The two stones, one dark and one light, were as inert as the river pebbles Baudoin had earlier compared them to. Nogaret glared venomously at the stones, one clasped in each hand.

"The fault lies *here!*" he growled.

"Could the Templars have performed some kind of substitution?" Peret asked.

"No!" Nogaret snapped. "These stones bear the sacred mark of the shamir. And yet they are dead! As dead as the man who—"

His voice broke off. All at once he snatched up the book and began riffling through its crackling pages, urgently searching for a dimly remembered passage. The others kept silent, baffled by his actions, but afraid to ask.

When he found the part he was looking for, Nogaret quickly scanned the page, silently mouthing the words as he read. Then he slammed the book vehemently shut, as though to imprison the unpalatable truth he had found there.

"That accursed Templar!" he spat. "He *knew* this would happen!"

"Knew *what* would happen?" Valentin asked.

Nogaret rounded on him furiously, as though he were personally responsible for this disaster.

"The authority to wield the *Urim* and *Thummin* can only be passed on by the priest, by the man who is guardian of the Breastplate. If he dies while in charge of it, his death robs the stones of their potency. Only one who has already been granted the same priestly authority can reempower them."

"So the Breastplate is useless," Baudoin said flatly.

"Do you accuse me of failure, fool?" Nogaret demanded, thrusting his face at his subordinate.

Baudoin fell back a pace. Seeing him silent, Nogaret gave a snort.

"I should have expected no better from one whose comprehension of the sorcerous arts is so limited by his meagerness of intellect," he said caustically. He took a deep breath to steady his passion before continuing.

"Without the *Urim* and *Thummin,*" he stated tightly, "we must empower the jewels individually, one by one, by alchemical means."

"Is that possible?" Valentin asked cautiously.

"It *must* be possible!" Nogaret insisted through gritted teeth. "Return to your castles, search your libraries, delve deep into every volume of occult lore in your possession. Then report everything you find to me."

"But who knows how long all this will take?" Peret objected.

"It will take as long as it must," Nogaret replied. "But time is on our side. Most of the Templars are already in custody, so they represent no threat. I will see to it that King Philip does not relent in his pursuit of them. Let them rot in prison or die at the hands of their torturers!"

His eyes were gleaming again, his anger transmuted into a fiery determination. "While they die, we shall grow in power and influence. This treasure and everything else they possess shall come to us and serve our ends. And then *nothing* shall stand in our way!"

Chapter Twenty-five

January-May, 1308

HAVING MANAGED TO STEER CLEAR OF THE ROYAL AGENTS rounding up Templars all over France, Arnault de Saint Clair made his slow way toward Scotland. It took him several weeks to reach the French border, and then only by doubling back northward to seek refuge in the Low Countries. By mid-November he had secured passage on a ship headed north—a Flemish merchantman bound for Aberdeen by way of Norway—not his first choice of route, but he dared not wait for another boat.

The sea voyage gave him time at last to consider his longer-term plans. It also gave him time to ponder the message of the mysterious Iskander—a name that had been mentioned, he finally remembered, in Jauffre's report of the Ethiopian embassage seeking a Western alliance. He had no idea whether the two Iskanders were one and the same, but the message of the one at Chartres had seemed to hint at an additional dimension in the task set for those guarding the Inner Temple—though Arnault had no idea how this new information fit into the more immediate plans to erect the Fifth Temple in Scotland. But at a very gut level, he had no doubt that it did fit.

Which made his first priority to consult with Luc and whatever other members of *le Cercle* he could find, to see what they might make of the message. And then he must find Bruce and assess the more practical aspects of the Scottish struggle for independence—for only in a stable and independent land would it be possible to erect the Fifth Temple at all.

He had hoped, since his escape took him by way of Norway, that he might obtain more recent news of Bruce from the Norwegian court, where Bruce's sister Isabella was queen. But the ship's brief stop in Oslo did not allow for more than token inquiries, and no contact with Isabella Bruce herself, so Arnault sailed for Aberdeen little wiser than when he had arrived. He did learn that Bruce—or so it was rumored—was wintering somewhere in Argyll. As for the Templars, he gathered that the Norwegians knew only vaguely that there had been some kind of trouble in Paris.

He arrived in Aberdeen just before Christmas, procuring a mount and heading south by way of Montrose, Arbroath, and Dundee, avoiding the worst of the winter snow by staying close to the coast. After crossing the Firth of Forth at Queensferry, he headed for Balantrodoch by the most direct route, riding into the preceptory's icy yard on the evening of Epiphany. His reception was cordial, for his arrival meant fresh news from France, and he soon was seated between Luc and Balantrodoch's master, Frère Walter de Clifton, being barraged with questions while he tried to consume a hot meal. After he had related some but not all of his adventures in fleeing France, and heard what little news was to be had locally, he retired with Luc for a more private debriefing. Luc's more detailed accounts of the past three months did not provide reassuring listening.

"In general, I can't add a great deal to what you heard at supper," Luc told him, as they settled before a modest fire in Luc's office with cups and a pot of hot mulled wine. "I *can* tell you, however, that the most recent news from France is not good. Apparently the sweep in October was extremely efficient, despite the fact that the officers of the Paris Temple knew or at least suspected that this was coming."

"They knew," Arnault agreed. "Gerard de Villiers took measures on his own initiative—which, as Preceptor of Paris, he was in a position to do. So did a few others. I don't know how much the Grand Master knew."

"De Molay can be pig-stubborn, when he wants to be," Luc said, shaking his head.

"I'll not argue that," Arnault replied. "I attended him the day before the arrests. All he was concerned about was the prestige of being in the royal funeral. He simply refused to accept what was coming."

"Well, it came," Luc replied. "We hear that thousands were taken into custody, all over France: knights, serjeants, lay brothers, clerics. It's being said that scores of our brothers have confessed to all manner of crimes, and we hear of tortures and threats of tortures. It's even said that de Molay signed some sort of confession."

Arnault dipped out another cup of mulled wine, more to warm his hands than out of any desire for the taste. "I'd heard much the same thing—I forget where. Have any of the other members of *le Cercle* checked in?"

"Christoph arrived in mid-November," Luc said, dropping his gaze. "He—thinks Jauffre may have been captured. But he isn't sure."

"Jauffre? Dear God. . . ."

"I'm afraid so. We've had no further news on that. Father Bertrand arrived at the beginning of December. After due consideration, we agreed that he and Christoph should go on to Dunkeld, to put them in close proximity to the Stone. I suppose you knew that Abbot Henry was taken by the English last summer—sent to imprisonment down in Wiltshire—but Bishop Crambeth is taking a direct hand in the protection of the Stone. He's given sanctuary to Christoph and Bertrand. They're posing as monks there at Dunkeld."

Arnault nodded distractedly, in total agreement with the strategy, though the news of Jauffre had taken him aback.

"And the relics they carried?" he asked.

"Safe, so far as we know," Luc replied. "There was a refuge already arranged for what Christoph carried, as you know; it lies there now. Father Bertrand brought Solomon's Sceptre. For the present, I've locked it in one of the vaults below. Were you to bring something?"

"Yes, I have Solomon's Seal," Arnault replied. "You'll want to lock it up as well." He sighed. "And you've heard nothing from any of the others?"

Luc shook his head. "No word yet. But it's early days. You've only just arrived, and you were meant to be the first. From what you've told me of conditions in France, they could come straggling in for months."

"If they weren't captured," Arnault muttered. "What about here? And in England? Will it spread outside France?"

"Hmmm, I take it that you've not yet heard about the Holy Father's latest pronouncement," Luc said sourly. "It seems there's a papal bull called *Pastoralis Praeeminentiae*. It calls for the arrest of Templars everywhere, not just in France, and orders an investigation of the allegations. Which means, it appears, that he's throwing us to the wolves—or to the king and Nogaret, which is much the same thing."

Arnault was slowly shaking his head, hardly able to believe what he was hearing.

"When did this happen?"

"Late in November, we're told, though we've yet to have sight of the actual decree. But word reached the London Temple about a fortnight ago, just ahead of the official notification to the English chancery. William de la More sent word immediately, to as many of our establishments as he could, but nothing has happened yet in England—and probably won't, at least for a month or two. The English king is traveling to France this month, to be married to a daughter of King Philip—but that probably means that pressure will be brought to bear, even if he were disposed to ignore the Holy Father's edict."

"*That* is *England*," Arnault pointed out stiffly. "This is Scotland."

"The distinction is a valid one," Luc agreed, "and not just because Bruce is kindly disposed toward the Order. With him still under excommunication, and Scotland subsequently under interdict, I doubt any Scottish bishop can be induced to enforce the order—at least not for a while. But it may be only a matter of time."

Shaking his head in disbelief, Arnault propped his elbows on the table, bowing his temples against the heels of his hands. "Dear God, this can't be happening. . . ."

Luc said nothing, only clasping a hand to Arnault's shoulder, helpless to give any other reassurance. After a few minutes, Arnault slowly raised his head.

"We must gather what remains of *le Cercle*," he said. "Send word to Christoph, and tell him that. In fact, go there yourself, when you've done what you can here."

"What will you do?" Luc asked, nodding his agreement.

"I must find Torquil," Arnault replied. "And Bruce. More than ever, I sense that much now hinges on him."

Briefly he told Luc about the mysterious message given him by the stranger called Iskander, at Chartres.

"*The Law will destroy you . . . the Law will set you free . . .*" Luc murmured, repeating what Iskander had told Arnault. "You said that was in your dream, at the Paris Temple—but how could he have known of that?"

"I don't know."

"And what Temple was he talking about?" Luc went on. "The actual Temple of Jerusalem, the Order . . . or the Fifth Temple? *Before the Temple, there was the Ark of the Covenant. . . . And before the Ark, the Covenant itself. . . .* The Covenant, the Tablets of the Law, the Word of God. . . ."

He looked up at Arnault. "Is he equating the Law with the Word? With the Tablets, maybe?"

"I don't know," Arnault repeated. "I'm hoping that one of *le Cercle* will be able to help us discover what it means— because I've been thinking on it for weeks, and I haven't. Clearly, the implications are far wider than what the Temple is currently facing."

Luc nodded, thoughtful. "Perhaps it does refer to the Fifth Temple, then."

"Perhaps it does," Arnault agreed, "because the original Temple long ago ceased to exist—and it may be that the Order, as we know it, cannot survive this. But the Fifth Temple can and must survive—*here,* in Scotland.

"And it will be an Invisible Temple, one not made with human hands—for I fear the time is coming, all too soon, when no Templar will be free to ride openly in any land, if the pope truly has abandoned us. But if our public face must vanish, there is still much we can do from behind a hidden face."

"I pray that you are right," Luc whispered, though his tone had taken on some of Arnault's earlier despondence. He sighed. "Have you any idea where to begin? For I confess that I do not."

Arnault nodded. "Only a beginning of an idea, but at least it is that. We have a little time, here in Scotland. We begin by presenting this to what remains of *le Cercle.*"

"That will take time—to gather them together," Luc pointed out. "God knows, some of them may be beyond gathering, at least in this life."

"We must pray that your fears will prove unfounded," Arnault said determinedly. "And in the meantime, we will do what we can to preserve or at least prolong the existence of the external Temple. If I can induce some of the brethren here to come away with me, I will take them with me to Bruce—and leave them with him, while I take Torquil with me to Dunkeld to meet with Christoph and the others."

"I concur," Luc said. "What would you have me do?"

"Try to persuade the others here to flee into the Western Isles," Arnault replied. "There is a place in Argyll, beyond Loch Fyne, inland from Loch Crinan. Nearby, there are monks of the foundation of Iona. Abbot Fingon told me of it. It would make a secluded staging area, for gathering together the scattering remnants of the Order, such as we can. Some from the Paris Temple will have been told to go there; others will join them, in the coming months and even years that it may take, to build ourselves a place in this land."

"I doubt that many will go," Luc said. "At least not yet. They will not believe that the Holy Father has abandoned us."

"Then we must pray that God will be merciful, when they are called before the rulers of this world," Arnault replied.

The following night, he rode out of Balantrodoch accompanied by three other knights: the only ones who were willing to put off their Templar habits and adopt the life of outlaws, for the others still were convinced that no harm could come to the Order, and that the pope would protect them.

Grigor Murray was one of those who joined Arnault, for he had witnessed the Paris riots and the growing uneasiness sparked by the visit of the king and his minister to the Paris Temple. With him came two of the younger knights, Mingo MacDonald and Douglas Lumsden. Arnault got to know them well in the next four months—for that was how long it took them to find Bruce.

During that winter, the second since Bruce's crowning as King of Scots, the fortunes of the Scottish cause vacillated between incipient disaster and occasional small strides forward. Because the new King Edward was mostly occupied with domestic unrest regarding his favorite, Piers Gaveston, Bruce was left free to concentrate on his own domestic opponents—especially the Macdougalls, the Comyns, and Argyll.

In autumn of the previous year, having made significant inroads into Galloway in the south, the rebel king had blazed northward—on the offensive, for the first time since seizing the crown—leading his army over the mountains in a bold move that enabled him to outflank an expeditionary force under John Macdougall of Lorn. In October Bruce had seized and dismantled the Comyn-held stronghold of Inverlochy. From there, he and his followers had gone on to raze the castle of Inverness.

The town of Nairn subsequently had been burned to the ground, and Urquhart Castle on Loch Ness had been reduced to rubble. Intimidated by Bruce's show of force, the Earl of Ross had sued for a truce, leaving the English defense of the northland resting on the shoulders of John Comyn of Buchan, Sir David of Brechin, and Sir John de Moubray.

By the spring of 1308, the king and his army had been in the field for most of a year. At the outset, his Templar guardians' primary concern had been to safeguard him on the battlefield, but the greatest single threat against Bruce's life had taken the form of a debilitating illness that had struck him without warning at Christmas. What had seemed at first to be nothing more serious than an attack of rheum had escalated to a raging fever that had come and gone for months, leaving the king exhausted and sometimes bringing on attacks of delirium. Encamped in the snowy wilds, with scant food and no medicine to hand, the king's devoted friends could only watch and pray over their stricken lord. Only now was it beginning to seem that he was past serious danger.

Late May of 1308 found the king and his company bivouacked on a hillside within sight of the town of Inverurie. Torquil and Aubrey had been out on a scouting foray for several hours, and returned to the fire near Bruce's tent as one of the camp cooks appeared with a steaming bowl, cocking his head in their direction.

"Brother Torquil, do ye think ye might persuade His Grace to eat sommat?" he asked.

"Is that soup you've got there?" Torquil replied. "Good! If he doesn't eat it, I will." He grinned. "Thank you, Andrew. I'll take it in to him and see if he's awake."

The king's tent was no larger than those of his men, but that made it easier to keep some semblance of warmth inside. While Aubrey waited nearby, Torquil quietly drew aside the tattered sheepskin that served as a door and ducked inside.

Bruce lay huddled under his mantle and several more heaps of tartan, on a crude pallet padded with bracken and several sheepskins. By the scant light of a tiny fire burning in a pot in the center of the tent, the king's face was a gaunt mask of jutting bones. His sunken lids were closed, but when Torquil would have withdrawn, he stirred and opened his eyes.

"What is it?" he murmured.

Torquil presented the bowl with a flourish, crouching down beside the pallet.

"Andrew of Dunskellie presents his compliments, Sire, and craves your opinion of his cooking."

"To see if it's fit for the rest of the army?" Bruce replied, doing his best to smile as he struggled to a sitting position against the saddle he was using for a pillow. "All right, let's have it."

Torquil sat with him as he ate, and did his best to answer the king's questions concerning camp morale.

"The sooner we can retake the initiative again, the better," Bruce commented between spoonfuls of soup. "I much regret that I've been such a burden, these past weeks. Have you heard further regarding the trouble with your Order?"

Torquil found himself glancing away, more concerned than he dared show the king.

"Little news reaches us here, Sire," he said noncommittally. "It—doesn't look promising."

"And you would prefer to be about their rescue rather than playing nursemaid to a sick king," Bruce guessed.

Torquil shrugged and did his best to smile. "We all have our parts to play, Sire. Sometimes, those parts seem somewhat indirect. But I do know that the Temple's fortunes are linked to those of Scotland—so serving Scotland's king also serves the Temple. And as a Scot and as a man, I am honored and glad to serve my king."

"You Templars *are* the diplomats," Bruce said with a smile—and took another spoonful of soup. Nor did he pursue the matter.

Torquil gave him further commentary on provisioning status and the condition of men and beasts in Bruce's army—anything to avoid admitting how anxious he felt on behalf of the Temple. But the Temple's plight was never far from his mind.

He knew that in France, at least, the formerly respected Knights of the Order had become universal objects of persecution. The last report from Brother Luc had detailed a grim catalog of imprisonments and interrogations. Hardest of all to bear had been the news that Arnault's young cousin Jauffre probably had been captured while assisting Christoph's escape. In addition to Christoph, he knew that Father Bertrand likewise was safely in Scotland, but he had not yet had word regarding any of the other members of *le Cercle,* including Arnault himself.

The possibility that Arnault, too, had been taken did not bear thinking about; for Torquil lately had learned that King Philip, to lend credence to his claim that he was acting in accordance with the law, had invoked the services of Guillaume de Paris, the papal inquisitor of France, who had authorized the use of torture in the examination of all Templar prisoners. Under duress, many of the brethren had confessed to crimes that included heresy, blasphemy, and sexual perversion: charges carefully calculated to stir the lurid imagination of a credulous populace, now rapidly becoming convinced of the Templars' guilt. Torquil knew that Arnault would never confess to such a pack of lies—but the consequences of *not* confessing were too terrible to contemplate.

Accordingly, Torquil had forced himself to concentrate on the more immediate dangers attendant on Bruce and his rebel army. While they waited for the king to recover, they had remained constantly on the move, deep in hostile territory, striving to keep their distance from the enemy. A clash at Huntly, a fortnight earlier, had ended indecisively after an exchange of arrow fire. The men were growing weary of being constantly on the defensive, and Torquil was no exception.

Bruce finished his soup and returned the bowl, lying back with a sigh.

"Please convey my compliments to Andrew of Dunskellie," he told Torquil wryly. "Never have I tasted a finer dandelion stew."

Before Torquil could frame a fitting response, there came an indistinct outcry from the edge of the encampment. Even as Bruce signed for Torquil to investigate, the Templar was on his feet and on the move.

Aubrey had already gone to meet two other members of the king's entourage, approaching with a wounded sentry supported between them.

"The Earl of Buchan!" the sentry gasped. "He's headed this way, with nigh on a thousand men!"

A babble of voices told Torquil that the news was already spreading through the camp, that men were rousing, arming, mounting up.

"Men of Carrick," he bellowed, taking command of the immediate situation. "Fetch the king's litter! Lindsay, get your men mounted. The infantry will march with the king while we provide the rear—"

"*No!*"

The unexpected voice cut incisively through the hubbub of alarm. Whirling round, Torquil was astonished to see Bruce himself standing at the entrance to his tent, supporting himself against the tent pole. Though he was thin as a wraith, the king's gray eyes burned with determination as he addressed his army with a volume that belied his haggard appearance.

"No, we'll not flee," Bruce went on. "For weeks we've had to let ourselves be harried like foxes before the hounds. The time has come to turn and show our teeth. Forget all thought of flight. Today we have a kingdom to win!"

This declaration drew a ragged cheer from those close by, but as the cheer spread rapidly through the ranks, Torquil shouldered his way to Bruce's side.

"Sire . . ." he began. "Robert—"

"Don't tell me what I shouldn't do," the king replied. "I've had my fill of hiding and retreating, and caution has served me ill." He drew a fortifying breath as he hauled himself straighter. "Forward is the only path left to me, and neither fear nor sickness will make me falter. Now, help me arm, and someone—fetch my horse! We're going to give Buchan the fright of his life!"

A wolfish grin transfigured his gaunt features as he made this declaration, and a ragged cheer went up from some of his men. Standing close to the king, Torquil could feel the force of the royal will emanating from him like heat from a bonfire. Excitement spread through the rebel ranks like wildfire as cavalry and infantry began forming up in ranks, hefting their weapons with purposeful intent.

Bruce stood firm as Torquil and an esquire buckled him into his hauberk and set his helmet on his head, once again crowned with a royal circlet. Robert Boyd fetched the king's sword, and offered it on bended knee. As Bruce's fingers closed around the hilt, his blue eyes lit with a possessive ferocity.

"Where is Brother Aubrey?" he demanded. "I want him

as my standard-bearer today! And Torquil—there you are! When we ride out, I want you at my other side. When we three lead the assault on our enemies, I promise you they will not stand against us! They probably think I'm dead," he added in an aside, "or at least at death's door."

"Not today, I think!" Torquil said with a chuckle, as horses were brought up—for Bruce's conviction was contagious. "Today we ride for Scotland!"

John Comyn, Earl of Buchan, cocked an ear at the sounds of a clash of arms ahead, reining back his steed as he turned to his standard-bearer.

"Excellent!" he said. "It appears our vanguard has engaged the enemy!"

A stir of anticipation raced through the front ranks of Buchan's heavy cavalry, ranged to either side. To his rear, the spearmen, archers, and clan levies started jostling forward, craning and murmuring as they pressed up behind the ranks of their betters, eager to catch a glimpse of the action.

Just then, a knot of horsemen burst from the trees ahead, bolting down the slope at breakneck speed, with weapons trailing and plaids flapping. Buchan took a second look and reined short with a curse.

"Hell's teeth, those are Brechin's men!"

The first of the onrushing riders converged in a sweaty lather of panic.

"Run for it!" one of them shouted.

Buchan grabbed for the bridle of the first rider he could reach and wrenched the horse around to a standstill.

"Who the devil are you running from, ye glaikit coward?" he bellowed.

"The Bruce!" the rider cried, white-eyed, trying to rip his reins free. "He's no nearer dying than you are! It was all a trick to lure us in. And now he's after us, thirsting for blood!"

Buchan's consternation caused him to release his grip.

"That's impossible!" he snapped, though he could feel the blood draining from his face.

"There he is now!" someone yelled, pointing behind them. "With a host o' Hieland de'ils at his back!"

Even as the cry rang out, the trees disgorged a hostile line of horsemen with weapons at the ready, Bruce himself conspicuous at their center. Mounted on a shaggy Highland-bred steed, sword in hand, he was flanked by two knights as tall as himself, with the battle standards of Saint Andrew and the royal lion of the Scottish crown snapping above their heads.

Bruce and his mounted entourage were backed by a formidable array of infantry, all of them apparently fired by their king's presence. To the horror of Buchan and his men, the assembled spearmen and archers formed up smartly into disciplined ranks behind their mounted captains, weapons at the ready.

"For Scotland and liberty!" Bruce roared—and gave the signal to charge.

The rebel host poured down the slope like a great wave, smashing into the ranks of Buchan's men with the penetrating force of a battering ram. Men and horses foundered and fell, impaled on thickets of spears, their screams mingling with the sound of battle cries.

Buchan's knights wheeled this way and that, vainly trying to defend themselves, but the rebels swarmed about them like wasps, giving no quarter. As the fighting grew heavier, a wail went up from the ranks of the defenders.

"There's no stopping the Bruce! Even death can't hinder him!"

Buchan's battle began to buckle.

"Stand your ground, damn you!" the earl cried.

But panic had already taken over, as Buchan's men began scattering, fleeing. His cavalry galloped off at full speed while his footmen were cut down from behind as they tripped and stumbled over one another in their flight. Bruce and his cavalry made ruthless pursuit, spreading carnage through the broken ranks of the enemy.

"On!" Bruce cried hoarsely. "Let's make an end of it, *here*!"

He tried to urge his own horse forward, but his strength was fast fading, and he suddenly paled and drooped over the pommel of his saddle.

"That's enough!" Torquil insisted, reaching over to yank in the reins of Bruce's horse. "The day is won!"

Together, he and Aubrey escorted the king from the field, leaving Boyd and Lindsay and Bruce's other lieutenants to mop up. Back amid the deserted confines of the camp, the two Templars helped Bruce from the saddle, Aubrey supporting him while Torquil removed his helmet. The king was grinning raggedly, though a feverish sweat had broken out on his brow.

"So, do you still think we should have retreated through the woods?" he asked.

Torquil answered with a slow shake of his head, but there was admiration in his voice. "You risk yourself too readily, Sire."

"So *you* say." Bruce managed a labored chuckle as Aubrey helped him sit. "I say that no medicine would so soon have cured me as this chance to show our enemies our mettle."

He drew a deep, somewhat labored breath. "Now that we've put Comyn and his cronies to flight, we'll harry this country into submission so that I may never be troubled from this quarter again. I must have the Highlands secure at my back."

"So we must, Sire," Torquil murmured. "I only pray you do not push yourself too far or too fast."

Chapter Twenty-six

May-June, 1308

Only when he was assured by his scouts and commanders that Buchan's army was utterly routed and his own position secured did Bruce agree to return to his sickbed.

Even from there, however, he continued to issue orders before taking a grudging nap. By evening he was up again, shakily doing the rounds of the campfires and warmly commending his men for their bravery, offering encouragement to those who were tired and far from their families.

To those who had been wounded he gave special attention, bringing comfort and fortitude by his presence. Casualties, happily, had been few, testifying to the completeness of the rebel victory.

It was after dark when a sudden cry from one of the sentries announced the approach of several armed riders. The newcomers were quickly surrounded by bristling guards, anxious of the safety of their king even here in the midst of his camp, but the lead rider reined in submissively and slowly dismounted as Aubrey pushed his way to the fore on the king's behalf, to investigate.

"Identify yourself," he started to order—and broke off as

the newcomer shook back his hood, merely chuckling, and a familiar pair of blue eyes gazed back at him.

"Arnault!" he blurted.

"It's good to see you, too, Aubrey," Arnault responded with a smile. "Is Torquil anywhere around?"

"Yes, but—" Aubrey was peering past Arnault, where more men were dismounting, men he had only seen previously with beards, and wearing Templar white. Two of them he knew well: Mingo MacDonald and Douglas Lumsden, youngsters like himself. The face of the third was vaguely familiar, but he could not recall the man's name.

"You've brought reinforcements," he noted lamely—then added, "Come, I'll take you to Brother Torquil."

"The last time I saw the king," Arnault said, as Aubrey gestured toward the back of a cloaked figure sitting by a fire, "he said I'd find him wherever the fighting was."

Torquil stiffened slightly, then turned and set aside a half-eaten bowl of porridge, grinning as he got to his feet.

"Well, it's about time!"

The two thumped one another on the back as they briefly embraced. Both had gone grayer in the two years since their last meeting, and new lines etched both their faces.

"Arnault, it's good to see you. How have you fared?" he asked quietly, not sure he wanted to hear the answer.

Arnault heaved a weary sigh, but did his best to summon up a smile.

"A good deal better than many. But before we say more about that, I must first ask you how it is with the king. Rumors in the Lowlands have put him at death's door from a winter illness."

"Thankfully, those rumors are weeks out-of-date," Torquil responded with a grin. "Today he celebrated his recovery by personally leading a highly successful foray against the Earl of Buchan."

Arnault's expression brightened. "Ah, then that explains

the stragglers we saw, coming here, and the atmosphere of high spirits about the camp. I've brought a few reinforcements," he added, at Torquil's look of inquiry at his use of *we*. "Only three—but as you know, three Templars are worth any thirty ordinary men." They both grinned. "If the king's receiving visitors, I'd better pay my respects."

"I'd join you," Aubrey interjected, reluctantly hanging back, "but I'm due on watch. You won't mind repeating yourself later, will you?"

"I promise to catch you up on all the news," Arnault replied, clapping the younger man on the shoulder. "Meanwhile, you might talk to the others. The two young ones don't know a great deal, but Grigor was in Paris with me for a while."

"*Grigor* was in Paris?" Torquil repeated, somewhat incredulously. "His French is terrible!"

"Aye, he hardly speaks it at all," Aubrey chimed in.

"He speaks it better now than he did," Arnault replied with a wink in Aubrey's direction. "I made him practice. Now, get you gone, cousin. Torquil and I must speak to the king."

Aubrey snorted and took his leave with a wave that was almost a salute. On their way to the royal tent, Torquil furnished Arnault with a concise account of their progress since Bruce's landing at Carrick.

"Our campaign had been gaining steady momentum when he fell ill at Christmas," Torquil concluded. "He's been a long time recovering, but fortunately, his enemies haven't been able to take advantage of his weakness—and now that he's convalescent, I don't foresee them regaining the initiative. As we saw today, the mere sight of him, sick or well, has become a weapon he can use against his foes."

"Then perhaps there's still hope," Arnault murmured, too softly for Torquil to overhear.

They found Bruce sitting by his campfire, dictating a letter to one of his clerks.

"Pardon the interruption, Sire," Torquil said as Bruce looked up, "but here's an unexpected guest seeking an audience."

"Brother Arnault!" The king did not rise, but his elation was patently genuine. "Praise God, you've returned to us in a happy hour! Only yesterday, you would have found me moping in my bed. Today you see us celebrating a triumph."

"So Torquil has been telling me," Arnault replied. "I understand that you sent Comyn of Buchan packing, with his men's tails between their legs. My congratulations."

"God grant we may have more such victories," Bruce said. "Will you take some refreshment after your journey?"

"Perhaps later, Sire—if you don't mind. Torquil and I have a great deal of catching up to do—and the sooner, the better."

"So be it, then. Of the little I have here at this camp, whatever you need is at your disposal. Later, you and I will talk."

"Yes, Sire. And thank you."

Once the two Templars had retired to a sheltered knoll, safely out of earshot of the rest of the company, Torquil was able to stop pretending he hadn't noticed the anxiety Arnault had been at pains to conceal since his arrival.

"So, how bad is it?" he said, trying to read the other's expression in the moonlight. "Is it true that Jauffre was captured?"

Drooping visibly, Arnault sank down on a rock, nodding.

"Torquil, I would give my right arm to deny it, but I can't. My one consolation is that his capture probably bought Christoph's escape—and the safety of the Shroud." Arnault briefly glanced away. "So far, Christoph and Bertrand are the only ones besides myself to show up at Balantrodoch."

"Dear God. . . ." Torquil sank down blindly beside Arnault. "Do you think the rest were taken, too?"

"It's too soon to know. If the others had the same kinds of problems I had, they might just be delayed." He shook his head. "Anyway, we need to meet with Christoph and

Bertrand and decide what to do. They've gone to Dunkeld, to be near the Stone. Bishop Crambeth has given them sanctuary. I think we ought to bring Aubrey as well."

Torquil blinked. "You do recall that he isn't yet a full member of *le Cercle*?"

"I think he's going to have to *become* one, and rather sooner than any of us thought. We no longer have the luxury of long apprenticeships."

"I suppose not," Torquil murmured, stunned. "I—don't think Bruce is going to want to let us go, though."

"He must," Arnault replied. "And I *have* brought him three other Templars to replace us. And gold. Of course, they can't replace all that we do—but they can certainly help to keep his physical person safe. That will have to do, for now."

Torquil let out an audible sigh. "You're going to have to tell him at least a little of why we're leaving."

"I intend to tell him everything. He already knows a great deal of it," Arnault added, at Torquil's look of shock. "In times as benighted as these, it serves no purpose to keep one another in the dark."

True to his word, he held nothing back when it came time to take Bruce into their confidence. Following Arnault's terse recital, the king was silent for a long moment, head bowed in thought.

"You are free to go, of course," he finally said, "though I would rather give up a hundred of my best men than lose either of you—or young Aubrey, for that matter. But I have seen enough in your company not to doubt what you have told me—and to take heart from the fact that what you do is for this land as well as your Order."

"We have long known that the needs of the two are intertwined," Arnault pointed out.

"I will accept your word for it," Bruce said with a smile. "I don't pretend to understand even half of what you've told me. But I will always be grateful for the help you have rendered in bringing me this far along the road. Accordingly, if there is anything I can do in return, you know you have only to name it."

"Then, simply carry on as you have done," Arnault replied. "For now, that is the best any man could ask. For our part, we will do what we must do, to prepare the way for our part in your final goal."

Bruce gave a wan smile. "The doing will be harder than the asking, I have no doubt. But my own objectives will remain unchanged: to set Scotland free from foreign domination. Only then will we be at liberty to establish a government where justice and respect for individual liberties will be the rule of law."

"If we succeed," said Torquil, "Scotland will become the envy and model of other nations for generations to come."

Bruce summoned a crooked smile. "Then, it seems we each have our own separate wars to fight, at least for a while—our edifices to build, our statutes to forge. But if— God willing—we are both victorious, the legacy we hand on to future generations will be something wondrous, indeed!"

"Amen to that!" Arnault said.

Aubrey confessed himself somewhat surprised to learn that he was being included in the foray to Dunkeld.

"I'd expected to stay behind with Grigor and the others," he said. "Shouldn't *someone* stay, who is known to the king? Besides, you don't need a junior knight like me along."

"Aubrey," Torquil said mildly, "in case you hadn't noticed—and apparently, you hadn't—you're no longer a junior knight."

"But, the king—"

"Your recognition of the need for his safety is part of the reason you're no longer a junior knight," Arnault pointed out. "But he'll be safe enough until we've finished at Dunkeld. After yesterday, the English won't be back right away. In the meantime, are you going to make me invoke your vow of obedience?"

"No, of course not. It's just that—well, I wasn't expecting—"

"This is about the Inner Order, Aubrey," Torquil said quietly. "We'll talk about it more along the way."

"Oh," was all Aubrey said.

Arnault spent most of the next day conferring with Bruce and then briefing the three Templars who would remain with the king. He, Torquil, and Aubrey left the following morning, lightly provisioned and mounted on sturdy Highland ponies.

They expected that the journey to Dunkeld might take as long as a fortnight, but a run of good weather enabled them to shave several days off that estimate. Only at the end did the weather worsen, so that they emerged from a thickening mist as they rode at last through the gates to the abbey yard adjoining Dunkeld Cathedral. It was just dusk on the Eve of Saint John.

"We're here to see Bishop Crambeth," Arnault told the young novices who came to take their ponies, since he saw no immediate sign of any of their Templar colleagues.

"Yes, m'lord," one of the novices replied, nervously eyeing the three travel-worn men in fighting harness. "What name shall I give His Grace?"

"Arnault de Saint Clair. He knows me."

"Yes, m'lord."

The three of them withdrew into the shelter of a roof overhang to wait as the ponies were led away and the one novice disappeared into a slype passageway. They had seen no sign of any English presence as they approached Dunkeld, so they probably were safe enough within its precincts. Because of King Edward's withdrawal down to London, and the ineptitude of the governor he had left to oversee matters in Scotland, the English presence north of the Border had become largely confined to the areas surrounding the four Lowland castles of Berwick, Roxburgh, Edinburgh, and Stirling. Many Lowland lords had taken advantage of that fact, including Dunkeld's bishop, Matthew Crambeth.

Crambeth had been less actively militant in his support of Bruce than men like Lamberton and Wishart and Scone's Abbot Henry, all of whom now languished in captivity in the south of England, but this more outwardly neutral stance had enabled Crambeth to retain his episcopal seat—and, in secret, to continue providing a safe hiding place for the Stone of Destiny. Here, as well, he had gathered around himself a body of like-minded clerics, quietly committed to fostering the independence of the Scottish Church.

It was to Crambeth that Arnault had told Luc to send the other surviving members of *le Cercle* as they checked in; and it was Crambeth himself who came out to meet them, simply dressed in the plain black habit worn by the cathedral's regular canons. He had been present on that night they had wed Bruce to the Stone of Destiny, between the king's two public crownings, and he had been the Stone's faithful guardian in the two years since.

"Brother Arnault, thank God you've arrived," he murmured, drawing the three newcomers to him with a shepherding motion. "And Brother Torquil." He nodded to Aubrey as well, though he did not know him. "Come inside, all of you. You won't attract such notice. I've already had the others summoned. The news bodes ill for your Order. Very ill, indeed. I'll tell you more when we're safely inside."

Arnault and Torquil exchanged wary glances as they passed into the cloister yard and along the east range, but they followed the bishop without question, Aubrey trailing them wide-eyed.

"I fear that several of the particular brothers you were expecting may have been arrested in France," Crambeth murmured as they walked. "It's known that a Brother Oliver was taken, and your Brother Gaspar is likewise missing. I quite liked him."

"Dear God. . . ." Torquil whispered.

But Arnault signed him to silence until Crambeth had led them on through the abbey church and into his own house, where Christoph and Luc were closeted with the two Templar priests, Bertrand and Anselmo, poring over a map. Luc was now clean-shaven like the priests, all four of them now garbed, like Crambeth, in plain black robes.

Beyond them, one more Templar sat slumped on a bench set against the wall: a white-faced Flannan Fraser, stripped down to a ragged arming tunic, having his arm tended by two white-robed Columban brothers.

"He's fine," said the taller one with flaxen hair, with a reassuring glance at Arnault. "It was only a dislocation."

Relieved—for the pair were Brothers Ninian and Fionn, from Iona—Arnault turned his attention to the more urgent question of the news Crambeth had mentioned.

"Christoph, what's happened?" he demanded, as soon as the bishop had closed the door behind them. "Are Gaspar and Oliver truly taken?"

Christoph slowly laid aside a pair of calipers.

"Oliver was, about a week after the arrests began," he said quietly. "They're holding him with the Grand Master and several other senior officers of the Paris Temple. We don't yet know about Gaspar, but it doesn't look good."

"Could he simply have been delayed?" Arnault asked.

"The rest of us scattered from the Paris Temple, right after you'd left," Anselmo said. "That's the last anyone has seen of him."

At a light rap on the door behind him, Crambeth turned to admit Armand Breville, Hugues de Curzon, and Hamish Kerr, the latter a fairly recent Scottish initiate of *le Cercle*. The three apparently had been here for some little while, because all were clean-shaven like the others, and robed in black.

"That's everyone who has shown up thus far," Christoph said, waving the three newcomers into the room. "Brother Aubrey, stay by the door, if you would, so that His Grace can join us here. Gentlemen . . ."

He gestured toward the benches and chairs around the table, taking charge, and Arnault dutifully sank down between Torquil and Brother Fionn as the others took places. At Torquil's gesture, Aubrey pulled a three-legged stool over beside the door and hunkered down on that.

Flannan remained on the bench against the wall, with his arm now in a sling, apparently in no little discomfort, for Brother Ninian stayed seated beside him. At Arnault's glance of question, Brother Fionn murmured, "He arrived a few hours ago. His shoulder had been dislocated for weeks. Putting it back was not easy—or pleasant. But he'll be all right."

Arnault grimaced in sympathy, but at least Flannan had won free. Gaspar, however . . .

He glanced at Christoph, reluctant to ask what he knew he must.

"If Gaspar has been taken," he said, when everyone had settled, "I'm obliged to ask which of the Treasures he was carrying."

A flicker of reluctance passed over Christoph's handsome face.

"The High Priest's Breastplate."

The words rang leaden, like a funeral bell, lodging in a queasy knot in Arnault's gut. Of all the Treasures possessed by the Temple, the Breastplate was one of the most precious, especially in their present circumstances, for it was the essential mystical counterpart to the Stone of Destiny. Without it, how could they hope to secure the foundations for the Fifth Temple?

"We don't yet know that it's definitely lost," Arnault found himself saying, though without much conviction.

"Who brought the news that makes you think Gaspar was captured?"

Christoph nodded toward Flannan Fraser.

"Flannan?" Arnault said, hopeful but dreading a response.

Flannan opened his eyes, but his gaze drifted to a patch of damp where the far wall met the ceiling.

"Each of us had devised a separate escape route," he said dully. "Gaspar planned to make for La Legue, on the north coast of Brittany. We had arranged that I should meet him there with one of our galleys, but a week went by—and then two—and he didna come."

He closed his eyes again as he went on, pain broadening his Scottish accent.

"I couldna wait forever. By late October, two French warships had started sniffin' round, so I had to sail or risk capture myself. Through the winter, I had the crew land me at different places on the coast of Brittany, in hopes I might pick up some trace of him—but I never did. And I nearly got caught myself, the last time I tried—which is how I got my shoulder hurt.

"I did have separate inquiries made at the places where other Templars are being held," he added, finally glancing at Arnault, "but there's nae sign of him. Which means that he's likely killed, rather than captured."

"It also means," Christoph said, when Flannan did not continue, "that the Breastplate may have fallen into the hands of our enemies."

Silence followed this declaration. The Templars looked thunderstruck, to a man. It was Ninian who finally spoke.

"There may be a way to at least find out."

All eyes turned toward the Columban brother as he left Flannan and came over to the table.

"The Breastplate is linked to the Stone of Destiny, yes?" Ninian said, standing with a hand on Arnault's shoulder.

"Of course."

"And though we do not have the Breastplate, we do have the Stone."

All of the Templars exchanged puzzled glances as they nodded.

"It is also, true—is it not?—that a mystical bond will have been forged between the Stone and those who presided at Bruce's enthronement upon it," Ninian went on. "Of those present both then and now, besides myself, that would be Bishop Matthew and Brothers Arnault, Torquil, and Luc. And Brother Gaspar was present, as well."

Those named glanced uncertainly among themselves.

"Brother Ninian," Christoph said softly, "what are you suggesting?"

With a faint smile, Ninian swept his arm in a gesture for all of them to rise.

"I think it might be best if all of us adjourned to the premises of the Stone. I shall explain when we are there," he added, holding up a hand to silence the questions that started to erupt. "Brother Matthew, perhaps you would go first, to make certain the way is clear. We shall follow in twos and threes."

A quarter hour later, all of them had made their way to the narrow crypt beneath the cathedral, converging on a small chapel beneath the east end, where the Stone now resided. The air was redolent with the scent of cinnamon, sandalwood, and the beeswax of the candles some of the brethren were lighting in the trefoil sconces set along the walls. Once again, the junior Aubrey was set to keep watch at the door.

The Stone itself lay beneath an altar made of wood, set over it like an overturned box and dressed with fair linens, silver candlesticks, and a cross carved with Celtic interlace. These Ninian bade them remove before directing four of the Templars to lift away the altar shell and move it into the undercroft, exposing the Stone to their view.

Not speaking, Brother Ninian knelt beside the Stone and

lightly laid his hand upon it, head bowed for several seconds, then rose and glanced around him.

"Brother Arnault, would you please sit on the Stone?"

The presumption took Arnault aback.

"I dare not. That is not my place," he began.

"It is the place of him who serves the Stone and its king," Ninian said calmly. "Such a man *must* dare, if he would work with the Stone to search for Brother Gaspar, wherever he may be, among the living or the dead. If the latter, you will need its power and protection."

Arnault felt his pulsebeat booming in his ears, making him feel a little light-headed as he glanced among the others, but not even Bishop Crambeth appeared to doubt that the request must be honored. The Bishop of Dunkeld, though neither of *le Cercle* nor even of the Temple, was proving to be a man of steady nerve and no little faith.

Not speaking, Arnault unbuckled his sword and handed it to Torquil, who wrapped its belt around the scabbard before laying it aside behind them. He drew a fortifying breath and let it out before seating himself gingerly upon the Stone, where Bruce had sat. Lightning did not smite him, and the Stone did not strike him dead.

Relieved, he took another deep breath, though he could not say he was as confident as he might have been, had he known what to expect. But he trusted the Columban implicitly—which was a good thing, because Ninian seemed to be inventing this as they went along.

At Ninian's direction, Bishop Crambeth came to stand behind him, providing a back to lean against, steadying hands set on his shoulders. Torquil and Luc came to stand to either side—for all three had been present on that night, in addition to Arnault and the missing Gaspar. Arnault could fathom the reasoning behind the arrangement, and that was reassuring. Ninian was rummaging for something in a waist pouch as the rest came to kneel around the Stone in a semicircle, expectant faces upturned.

"Let us begin our work," Ninian said softly, lifting his closed right hand before and above Arnault's eyes, perhaps a handspan away. "In the name of our blessed Columba and Cra-gheal, the Red-White One, I ask you to commend yourself to their protection and to the Grace of the Three, and to gaze upon this stone, from the shores of the Holy Island of Iona."

He opened his hand to display a sea-polished pebble the size of a seagull egg. "And as you gaze upon it, dear brother, I ask you to focus all of your heart and soul and mind upon that one, all-encompassing task of these next few moments, where time has no meaning . . ."

Arnault gladly obeyed, fixing his gaze on the sea pebble and letting himself drift with Ninian's voice, a part of him reconnecting with the peace and serenity of life on Iona with the gentle Columbans and their saint.

"Make yourself one with the Stone on which you sit," Ninian went on, "wherein resides the Sovereignty of this Land, and the hallowing of its king, whom you serve . . . and who serves the Land, and the Lord of that Land and of its king, and the building of His Fifth Temple, which shall be built not with human hands but with the love and the will of those who serve God and His creation. . . ."

Ninian's voice seemed to ebb and flow like the tides, gently submerging Arnault in the embracing warmth of a pool of sound and taking him into a detached, floating space where only the pebble and the voice remained. As the pebble slowly began moving downward, Arnault's eyes followed without resistance, consciousness likewise descending into ever-deeper realms of receptivity and awareness.

By the time the pebble touched his open hand, his eyes had closed and he had surrendered utterly to the peacefulness in which he was enfolded. Only the faintest thread of Ninian's voice remained outside of that centered expectation into which he had descended, gently nudging him now toward the task set before him.

"Your brother Gaspar is linked to the Stone as you are," Ninian whispered. "Reach out for him. Call to him. See the place where he now dwells. . . ."

At that bidding, Arnault found himself standing in spirit before a heavy door set deep within a rounded arch. The door stood slightly ajar.

Slowly, hesitantly, he pushed it open and stepped through. Beyond lay a chapel, lofty and full of light. The far wall was pierced by a sun-flooded window like a jeweled flower, before which stood an alabaster statue of the Blessed Virgin, crowned with roses still kissed by the morning dew. Bright lancet windows cut the walls to either side, throwing swaths of rainbow light that intersected in midair like a pair of crossed swords.

Beneath this crossing of light, a white-cloaked figure in Templar livery knelt in an attitude of adoration, bearded face upturned toward the Virgin, amid a hush so profound that all nature seemed to hold its breath. The face in profile was faintly luminous, serenely contemplative, and suffused with gentle wonder. The hawklike features belonged to the man Arnault had come to find.

"Gaspar," he called softly, reluctant to disturb the silence. "Gaspar, I must speak with you."

Gaspar slowly turned his head and blinked, like a sleeper awakening, but he seemed not at all surprised at Arnault's presence. A welcoming smile crossed his lips, almost as if he had been expecting the younger man's coming.

"For as long as I can remember, I've been wanting to go home," Gaspar confided. "To return to the place where I took my first vows, and where I was baptized as a babe, is to feel myself reborn. That you should come to visit me here makes my joy the more complete."

The prismatic light from the rose window encompassed him like a halo of jewels as he stood, dappling his white mantle with rainbow glints. To Arnault it seemed almost blasphemous to disturb the peace of this place, but the urgency of his quest had left him no choice.

"It is duty that brings me here," he said quietly. "There are things I must know, on behalf of the Order—questions only you can answer."

A shadow flickered across Gaspar's face, like a premonition of pain, but Arnault forced himself to continue.

"Where now is the Breastplate which *le Cercle* committed to your care?"

Regret lit behind Gaspar's eyes, leaving them cold and bleak. The warm glow of the chapel collapsed into wintry chill as a harsh series of cracks shivered the windows, and broken glass fell like rain, filling the air with dissonant chiming. Even as Arnault recoiled, the chapel itself disintegrated.

Splintered images swirled around him like leaves in a whirlwind, seizing him and spinning him into darkness. When it cleared, he found himself standing not in a chapel, but on a high, stone-built bridge.

At his feet lay the reeking carcass of a horse newly dead. A few paces off, two armored figures struggled breast to breast, their locked swords slippery with blood. The older of the two was Gaspar; the beringed hand of the younger twisted and disengaged as he whirled out of Gaspar's reach and another darted in.

Gaspar was gasping with exertion. This new opponent was but one of a succession he had fought off, only to have another, fresher foe take his place from a pack of nearly a dozen armed men clumped near the bridgehead, swords at the ready, awaiting their turns. As he fought off more of them, Gaspar glanced longingly at the chance of escape behind him, but before he could decide to run for it or resume the fight, his current adversary made a lightning lunge, driving his blade up and under the Templar's laboring ribs.

The blade twisted as Gaspar wrenched away from it in reflex, doing more damage. He knew the wound was bad, but he kept fighting, for he had no choice. And when he knew his strength was nearing an end, and that death was edging nearer, he drew back and reversed his sword end for end to hurl it desperately at a rider sitting a tall bay at the bridge-head.

He dimly heard the clangor as it hit the cobbled pavement, but by then he was spending the last of his strength to twist around and fall hard against the edge of the bridge's parapet. As he tumbled over, and he felt consciousness and life slipping free, his lips were moving in a plea for Heaven's mercy, and his last conscious act was to sketch the sign of his faith in final commendation to the God he had tried to serve.

And Arnault plunged after him. As the murky water closed over his head, his groping fingers found Gaspar's, but an icy darkness enveloped him, flooding into his lungs. United with Gaspar in watery death, he felt himself sinking under the weight of the current until his body struck bottom with a jolt.

Gaspar's hand left his, and the river vanished. Arnault gasped for breath, and drew blessed air into his lungs. When his vision cleared, he again was standing with Gaspar in the light-drenched chapel. The older knight now wore the guise Arnault remembered from the morning of their departure from Paris, clad as a simple soldier.

"You have seen my ending in body," he said with a trace of sadness. "I ran my course, gave my all, but I could not win free. Yet I do not regret losing my earthly life in the service of the Order. If my prayers were answered, the river carried my body to the sea—and with it, what I tried to safeguard for the Temple. But I do not know its fate after that."

"Nor do I," Arnault replied, though it occurred to him that he had recognized the man on the horse, at whom Gaspar had thrown his sword. If Guillaume de Nogaret had somehow retrieved the Breastplate from Gaspar's body . . .

"I don't know," Arnault repeated, "but I intend to find out.

Meanwhile, no one can fault you for your courage, Gaspar. You gave all you had, against terrible odds. I regret the necessity to make you relive it."

"And *I* regret that this knowledge is of so little use to you," Gaspar replied.

"Perhaps it will be of more use than you think," Arnault said, putting all the comfort and assurance he could muster into his words. "Let others be the judge of that. Believe me when I tell you this battle is far from over!"

He clasped the other Templar's hand and wrist in his own as knight to knight, in farewell, for he could feel the Stone calling him back to his own body.

"On behalf of your brothers of *le Cercle*, I give you thanks," he said to Gaspar. "May God, in His infinite mercy, make your peace henceforth abiding. Good-bye, my brother—and my friend."

With these words, he released his grip and the link. The instant of parting turned the world briefly askew, ending with an almost-physical jolt. When Arnault opened his eyes, he was sitting on the Stone again, gazing at a sea pebble in his hands.

Chapter Twenty-seven

June, 1308

ARNAULT KEPT HIMSELF A LITTLE DETACHED AS HE REported what he had experienced, sighing inwardly to see the hope in their eyes give way to grief, anger, and frustration. Before settling in to analyze his revelations, they adjourned back to Bishop Crambeth's house. Though their subsequent business largely concerned the Order—and its secret workings, at that—Crambeth was permitted to stay, since he was the Stone's guardian.

"If that was, indeed, Nogaret himself who caught up with Gaspar," Christoph said, when they had gathered again around the bishop's table, "I think we must assume that he now has the Breastplate."

"How could he have known?" Hugues wondered aloud. "Why pursue Gaspar, in preference to any other Templar fleeing the Temple that morning?"

"Does it really matter why?" said Father Bertrand. "Though I certainly agree that I would like to know how he knew."

"Is there any chance that Nogaret did *not* recover the body?" Flannan asked, his face still taut with discomfort from his injured shoulder.

"Very little, I should think," Christoph said. "Clearly, Gaspar did his best to prevent his body from being taken—and with it, what he carried. However, he was wearing mail. I think it most unlikely that the current was strong enough to carry him away."

"Perhaps," said Armand Breville, speaking for the first time, "we should examine this account from another angle."

All eyes turned in his direction.

"It is clear that Gaspar did not survive," Breville went on, "but I wonder whether we dare to assume that he was taken by agents of the French crown."

"Nogaret led them," Flannan pointed out. "If *he* is not an agent . . ."

"Oh, he is Philip's agent—make no mistake," Breville replied, "but Philip may not be his only master. If Gaspar had been captured or killed in any official capacity, much would have been made of it, especially given what he carried.

"But Nogaret has taken great pains to keep the matter secret. In him, I think we are looking at an enemy far more knowledgeable and far more dangerous than either the King of France, the Inquisitor of Paris, or even the Holy Father."

Hamish Kerr turned to him in some surprise. "You now count the Holy Father as our enemy?" he asked.

"He has allowed the arrests to go forward," Breville pointed out. "And he has excommunicated your king, and placed your country under interdict."

Christoph lifted a hand in a gesture indicating that the exchange had best be dropped.

"Enough, Armand. What makes you believe that Nogaret is so dangerous? I point out that he is one man."

"And had assistance in running Gaspar to ground—men who may have been more than mere retainers." Breville turned to Arnault. "Would you do me the favor of examining your own memories more closely?"

"Certainly. Which details do you wish me to consider?"

"You mentioned that one of the men Gaspar fought was wearing a ring on his sword hand. Were any of the other men wearing rings?"

Casting back in memory, Arnault realized that many of them were.

"Yes, several."

"Do you think that any of these rings might have been alike? Can you describe any of those rings?"

"They were gold, with . . . black stones," Arnault reported, eyes closing as he strained for detail. "Signet rings," he decided. "Gaspar only got a real look at one, but . . ."

He pressed Ninian's pebble to his forehead, trying to visualize the ring on the hand of the man who had given Gaspar his mortal wound, doing his best to maintain the balance between what he had *actually* seen, and what he simply *wanted* to have seen.

"The detail is harder to make out—it was only dawn—but it . . . looks to me like some kind of . . . bird!"

He broke off abruptly and opened his eyes, stunned.

"Armand, it was a black swan!"

"I perceive we are of one mind," Breville observed, nodding. "It is what I feared." Raising his voice, he addressed the rest of the company. "The signet Brother Arnault has just described is the badge of the Brotherhood of the Black Swan. For those of you who have not heard of it, they are a fraternity of black alchemists, without scruples or any moral sense, whose aim is to wreak havoc among the forces of Light."

"Do you know Nogaret to be one of them?" Hugues asked.

"Not specifically," came Breville's reply. "But I have another name for us to conjure with: Bartholeme de Challon."

"I have heard that name," Luc said, as Torquil, too, pricked up his ears. "Pray, continue."

"Some of you will have heard parts of this story before," Breville explained. "How a French knight by that name, displaying a signet ring emblazoned with a black swan, appeared at the English court last year and ingratiated himself with the English king. Soon after, he attended a royal banquet at which a pair of black swans were featured as heraldic relics upon which the old king and others, including the then-Prince of Wales, swore a grand oath to spare no effort until the rebels of Scotland were vanquished.

"This Bartholeme de Challon subsequently joined the English king's household retinue, and became a close confidant of John Macdougall of Lorn. The pair traveled to Scotland with the English invasion force, where their arrival coincides with the commencement of a series of sorcerous attacks directed against Robert Bruce."

"This is true!" Torquil murmured. "I was with Bruce!"

"At Methven," Breville continued, "the English army was supplied with uncannily exact information that led them straight to Bruce's encampment. Both Challon and Lorn were present on that campaign. The English army then traveled west, shortly before the battle at Dail Righ, where some of our Templar brothers first sighted a malignant entity in the form of a great black bird.

"This same demon-bird attacked the king after his landing at Turnberry Point, where Brother Torquil was hardpressed to drive it away, but he did it serious damage. That incident marks the end of these attacks, so far as we know," Breville concluded, "and I have since confirmed that Bartholeme de Challon later returned to France, much reduced in health, only recently returning to court—and to the service of Nogaret, quite possibly with the intention of playing an active part in the arrest of the Templars."

This conjecture raised a murmur that quickly ceased as Hugues de Curzon spoke.

"It seems, then, that at least one of us must go back to France, to learn more about this Bartholeme de Challon and the Knights of the Black Swan," he said. "I notice that you do not link him specifically to the men who apprehended

Gaspar. Do you anticipate that he could lead us to those who did?"

"Perhaps," Breville said. "In any case, this falls to me. I fear the fires of the Inquisition far less than I fear what will become of our brotherhood, if we fail to recover the Breastplate."

"Could these Knights of the Black Swan actually *use* the Breastplate?" Father Bertrand asked thoughtfully. "Has it not become attuned to a selected few amongst us, like Arnault and Gaspar, so that others could not harness its powers without a like attunement?"

"That *might* protect it," Father Anselmo conceded. "But if they could not control it, might they take steps to destroy or damage it, in order to deprive us of its benefits?"

"I doubt they would go so far—at least not immediately," Arnault said. "Those who embark on the Dark Roads do so because they crave power. Our enemies are more likely to cherish the Breastplate as long as they think there's a possibility of mastering its mysteries for themselves."

Hamish Kerr was shaking his head worriedly. "Could they really do that?"

"I hope not," Christoph said. "The Breastplate is a priestly artifact. The authority to invoke its powers comes only through sacramental transmission—by the shared fact of a religious vocation or by the laying on of hands. But I wouldn't swear there isn't a way to circumvent this requirement. And we can be quite sure that if such a method exists, our enemies will find it."

"In that case," said Breville, "the sooner I leave for France, the better."

"And what becomes of our intention to raise the Fifth Temple?" Father Anselmo asked. "We do still have free access to the Stone of Destiny. Might it be possible, do you think, to substitute some other priestly hallow for the Breastplate, in order to set the foundation of the Fifth Temple?"

"Possibly," Christoph conceded, when no one else spoke.

"But it could take years to discover what and how. The Breastplate was fashioned in strict accordance with instructions given by God. Its powers are directly ascribable to the *Urim* and *Thummin,* the Lights and Perfections, which spring from celestial origins. No other artifact in the history of the Hebrew people has such powerful associations with the Divine Word of God, with the possible exception of the Tablets of the Law and the Ark of the Covenant."

The mention of the Law smote Arnault like a physical blow.

The Law will destroy you; the Law will set you free. . . .

He started up involuntarily, and blurted, "That's it! That's what Iskander was talking about!"

All eyes turned his way.

"Who is Iskander?" Breville asked, though Luc and Torquil began nodding excitedly.

Arnault recounted his encounter at Chartres, for the benefit of those who had not yet heard the tale.

"His words almost had the ring of Holy Writ—certainly the resonance of prophecy," Arnault said. *"Before the Temple, there was the Ark of the Covenant. And before the Ark, there was the Covenant itself. The voice of God spoke, and the Tablets of the Law received the sacred Word. And the power of the Word shall abide forever, though the Tablets themselves crumble into dust. . . .*

"And then he said that there is hope for redemption, but only at a price—and the answer lies in Jerusalem. He said, *The First Temple was raised in accordance with the Word. In the place where the Temple was raised, you will find the answers that you seek. Hope dwells for all eternity in the City of God. . . ."*

No one spoke for several breathless seconds, until finally Father Bertrand said, "Arnault . . . what do *you* think he meant?"

"I think he meant that even without the Breastplate, we may still be able to erect the Fifth Temple," Arnault replied immediately, with no shred of uncertainty. "But to do it, we must recover some relic of the Tablets of the Law. And to do *that,* someone must make a pilgrimage to Jerusalem."

The range of expressions that greeted this assertion included interest, confusion, and doubt.

"Some relic of the Tablets?" Hamish Kerr murmured "Does such a thing exist?"

"It's a very large gamble. . . ." Bertrand muttered under his breath.

Even Christoph sounded dubious.

"Arnault, are you really prepared to trust the future of the Order to the word of this chance-met traveler?"

"I don't think the meeting was chance," Arnault said. "Not when you link it with my dream, and then the words of the dying Jew, the night before the arrests: *The Law will destroy you. The Law will set you free.* Iskander spoke those same words to me when we met. He *knew!* And then, when he spoke of the Ark, and the Word, and the Law . . . What else could it mean?

"If Armand can ferret out this Bartholeme de Challon—who may or may not have access to the Breastplate—well and good. But while we wait for that *perhaps* to happen—*if* de Challon has it, and *if* it can be retrieved—this is another avenue for us to try. It can do no harm—and if the Breastplate cannot be retrieved, it may be our only hope."

"I'll go with him," Torquil declared. "I think he's right; and two will be safer than one. Arnault and I are able to move with relative ease in that part of the world. It *is* a gamble. But it's also a second chance if the Breastplate can't be recovered."

When no one gainsaid him, Torquil said, "I propose that Aubrey be given charge of Bruce's protection. Bruce knows and trusts him, after all, and knows that he acts for the Order—and he's certainly earned *my* trust in the past year and more."

He did not look at Bishop Crambeth for concurrence, but

the others universally were nodding their agreement, well aware that he was speaking of a trust that could only be encompassed within the trials and vows of full membership in the Inner Order.

"It's settled, then," Arnault said. "We'll make the necessary arrangements before we leave."

"There's one further thing," Torquil said. He pulled from his belt the dirk given him by Abbot Fingon, sheathed with its broken blade, and glanced at Brother Ninian.

"I'd like to pass this on to Aubrey, since he's to become Bruce's protector for the next little while," he said. "I'm afraid I broke its blade, fending off that demon-bird at Methven, but perhaps you can help him discover how to make it an effective weapon again. It snapped off near the hilt. Perhaps it can be reforged."

Raising an eyebrow, Ninian leaned across the table to take the weapon from Aubrey, touched the blue hilt-jewel briefly to his forehead, eyes closed, then smiled and handed it to Aubrey.

"It can be done," he said to the wide-eyed younger man. "And you will be a worthy successor."

"Then, it's settled," Arnault said quietly. "Torquil and I are for Jerusalem, Aubrey's for Bruce, and Armand is for France—and God help us all in our undertakings!"

Chapter Twenty-eight

1308-1310

THE PAIR SET OUT FOR THE HOLY LAND BY WAY OF FRANCE, traveling as far as Brest with Christoph and Father Anselmo—and ended up lingering in France until the following spring, for the worsening plight of the Order held them with a dread fascination that made them reluctant simply to abandon their brethren. In May, they learned, a congregation of some two thousand nobles, clergy, and commons had gathered in Tours to hear Nogaret harangue about the depravity of the Order—and had recorded their whole-hearted assent that the Templars should be forced to confess their sins. The pair made particular efforts to discover the fates of Jauffre and Oliver, but to no avail.

They did learn that rumors of a confession by the Grand Master were true, though they also heard that only torture had produced it. Confessions had also been obtained from a number of other high-ranking officers of the Order—various senior preceptors of provinces and even Hugues de Paraud, the Visitor of France. Virtually all of these men had later revoked their confessions, for having been extracted under torture; but since retraction would have seen them burned as relapsed heretics, every one of them had soon returned to his original confession.

Meanwhile, the relentless interrogation and torture of other Templars continued, yielding an increasingly damning accumulation of confessions extracted under extreme duress. In addition, Pope Clement began insisting that arrests and interrogations proceed in other kingdoms. The threat of the stake was ever-present, and lodged itself in Arnault's soul, even when he and Torquil at last left France and turned their sights toward Jerusalem.

It took the two men more than a year to cover a distance that previously would have taken hardly a third that time, for the disappearance of the Templar fleet had left the Mediterranean exposed to the threat of pirates and corsairs, even in the close coastal waters off France and Italy. Arnault and Torquil knew where a few of the Templar ships had gone— and what they had carried—but most had simply disappeared as the news of the arrests in France spread, for their crews had little relish for the notion of surrendering their cargoes and their persons into the less-than-benign attentions of the Holy Inquisition and its torturers.

In the absence, then, of Templar transport, the pair had been obliged to secure passage where they could. Traveling in the guise of pilgrims, and with Torquil's bright hair drabbed with dark dye, they drew little notice, but their journey had been an arduous one, nonetheless, beset by delays, occasional near encounters with hostile galleys, and shortages of food and water—and occasional nightmares, on Arnault's part, about Templars consigned to the flames. Their present vessel was a Genoese trader, a wallowing, broad-beamed merchantman that had taken twelve days to make the crossing from Limassol—headed, at last, for the ancient port of Alexandria. From there, it was still some weeks' journey to the Holy City of Jerusalem.

Before dawn on the morning they hoped to make landfall at last, Arnault clawed his way out of fitful sleep and the worst nightmare yet—so vivid that it sent him blindly retch-ing to the rail to puke up the acid contents of his mostly empty stomach. When he at last could see again, Torquil was standing beside him, offering the dipper from the water barrel kept amidships.

"Another nightmare?"

Nodding, Arnault took the dipper and tried to rinse away the sour taste from his mouth. After spitting that over the side, he drank the rest down greedily. Even lukewarm and slightly brackish, at least it eased the sour, parched sensation that lingered at the back of his throat.

"It was Jauffre, this time," he rasped after a moment, his gaze unfocused out over the water as he handed the dipper back to Torquil. There was no wind in this predawn stillness, and the rhythmic dip of the oars made a soothing, reassuring counterpoint to the slap of wavelets against the hull. When he did not say more, Torquil took the dipper back to the water barrel, then returned to his side.

"Do you want to talk about it?" he asked.

"No. But I think I must." Arnault lowered his forehead into one hand, closing his eyes.

"I think they've burned him, Torquil."

"Dear God. . . ."

Arnault raised his head to gaze out again at the rosy dawn beginning to stain the horizon, wiping his mouth with the back of a sunburnt hand.

"I've dreamed about burnings before; you know that. But this was different. It was specific. It was much, *much* too real."

"Go on."

"He was . . . in the square before some great cathedral—not Notre Dame or Chartres, I don't know where—and he was not alone. Erected in the square was a veritable sea of stakes—scores of them, maybe fifty or sixty, sticking up like the masts of so many ships.

"Except that each stake had a human being chained to it,

with resin-soaked wood and kindling piled knee high around each one." Arnault's voice had dropped to a whisper.

"They had been most cruelly used, Torquil. Hardly any were unmarked by the evidence of deprivation, terrible tortures. And nearby, fire baskets nursed the waiting torches, filling the air with the reek of sulfur and burning pitch."

He had to stop to swallow before he could go on.

"There was . . . a large, unruly crowd gathered to witness the spectacle, jeering and jostling for the best vantage points . . . and prelates and priests who condoned the thing about to be done . . . and then the whiff of smoke and brimstone and ash, as the pyres were torched—and all too soon, the roar of the flames, and the stench of roasting flesh. . . ."

A sob caught in Arnault's throat, and he buried his face in his hands, but he continued to speak.

"They uttered hardly a sound," he managed to whisper. "A few were defiant to the end, shouting out the innocence of the Order . . . but most simply bore their pain in stoic silence." He shook his head.

"Pain. . . . Can that simple word even begin to describe it? Yet most uttered no more than a gasp or a moan, as the flames began to lick at their flesh. I—do not think I could summon such courage, in the face of such a death. . . ."

Torquil said nothing, only clasping a hand to Arnault's biceps as the other man's shoulders shuddered in silent weeping. His own vision was blurry with tears, breath catching in his throat, and he tried not to imagine what it had been like—for the men in distant France as well as for Arnault.

After a little while, as the pink of dawn faded to the bright splendor of the sun-ball itself lifting above the eastern horizon, Arnault recovered himself sufficiently to raise his head. Nothing could reclaim what had happened, bring Jauffre back—and he was all too certain that he had dreamed true.

As it was, he and Torquil both knew they were working against time. At first traveling mostly on foot, and with only their own resources of wit to sustain them, they had come so

far only by being constantly on their guard; for spies and in-
formers were everywhere, and the arm of the Inquisition
was long.

The strident crow of a cock in one of the poultry cages put
an end to Arnault's ruminations. A breeze was rising, and the
ship's sailing master emerged from his canopy on the forecastle and began barking orders at his sleepy-eyed crew.
Torquil disappeared briefly, presently rejoining Arnault at
the rail with two meager rations of hard bread.

"Enjoy it while it lasts," he recommended with a grimace.
"If Saint Anthony and Saint Jerome ate locusts in the desert,
I don't suppose a few weevils will hurt us. That's all the
food we have left till we reach landfall."

"How encouraging you are," Arnault murmured, frowning as he knocked his bread against the rail. "Fortunately,
our captain is predicting we'll sight land before midday."

"I'll believe that when it happens," Torquil said with a
skeptical snort, and gnawed off a corner of his own crust. He
did not bother to attempt dislodging the weevils.

Both men had lost weight from months of living on the
edge of poverty. The pilgrim's robes they had assumed at the
outset of their journey were now stained and tattered with
use. Their weapons at present were wrapped in canvas and
disguised amid the spare blanketing and tent poles and pilgrim staves stashed by the area of deck they had staked out
early in the voyage—though everyone aboard knew them to
be soldiers, even if on pilgrimage, and well armed. It occurred to Arnault that, ironically, they probably were safer in
the Moslem lands toward which they were bound than in the
Christian countries they had left behind.

Their stalwart ship continued to plow its slow way
through the waves, under sail since the rise of the breeze
with the dawn. Most of the passengers sought whatever
shade they could find from the glare of the morning sun,
some sheltering under wide-brimmed hats or the hoods of
desert *djellabas*. Torquil had dozed off with his head resting

on his forearm. Arnault was just wondering if he ought to do likewise when there came a cry from the masthead.

"Land ho!"

The cry roused everyone on board. While the members of the crew scurried to adjust the sails, the passengers hurried forward, peering narrowly at the distant horizon. Taller than anyone else aboard, the two Templars were first to spot a tiny sliver of yellow squeezed between the sea and the sky.

"*Egypt!*" Torquil breathed on a sigh of triumph.

With everyone else aboard, the two of them stayed glued to the rail, watching the outlines of Alexandria come into sight. Both had been there before. As the ship's master came to watch from the rail beside the two, Arnault paid compliment to the master's navigational skills.

"In former times, it would have been easier," the captain responded with a shrug, nodding toward an island ahead that was linked to the city by a broad causeway.

Another of the pilgrims, a German monk from Wurzberg, turned his head in curious inquiry. "How so?"

Arnault pointed to the tower that rose tier upon tier from the closest point of the island.

"That is the great lighthouse," he explained. "It's sometimes called the Pharos, because that's the name of the island on which it's standing. In times past, its beacon shone night and day, marking the safe route in and out of the harbor."

"It's a lighthouse?" said a traveler from Parma.

The captain squinted at the speaker as though he were slow-witted. "Don't tell me you haven't heard of the great lighthouse of Alexandria. It was one of the Seven Wonders of the ancients."

"It's a miracle that it's still standing," Torquil said, gazing at the lofty structure. "The lowest of its three sections was square, the middle section octagonal, and the topmost stage circular, the whole of it rising to a height of several hundred feet. The marble surfaces were stained with time, and here and there the masonry was visibly crumbling.

"So, why is there no light now?" the German monk asked.

The captain shrugged. "The Arabs didn't understand the purpose of the reflecting mirror. They carried it off and never replaced it. Now, no one even bothers to light a fire up there by night."

To Arnault's searching eye, the lighthouse looked considerably more derelict than he remembered from his last visit to Alexandria.

"It looks like it's starting to collapse," he remarked.

"A recent earthquake shook it up badly," the captain said, "and no repairs have been planned so far." He sighed gustily. "It's a sad sight for a sailor to see such a beacon sliding into ruin. The Arabs aren't seafaring folk. They're far more concerned with their new capital at Fustat, on the Nile."

Beyond the island of Pharos, at the far side of the harbor, Arnault recognized a pair of huge obelisks that dominated the surrounding buildings: called the Needles of Cleopatra, brought here from a southern city in honor of the famous queen. But for Arnault, all at once they were eerily reminiscent of the twin towers of Notre Dame, reminding him yet again of the horrors that were taking place back in Europe.

The deck shifted beneath their feet as the ship tacked westward.

"Why are we turning away from the harbor?" the Italian traveler inquired.

"The great harbor is reserved for the Faithful," the captain said with a sour grin. "We Infidels have to use the smaller harbor, up ahead—and we'll be charged extra, even for that privilege."

As they cleared the harbor mouth, the crew dropped sail and used the oars to guide the vessel to the dock. Galleys and merchantmen from a dozen lands jostled by the quayside, here to trade metals, grain, spices, and silk.

Beyond the warehouses and customs offices that lined the harbor, the sunlight against marble-and-plaster buildings reflected with such brilliance that it almost hurt the eye to look at them. Off to the south, the silver sheen of Lake Mareotis and the canal that connected Alexandria to the Nile flashed mirror-bright. Though it was no longer Egypt's capital, Alexandria was still a bustling city. When Arnault and Torquil disembarked, traveling packs over their shoulders, they were almost swept away in the boisterous crowd that was milling around the harbor.

A polyglot hubbub dinned in their ears as they walked, the mixed tongues of Arabs, Berbers, Copts, Melkites, Italians, Frenchmen, and Germans. Jewish merchants and Arab traders vied with one another to offer the best price on the newly arrived goods, while officials acting on behalf of the city's governor supervised the unloading and collected duty on the cargo.

The streets beyond the waterfront were only slightly less congested, but Arnault made his way through the city as confidently as if he were walking down the avenues of Paris, Torquil sticking close beside him. When he came to the house he was seeking, he found the door ajar to let the air flow freely on this hot day.

Arnault tapped twice and stepped inside. Torquil followed, careful to close the door securely behind him.

Inside, a shaggy-haired man was hunched over a workbench beside an open window on the far side of the room, applying a small, pointed instrument to the edges of a disk of copper. Only when Arnault was standing right over him did he look up and then leap to his feet, dropping his tools. His look of shock turned to one of joy when he recognized the face of the intruder.

"Arnault!" he cried, flinging his arms around the knight and pressing him to his breast. "My dear friend, I had not foreseen to greet you again before Heaven!" He spoke in broken Latin with a thick Coptic accent, but that did nothing to obscure the hearty affection in his voice.

He released his hold and stepped back. "I have heard of the great badness taking place, of your slain brothers. Surely God Himself has placed a protection over you, to bring you safely here."

"I believe that truly," Arnault said, summoning a smile at the remembrance of other times, other greetings.

"But, who is this?" said the shaggy man, tugging at his curly, gray-streaked beard as he scrutinized Torquil.

"This is Torquil Lennox, one of my confreres," Arnault explained. "Torquil, this is the good friend I told you about: Matthias the coppersmith."

Torquil was wary that he might be swallowed up in another of the Copt's enveloping embraces, but to his relief Matthias merely bowed and beckoned the two men to follow him into a back room. Here he fetched figs, dates, olives, bread, and wine, pressing them not to speak further until they had eaten.

"You look as if you had fasted a year," he complained, with a reproving shake of his head. "I cannot bear to behold you until you have filled your bellies—though you may tell me of the tedium of your voyage, if you wish."

They eschewed tedium in favor of eating. Matthias, once he was satisfied that they were properly fed, consented to listen to their tale. Without revealing the true purpose of their journey, Arnault told him of their destination.

Matthias tugged at his unruly beard with one hand, absentmindedly juggling a date with the other.

"A long way lies ahead," he said, "but at least now you will not fail from starvation on the first leg. Now that the Holy Country is under the rule of the Mongols, there are new things to fear. The trade routes still thrive, but there is more unruliness, more danger than before."

Torquil knew that the Mongols had swept down through Baghdad and taken Jerusalem itself, overwhelming the

Arabs just as the Arabs had swept across the Christian land centuries before. Whether that would make their mission easier or more hazardous, Torquil had no better idea than the coppersmith.

"Only when we get there will we know what is going to happen," Arnault said, with a philosophic shrug. "We must go, regardless—and there's no sense trying to play the prophet."

"Ah, but what money I could make in the markets, if I could." Matthias grinned as he tossed the date into his mouth and chewed. "Still, whoever rules where, trade goes on as rightly as the winds blow. A caravan departs for Mecca in two days' time. For two poor pilgrims such as yourselves, even Christian ones, to place themselves under its protection for part of their journey would be no very strange thing."

"That gives us a couple of days to gather some further intelligence," Torquil said.

Matthias made a disgusted noise at the back of his throat. "It gives you two more days to eat," he insisted. "In Jerusalem or in Mecca, the great God wants to be worshiped by men, not skeletons."

In spite of all the hardship and danger that lay ahead, Torquil could not help chuckling at the Copt's good humor, and Arnault found himself heartily joining in.

Chapter Twenty-nine

1310

THE TWO TEMPLARS SET OUT EASTWARD, FOLLOWING THE ancient trade route between Egypt and Arabah, which had been known to the Romans as the Via Maris. On foot, it was a long, hard journey, compounded by the necessity to keep their true identities a secret from those around them; for Western knights would find no welcome among those who had been their sworn enemies.

Accordingly, the pair had maintained their guise as pious Western pilgrims, their travel scrips adorned with a variety of pewter pilgrim badges and the cockleshell emblem betokening a visit to the shrine of Saint James at Santiago de Compostela. For desert travel, this attire was modified by the addition of hooded burnoose and *keffiyeh,* the sun-shielding head covering that also served as protection against blowing sand.

Their swords they disguised amid the bundle of poles and stakes that supported their tiny travel tent; the dirks they wore beneath their robes were formidable stabbing weapons, almost as good as a short sword, and could be explained by Torquil's Scottish origins. Such blades were entirely reasonable accoutrements for travelers on the pilgrim routes; and the iron-shod pilgrim staff that each of them carried could also serve as quarterstaff or even halberd for defense.

Even as pilgrims, their travel must be wary. Moving from oasis to oasis, village to village, the two of them traversed the arid wastes of the Nile Delta like men crossing a dangerous river by a series of precarious stepping-stones. When possible, they traveled in the company of caravans, for safety and anonymity lay in numbers, and the Muslims respected the institution of pilgrimage even by those of other faiths. Only after many weeks of travel did the two Templars at last enter the wilderness of Judah, the southern gateway to the Holy Land.

The timeless landscape had changed but little since their last sojourn there, nearly twenty years before. Two days' journey to the north, by Arnault's reckoning, lay the heavily salted waters of the Dead Sea. Nearer at hand, bleak desert surrounded them on all sides, stretching to every horizon in wind-scoured ridges of sand and stone. Arid breezes raked up sheets of grit that stung the eyes and clogged the throat. Here and there, rocky crags and sheer escarpments reared up like cyclopean ruins.

The leader of their present caravan, a Muslim captain named Qasim, was in the pay of a consortium of merchants whose goods he had been hired to protect: coffee and copper, honey and salt bars, bales of cotton, carpets, leather, and ivory. So far, the only hazards had been hunger and thirst and the danger of losing their way. From these, Qasim had protected them well. He knew every spring and well along the route, and where to stop to renew their supplies. And he knew the stars in the sky as well as a man knows the rooms in his own house.

In addition to the armed guards and the drovers who cared for the pack animals, and the merchants themselves, a score of other pilgrims accompanied the caravan, Jews as well as Muslims, and even a few other Christians. But though it was Qasim's duty before Allah to protect all these human charges, they received none of the personal attention he gave to the animals—the camels, mules, and donkeys, at least two hundred of them in the long train, in addition to the horses of his men—all of them giving off a pungent reek in the desert heat. Qasim was being paid to see that the goods reached their destination safely—and for that, he must keep his pack animals fit and strong, regardless of what happened to the people. Arnault and Torquil had observed the care with which he inspected each animal at the beginning and end of every day, overseeing their care and feeding, making sure none suffered from saddle galls or foot problems.

"I suppose we ought to tell Qasim we're leaving in the morning," Torquil said to Arnault, as the two of them trudged along beside their pack donkey. "On the other hand, I doubt he'd much notice our absence, if we just slipped away. We've only two legs after all—not four."

"Aye, he does love his animals," Arnault agreed. They spoke in court French, unlikely to be understood by any of their companions, and had been careful not to reveal that they both were fluent in Arabic, Arnault more so than Torquil. "Concern for animals is a virtue of their religion. I've heard it said that Mohammed once cut the sleeve off a robe he was wearing, rather than disturb a sleeping cat."

"Did he, really?" Torquil replied, falling silent to think about that as they continued to trudge along.

Off to one side, Arnault watched a miniature whirlwind touch down briefly and stir up sand, then lift again and spin off in another direction.

"If you're reluctant to leave the caravan, just say so," he said, after another little while. "It does mean striking out on our own, but I can't help feeling we'll be safer, now that we're getting nearer our goal. I campaigned in this vicinity when I first took my vows. It's looking more and more familiar."

"You couldna prove it by me," Torquil quipped, for his own experience in the Holy Land had been somewhat more limited than Arnault's. "We haven't any deserts in Scotland.

Still, it's certainly true that every day we stay with the caravan, we run the risk that someone is going to discover who we really are. I don't think they'd be so hospitable to a pair of Western knights as they have been to two innocent fellow pilgrims."

"Aye, they do respect a man who undertakes a holy journey, as they themselves are doing—even though we're Christians. It helps that all of us are People of the Book—Christians, Muslims, and Jews. A pity we keep having to fight wars to remind ourselves of that."

"Aye, it is." Torquil squinted against the sun to scan the distant horizon with disfavor. "I confess I'll be glad to put this rough country behind us."

"Aye, this is typical bandit territory," Arnault agreed. "Far enough into the desert to be clear of military patrols, yet still within reach of civilized outposts when they need a source of supplies or access to a market."

A growing plume of dust was rising in the wake of the pack animals, increasingly bothersome as the caravan passed through an area of finer sand, approaching a ridge of higher ground. The two men fell silent, the better to listen, veiling the lower halves of their faces in folds of their *keffiyehs*. But as they continued trudging along, both men kept increasingly sharper watch on the cliffs and ridges ahead. It was Torquil who first spotted the telltale flicker of movement partway up the side of a neighboring crest of high ground—though Arnault was already turning in that direction as Torquil focused his full attention on what he thought he had seen.

"Uh-oh," he muttered. "Did you see that? I think we may have company."

He jutted his chin vaguely toward the spot in question, though he did not change the carriage of his head. Narrowly scanning the ridge in his turn, Arnault was able to pick out two bearded faces peeking out from behind a scrim of tumbled boulders.

"Do you see them?" Torquil murmured.

Arnault half turned his face back toward the younger knight, but his eyes never left his quarry.

"I see them."

"What do you think?"

"I think," said Arnault, "that we had better warn the captain. I would guess that they're assessing our numbers. Make sure our swords are accessible, but don't uncover them yet."

Leaving Torquil with the donkey, Arnault headed toward the front of the caravan, extending his long-legged stride to move quickly without appearing to be in a hurry. Qasim had been riding up and down the caravan, and was currently toward the front, mounted on a wiry chestnut mare as lean and weather-hardened as her master. He turned in the saddle as Arnault came abreast of him and laid a hand briefly on his stirrup, at the same time pulling down the swath of fabric veiling his lower face.

"We are being watched," Arnault announced in brisk Arabic. "Two men lurking in the rocks atop that hill." He jutted his chin in that direction. "I very much doubt they are alone, or that their intentions are benign."

The caravan captain gave him a supercilious look but kept his mare moving forward. If he was surprised at Arnault's sudden display of fluency, he gave no sign of it. Casually, seeming merely to adjust his headcloth, he bent his gaze on the ridge the Templar had indicated. But during Arnault's progress up the line of march, the two scouts had disappeared.

"Your eyes play tricks on you, infidel," Qasim murmured contemptuously. "You are not accustomed to the brightness of the sun."

"Look again," Arnault insisted, "and then look around us. Is this not a perfect spot for an ambush?"

Qasim scowled. "How would you, a pilgrim, know of such things?"

"I was once a soldier, until God led me into the ways of peace," Arnault improvised. "I am making this pilgrimage to atone for the sins of my past."

"Allah loves a soldier," the Arab responded with a curl of his lip. "The Prophet Mohammed—blessed be his name—rode at the head of his army and conquered half the world. You cannot say the same of your Nazarene."

Arnault bit back his exasperation and cast a sidelong glance at the ridge. This was no time to argue religion. He spread his hands in a gesture of conciliation.

"Should a wise man not accept true counsel, whether it comes from a caliph or a beggar—or even from an infidel?"

The Arab once again scanned the ridge with eyes long accustomed to the desert glare.

"You were a soldier, you say?"

Arnault nodded. "Do you see something?"

"I see that there are carrion birds among the rocks and thorns to our right," Qasim noted grimly, "but none upon your ridge to our left. They anticipate the dead, perhaps, and avoid the living."

Suddenly clapping heels to his horse's sides, he wheeled the animal around and raised his arm as he gave a ululating cry. His horsemen scattered from where they had been riding in bunches amid the line of march, respacing themselves along the line, and the caravan lumbered to a halt. Donkeys jibbed and camels jostled one other with bad-tempered snorts. Querulous protests broke out among the merchants.

"Why are we stopping here?"

"This is no place to make camp!"

Before Qasim could bellow for silence, a warbling chorus of battle cries split the desert air as the western ridge came alive with ragged shapes, mostly on foot, the desert sun glinting off a motley assortment of swords and javelins. Brandishing their weapons, the bandits yelled and stamped their feet.

"We do not take fright so easily as that!" Qasim declared. "If these dogs want booty, they'll have to fight for it!"

Drawing a thin, curved sword, he barked out a staccato string of orders. Goaded by urgency, the twelve men under his command swiftly marshaled the caravan into a tight circle.

Donkeys, mules, and camels were forced to their knees, form-ing a living barricade. The merchants and pilgrims took shel-ter among them while the Arab guards drew their weapons and braced themselves for defense.

Arnault joined Torquil and their fellow travelers in the mid-dle of the circle. Torquil was hesitating over the wrappings that disguised their swords. Howling like dervishes, the ban-dits left the shelter of the rocks and poured down the slope to-ward the caravan. In a lightning tally, Arnault counted two dozen black-robed figures on foot, led by three men on horse-back.

"This doesn't look good," Torquil muttered. "Other than Qasim's men and ourselves, I doubt there're half a dozen amongst the rest of us who can fight—and if *we* fight . . ."

"I fear it's a little late to be worrying about our disguise," Arnault replied, as he whipped the wrappings from his sword and pulled it from the scabbard.

Some of Qasim's horsemen were armed with bows as well as swords—wicked little recurves with the power to pierce armor—and loosed off a volley of arrows. The brigands, though they wore no armor, were undeterred, and closed in, howling, as they flung themselves at the barricades. Half a dozen in the first wave were cut down in their tracks. But as the range became too close for bows, and more bandits came surging forward with swords and javelins and even cudgels, Qasim's men charged into them with swords, slashing and hacking.

Two of the caravan's defenders fell wounded. A number of the Muslim pilgrims dropped to their knees and began offer-ing up wailing prayers to Allah. Pushing their way through the mostly unarmed travelers, naked broadswords now in hands, Arnault and Torquil raced to join Qasim and his men. The car-avan captain flashed them a sharp look, but didn't question their aid.

"You say you were a soldier," he shouted to Arnault between hacks at attackers. "I hope you have not forgotten the art!"

Bandits were swarming on all sides. A pilgrim screamed as a bandit stabbed him from behind. Arnault and Torquil ran to where the attackers were most numerous and drove them back with bloody sweeps of their broadswords. When one of the riders tried to overleap the barricade, Arnault brought the horse down with a crashing blow of his sword pommel to its skull. Its rider went flying, and Torquil cut him down before he could recover from his fall.

Fighting back-to-back, they could hear Qasim alternately bellowing encouragement to his men and raining curses upon his enemies. An enemy horseman rode straight at him, but the Arab captain yanked his nimble steed aside and flung a dagger that caught the raider in the back as he rode past.

Inspired by his example and that of the two Christians, the Arab merchants and pilgrims plucked up their courage and joined in the fray. Some used their staves while others snatched up rocks to use as makeshift weapons. Two of them were cut down at once by the swords of the bandits, but the others fought on, spurred by a potent mix of faith and desperation.

Their determined resistance caused the raiders to waver. But before greed or fear could decide the issue, an eerie, long-drawn howl began to penetrate the fighting din. As the howling grew louder, rolling across the sand like the voice of a mighty djinn, both sides faltered to a standstill, recognizing a mutual danger they knew only too well.

All eyes turned toward the east, where a huge wall of yellow sand had swallowed the horizon and was rolling toward them with the speed of a racing camel. Great clouds of grit billowed and churned in its heart, while near at hand, the dust was already starting to rise before the wind.

The bandit leader gave a yell, wheeling his horse to flee. His remaining followers broke and ran, scurrying like rats for the shelter of the rocks. The surviving members of the caravan hurled themselves flat among their kneeling animals and buried their heads in their desert robes. The sandstorm was upon them within a matter of seconds, blotting out the sun.

Torquil had heard Arnault's tales of such storms, but never had he experienced one himself. The storm shrilled around them like a chorus of demons as a wall of sand and wind swept over them like a giant wave, buffeting them without mercy as they crouched in the meager shelter of two kneeling camels. Blinding sand whipped about them in gnashing clouds, as if the desert had risen up like a plague of insects, trying to devour them with a million tiny teeth.

Coughing and choking, Torquil dragged another fold of his cloak over his mouth and nose and sucked as much air as he could through the fabric, trying not to gag. Under his *keffiyeh*, he could feel tears streaming down his cheeks from grit in both eyes, but blinking did little to clear them as long as the wind blew.

The storm raged about them for what seemed an eternity. Through their tearing eyes, they could see no farther than a few inches away. Just when Torquil was convinced he must suffocate, a new noise began to pierce the roaring of the storm, which slowly began to slack off.

Sustained and silvery, the sound much resembled the bird-like note of a flute—surely too frail to penetrate the ferocious wind, yet it resounded as clearly as if it were echoing down the aisles of an empty chapel. Their breathing eased as the wind gradually ceased battering their backs.

Cautiously, through the tear haze, Torquil cocked an eye above the folds of his robe and saw that the storm was, indeed, abating. He was about to lower his head again, wiping at his cheek with the back of a grimy hand, when he caught a startling glimpse of something bright, like sunlight flashing off polished metal.

Patches of sky reappeared. The eerie twilight dissipated as the storm moved on. The sand drifted down and settled, leaving the air clear again. The blessed silence, after the storm, was a benison to all.

A little unsteadily, Arnault heaved himself up and began shaking the grit from his garments, wiping at his cheeks, coughing to clear his lungs. Torquil followed suit. All around them the Arabs were getting to their feet, giving thanks to Allah. Hurriedly the guards and the drovers set about checking that their beasts were uninjured and their goods intact.

There was no sign of the bandits other than the dead they had left behind. It was as though a huge hand had descended from the heavens and swept the earth clean of their presence. Torquil was still puzzling over the mysterious flash he had seen when an exclamation from Arnault alerted him to the approach of fresh company.

A solitary figure was emerging from the heat-shimmer in the east. Like them, he must have been overtaken by the storm only moments before, yet he strode with the easy confidence of a man who fears nothing that nature can send against him. He was of medium height, his lean frame enveloped by a rough-woven burnoose the color of the sand, its hood casting his face into featureless shadow. His sandal-shod feet carried him toward them with the firmness of a soldier on the march.

The other pilgrims eyed the approaching figure with suspicion, pointing and muttering uneasily. Qasim directed several of his men to be on guard. As the newcomer drew nearer, a sinewy arm emerged from the folds of the burnoose to pull back the hood, from which emerged a shaven head above a handsome, beardless face the color of old mahogany. The fine planes of cheekbones and jaw recalled statues Arnault had seen in Egypt, but it was the man's dark-eyed gaze that made him stiffen and catch his breath.

"You know this man?" Torquil said under his breath, in French.

Arnault slowly nodded. "It's the very man we came to find," he whispered. "Iskander, whose summons has brought us here in quest of a miracle."

Chapter Thirty

1310

A BUZZ RIPPLED THROUGH THE MUSLIM RANKS AT ISKANder's approach. Bristling with suspicion, some of the caravan guards made ready to bar his way with drawn swords, but Qasim hissed at them to stand aside.

"Do you not know a holy man when you see one?" he said, making a *salaam* as the newcomer passed him by with hardly a nod, his dark gaze fixed on Arnault.

When the man had come within a few paces—he did not appear to be armed—he inclined his head, approval and faint humor in his dark eyes.

"So you have come at last," he said in Arabic, rather than the French he had spoken at Chartres. "As I knew you would."

"If you knew I would come, then you know that I had little choice," Arnault replied in the same language. "But how did you find me in the midst of this desert?"

"In the same manner I found you before," came Iskander's cryptic answer. "You and your companion," he added, with a nod of his chin in Torquil's direction. "Another man might have chosen to come alone."

"This is my brother-in-arms," Arnault said, not naming

Torquil because of Qasim's presence—and wondering if his own name was even known to Iskander. "He is here because he would not have it otherwise."

"Then you are more fortunate than many," Iskander said. "Come."

Swiftly Arnault and Torquil gathered up their meager gear, giving their donkey into the care of one of their traveling companions. They were at the point of following after Iskander when Qasim hesitantly approached them.

"The caravan must move on," he said. "This is dangerous country. We dare not wait for you."

"Nor do I ask that you should," Arnault said. "We must part now. Thank you for your protection."

"You know this holy man?" Qasim persisted.

Arnault smiled faintly. "I know him."

The caravan master's gaze flicked from Arnault to Torquil and back as he shook his head. "They say that Allah protects his own—and children and fools. Go, then. Whatever fate has been ordained for you, I do not believe that we shall meet again."

With a sketched *salaam,* he turned on his heel and strode off, bellowing orders. As Arnault and Torquil headed after Iskander, a flurry of activity erupted as drovers and pilgrims goaded the pack animals to their feet, shouting to one another as they thumped the loose sand from their belongings and checked their baggage harness.

With the exchange of a speaking glance, the two Templars left it all behind, casting their lot with Iskander. Arnault studied him from behind as he and Torquil trudged after him. The mysterious stranger had been at the center of many a conversation between the two of them during the long months it had taken them to come to this moment.

Now that they had found him—or he had found them—Arnault wondered whether he had made the right decision. But Torquil appeared nonplussed at actually meeting Iskander. Seeing his faint smile, Arnault found some of his own earlier reservations slipping away—but Iskander himself remained an enigma, thus far, and Arnault was reluctant to press him for information just yet. Besides, he didn't think he had the breath to talk and also keep up the pace the stranger set.

They soon lost sight of the caravan as Iskander led them into the dusty hills. The ground was stony and rough, the footing often treacherous. Their guide paused occasionally to glance back at them, a faint smile on his lips, but he did not speak, and he did not pause long enough for them ever to come abreast of him.

An hour's march brought them to the mouth of a jagged ravine. At its far end, a dense outcropping of greenery showed intensely vivid against the arid backdrop of the surrounding terrain. As they drew nearer, another human figure stepped out of a fissure in the side of the ravine, robed like Iskander, and stood statuelike to await their arrival. He was shorter than Iskander, and slighter of build and probably somewhat older, but with the same liquid-dark eyes and fine skin like burnished old wood.

"My servant, Berhanu," Iskander explained as they approached, speaking French. "He shares my counsels even as he shares my labors. Though he understands your Frankish tongue, he cannot speak it. Being mute, he communicates only in signs."

Berhanu smiled and accorded them a grave gesture of greeting, making the *salaam* usual for this part of the world, but then adding a little bow over palms pressed together before his breast.

Arnault returned the bow, and said, "I am Arnault de Saint Clair, and my companion is Torquil Lennox."

Iskander inclined his head, then spoke briefly to Berhanu in a language Arnault had never heard before, to which his servant responded with nods and hand gestures too swift for the inexperienced eye to follow.

"Food and drink await us," Iskander informed the knights.

"Come. You will have many questions, which are better answered when we have taken refreshment."

A further brief walk along the ravine brought them to a set of ancient ruins surrounded by cedar trees. Three well-fed mules and a pair of donkeys grazed placidly on the lush grass growing up between the stones. From nearby came the blessed sound of trickling water, reminding both Templars how long they had been walking, after the sandstorm. At their glance in that direction, Iskander pointed out a rivulet welling from a cleft in the wall of the ravine, which pooled in a small, rocky basin and then was channeled downhill along a shallow course of stones, eventually running dry amid the rocks.

They paused to drink from the basin. The water, Torquil discovered, was blessedly pure and cold. Following the example of Iskander, he and Arnault washed faces and hands, only reluctantly abandoning the water for the shade of one of the crumbling walls, where Berhanu had set out bread, cheese, and dates, along with more of the fresh, cold water.

The Templars accepted the food with thanks, surveying the ruins as they started to eat. On the wall above Iskander's head, a lingering patch of fresco work displayed a still-bright symbol of a *Chi-Rho*, the Greek letters superimposed one on the other in an emblem formed by the first two letters of the name of Christ.

"In the days of the Roman emperors, this was home to a band of early Christians," Iskander explained, noting the direction of their gaze. "Its builders came here to escape persecution—as do you."

Torquil glanced at Arnault, wondering how much the other man could actually know of their affairs.

"Who *are* you?" he blurted.

"Brother Arnault will have told you my name," Iskander replied with a shrug, around a mouthful of date. "Beyond that, I am what you see."

"What I see," Torquil replied, frowning, "is what you are

not. You are not an Arab. Neither are you of Latin blood. You speak the *lingua franca* fluently, but not as one who learned it from birth. So where do you come from? And what language is your mother tongue?"

"So many questions," Iskander said, with a glimmering of humor. "I was born in Gondar, in the northern province of the kingdom of Ethiopia. The native speech of my homeland is Ge'ez, and many neighboring lands speak Arabic, but those who serve the Church must learn both Greek and Latin. And of course, I have learned your Frankish speech."

Ethiopia.

Torquil registered a blink of surprise, aware of how little he knew of that far-off African kingdom, so distant from his native Scotland that its very name carried the resonance of legend. He and Arnault had spoken of it more than once, during the long months of their journey here, intrigued by the possibility that the Iskander of Chartres Cathedral might be the same Iskander mentioned by Jauffre in connection with the Ethiopian embassage of 1306. But this in no way explained why either Iskander should be interested in Templar affairs.

"This raises more questions," Arnault said tentatively, obviously thinking along lines similar to Torquil. "At Chartres, you called yourself friend and referred to me as brother. May I ask why?"

"Because that is what you are. Like you, I am a Knight of the Temple of Solomon. A Templar."

As Arnault and Torquil exchanged startled glances, Iskander drew apart the neck of his burnoose to reveal an egg-sized medallion of dark wood strung on a slender leather thong. Into its face was carved a Templar cross, and on its other side, as he turned it for them, a finely carved depiction of the Templar seal, with two knights riding on one horse.

Opening his hands, Iskander then showed them small cruciform tattoos at the base of each palm. His feet bore similar markings atop the instep, betokening the wounds of crucifixion. Mouth agape, Torquil suddenly found himself quite certain that there would be a fifth tattoo on Iskander's side, beneath the flowing robes. The look on Arnault's face, when Torquil glanced at him, suggested that he probably had come to the same conclusion, and that he, too, was both taken aback and curiously intrigued by what all of this suggested.

"I see that I must explain," Iskander said, smiling at their mute astonishment. "The tale begins more than a century ago. At that time, Ethiopia was ruled by a king called Harbay, who had a younger half brother called Lalibela, though they were by different mothers. Lalibela's mother was a prophetess; when he was only an infant, she saw a great swarm of bees hovering around his cradle without injuring him. From this sign, she knew that the child was born for greatness, and gave him the name, which means *The bees recognize his sovereignty.*

"When Harbay heard this prophecy, he began to fear for his throne and made several attempts to kill his younger brother. At last, prompted by God in a dream, Lalibela fled Ethiopia and made his way to Jerusalem, where he presented himself to the Knights of the Order of the Temple. Christianity came early to my land, of course," he offered as an aside, "though we follow the Patriarch in Alexandria. Some of our customs differ somewhat from those of the West." He briefly displayed his palms again.

"In any case, the superiors of the Order examined Lalibela and, finding him worthy, agreed to receive his vows. In due course, his spiritual gifts commended him to the *Maître* of the time, who became the prince's mentor and initiated him in the mystical disciplines necessary for one called to service among the inner guardians of the Light—yes, those you refer to as *le Cercle.*"

Torquil glanced quickly at Arnault, who had stiffened at this revelation.

"This is information of the most privileged kind," Arnault said softly.

"And it is safe with me," Iskander assured them. "Remember that I, too, am a sharer of the wisdom of Solomon. We have sworn a common vow."

In the air before them he sketched a sign, which manifested briefly as a shimmering glyph of light. Torquil caught his breath, for it was the sigil of an adept of the highest degree. Arnault raised an eyebrow but merely nodded silently, still tight-lipped as Iskander resumed his tale.

"Lalibela remained in Jerusalem for twenty-five years, under the tutelage of his Templar masters. At the end of that time, upon the death of King Harbay, he returned to Ethiopia to assume the throne. When he left, he took with him not only the wisdom he had gained from his masters, but also several knight-brothers who had become his disciples. Thus was instituted the Ethiopian branch of the Templar Order, whose special charge it was to safeguard the mystical heirlooms of the Ethiopian royal line. One was the Mirror of Makeda; the other was the Ark of the Covenant."

Both men's jaws had dropped at this declaration. Arnault was the first to find his tongue, and only with difficulty.

"But—the Ark has been lost for . . . several thousand years. You're saying it ended up in Ethiopia?"

"Yes. Makeda's great-grandson had it brought there," Iskander said.

"And who is Makeda?" Torquil dared to ask.

Iskander seemed almost amused by the question. "The scriptures do not name her, but amongst your people she is known by her title: the Queen of Sheba."

"Of course," Arnault murmured, faintly nodding.

"These revelations should come as no surprise," Iskander said. "The history of the kingdom of Ethiopia and the history of the Templars are both rooted in the same event: the raising of the First Temple by King Solomon the Great."

Arnault and Torquil watched him pour tiny cups of steaming, fragrant coffee that Berhanu brought, hanging on his every word as he continued.

"The First Temple was built to house the Ark of the Covenant, and the Ark was made to house the Tablets of the Law," Iskander said, passing a cup to each of them. "When Solomon set out to build his great temple, he sent messages throughout the known world, calling for the materials he required and offering gold and silver in return.

"Amongst those who responded to this call was an Ethiopian merchant named Tamrin, who came to Solomon offering red gold and sapphires and black wood that could not be eaten by worms. Tamrin was amazed at the splendor of Solomon's kingdom, and the wisdom of Solomon himself. When he returned to Ethiopia, he gave such a glowing account of all he had seen that Queen Makeda resolved to go and see these marvels for herself.

"She set out with a great caravan laden with gifts and riches. When she arrived at Jerusalem, Solomon received her with great honor. Captivated by her beauty, he later sought her love. This she freely bestowed, likewise embracing the faith of Israel, which she had come to revere.

"She returned to Ethiopia carrying a royal prince in her womb," Iskander went on. "When this child, Prince Menelik, grew to manhood, he journeyed to the court of his father, who received him with delight. But Queen Makeda grieved for her absent son. Out of pity for her tears and prayers, an Angel of the Lord came down and breathed upon her mirror. The Mirror became a window of vision that enabled her to watch over her son at a distance—and it remains a vehicle of divination to this day."

"But what of the Ark?" Arnault said impatiently.

"Yes, the Ark." Iskander smiled faintly. "It has been claimed by some that when Menelik was preparing to return home, some of his traveling companions stole the Ark and secretly made away with it. Those claims, however, are wide of the mark. Having failed to persuade Menelik to remain at his side, Solomon presented his son with the altar covering from the Ark as a parting gift—not the Ark itself. It was not until two generations later that the actual Ark came to Ethiopia—and by a different route entirely.

"When Jeroboam was king of Judah," he continued, "the Egyptian pharaoh Sheshak I declared war on the Hebrews. When the Egyptian army attacked Jerusalem, the High Priests, fearing the worst, removed the Sacred Tablets from the Ark and hid them in a secret sanctuary deep beneath the Temple Mount in Jerusalem. Sheshak demanded a great tribute in gold and silver as a price for sparing the city. To satisfy this demand, Jerusalem was stripped of all precious objects, including the Ark with its housings of gold. Sheshak took the tribute and returned home, where the Ark was placed in his treasury as a tribute of war.

"Menelik's grandson, also of that name, had just ascended to the throne when he learned the news. He spent three days fasting and praying before setting out for Thebes. Guided by Makeda's Mirror, he and his companions were able to penetrate Sheshak's tribute vaults and retrieve the Ark. As the Israelite kingdoms were still in disarray, Menelik II brought the Ark back to Ethiopia and installed it in a tabernacle in Aksum, where it remains to this day."

As he fell silent, the Templars allowed themselves to breathe at last.

"A remarkable story," Arnault said.

"It remains for you to finish it," said Iskander. "Or die in the attempt."

Arnault felt a chill along his spine. "How could I finish such a story?" he asked. "Surely you aren't saying that we must find the Ark?"

"Not the Ark, but what it contained."

"The Tablets of the Law? But you said they're no longer in the Ark."

"No, they lie beneath the Temple Mount, where they must remain. There, as well, were placed certain manuscripts containing much of Solomon's wisdom. That is what the founders of our Order were looking for, when they first came to Jerusalem, and those who discovered this repository took up the charge to safeguard it. Thus was born the inner order of the Temple—what was to become *le Cercle*. And from this source must come the founding of the Fifth Temple, the Temple not built with human hands, which you are charged to erect."

"But, how is that possible?" Torquil murmured. "If the Tablets must remain . . ."

Iskander smiled faintly. "Tell me, either of you, did you ever wonder what became of the Shards of the First Tablets of the Law, which Moses cast down and shattered after he had come down from Mount Sinai?"

Both Arnault and Torquil stared at him blankly.

"No? Well, I shall tell you. They were placed in the Ark with the new Tablets of the Law, which was later hidden beneath the Temple Mount in Jerusalem. When the Ark was taken elsewhere, the Tablets and Shards were left behind, anchoring the site of the First Temple—for it is the *Shetiyyah*, the foundation stone of the world. Beneath the *Shetiyyah* is the *Bir el-Arweh*, the Well of Souls, where it is said that the voices of the dead can sometimes be heard, mingled with the sounds of the Rivers of Paradise.

"There the Tablets and the Shards lie, still. The living intrude at their peril. But with care and daring, a righteous man may enter those sacred precincts and remove one Shard only . . . and this he may use to erect the Fifth Temple. *The Law will destroy you . . . the Law will set you free.*"

Neither of his listeners spoke when he had finished, wideeyed and fearful to break the spell he had woven with his words. Arnault finally dared to clear his throat, reluctant to clarify what he thought Iskander was proposing.

"What you are saying, then, is that these—broken fragments of the original Tablets of the Law . . . were preserved with the second set of Tablets?"

"Yes. And having been writ by the Finger of God, encompassing His sacred Word, even the fragments became sacred things, hallows in their own right."

"And we must retrieve one of them . . . ?"

"Yes. But heed this caution: One fragment, and one fragment only, will serve to anchor the Fifth Temple. When the moment of choice is upon you, be sure to choose aright. The price of error," he concluded, "is death."

"How will I know?" Arnault asked, bewildered. "Can you help me?"

Iskander shook his head. "It is not I who have been appointed. But I can offer one thing that might prove efficacious. Whether it suffices will depend upon your faith and your own powers of discernment."

From the breast of his robe he extracted a flat leather case suspended about his neck on a stout leather thong, longer than the Templar medallion he had shown them before. He opened the case and took out a flat circular object the size of a man's palm, wrapped in a double thickness of silk. This he carefully parted, to reveal a large silver disk attached to a rather substantial silver chain.

The visible side of the disk glittered with uncut sapphires set amid scroll-patterns of strange, flowing script. The obverse, as Iskander lifted it by the chain, was polished to mirror-brightness, suggesting the clarity of water. At its very sight, Arnault's deeper sensibilities quickened, starting to draw him into it—until he blinked. Even without touching it, he knew the disk to be an item of great antiquity, and even greater power.

"The Mirror of Makeda," Iskander said. "I am its guardian."

"And this is how you found us," Arnault guessed. "And how you found me, at Chartres."

"Today—yes," Iskander confirmed. "But at Chartres, I knew you because you were the bearer of Solomon's Seal. The mystical resonances were almost overwhelming. Having found you once, it was not difficult to find you again, even without the Seal—even in the midst of the desert."

He gave the chain of the Mirror into Arnault's hands, watching as the Templar held it up for inspection with reverent awe.

"The Mirror is no mere scrying tool," Iskander cautioned. "It responds more strongly to the unspoken desires of the heart than to the conscious commands of the will. To interpret what you see aright, you must learn to discriminate between images which are merely images and those whose significance is symbolic. You are free to put the matter to the test."

Thus cautioned, Arnault folded the Mirror between his palms and closed his eyes, touching his fingertips to his forehead as he breathed a silent prayer.

Lord, open my unseeing eyes. To You Who gave sight to the blind do I yield all desire to see. Show me what You will, or nothing at all. . . .

He lowered his hands and opened them as, emptying his mind of all conscious thoughts, he bent his gaze to the polished face of the Mirror. Its surface at first appeared blank— a bright-flashing roundel cupped between his hands. As he continued to gaze in and through it, however, its quicksilver luster evaporated, leaving the Mirror dull and dark as old iron.

"Keep watching," Iskander whispered.

A few seconds later, a sudden slit of light burned itself across the center of the disk, dividing the Mirror in two. The slit slowly widened, like a pair of doors. Beyond the threshold, red-and-yellow streamers of flame flickered and lashed like dragons' tongues, so that it seemed to Arnault that he was gazing into the depths of a fiery furnace.

The flames mounted higher, twisting and turning like a tangle of salamanders. In the midst of the conflagration, Arnault glimpsed the shimmering outline of a human form. The form split and multiplied into four identical counterparts, one of which advanced on Arnault, filling his field of vision with its incandescent presence. Two blazing eyes gazed out at him from a fiery face mere inches from his own, and a voice like a flourish of war horns sounded in his ears.

> *He who hungers after the Law must face the Trials*
> *of Chaldea.*
> *He must tread under foot the fires of judgment*
> *And fear not to set his hand into the lion's mouth.*

With the pronouncement of these words the Mirror went blank. Arnault was left momentarily transfixed. Belatedly he became aware that his companions were both gazing at him intently. He gave himself a slight shake and offered the Mirror back to Iskander.

"Did you see anything?" Torquil asked.

"Yes," Arnault said. "But the meaning of what I saw will bear some thought."

"So it will," Iskander said. "But traveling on foot—as we must, starting a day's ride from here—it will take us twelve days yet to reach Jerusalem. You have that much time to read the riddle and decide what to do."

Chapter Thirty-one

1310

A FORTNIGHT LATER FOUND THE THREE OF THEM IN THE hallowed quiet of the Garden of Gethsemane, as the midnight hour approached. On the high ground above, a wind from Galilee sighed among the age-old groves for which the Mount of Olives had been named.

Arnault, Torquil, and Iskander sat huddled in their cloaks amid the ruins of a former shrine, each wrapped in his own thoughts. None of them spoke a word, though the two Westerners had formed a bond of trust with their Eastern brother during their shared journey of the past two weeks—and with the mute Berhanu, who would be waiting at their modest lodgings near Herod's Gate, watching over their few belongings in their absence.

Somewhere farther down the hillside a night bird called. Glancing over at Arnault, Torquil could not begin to foresee how the night might end. It seemed strange to reflect that in several hours' time the sun would rise on a new day. It was harder still to accept that by then, this part of their mission would all be over—for good or for ill.

Gethsemane lay at the upper end of the Kidron Valley. On the far side of the ravine, a dim chain of flickering watch lights marked the eastern perimeter of Jerusalem. The centuries that had seen the Holy City razed and rebuilt many times over had left the Mount of Olives untouched, at least since the time when the Son of God had prayed in this garden. It occurred to Torquil that the trees clothing the lower slopes might well be direct descendants of those which had borne silent witness to Christ's torment, betrayal, and triumph, more than a millennium before.

Three hundred yards to the west, dwarfing all surrounding landmarks, the great mass of Mount Moriah, the Temple Mount, loomed against the heat-hazed starry sky. Lifting his gaze, Torquil traced the graceful silhouette of the Dome of the Rock against the horizon. Other outbuildings formed a serrated line on either hand, with nary a cross to be seen. Though the once-proud fortifications of the Crusader Kingdom had been left to crumble into decay under Moslem rule, the sanctuary on the Rock remained in scrupulous repair.

It occurred to him that no other place on the face of the earth, perhaps, had such intense spiritual associations for so many. Separate in their individual beliefs, Jews, Christians, and Muslims were united in their reverence for the Temple Mount. For Jews, it was forever hallowed as the site where the First Temple had been built by King Solomon the Great. For Muslims, current masters of the Mount, the great rock beneath the Dome marked the place from which the Prophet Mohammed ascended on his Night Journey to Paradise. For Christians, it was the place from which their Messiah had revealed Himself to the world, preaching His message of salvation and eternal life.

More than a mere location, then, the Temple Mount—and the very concept of the Temple—was a matrix for mankind's ongoing quest toward the Divine; and behind this abstraction lay a still greater reality and a greater hope. Iskander had named its physical manifestation the *Shetiyyah*, the foundation stone of the world, whereon was centered all of human longing to be one with the Divine. And one day, if

Arnault succeeded in his night's mission, there would arise yet another Temple, greater than all its predecessors thus far—and even that would be but the next increment in mankind's yearning toward Divinity: the eternal Dream made real.

But for now, the whole world seemed veiled in darkness. The last party of ordinary pilgrims had left the Garden some time ago, their devotions accomplished, their reverences paid. So far as Torquil could tell, only he and Arnault and their Ethiopian brother remained, indistinct even from one another in the rustling gloom.

Arnault, too, was contemplating their circumstances, increasingly aware of being cut off from his companions by more than darkness. Iskander had warned him that the quest for the Tablets was his and his alone.

"The first test will be to find the entrance to the secret sanctuary," the Ethiopian brother had declared. "If you succeed, you must put aside all earthly things and set your mind on the things of Heaven. Only then will you be able to see your way clearly."

When Torquil had proposed accompanying Arnault, Iskander was adamant that Arnault must go alone.

"Where one man may tread safely, two may fall to ruin," he told the younger knight. "Brother Arnault's mind must be free from all distractions, his thoughts united to a single purpose. For his own sake, as much as yours, nothing must distract him from his goal."

But Torquil was not yet reconciled to the prospect of being left behind.

"Finding this hidden entrance could take some time," he murmured close to Arnault's ear. "Shouldn't we get started?"

"Not yet. Iskander says we must wait for a sign," Arnault reminded him.

"What sign?" Torquil murmured under his breath, increasingly impatient.

There was no moon. Night after night on the road north from Hebron, they had watched it wane, growing thinner and thinner until it finally disappeared.

Now was the turning of the lunar cycle, the waning moon become a waxing one—augury for auspicious beginnings. The heavens themselves were a featureless void, obscured by a heat haze that masked the desert stars. Nonetheless, Iskander sat gazing up at the sky as though he expected a host of angels to appear.

"I guess he knows what he's looking for," Torquil muttered dubiously.

Even as he spoke, a falling star penetrated the haze, dropping toward earth in a brief blaze of glory. Iskander stirred.

"It is time," he said softly.

Leaving the garden behind, they struck out along a well-trodden path leading down into the Vale of Kidron. The distant glimmer from the torchlight on the walls above gave faint illumination to the path leading southward along the base of the Mount. Halting in the shadow of a tall outcropping, Iskander turned to lay a surprisingly gentle hand on Arnault's forearm, his lips but a breath away from Arnault's ear.

"I have brought you this far," he whispered. "Now you must be our guide."

He took the Mirror of Makeda from its casing and presented it to Arnault, shaking out the Mirror's silk wrapping to fold it into a narrow strip as Arnault silently slipped the chain over his head.

"I shall use this band of silk to bind your eyes," Iskander informed him, as Torquil looked on. "Sight will not avail you in this task. Only faith can discern the threshold of the Hidden Door."

The cloth was heavily embroidered with mystical symbols of protection and enlightenment. Arnault could feel them under his fingertips as he held it in place over his eyes and Iskander secured it at the back of his head. A moment later he felt the Ethiopian's lean hand on his right shoulder, and Torquil's briefly touching his other arm in reassurance and leave-taking.

"May God be your guard and your guide," Iskander whispered. "May His angels keep watch, lest you dash your foot against a stone."

Both touches ceased. Arnault took a moment to collect his thoughts. Like so many birds of the air, they came to rest, briefly fluttering and then settling into stillness. The stir of a breeze against his face was like the touch of light fingers as he drew a deep breath, marshaling his deeper faculties of perception.

O God, be Thou as a lamp unto my feet, he prayed silently, *and as a watch in the night. Lead me, as a shepherd leads his sheep, into the shelter of the fold. . . .*

Another breath he drew, then hesitantly probed forward with one foot, then the other. Gathering assurance, with the mirror dangling against his chest, he moved forward with hands outstretched until his palms met stone.

At this, he abandoned himself to Providence, feeling his way among the rocks with his sandaled feet, moving this way and that, like a ship yielding to the wind, until all at once his fingertips brushed something that gave off a jolt of energy.

Surprise made him recoil, but only momentarily. He reached out a second time, and again experienced the needlelike prickle of power. The sensation spread throughout his body, setting his nerve ends tingling.

"Here," he called softly to his companions, barely breathing the single word.

When he sensed them beside him, he described what he had felt.

"There is a final test to make," Iskander said, moving behind him. "Permit me to unbind your eyes."

When the blindfold had been removed, Arnault tilted his head back to stretch his neck and saw, to his astonishment, that the heat haze had vanished, leaving the sky ablaze with stars. The Mirror on his breast caught and magnified their light, casting a silvery shimmer over the adjacent rock face, like the moon come down to earth—the moon that would not be, until a fortnight had passed.

The unearthly brightness was dazzling. Squinting, Arnault lifted both hands to shade his eyes. It was a moment before his vision adjusted, but what he saw made him catch his breath. Before him gaped a fissure in the rocks, wide enough to admit a man, its outline limned by a pearly sheen of starlight.

"There! Do you see it?" he asked, lifting one hand in that direction.

"I see nothing," Iskander said from behind him, "but your faith has given you vision. Now the way lies open. Take nothing with you but the Mirror, which alone must suffice to guide and protect you. We will remain here and pray for your safe return."

Wordlessly Arnault removed his sword and dirk and handed them over to Torquil, likewise removing his sandals, for he knew he was to tread on holy ground. His *keffiyeh* he retained, for he sensed it was meet to keep his head covered, for much the same reasons that he would go unshod, but he divested himself of his burnoose before stepping up to the fissure.

Though the opening remained outlined with a faint glow, he could discern only darkness beyond the threshold. After lightly touching the mirror to bolster up his nerve, he took a deep breath and stepped through the jagged arch.

A wave of dizziness rolled over him and wrenched at the pit of his stomach, as if the floor had suddenly dropped away beneath him. His bare toes instinctively curled for a better grip on the floor, and he flung out his hands to break a fall, scuffing the knuckles of one hand against the rock. Then the world righted itself, and he felt firm ground beneath his feet again.

Where he was, however, he had no clear idea. Glancing back and all around, he could not see the doorway through which he had passed. All around him he sensed a towering weight of stone, but he was by no means certain that he was standing in the flesh beneath Mount Moriah, or whether he had crossed over into some mystical realm between the physical world and the world of the spirit.

It occurred to him then to wonder how he was seeing anything at all. In that same instant, he realized that a faint illumination was emanating from the Mirror on his breast, like moonlight on water. As his eyes adjusted, the glow revealed that he was standing at one end of a barrel-vaulted passageway—or was it the passage itself that glowed as well?

He started down it. Far at the end of the passage, becoming more distinct as he approached, a looming figure began to take shape, silent and motionless, human in form but larger than human in its proportions.

Venturing closer, Arnault realized that it was a statue, curiously fashioned out of several different materials. The statue's head was made of gold, finely wrought, but its breast and arms were of silver, while its lower trunk and thighs were made of bronze. The statue's thick legs were iron, its feet sculpted from a mixture of iron and clay.

The feet of clay triggered the pertinent memory from scripture, from the Book of Daniel. Gazing up at the statue, Arnault found himself remembering how Nebuchadnezzar, King of Babylon, had envisioned such an entity in a dream, interpreted by the prophet as an apocalyptic symbol of future events.

Even as this thought crossed his mind, his eye was drawn to an inscribed plaque on the statue's broad breast. Dismay briefly seized him as he leaned closer to make out the words, for he read little Hebrew, but the very act of leaning closer caused the Mirror on his breast to cast a bright reflection upon it—and suddenly, he could read the words with ease.

Who shall ascend into the hill of the Lord?
or who shall stand in His holy place?
He that hath clean hands, and a pure heart;
Who hath not lifted up his soul unto vanity.

He recognized the passage. It came from one of the Psalms. In this otherworldly setting, the words somehow took on the resonance of a warning.

But, a warning of what? Arnault asked himself.

Pondering the verse's meaning more deeply, he realized that he was being challenged to prove himself worthy to proceed. He could almost hear Torquil's trenchant Scottish voice asking, "If this is a trial, who is the judge?"

The word *judge* struck a chord in Arnault's thoughts. The Sacred Tablets of the Law had been handed down to God's chosen people as a prescription for righteousness.

And God Himself was the Judge to Whom every member of that community was ultimately accountable. Given the universal frailty of human nature, what man would dare enter into the court of Heaven declaring himself wholly blameless? Indeed, when had any human being save One ever attained perfect obedience in the spirit of perfect love?

Renouncing all self-justification, Arnault lowered himself to both knees and bowed his head over folded hands in an attitude of abject humility, offering up all his frailties and failings.

Thou art my Lord and my God, he prayed. *Into Thy hands I commit my spirit, trusting not in my own righteousness, but in Thine abiding mercy. . . .*

In the silence he could hear his own heartbeat, his pulse throbbing in his ears. Then a warmth enfolded him like a benison and a Voice entered his thoughts, breathing a fragrance of benison into his soul.

I am the door: By Me, if any man entereth in, he shall be saved. . . .

It was as though he were hearing the words afresh, at the

moment of their first utterance, ringing clearly across a gulf of earthly time. Drawing resolve from these words, Arnault was emboldened to open his eyes and raise his head. From his kneeling position, face upturned toward a faint light being reflected from the Mirror on his breast, he glimpsed something that had not been visible when he was standing upright: an arched recess in the wall behind the statue, previously hidden in the shadows cast by the statue's looming bulk. Just discernible within the arch was a door.

He started to get to his feet, but paused with one knee still bent as a dull glint of metal drew his attention toward the statue's right foot. Leaning closer, he saw it was an iron key embedded in the clay at an angle that would not have been discernible from above.

Carefully, with due respect, he reached out and pried it from its matrix. It seemed quite an ordinary key, but he knew it could not be but extraordinary in this place. He weighed it in his palm as he hauled himself fully erect and sidestepped the statue, advancing to the wall behind to run his hand along until it found the portal. Here the glow from the Mirror revealed another inscription, which he was able to read at once:

There are many paths, but only one true way.
He who loses himself will never find it.

Chapter Thirty-two

1310

BRACING HIMSELF TO MEET WHATEVER NEW CHALLENGE might lie behind the door, Arnault fitted the key into the keyhole. The lock yielded with a crack like breaking ice, and the door moved slightly beneath his hands.

Almost light-headed with the tension, Arnault carefully pushed the door open. When no immediate danger threatened—though he could not see far into the chamber beyond—he stepped warily over the threshold.

The glow from Makeda's Mirror revealed a small, square cubicle with three other doorway arches confronting him to left, right, and center. Each doorway gave access to a shadowy maze of short-angled passageways. Standing in the cubicle, Arnault closely examined each of the doorways in turn, running his fingers over the doorposts and lintels. Neither sight nor touch revealed any clue to suggest which way he ought to go.

He paused to reconsider the inscription, suspecting that the answer might well lie within it:

. . . many paths, but only one true way. He who loses himself will never find it. . . .

But though he sifted the lines word by word, and phrase

by phrase, he could tease out no hint of hidden meaning. It appeared he must proceed by trial and error, and pray that an error would not be his undoing.

Again he considered the three doorways, then chose the center one, reckoning it to represent the straight and narrow path that was recommended as the goal of a righteous man. He soon found himself in the midst of a tangle of cross corridors, and knew that if he went on without marking his choices in some manner, he was sure to go astray if he must retrace his steps.

He had nothing to use, however, and nothing metal besides the Mirror with which to try scratching a mark—and he dared not risk damaging that. The floor was too uneven and stony for his bare feet to leave footprints, and there were enough loose stones on the ground that trying to set some pattern at each turning would be nigh impossible.

He considered leaving marks in his own blood, but even that presented difficulties, with no blade to make a cut. He supposed he could gouge his flesh with a sharp stone, or even use his teeth to draw blood, but somehow smearing blood on the walls seemed like a desecration in this place.

He was agonizing over what to do when he realized he was straining to see much farther than the length of his arm. To his dismay, he realized that the Mirror's light was fading.

Chilled, for he already was deep into the heart of the mountain, he lifted the Mirror from his breast to take a closer look—and made an even more disconcerting discovery: Though he was gazing directly into the Mirror, its surface gave back no hint of a reflection.

He recoiled in surprise. Doubting the evidence of his own eyes, he tilted the mirror this way and that, seeking a new angle of vision, shifting his position as he tried to distance himself from the nearest shadows. Not until he turned himself around did he find that his image suddenly reappeared within the Mirror's frame.

The sight stopped him short, staring. On an impulse he

pivoted aside. The Mirror promptly went blank. Further experimentation established that his image was only visible as long as he was facing back the way he had come—which, he suddenly realized, was consistent with the inscription at the door that led to the three choices:

There are many paths, but only one true way.
He who loses himself will never find it.

Which now made things perfectly clear: His reflection was present in the Mirror only when he was facing the proper direction—and the Mirror was showing him that direction by showing him himself. Having now found himself, he must continue to keep his own image before him.

The revival of his faith rekindled the Mirror's fading light. Holding the polished disk before him like a lantern, he strode out confidently, and soon had returned to the intersection where he had made his first choice.

Again standing before the three arches, he held the Mirror to the left and to the right. Only darkness showed at the left, but his face was clear and bright as he moved the Mirror before the right-hand archway.

A righteous man shall walk the right-hand path, he murmured under his breath, recalling one of the first precepts taught to any warrior in the service of the Light.

He set out confidently in that direction. The shadows fled before him, banished along with his doubts. Responsive to the Mirror's promptings, he threaded his way through a labyrinth of tangled passages, now confident of reaching his intended goal.

The silence seemed to weigh more heavily as he progressed; centuries of dust befuddled his nostrils. As he rounded yet another bend in the labyrinth, a breath of warmer air seemed to rise up before him; around the next bend, he began to discern a crimson glow ahead.

The air grew hotter, laced with the acidic tang of hot

metal. A muted crackle and roar now began to niggle at the edges of his hearing, like fires playing round a forge. A moment later, he emerged into an area of open space.

Before him stood a pair of iron doors, like the gates to a furnace, outlined by a fiery glow from within. Feeling their heat, which came from the doors themselves as well as what lay beyond, Arnault recalled the words of warning the Mirror had given him the first time he used it, spoken to him from out of the flames:

> *He who hungers after the Law must face the Trials*
> *of Chaldea.*
> *He must pass unscathed through the fires of judgment*
> *And fear not to set his hand in the lion's mouth.*

At once, he made the biblical connection. The Trials of Chaldea, like the statue of many parts, had their place in the Book of Daniel. Through the intercession of an angel of the Lord, the prophet and his companions had survived the fiery furnace and the lion's den. But would the Angel of the Lord intercede for a Knight of the Order of the Temple?

As he hesitated before his own indecision, the sullen roar of the flames grew louder as, with a deep, sonorous clang, the doors to the furnace began slowly to open. Heat billowed forth in sulfurous gusts, like the exhalations from an inferno, causing Arnault to shield his face with an upflung arm.

Beyond the threshold of the forge, he could see a raised causeway extending out over the liquid swirls of flame and smoke, as deep and tumultuous as the mouth of Hell. Paved with smoldering coals, the causeway glowed mottled black against a lurid background of scarlet and gold, with tongues of flame crackling along its borders like hungry imps.

Retreating a step before the onslaught of heat and light, Arnault could feel the sweat beginning to pour from his brow and trickle down his ribs; yet here, clearly, lay the path he must tread. The very notion filled him with dread. In his dreams and nightmares he had shared the mortal anguish of his brother Templars condemned to the stake, shrinking from the anguish of the flames that ate away skin from flesh and flesh from bone. Rarely a night passed that some hint of their torment did not touch his dreams.

Yet he forced himself to approach the mouth of the forge, dragging an edge of his *keffiyeh* up to wipe the sweat from his eyes and brow and then, as an afterthought, drawing it across his lower face, tucking the end into the cords that bound it, hoping that this scant protection might at least make it easier to breathe. The heat smote him like a hammer, still causing mortal flesh to cringe aside in instinct, but if his brothers had endured the flames for the sake of the Order, he could not but do likewise. Still shielding his face partway under his upraised arm, he set a bare foot firmly on the near end of the bridge.

The surface was hot, but it did not sear his flesh—at least not yet. Determined not to yield to his dread, he drew cautious breath and began edging forward, one step at a time. Smoke snaked up around his ankles, and the heat intensified, as he moved resolutely forward.

The heat from the bridge began to raise blisters on the soles of his feet as dragonets of flame snapped at him from both sides, singeing his garments and the hairs on his forearm. Acrid fumes forced their way past the cloth covering his mouth and nose, causing him to wheeze and choke. Limping and staggering, gasping for breath, he could only pray that he might reach the other end of the causeway before his strength gave out.

If only he could simply *see* how far he still had to go. The very air seemed on fire. More than half-blind, he struggled on until a sudden whirling blast forced him to a standstill, stranding him on an island in a sea of flame. Dismayed, driven to the limits of his endurance, he all but gave himself up for lost.

Arnault, have faith in God!

Scorched and half-suffocated, Arnault started at the sound
of his name, squinting ahead through tearing eyes to glimpse
a light-limned figure moving toward him through winding
sheets of flame. His wonder gave him fresh hope, and he
made himself take another step, then another.

The other drew nearer, lightly moving through the flames
as if they were no more than swaths of tall grass in a spring
meadow. His hair lifted on the fire-breeze, but his white garments went untouched by the fire that blazed round him on
all sides. While he was yet a short way off, a gust of burning wind flung back his mantle, revealing a red cross *pattée*
on the breast of his tunic. Youthful and handsome, the Templar's bearded face was one that Arnault knew very well.

"*Jauffre!*" he cried.

Further speech failed him. Jauffre, with a smile of deep
affection, turned and beckoned with a sweep of his arm.
Beyond him, through the heat-shimmer, Arnault saw three
more white-robed figures striding through the fiery storm.
Two of them were fellow Templars whose martyrdom Arnault had witnessed in his dreams—or in his nightmares.
Likewise robed in white, the third loomed a full head taller,
with hair like flame and eyes that seemed to plumb the very
depths of Arnault's soul, radiating a puissance only thinly
veiled by his semblance of human form. The flames that
trailed behind him gave just a hint of fiery wings.

Enraptured, heedless of his own peril, Arnault sank to
both his knees, pierced to the soul by the other's beauty. His
parched throat could make no sound, but his heart sang out
as his arms lifted in greeting.

*Hail, holy Michael, great captain of the hosts of Heaven!
Hail, Cra-gheal, the Red-White One, bearer of the sword of
victory!*

At a sign from their angelic captain, Jauffre and the other
Templar martyrs formed a shining company around Arnault,
their presence like an encircling shield wall, shutting out the
flames of the inferno. As strong hands raised him tenderly to

his feet, he felt all his pain fall away in a single healing instant. The angel spoke in a voice of breathtaking melody:

> *These are they which came out of great tribulation,*
> *and have washed their robes,*
> *and made them white in the Blood of the Lamb.*
> *They shall hunger no more, neither thirst anymore,*
> *neither shall the sun light on them, nor any heat.*
> *Commend thyself to their fellowship,*
> *and they will gird thee for the battle yet to come.*

A fragrance like attar of roses swept over him, ravishing his senses with holy rapture. When he recovered himself, the angel had vanished, but the three Templar martyrs remained.

It was Jauffre who was the first to address him, drawing his sword and placing it in Arnault's right hand.

Receive the sword of righteousness, he told Arnault. *Wield it in defense of the Law.*

The second knight-brother now bore a shield, which he presented to Arnault in his turn.

Place upon your arm the buckler of valor, he said. *May it avert the malice of the Enemy.*

The third brother carried a helmet under one arm. This he placed on Arnault's head, saying, *Be crowned with the helmet of truth. May you find what you seek.*

"I give you my abiding thanks," Arnault told them, saluting the three with the sword. "As long as the Order endures, in whatever place, know that your sacrifice will never be forgotten."

He and Jauffre exchanged the fraternal kiss of peace, the latter folding him briefly in a fierce embrace. With that, the three Templar martyrs faded from his sight and the lingering fires flickered and winked out. Left alone, helmed and armed with sword and shield, Arnault found himself standing in a place of mystery.

Light from the Mirror of Makeda cast a silvery circle

about his feet. Outside its narrow radius lay darkness. As he attempted to orient himself, there came a soft, heavy thud from somewhere off to his left.

He stiffened and turned in that direction, scanning around him. In a heartbeat, there came a shadowy surge of movement from off to his right. He dropped to a crouch, tightening his grip on sword and shield as he glimpsed two bestial shapes prowling beyond the circle of light.

The creatures were larger than ponies. Arnault's nostrils picked up a rank waft of animal breath. Raising his guard, he slowly pivoted this way and that. As he did so, a Mirror glint registered two pairs of shining amber eyes.

With a sudden roar, a great feline shape came bounding out of the shadows. Arnault's shield took the brunt of the attack, but claws like daggers shredded the sleeve of his robe, narrowly missing his arm beneath. He lashed out with his sword and scored a bloody line along one tawny flank.

The lion veered off with a yowl of pain and rage. Its mate leapt in to take its place. Her charging weight knocked Arnault off-balance, and he staggered and fell, landing flat on his back.

Snarling, the lioness lunged for his throat. Fending her off with his shield, Arnault thrust at the creature's underbelly—and penetrated deep. With a mortal scream, the she-lion recoiled, wrenching the sword from his grasp.

Before he could retrieve it, the male lion rushed in. Arnault went rolling under a heavy blow from a powerful paw, finishing flat on his back and with the lion pinning his shield arm under its full weight—and recoiled from a blast of lion breath as gleaming fangs suddenly yawned mere inches from his face. In sheer desperation, he made a tight fist and lashed out at the lion's mouth with all his strength, bracing himself to feel the daggerlike teeth crunch down on his hand and wrist.

To his amazement, nothing happened. The lion stood

transfixed, at the height of its fury, its frothing jaws agape. It was as if time itself had been suspended.

Hardly daring to breathe, watching its eyes, Arnault withdrew his fist from the lion's maw. The creature remained motionless, then turned semi-transparent before melting away like smoke into the surrounding darkness.

First the fiery furnace, and then the lion's den, Arnault thought dazedly, as he heaved himself up onto his elbows.

He now could see no trace of either lion. Not a sound could he hear besides his own rasping breath and the pounding of his heart.

Making a conscious effort to steady his breathing, he briefly stretched to retrieve the sword. As he did so, the air became suffused with a shimmering sapphire glow, magnified by the Mirror on his breast, which pushed back the darkness to reveal a circular chamber hollowed out of the rock.

He hauled himself to a sitting position, still breathing hard. The chamber seemed to be configured as a chapel. On the far side stood a stone altar draped with a linen cloth of snowy white. A seven-branched candlestick adorned either end, with a gilded casket resting between them, its lid peaked like the roof of a house. The casket itself was the source of the celestial blue glow, and radiated enormous power.

Laying the sword aside, Arnault likewise put off the buckler and got to his feet, also removing the helmet, for there was no doubt in his mind that the casket contained what he had come to find. Its allure was as irresistible as it was potent, drawing him to kneel before the altar and humbly abase himself. He then rose up on his knees and lifted his head to examine the casket by its own sapphire light.

There was no lock that he could see. Instead, the box was embellished with scrolls of Hebrew script and cabalistic symbols of warding. The writings echoed the many cautions that Arnault had received from Iskander in preparation for this night's work.

"The Sacred Tablets were inscribed by the Finger of God," the Ethiopian brother had reminded him. "The *Shekinah*, the Divine Presence, the very *Ruach* that brooded upon the waters and brought forth life. Even broken, the Shards are perilous to look upon, so long as all the pieces remain gathered together in one place. If you value your sight, rely on the Mirror to show you what you need to see."

With this warning in mind, Arnault averted his gaze before venturing to tilt back the lid on the casket. Intense sapphire light shone out like the opening of a great eye, dazzling as the midday sun, so powerful that it rendered the casket semitranslucent. He breathed a prayer from distant Iona as he moved closer on his knees.

> *God and Christ and Spirit Holy,*
> *Be protecting me as Three and as One,*
> *From the top tablet of my face*
> *To the soles of my feet. . . .*

Squinting against the brightness, Arnault took the Mirror of Makeda in hand and carefully extended it over the open casket, its face angled to reflect the contents—which were, indeed, the Tablets of the Law. Atop the thickness of the Second Tablets, the Shards of the First Tablets had been arranged in accordance to their unbroken form. Even with his eyes growing accustomed to the brightness of the casket itself, the script was so bright that Arnault was forced to squint before he could attempt to decipher its reflections—not only fragmented, in a language and script not his mother tongue, but reflected in reverse. Iskander's words reverberated in the back of his mind like a warning bell.

One fragment only will restore the Temple to eminence . . . and the price of error is death. . . .

Drawing steadying breath, by dint of concentration, Arnault singled out each Commandment in turn and considered its full meaning, beginning with the ones most apt to be applied to the Temple by their accusers, carefully testing the weight of each injunction against the truth.

Thou shalt not make unto thyself any graven image? No, the Templars had never worshiped idols, whatever their accusers might claim.

Thou shalt not kill? In time of war, the Templars most assuredly had fought and killed in defense of their faith, but they had never been guilty of murder—which was the actual meaning of the word.

Thou shalt not bear false witness against thy neighbor.

Even as Arnault read the words, he was seized by a sense of certainty. The gross charges being pressed against the Templars were based not on truth, or even individual failings, but on lies deliberately fabricated by their enemies. Surely vested in this commandment was the very essence of the danger which threatened the Order.

He pondered a moment longer, briefly examining the other seven Commandments, but after reflection, he remained convinced of his choice. Drawing a deep breath, he reached into the casket and laid his hand on the chosen Shard.

Despite his faith, he half expected immolation to follow. Instead, the radiance slowly faded back, as if gathered to its source. Heart beating hard, Arnault lifted the Shard from its resting place, closing it in his hand, and reverently thrust it into the bosom of his robe. Then, feeling suddenly very weary, he sank back on his hunkers and closed his eyes, breathing a profound prayer of gratitude.

Even as his thoughts ascended toward the Divine, he was once again seized by the sensation of soul-flight. With it came a rushing sound, as of a great wind. Weightless as a feather, he let it bear him where it would. When at last he felt ground beneath him, he slowly drew a deep breath and opened his eyes.

To his surprise, he was standing before a sky flushed with the first hints of dawn, at the mouth of the fissure where he first had entered Mount Moriah. Whether his own feet had carried him here, he had no idea. Half-doubting the evidence of his own eyes, he pressed a hand to his chest and felt the irregular outline of the Sacred Shard. Somewhat dazedly, he staggered out into the open air.

Torquil and Iskander were waiting, the latter looking not at all surprised to see him there. Torquil flung a supporting arm around his drooping shoulders and bore him up as his knees started to give way.

"Are you all right?" he asked anxiously. "Did you find—?"

As the question faltered on his lips, Iskander exclaimed, "He lives, does he not? What need have we to ask more?"

Arnault sensed, rather than heard, a rumbling sound behind him. When he turned to look, he could see no trace of the fissure.

"God has closed the door," Iskander said. "Let us hope there will be no need for any man to open it again before the Last Day."

"Amen to that!" Torquil agreed.

The light was broadening in the east.

"We'd better be gone," Arnault murmured, "before the city wakes."

Berhanu welcomed their return with shining eyes. After they had barred the door of their hired chamber, Arnault divested himself of the Mirror of Makeda and gave it back into Iskander's keeping.

"Thank you for entrusting me with it," he said. "Without its guidance, I could not have survived."

"It was my privilege to be of service," Iskander replied. "In return, I give you something of a different nature, which you may take away with you."

With a soft word, he bade Berhanu fetch what appeared to be a small pillow of scarlet silk, as big as a man's hand.

In truth, the scarlet proved to be a casing for a folded wad of natural silk which, when shaken out and spread upon the floor, showed drawings of big-eyed saints and angels inked in red and black, interspersed with lines of writing in an odd, angular alphabet. All of this was contained within patterns of tracery that bore a close resemblance to some of the Celtic designs Arnault and Torquil had seen on Iona.

"Among my people," Iskander explained, "paintings such as these are known to have healing virtues. Usually, they are made for a specific person and done on parchment sized to the height of that person. If one is being particularly faithful to tradition, the parchment is made from the skin of an animal sacrificed as a substitute for the person, usually a lamb. This one, however, has been done on silk, as you can see, so that you may use it to wrap around the Shard to protect it—though it is still the length of a man. It is Berhanu's work," he added, with a smile at the mute servant.

Duly impressed, both Arnault and Torquil bent closer to study the work.

"Berhanu, you are very skilled," Arnault said, glancing up appreciatively. "Iskander, can you explain some of the symbolism?"

"Yes, this is Michael, our patron, whose wings enfold those who serve him, and these are the names of the three nails of the Cross that pierced our Lord's sacred flesh," Iskander said, pointing out parts of the design. "This is *Chä-Danat, ChäRodas,* and *ChäAdera.* Their presence imparts powerful protection. And this heart, pierced by the Crown of Thorns, signifies that you must ask from the heart, if ever you should need to invoke the cloth's healing powers, for God will heed such prayers."

Arnault accepted the gift with deep gratitude, helping Iskander to refold it and return it to its carrying pouch, after which he brought out the Shard to lay it atop the pouch for Iskander's inspection. By daylight, it appeared to be of some bluish, faintly translucent material, deeply incised with the Hebrew letters of the ninth Commandment.

"*Lo sa-aneh v'ray-achor,*" Iskander murmured, reading it aloud. "*Thou shalt not bear false witness.* Truly, an inspired choice. I shall pray it serves you well."

Arnault slipped it into the silken folds of the pouched talisman and tucked the pouch into the bosom of his robe.

"We are extremely grateful for your assistance, Brother Iskander," he said. "Please God, it will assist us in establishing the Fifth Temple, but we still have a long road and many battles ahead of us. Will you not accompany us back to Scotland?"

The Ethiopian brother shook his head. "Regretfully, I cannot. Like you, I answer to superiors who are waiting to hear the outcome of this venture."

"Not, I hope, before we've rested and shared a final meal, then," Torquil said.

A rare smile illumined Iskander's chiseled features. "Tomorrow will be soon enough for us to set out on our separate roads. Thereafter . . ."

He paused and shrugged. "Only the great God knows whether we shall meet again in the body. But when you go up against your enemies, be assured that my brothers and I will be with you in spirit."

Chapter Thirty-three

Spring, 1312

IT WAS THE SPRING OF 1312 BY THE TIME ARNAULT AND Torquil stood once again on French soil: a year and more of impatience, boredom, and growing anxiety punctuated by incidents of peril, but at least the dangers they faced were impersonal, unlike what they knew awaited them and what so many of their incarcerated brethren were enduring.

They had heard little news of the state of affairs in France or Scotland during their absence; and even what they learned in Alexandria, before taking ship for their return, was at least six months old. Once they landed at Marseilles, however—again attired in the long, coarse robes and sheepskin mantles more usually affected by pilgrims—they found the port abuzz with gossip of Templar trials and tortures and burnings, and the expectation that the pope, presently resident at Vienne, at last was about to make a pronouncement regarding the fate of the Order.

"I wonder if we ought to detour to Vienne," Torquil murmured aside to Arnault, as they sheltered from a spring hailstorm in the lee of a doorway, on their way out of the city.

Arnault shook his head, squinting under the wide brim of his leather pilgrim hat. In addition to the pilgrim badges they had started out with, both now displayed withered sprigs of Jericho palm, and cockleshells dangled from their iron-shod pilgrim staves, betokening completed pilgrimages both to Jerusalem and to Santiago de Compostela—though, in truth, they had not delayed further to stop in Spain, and their Jerusalem pilgrimage had been far from conventional.

Their swords still were wrapped and bundled with their tent accoutrements, which Torquil carried slung across his back, but their dirks were nearer to hand, hidden beneath their robes as before. Arnault had shouldered a second pack with their foodstuffs; and of course, the Shard of the Law still resided next to his heart, wrapped in its Ethiopic silk, though carried now in a leather pouch he had stitched early on the voyage home.

"I'll grant you, it's tempting to want to be present when the judgment is rendered," Arnault said, "but we can't afford the delay." He kept his voice low, even though the street was empty. "Better that we continue on to Paris, where we have a better chance of meeting up with friends. There's more risk there, perhaps, but we know the city, and we know the hiding places."

"There *was* that report of fugitive knights hiding in the woods outside Lyon," Torquil offered. "That's very close to Vienne."

"Yes, and I expect they're long gone by now. That was six months ago." Arnault squinted up at the hail, which was abating. "I don't know why we bothered to take shelter. After simmering in the desert for the past several years, you'd think we'd be glad of a chance for a soaking."

Torquil grinned, teeth flashing in a beard now gone more gray than red, though not nearly as gray as Arnault's. He had discovered, on the voyage back, that he no longer needed to drab its once-distinctive color.

"You're right. It was only a thought. Anyway, if the Holy Father *is* about to announce his decision, I'm sure we'll hear about it somewhere along our way."

They continued to piece together a chronology for the past several years, as they headed north out of Marseilles. Of affairs in Scotland or, indeed, any word of Bruce, they could gain not a jot of information this far south, but many of their fellow travelers had definite opinions about the Templars. Much was patently incorrect, simply reiterating the old rumors and innuendoes. But hints of a curious side intrigue emerged during conversation with a traveling friar, the day after their arrival, suggesting that the council currently meeting in Vienne to decide the fate of the Templars was the result of a deal made between king and pope.

"Personally, I don't think the Templars are guilty," the friar said, "but the king is determined to be rid of them. There was rumor last year that he threatened to revive the old charges against Pope Boniface VIII unless Clement agreed to condemn the Templars. Whether or not that's true, the king withdrew the charges, and the Holy Father has convened this new council. They say a verdict is expected very soon."

Arnault was shaking his head. "Well, I suppose it must be resolved eventually. Has there been no defense?"

The friar shrugged and had another pull at his ale. "I think the heart has gone out of them. Too many have died, and suffered unspeakable tortures. Certainly, no fair trial is possible."

In light of this appraisal, Arnault and Torquil did not regret their original decision to steer well clear of Vienne. Nor had their spirits been lifted by the accounts they heard of the tortures inflicted on many of their captive brethren—and the growing realization that upwards of a hundred of their fellow Templars already had been burned as relapsed heretics, for recanting confessions extracted under torture. In the worst incident, confirmed by a fellow fugitive they met in Nevers—who was able to provide them with a pair of horses and a meal—more than fifty men had perished at the stake, protesting their innocence to the last.

"Jauffre would have been one of those," Arnault had murmured, a little while after they had left Brother Pierre. And
God alone knew how many more of the doomed men the
pair of them had known personally.

At least with the horses, they made better time after that,
though the beasts were nothing like the fine Templar mounts
that once would have been their due. But the long-dreaded
news from Vienne caught up with them in Orléans, on a fine
day in April, that a verdict had been rendered, a papal bull
promulgated. That afternoon, they reluctantly joined a
jostling, uneasy crowd gathered in the cathedral square to
hear the verdict read, meekly doffing their hats like everyone else as papal guards escorted a bishop's chaplain to a
place on a balcony near the cathedral.

"From this day forth," the chaplain declared, unfurling a
parchment scroll with the papal seal dangling, "by the decree of His Holiness, the Order of the Temple is suppressed.
All their rights are withdrawn and all their lands are forfeit.
Following is the text of the papal bull, *Vox in excelso*."

He then began to read in Latin. Few present would understand the words, but all knew what the decree portended.
The word had spread far and wide that the Templar Order
was not simply to be purged; it was to be destroyed.

The first part of the text set the stage, telling how the
pope, at about the time of his election as Supreme Pontiff,
had received secret intimations against the master, preceptors, and other brothers of the Order of the Temple and
against the Order itself. Therefore, it was against the Lord
Jesus Christ Himself that they fell into the sin of "impious
apostasy, the abominable vice of idolatry, the deadly crime
of the men of Sodom. . . ."

The decree went on to outline how the pope, like so many
others, had not wished to believe the charges at first. But
what had changed his mind about the guilt of the Templars
had been the revelations of a faithful son of the Church,
". . . which seemed to be proved by the many confessions,

attestations, and depositions of the Visitor of France and of the many preceptors and brothers of the Order in the presence of many prelates and the inquisitor of heresy. . . ."

In addition, through "spontaneous" confessions, a number of individual members had been convicted of such heresies, crimes, and sins as to render the Order very suspect, the infamy and suspicion making it "detestable to the holy Church of God, to her prelates, to kings and others rulers, and to Catholics in general." It was also believed that from now on, there would be no good person who wished to enter the Order, and so it would be made useless to the Church of God and for service to the Holy Land, for which services the knights had been dedicated.

"Therefore, with a sad heart," the papal chaplain went on, "not by definitive sentence, but by apostolic provision or ordinance, we suppress, with the approval of the sacred council, the Order of Templars, and its rule, habit, and name, by an inviolable and perpetual decree."

From the corner of his eye, Arnault saw Torquil look down, swallowing with difficulty, for this surely was the death knell of the Order.

"We entirely forbid that any from this time forward should enter the Order, or receive or wear its habit, or presume to behave as a Templar. If anyone acts otherwise he incurs automatic excommunication. In addition, we reserve the persons and the property of the Templars for our own disposition and the Apostolic See. . . ."

With a few more words, it was done. Utter silence followed this pronouncement, such that even far across the cathedral square, the rustle of parchment could be heard as the papal chaplain rolled up his scroll, turning away to converse quietly with two waiting prelates as a belated murmur of conversation rippled through the crowd. To Torquil, it would have seemed more fitting if such a condemnation had been marked by a clap of thunder or some other omen of doom. A few scattered cheers and catcalls rang out, but even

these lacked force, as if most of the crowd had already consigned the Templar Order to oblivion.

In twos and threes, the people began to disperse, their talk
at once returning to the business of their own daily affairs.
For them life would go on as it had before, but for the two
Templars unbeknownst in their midst, life would never
again be the same. From henceforth they would forever be
fugitives.

Neither Arnault nor Torquil said a word until they were
well away from the square, retrieving their horses from the
inn where they had left them.

"Clement actually did it," Torquil said softly, as the two
of them tightened up their cinches and prepared to leave.
"He threw us to the wolves."

"You actually thought he might have a last-minute attack
of courage?" Arnault asked, securing the last strap on the
pack behind his saddle.

Torquil sighed and shook his head, leaning briefly on his
horse's rump to gaze across at his companion. He had
known the words to expect, but he had not reckoned on their
effect. That the Templars should have been thus disowned
by the church they had fought to serve and protect made him
feel desolate and orphaned, as if his own father had turned
his back on him in his hour of need.

"I suppose I hoped that something would happen at the
last minute, to change the inevitable. This is the work of
King Philip, you know. And probably Nogaret."

"Oh, well do I know," Arnault replied.

His voice was wistful, his gaze flicking momentarily into
some dimension visible only to himself as one hand brushed
the faint bulge of the pouch under his robe, where he carried
the fragment they had retrieved from beneath the Temple
Mount. In that instant, Torquil was struck by the irony that
Arnault should be carrying one of the broken fragments of
the first Tablets of the Law, and wondered what law the
Templars might have transgressed to merit their fate.

And how, now, was the Law to uphold them, as both Iskander and an aged Jew had promised? Was Arnault drawing comfort from the sights and images he had witnessed beneath the Temple Rock? Or was he beset by fear that, for all they had accomplished, they were returning home too late?

"What now, then?" Torquil asked quietly.

"Now we ride on to Paris," Arnault said, "and see what can still be salvaged. We have yet to learn how things fare in Scotland. After today, more than ever, that remains our only hope for a safe haven. Here in France, the past is a closed country to us now. We must hope that our Scottish brethren have been more successful."

With that, he turned to lead his horse out of the yard, Torquil following behind, both of them carrying their pilgrim staves in their free hands as they shouldered through the crowds, for it was market day. They had traversed the adjacent street and were headed toward a crossroads ahead when Torquil noticed the beggar trailing behind them with a purposeful air.

"I see him," Arnault murmured, before Torquil could speak.

Shoulders stooped beneath a grimy mantle of rags and patches, the beggar made an oblique approach, rag-bound feet deceptively nimble, for only belatedly did Torquil notice how quickly he—or she—was moving; for it was not even clear whether the figure was man or woman. A sack-cloth hood shrouded the other's bent head, as if to conceal some hideous disfigurement, and a bandaged hand was locked around a staff that was also a crutch. The other hand reached out of a ragged sleeve toward the Templars, grimy palm outspread in appeal.

"Alms, good pilgrims, for the love of God . . ." a rasping voice whined.

Torquil was already fumbling in his scrip for a copper or two, intending to be rid of the stranger as quickly as possible, but the beggar's next words made him falter with his hand inside.

"The Circle remains yet unbroken."

In the same moment that those words were softly spoken, the mendicant tilted his head, allowing a glimpse of the face within the muffling hood. Beneath the smearing of dirt that formed part of his disguise, there was no mistaking Armand Breville.

"Affect not to know me," Breville whispered, even as he thrust his hand more emphatically under Torquil's nose, "but your pilgrim heart is moved to charity. Continue on. I'll find you. And be wary of *them*."

Arnault was already turning away, face composed, immediately in character. Torquil, by now with a copper in hand, tossed it toward the "beggar's" outstretched hand and continued on; but both of them noted the direction of Breville's chin gesture as he cringed, fumbling and dropping the coin, then scrabbled among the horses' legs to retrieve it.

"There in the doorway," Torquil murmured.

"I see them," Arnault replied.

"Be sure you are not followed," Breville whispered urgently.

The two led their horses on, feigning to pay no further notice to Breville or the two city guards lounging in the distant doorway. At a square at the end of the next street, they paused at a fountain to water their horses. Arnault used the stop to pretend concern for one of his horse's front feet, calling for Torquil's consultation as he lifted the hoof and prodded at the frog.

"Any sign that we're being followed?" he whispered.

"No."

"All right, we'll linger for a few minutes, then move on."

When they had mounted up, they continued on along the street headed north, picking their way slowly through a modest market-day crowd. At the next intersection, the ties on a scrawny-looking pack pony had come asunder, and a large, amiable-looking man was scrambling to retrieve his belongings before a pack of urchins made off with anything.

"All right, you lot, get away!" he cried, snatching a pot from under one young lad's nose. "*You,* drop that!"

As another boy darted in to seize a fallen sack, Torquil gigged his horse forward to grab the child by an upper arm and wrench him around, giving him a quick shake to make him drop the sack before releasing him. Arnault had crowded right behind him, and the arrival of two mounted men on the scene sent the remaining children scattering.

A smile creased the face of the big man as he retrieved the last of his belongings and glanced up at his rescuers.

"My thanks, good pilgrims," he declared—and flicked a glance to one side, where Breville was motioning them from the opening of another street. "You'd best not linger," he added in a lower voice.

They took his advice, though they were careful not to appear too eager. Heading off the way in which Breville had disappeared, they followed him down a crooked alley that headed deeper into the winds. When they rounded the next turning, Breville was holding open the door to a small stable shed. At his urgent gesture, they quickly dismounted and led their horses inside.

"Bring your baggage and say nothing," he whispered, as he barred the door behind them. "Jacques will delay pursuit, if you were followed."

In the next little while, Arnault and Torquil followed him through a winding maze of narrow streets and tenements, to skirt finally along the riverbank. There, casting off the mendicant's posture that was part of his disguise, Breville led them briskly behind a privy shed, where he ducked into what appeared to be the mouth of an ancient drain. Just inside, he bade Arnault and Torquil help him heave at a crack between two paving slabs.

One of the slabs shifted, exposing a dark cavity below. As they pushed it wider, a dank reek of weeds and river water filtered up from the gap. Wider still, and they could see a narrow stairway descending into the blackness below.

"Not the best of arrangements," Breville murmured, fitting his lower body through the opening, "but it serves its purpose. Follow me."

As he disappeared into the darkness, Arnault and Torquil followed without hesitation. Pausing in an alcove half a flight down, Breville produced flint and steel and set alight an oil-soaked torch left ready to hand, then motioned for his companions to close the hatch above them, by means of an iron ring set into the underside of the stone slab. Only once the pale square of daylight had been shut out and they were continuing down did Torquil venture a whispered question.

"What is this place?"

Breville showed teeth in a thin smile as they came to the level at the bottom of the stair. "The remains of a Roman sewer. Like the Christians of a former age, we have taken refuge underground in order to escape our oppressors."

He beckoned them off along an arched passageway, its walls blotched with damp and algae. The flickering torchlight showed other passages vanishing into obscurity on either hand, but after a few turns they arrived at a decrepit-looking wooden door. When Breville gave two sharp knocks, followed by a third, the door swung open, revealing a cramped chamber beyond, lanternlit and nearly filled by three standing figures.

"Christoph!" Arnault breathed. "And Hugues, Father Anselmo! What on earth are you doing in Orléans?"

"Meeting up with you," Christoph said with a faint smile.

"But—how did you know we would come here?"

"In much the same way we feared our enemies might detect your presence," Father Anselmo said, motioning both of them into the little room. "We have confirmed that Nogaret now possesses the Breastplate of the High Priests of Israel, which would have a powerful affinity for the Tablets of the Law—or one of the Shards of the Law."

"Fortunately, he has no reason to suppose that anyone was trying to retrieve one of the Shards," Hugues said, "so there was no reason for him to look. Furthermore, we don't believe he has yet learned to harness the power of the Breastplate."

"But we couldn't be sure of that," Breville said, "and eventually, he may well discover how to bend it to his will. Hence, the need for caution.

"As for how we found you," he concluded, smiling faintly, "fortunately, we have another artifact with an affinity for the Shards—and we know how to use it." He glanced back at Hughes, who held up a scarlet pouch the size of a man's two fists.

"The Seal of Solomon," Hugues said, hefting the pouch. "We also had a link to you, through *le Cercle*. We used the two to scry for you on a monthly basis, beginning about a year after you left France. Eventually, we caught a glimpse of you—and the Shard. After that, it was a matter of staying out of official clutches until you returned. I suppose you've heard what's been transpiring in your absence?"

"Today's decree, most certainly," Arnault replied. "Of Bruce, very little—though I assume we would have heard if he were dead."

"Indeed," Christoph said, gesturing for them to take seats on the dusty floor. "Sit, and we shall endeavor to bring you up-to-date."

Over cups of sour wine and a loaf of stale bread and rock-hard cheese—all of which tasted like banquet fare, for being shared among long-parted brethren—they heard the latest news of Scotland and the Order.

"You knew Bruce had convened a parliament at St. Andrews, I believe," Hugues said. "That was the year you left for Jerusalem. Later that year, Edward of England ordered the Scottish bishops to enforce the pope's order to arrest all Templars in Scotland. Lamberton, in particular, was under parole, and had no choice but to obey, especially since a papal legate had accompanied Edward's orders. Curiously enough, he could find only two Templars in all of Scotland, and they could account for none of the treasure we were alleged to have there."

Smiling faintly, Arnault nodded. "I don't suppose you know who those two Templars were?"

"As a matter of fact, we do," Father Anselmo said. "Walter de Clifton, the Master of Scotland, and a knight called William de Middleton. When pressed for details, they claimed their brother knights threw off their habits and fled across the sea—which, in fact, is no more than the truth. What they neglected to mention was that some of them took much of the wealth from the Scottish treasury to Ireland, where it is being used to buy arms for Bruce. Others fled to the west of Scotland, as was suggested by one of their brother knights some months before, and they abide there now, awaiting further instructions."

Grinning broadly, Torquil glanced at Arnault.

"I wonder who could have told them to do that?" he said.

"Obviously, a man of discerning judgment," Arnault replied, with a faint, droll smile. "But, what of Bruce himself? Is he well?"

"Aye, well enough," Christoph said. "He continues to make modest gains, though four of the most important castles in Scotland remain in English hands."

"Those being?" Arnault asked.

"Edinburgh, Stirling, Berwick, and Roxburgh," Hugues said promptly.

Arnault nodded. "That's hardly surprising. Even Edward understands that as long as he holds those, Bruce cannot truly be said to reign in Scotland. But that's no more than I expected, at this stage. What of the situation here?"

Christoph shook his head. "Not good. We reckon that at least one hundred of our brethren have perished at the stake, and hundreds more are still in custody, many of them under torture. The Bishop of Sens burned fifty-four in a single afternoon." His glance flicked away. "I regret to report that your cousin Jauffre was one of them."

Arnault bowed his head, but he had known of Jauffre's death.

"The priests Pierre de Bologna and Renaud de Provins had offered to defend the Order at Auvergne," Christoph went on, "assisted by two knights, William de Chambonnet and Bertrand de Sartiges. As a result, nearly six hundred confessions had been retracted.

"About that time, Philip de Marigny was appointed Archbishop of Sens, which has jurisdiction over the bishopric of Paris. He was twenty-three years old at the time of his appointment. Curiously enough, he is also the nephew of the king's chief minister of finance—so it is hardly curious that, within a month of his appointment, under instructions from the king, he had convened a provincial council at Paris, invoking his right to judge individual Templars under his jurisdiction. He adjudged them relapsed heretics, since they had recanted their confessions, and sentenced them to death.

"Pierre de Bologna got wind of the plan and tried to stop the proceedings, but to no avail. The executions went ahead, and the news of them shattered morale amongst the brethren. The defense collapsed when Pierre went missing—killed by his gaolers, we think—and Renaud was removed to face charges in the archbishop's court.

"There were more burnings after that, which took the heart out of further defense. We had hopes it might revive last year, when seven armed knights rode into Vienne in full habit and offered to defend the Order, but they were arrested—and released a little later, because of the threat of another two thousand brothers hiding in the forest nearby; but that episode made it clear that we could not hope for a fair hearing.

"Since then, there have been rumors of further secret intrigues involving King Philip and his cronies, and possible deals struck between him and the Holy See. The bull you heard read earlier is but the beginning of the end, I fear. There are several more bulls reportedly in preparation, that will parcel out our possessions and decide the fate of those brothers still in custody."

A heavy silence met the end of this recitation. After a moment, Arnault pushed his cup away and let out a sigh.

"What is it you intend to do next, then?" he asked quietly. "And more to the point, what is it you wish *us* to do? For I have the distinct impression that merely taking the Shard to Bruce is no longer your primary intention."

Breville leaned forward. "May we see the Shard?"

"Of course."

Eagerly they watched as Arnault pulled the Shard's pouch from under his tunic and opened it. Even nestled in the silk of its Ethiopic wrappings, the holy relic set the air a-shimmer with unseen ripples of power. A collective sigh of relief whispered among them as Arnault exposed it to view, but none made any attempt to touch it. Even Breville merely held a hand over it for a moment, eyes closed, before signing for Arnault to put it away.

"It may, indeed, serve for what we have in mind," he breathed. "All the while you have been gone, we have lived in hope. Now you bring us proof that our hopes remain green."

"What hopes?" Arnault said, when Breville did not elaborate.

After a glance at Breville, Christoph continued.

"We mentioned that we had confirmed Nogaret has the Breastplate, and that we believe he seeks to subvert its power. We have also determined that he does, indeed, have the backing of the Knights of the Black Swan—and is, in fact, their leader. Our investigations have established that some of them were with Nogaret when he hounded Brother Gaspar to his death."

"Not that this comes as any surprise," Torquil muttered under his breath.

"No," Christoph agreed. "But with Black Swan resources at hand, in addition to his own, it is very likely that, sooner or later, Nogaret will, indeed, master the Breastplate. So long as that possibility exists, anything else we attempt to do would be at risk."

"So, what are you proposing?" Arnault asked. "A direct assault on Nogaret?"

"Precisely," Breville replied. "But this may not be as daunting as you might suppose. I am not suggesting that we storm some royal enclave to get at him. There is evidence of dissension in the ranks of his subordinates. The French lord who was previously so active in Scotland, Bartholeme de Challon, seems to have fallen into disfavor, and has withdrawn to his ancestral castle near the German border. Meanwhile, Nogaret has spirited the Breastplate away to his own citadel in the hills of the Rouerge."

Arnault and Torquil exchanged glances.

"You know this citadel?" Arnault asked.

Breville nodded. "Somewhat. Superficially, it appears to be derelict—but appearances, especially in this case, are deceiving."

"Physical defenses first, then," Arnault said. "What size garrison?"

"Perhaps a hundred," Breville said. "Probably less."

"Can we raise that many?" Torquil said, glancing at Christoph.

"I doubt it," Christoph replied. "Thirty to forty, perhaps. But it's the esoteric defenses that worry us far more. At any given time, several Knights of the Swan are present in the citadel. The whole place is bound fast with dread enchantments, barriers that will halt a man in his tracks if he comes without Nogaret's express consent. He is well versed in the demonic arts, and has terrible allies watching over him."

"Allies that will bow before the Shard," Arnault said coldly. "He has used the law of man to topple the Order; now let him answer to the Law of God!"

The others glanced among themselves, then back at Christoph, who slowly nodded. "We had prayed that would be your answer," he murmured.

"And we must continue to pray that Nogaret will not find the means to usurp the virtues of the Breastplate before we can attack," Breville replied. "That has been his aim since it first fell into his hands."

"That is a chance we have to take," Christoph replied. "Now that we have a worthy weapon to hand, we must strike a hard blow in defense of all we hold sacred and true!"

"What about this Lord Bartholeme?" Torquil asked.

"One battle at a time," Arnault said. "Go, Christoph, and summon our brothers for war."

Chapter Thirty-four

April, 1313

T HEIR PREPARATIONS TOOK SOME MONTHS. DURING THAT
time, while they gathered and prepared a force sufficient to
take on Nogaret in his mountain citadel, Arnault sent several
coded messages to Aubrey, traveling with Bruce, and received several in response, reviewing the state of affairs in
Scotland. Only modest progress had been made during the
several years of Arnault's absence, but the new year brought
several notable successes.

Bruce took Perth in January of 1313, by means of an audacious night assault with rope ladders fitted with grappling
hooks; and in February, besieged Dumfries castle was
starved into surrender. Early in April, news had come of the
death of John Balliol, whom some still supported as Scotland's rightful king ahead of Bruce. Though a son remained
to persist in the Balliol claims to the Scottish crown, the
passing of the father effectively removed the last stigma
from Bruce truly assuming his crown—if he could take the
remaining four great castles of Scotland.

Meanwhile, the fate of the Temple had continued to grind
toward a conclusion that now appeared to be irreversible. A
second papal bull had followed on the heels of the first—*Ad*

Providam, which assigned to the Hospitallers all former Templar properties saving those in Spain and Portugal. A third bull, *Considerantes,* had followed only a few days later, which reserved the fate of certain individual Templars to the pope alone. That the Grand Master, Jacques de Molay, should be so named was understandable—along with Hugues de Paraud and two other senior preceptors. But Oliver de Penne had also been singled out for papal attention—the sole member of *le Cercle* now in custody.

"He will confess to nothing," Christoph had declared, on hearing of the bull.

But all of them knew that the price of holding that resolve was apt to be costly, in terms of the tortures that might be brought to bear; and they lamented the fact that, at least for the moment, they could do nothing for Oliver save to pray for him.

By late April of 1313, however, a core of members of *le Cercle* were ready to proceed against Nogaret. They had held their peace throughout the previous winter, carefully assembling their selected force and gathering the necessary intelligence—and had mostly avoided the vicinity of Nogaret's stronghold, lest they arouse suspicion. Their first sight of its approaches but confirmed what Breville had been telling them through the previous winter.

Though April was nearly past, this isolated part of the country looked for all the world as if some terrible enchantment had kept spring at bay, with nary an anemone or moss flower daring to take root in the crevices among the rocks. Instead, diseased-looking lichens stained the hillsides in bilious yellow patches, occasionally punctuated by the desiccated remains of a dead thorn tree, forbidding as a corpse left to swing on a gibbet.

"They say that all of this has happened in the past three years," Breville remarked across the rump of his horse, as he led Arnault, Torquil, and a score of additional knights single file through a maze of tumbled boulders. "It's all due to

Nogaret, of course—though the local folk know nothing of that. When it began, he went to great lengths to make it seem that this area is under a curse—and burned a few harmless old women as scapegoats. But it's his own sorceries, worked to hedge it round with circles of power, that have blighted the surrounding landscape."

Riding directly behind Breville, Arnault and Torquil could feel the unwholesome influence pervading the very air. A glance behind them confirmed that the others felt it, too, eyes restlessly searching the surrounding hillsides, gloved hands never far from sword hilts and bows.

None of them wore any outward sign of who and what they had been, though all were clad in mail beneath their heavy mantles, and each had a helm at his knee. Summoned by secret signs and coded messages, often relayed by unsuspecting couriers, they had come from scattered refuges throughout France, making their way individually to the rendezvous point: a forest camp now two days' journey behind them.

Now they rode forth as a military company. Since breaking camp early that morning, they had adopted the stealthy secrecy of a skirmish force advancing through hostile territory. Breville had acquainted them with the particular details of their mission the night before. Given the danger, not only of their mission but of being in France at all, it was no time to be circumspect with the truth concerning the issues at stake, though he had spared them needless details that would only frighten some of them.

"Since the founding of our Order, we of the Temple have always been guardians of a higher wisdom," he had informed them. "We worship and serve God according to these higher mysteries. The responsibility for guiding the Order in such matters has secretly been vested in an Inner Circle charged to carry forward this wisdom. If some of you have not been made aware of these facts before now, it was as much for your own safety as for the safety of the future."

He had told them as much as he dared, and Christoph had confessed those who wished it, likewise fortifying all of them with Holy Communion in the silent, predawn darkness before they set out. Although most of the men had not previously been introduced to the esoteric trusts of the Order, all had professed themselves willing to place themselves unreservedly at the service of those who had summoned them. In Christoph, they recognized a senior in the Order, now an ordained priest as well as a knight, though he rode as a knight today, mailed and armed like the rest of them. To those who survived the assault on Montaigre, more yet might be revealed.

On Breville's advice, they had elected to approach Castle Montaigre from the north. It had been one of the hardest marches Torquil could remember, saving only their experiences in the Holy Land. No clear trail marked the way through this wasteland of scree and boulders; and so close to the castle, nothing lived or moved except noxious insects, toads, and poisonous reptiles. All other creatures had long ago fled the area, driven off by the region's prevailing aura of malignancy.

Men of lesser fortitude would have turned back many hours ago, defeated by the air of desolation hanging over this region, but grief and hardship had so tempered the natures of these surviving Templar Knights that their hearts and souls were armored against the weapons of their enemy. More than once they had fetched up against unseen walls of power, erected to repel all intruders; but each time, the barricades had melted away in the presence of the Shard.

Now the company advanced in determined silence, ever watchful, ever mindful of the sufferings inflicted on their brethren by the man who had taken refuge in this place. All knew that even greater dangers remained still in store, but they also knew that the only route to saving the Order lay ahead of them, not behind.

Below them to their right, they began to catch glimpses of

a well-defined road running level along the valley floor. The previous night, Breville had pointed it out on the map he had drawn to brief them.

"The road from Aurillac to Bezier passes within a mile of the castle," he had said. "Nogaret's men use it regularly to bring in supplies, but they never approach the castle directly. Instead, they've made a secret entrance for themselves around the back of the hill, well out of sight of any chance travelers along the main route. We believe that any esoteric defenses at that point may also be reduced, precisely because they do use it with such regularity.

"But we won't know until we get there," Breville had warned his listeners. "What I do know is that this represents the only chink in the castle's defenses I've been able to detect. So be on your guard, and keep saying your prayers."

The afternoon wore on. Chill shadows began to creep across the ground. The Templar party crested the top of a shoulder of high ground as the sun was sinking out of sight behind the western hills. And beyond, perched in a saddle of higher ground, they caught their first distant glimpse of Castle Montaigre. Bathed in the glow of an ominous sunset, its squat turrets looked as if they had been dyed red with blood.

Pausing not at all, Breville led the company on, over the crest of the rise and down into a trough of stony ground, where they came upon a pathway worn smooth with frequent usage. The trail bed was too unyielding to register footprints, but animal droppings along the way marked it as well trafficked.

Breville glanced right and left, gauged the failing light, then motioned the company off the trail and into a small clearing some little way from the trail.

"From here, we go on foot," he said, dismounting and removing his mantle. "What we seek is perhaps a mile ahead. Leave anything that will hamper your movement or make a sound, and be ready for anything. It's been several weeks since I was here."

Leaving one of the older knights to stay with the horses, the rest of the Templar party shed their mantles and set off along the beaten track, into what seemed a vale of gloom far deeper than ordinary night. Presently they came upon a pair of tall boulders that straddled the path like the piers of a gateway. Ahead, low voices and harness clinks and a dusky fire-glow warned that they were approaching the end of the trail. At a signal from Christoph, the main Templar company fanned out to take cover among the rocks while Breville, Arnault, and Torquil edged stealthily forward to investigate.

Near at hand, several dozen lean horses and mules milled about within the compass of a stout wooden paddock. A stone's throw farther off, the tumbledown foundations of a long-deserted village lay scattered along the base of a low cliff. In the midst of these ruins, set solidly against the cliff, stood what appeared to be a new, strongly built edifice the size of a gatehouse, its front pierced by a stoutly reinforced gate. Outside, a trio of sentries in leather and steel could be seen leaning indolently on their spears.

The three scouts rejoined the rest of their party, relaying their findings to Christoph in whispers.

"The sentries are the least of our worries," Arnault warned. "The gate looks strong enough to resist anything less than a battering ram, even if it hasn't been magically reinforced. But the building does connect directly to the cliff face—which must be where the tunnel system goes into the mountain."

"It seems that we must force the gate, then," Christoph said.

"Maybe not," Torquil replied. "Maybe a diversion would trick them into opening the gate themselves."

"Precisely my thought," Breville agreed, with one of his tight smiles. "Brother Arnault, Brother Torquil, if you are with me, I believe I have an idea."

*   *   *

The three members of the Decuria chosen to assist Nogaret in the planned night's work waited in his tower sanctum with ill-concealed expectancy, black-robed and ceremonially prepared by weeks of divers disciplines. Nor was it the first time they had made such preparations; for thus far, the High Priest's Breastplate had refused to yield up its secrets.

The vaulted chamber was decked out with blasphemous splendor, illuminated by dozens of brass lamps. Drapes of heavy black silk masked the adjoining windows, stirring now and again when a slight draft would set the fabric undulating like the skin of a reptile—though the draft did not come from outside. A square, squat altar dominated the center of the room, covered with a black velvet pall whose sides were embroidered with alchemical symbols in flame and gold that seemed to twist and writhe in the lamplight as if they had a life of their own.

Centered on the altar stood a brazier of live coals. An iron trivet over the coals supported an alembic of blown glass, inside of which a mixture of boar's blood and swine's gall was gently warming. Thick tallow candles guarded either side of the brazier, stuck onto prickets set into sections of carved boars' tusks.

The stone floor of the chamber had also received exacting preparation, swept clean and inscribed with three magic squares drawn one within the other at right angles, with each chalked square symbolizing one of the three alchemical planes. The innermost square, which enclosed the altar, represented the four pillars of Hell, while the outermost symbolized the four material elements. Linking the two together, the intermediary square represented the principles of alchemical transmutation known as the four Keys of Zosimos, its salients aligned to the cardinal points of the compass—which were guarded by four yellowed human skulls set facing outward: the skulls of Cathar suicides, retrieved from a mass grave in the castle courtyard.

Tight-wound and impatient, Valentin de Vesey crouched

down to adjust the gaze of one of the skulls—and inhaled with a hiss as the candlelight glinted from the signet ring that he, like his fellows, wore on his right hand, as an electric tingle seemed to dart up his arm and spread through his torso, centering in his groin.

The tension building in the room was becoming harder to relegate to the balance point that was required for the night's disciplines. The very air was charged with subtle whisperings just outside the range of human hearing—a subtle susurrus that stirred the blood with a taut, predatory quickening of pulsebeat coupled with a cerebral hunger and sheer animal lust.

Indeed, the song was but an echo and a memory of the very real siren song that had beguiled all three men repeatedly during the past weeks of their preparation. For each of them had been allowed to taste of the carnal pleasures to be found in the embrace of the demon resident in Nogaret's ring, which—for a price—could and would take the form of a demon-lover whose appetites swept a man into sated oblivion. Amid the whispers, Valentin de Vesey found his body stirring to the memory of that embrace—and a sidelong glance at his companions, Baudoin de Champiere and Peret Auvergnais, suggested that they, too, were remembering.

In a swirl of shadowy draperies, Nogaret himself entered the chamber. His appearance instantly focused the resolve of all three of his waiting acolytes. The Magister of the Decuria was crowned with a conical headdress swathed with black gauze that veiled his face and partially covered the High Priest's Breastplate, its gold and variegated gems glittering against the black of his robes. In his left hand he carried an animal mask of beaten gold, long-snouted and sharp-eared in the likeness of the Egyptian demon-lord Set; in his right he bore a shallow oblation vessel containing the ruby demon-ring, which had already sealed the fate of so many, threaded on the golden chain by which Nogaret customarily wore it. It was this demon's siren song that so stirred the blood of those gathered in the chamber, and which now caused every eye to dart to the ring as Nogaret set it and the mask upon the altar, turning then to fold back the veil over his face.

All three of his acolytes stifled gasps to see him, for the dread forces to which he had exposed himself since acquiring the High Priest's Breastplate—and especially in the past twenty-four hours, sequestered in preparation—clearly had taken their toll. Nogaret was wan and sunken of cheek and his bloodshot eyes burned with a feverish intensity that reminded Valentin of the eyes of the skulls that ringed the room. The master's beringed hands looked almost skeletal, the nails as yellow as a vulture's talons.

"I am confident that tonight's endeavor will meet with success," Nogaret announced in a voice that creaked of the grave. "Tonight, at last, we shall reap the fruit of five years' unremitting study and toil."

He had to pause to cough and clear his throat, one trembling hand resting momentarily on the salver bearing the ring and the other caressing the gemstones of the Breastplate in a gesture that somehow became obscene.

"Without access to the powers of the Lights and Perfections," he continued, "the Breastplate of Aaron has been like an empty vessel. But not for much longer. One final *conjunctio* is needed to perfect the Ring of Ialdabaeoth as a *vas philosophorum*. With this ring binding the dual power of the *Urim* and *Thummin*, the puissance of the High Priest's Breastplate will at last be ours to command!"

Baudoin clasped his hands together, bidding the lust straining beneath his will to be contained yet a while longer. Like all of them, he had made his pact with the demon of the ring, paid its price, been the recipient of its favors. The ring itself, created to capture and hold one minor demon, had previously been a useful but limited tool. Now, however, Nogaret and his associates of the Decuria had used their alchemical arts to expand the ring's capacity, transforming it into a crucible of destruction, capable of sustaining and channeling the fires of hell itself. All that remained was to tap into the source.

"Yours was the inspiration, Magister," Valentin declared unctuously. "We await the fulfillment of your vision."

Nogaret acknowledged the tribute with a nod. Beckoning his associates to join him at the altar, he lifted the ring by its chain and lowered it carefully into the alembic. Warm boar's blood curdled round it, and the embers beneath it flared, enveloping the vessel and the ring in a murky amber corona as Nogaret opened his hands in a gesture of invitation.

"Great Lucifer, Patron of Slayers, be present in our midst!" he whispered. "Glorify yourself through this act of desecration. Into your hands do we render this ring of Power, together with the vessels of your Enemy. By the mysteries of blood and fire, make them both your own!"

He sketched a symbol of power in the air over the mouth of the alembic. With a susurrant hiss, the ring—or the demon in the ring—began to drink of the boar's blood. As the fluid steadily drained away, leaving the ring cleanly exposed, the ruby depths of the stone began to glow with deep-seated crimson fire.

The fire intensified, setting the alembic aglow and bathing the room and its occupants in scarlet radiance. Nogaret's pale eyes glittered hungrily, and a rapturous sigh escaped his thin lips.

"Yesss," he crooned softly. "Soon, soon we shall be like the *Nephilim* of old, shaping the world to suit our pleasure. . . ."

Chapter Thirty-five

April, 1313

OUTSIDE THE TOWER, SILENT AS GHOSTS, THE TEMPLARS infiltrated the ruins to the east of the castle gateway. The main party, under Christoph's command, faded into the shadows and drew their weapons, ready to rush the gate when the time came. Arnault, Torquil, and Breville edged closer still, dirks and daggers taken quietly in hand. From this vantage point, they could hear the conversation of the guards.

"I tell you, something big is happening tonight," the sergeant said to his two companions, casting a nervous glance back through the gate.

"How do you know?" asked the taller of the pair.

"Didn't you hear the row in the pig run this morning? That was Claude and Henri, butchering the black boar."

"What, that brute they've been feeding up on blood meal and gibbet meat?"

"The same," the sergeant confirmed. "And it all had to be done a certain way—master's orders. Fairly reeks of sorcery, don't it? It wouldn't surprise me if the master and those three lordly friends of his were planning to conjure up the Devil."

Arnault fancied he could feel a chill run up his spine. Far

from doubting the sergeant's lurid speculations, he feared they might be perilously close to the truth.

The nudge of Torquil's elbow in his ribs made him glance in that direction. The younger man's tight-lipped expression suggested that he was thinking much the same thing. Had Nogaret and his minions at last found some way to work their will on the High Priest's Breastplate, either to profane it or destroy it? If so, there was not a moment to lose.

Clapping a hand on Breville's shoulder, he gave him a nod and a jut of his chin. Breville nodded in return, eyed the direction of the guards' voices again, then dropped to a crouch and made a dash for the rear of the mule paddock. Slipping between the railings, he edged his way around to the gate and lifted the loop of rope that served as a makeshift gate latch, then withdrew to a patch of shadow as the gate swung slightly ajar.

The mules paid no heed. Arnault and Torquil exchanged resigned glances, then delved into their pouches for the supply of pebbles they had gathered earlier. Chucking a few into the midst of the animals produced the desired result, causing several mules and horses to startle, jostling their companions. One of them bumped against the gate. When it drifted open, one mule and then another began tentatively nosing their way out of the enclosure.

Half a dozen beasts had cleared the gate before the sentries noticed. With exasperated oaths, the men laid down their spears and ran to recapture the straying animals—who only scattered the more readily, spooked by the commotion.

Crouched low behind a ruined wall, where one of the mules was nosing at a patch of greenery, Arnault waited until one of the men was reaching for the animal's halter before silencing him with a lightning pounce and dragging him out of sight.

Working fast, he stripped off the man's mantle and helmet, then bound his hands and feet and gagged him securely. By the time he finished, Torquil and Breville had likewise claimed their victims. Breville's man was semiconscious, stirring, but rather than hitting him again, Breville clamped a hand across his mouth and set his dirk to the man's throat, one knee bearing down on his chest, while Arnault bound his hands and Torquil slung on one of the appropriated mantles. Nogaret's guards wore expensive livery.

"What's the watchword?" Breville demanded of their captive. "Tell me, and I may refrain from killing you."

Struggling under the hand clamped across his mouth, the man shook his head, eyes going wild as Breville shifted the dirk under the skirt of the man's chain mail, cold steel flat against the man's belly.

"Don't think for an instant that I'm bluffing," Breville said coldly. "Tell me, or I'll gut you like a fish and leave you to die with your entrails spread out on your lap!" He applied sufficient pressure with the point of his blade to puncture shirt and skin, giving a twist to make sure the man felt it, smothering the sob that rose in his victim's throat.

"The word?" he urged fiercely.

The man cringed from the blade, eyes screwed shut as he braced himself for the fatal thrust, but instead Breville leaned closer to his ear.

"I'll ask only once more," he whispered, cautiously easing his hand from the man's mouth. "Tell me—and I'll let you live. It's more than *he* would offer."

"N-no—please! *G-gallows bait*," came the strangled, anguished sob. "It's 'gallows bait'—I swear! Oh, God, he'll feed me to the demons!"

Hearing the ring of truth, Breville was satisfied. Withdrawing his blade, he dealt the man a stunning blow to the temple and set about applying a gag. A few seconds later, wearing guards' mantles, he and Arnault moved out into the open among the milling mules and began waving their arms. Torquil hung back, lest his accent betray them.

"We could use some help out here!" Arnault called in a gruff voice. "The bloody mules have got loose."

He kept a mule between him and the gate as a watch port in the door snapped open, revealing a suspicious eye.

"It's about time!" Breville snapped. "Will you lot get off your spotty backsides and give us a hand? You'll make us all *gallows bait!*"

His invocation of the watchword had the desired effect. There came the heavy clang of a large bolt being drawn, after which the port swung inward to let three more men-at-arms come sauntering out.

"You simpletons!" the leader sneered. "Can't you even catch a—"

An arrow fired from the nearby rocks took him cleanly in the throat before he could finish. Even as his companions recoiled and groped for their swords, looking around wildly, the lurking Templar force exploded from cover and charged the open door.

The port crashed inward. Surging across the threshold, the Templars in the van came face-to-face with the rest of the castle's gate watch. A sharp flurry of swordplay drove the defenders back into the tunnel leading from the rear of the gatehouse.

"After them!" Breville shouted. "There'll be another gate between here and the main keep!"

Torquil led the pursuit through the bowels of the hill, the others close on his heels. The predicted guard port at the upper end of the tunnel gave access to a warren of storerooms, where fleeing guards were frantically trying to close a door, but the Templars were on them before they could secure it. Daunted by the assault, the defenders turned tail and ran, shouting for reinforcements as they fled.

The alarm spread through the lower levels as the Templars pushed on through the cellars and burst into the kitchens. Cooks and scullions fled before them as, pressing on, the Templars emerged into a courtyard on the east side of the castle compound—just in time to see defending guardsmen disappearing into the castle's south wing. Glancing in that direction, his hand on the Shard of the Law in its pouch next to his heart, Arnault was not surprised to catch an impression of heavy shadow shrouding the tower that anchored that range.

"He's in the tower, and he's working right now!" Arnault cried, already breaking into a run in that direction. "Please God we're not already too late to stop it."

Even as he spoke, a shout rang out and a stream of men-at-arms came pouring out of the barracks on the north side of the court, torchlight splashing off a thicket of naked swords. Forming ranks, the Templars braced themselves to meet the attack.

Meanwhile, in the dark sanctity of the south tower, Nogaret had removed the High Priest's Breastplate and set it before the alembic on the altar.

"All hail to mighty Lucifer, Prince of Darkness!" he declared. "In his name do I claim this artifact of power as a trophy of war! Lest mine enemies seek to ransom it, I now cast out the source of its former virtues."

He bent to remove the lifeless stones of the *Urim* and *Thummin* from their pockets at the back of the Breastplate. As he did so, there came a sudden outburst of noise from outside.

Baudoin started up with a curse. Peret dashed for the nearest window and yanked the drapery aside.

"So much for precautions of secrecy!" he barked over his shoulder at Nogaret. "Someone's breached our defenses."

"That's impossible!" Nogaret snapped.

He rushed to the window to see for himself. Confused shouts and the clatter of weaponry rang out from below. All at once, a fierce cry rose above the din.

"To arms, brothers! *Non nobis, Domine! Non nobis, sed Nomini Tuo da gloriam!*"

Nogaret reeled back, his face contorted with disbelief and hate.

"Templars!"

"*Templars?*" Valentin echoed blankly. "But I thought—"

"That they were all imprisoned or dead?" Peret snarled. "Think again!"

"Well, they couldn't have forced a way in here by mere strength of arms," Baudoin retorted. "They must have some relic of power in reserve. We must stop them before they penetrate any farther!"

"Just what would you suggest?" Valentin said disdainfully.

"The ring, of course!" came Baudoin's reply.

The Ring of Ialdabaeoth, suspended in the alembic, was glowing like a mote of fire at the heart of a volcano, power pulsing from it in palpable waves.

"*Stop!*" Nogaret thundered, as Baudoin took a step toward the altar.

Baudoin rounded on him, face suffused with anger. "Why do you even hesitate?"

"Fools! We need all the ring's energy to quicken the Breastplate!" Nogaret spat back at him. "Do you imagine that I have no other weapons to hand?"

He darted back to the altar and removed from a hidden compartment at its base a small, round box like a pyx, made from carved bone. His hands trembled as he twisted off the lid to reveal a dusky gray powder like volcanic ash.

"What is this?" Peret murmured.

"Watch, and learn," Nogaret replied.

Muttering a series of cantrips under his breath, he circled the altar widdershins to cast a pinch of dust over each of the four Cathar skulls watching the room's four quarters.

"Awake and arise, *Perfecti!*" he commanded, when the circle was complete. "Awake and arise! An ancient enemy is without! Smite them where they stand, and take your vengeance!"

A thin, distant-sounding wail quickly overlaid the din of fighting from outside, and a vaporous cloud began to manifest inside each of the four skulls, dancing with motes of scarlet and blue deep within the eye sockets. Then all at once the vapors spewed forth from between the grinning jaws and surged upward, taking on the shadowy semblance of human forms, hollow-eyed and gaunt, trailing ragged grave clothes.

"Hear me and obey!" Nogaret ordered, stabbing a hand in their direction. "Templars have breached the outer baillie! I command you to summon the *bonhommes* to defend the citadel!"

Shreds of black silk flew in tatters from the windows as the Cathar wraiths swooped out into the night. At once Nogaret rounded on his subordinates, motioning them back to their places with a sweep of his arm.

"We must resume work! Compose yourselves!"

Out in the courtyard, Templars and defenders alike were buffeted by a blast of freezing wind as four spectral shapes plummeted from above and fell upon the living with eldritch shrieks. One of them swooped very near Torquil and laid hands on one of the Templar attackers, eliciting a heart-chilling cry of terror and agony as the man crumpled. As the specter wheeled skyward to swoop again, its icy shoulder struck Torquil a glancing blow that hurled him to the ground. The glimpse he got of its lambent eyes left him all but paralyzed for several pounding heartbeats before he could even dare to lift his head.

The air rang with the shrieks of the specters. Nearby, Arnault, too, was cowering under a raised arm, glancing about wildly for some respite from the attack. The crack of sundering stone split the air, cacophonous counterpoint to the specters' cries. In the next instant, the cobbled paving of the courtyard was ruptured by a zigzag pattern of glowing, branching seams that seemed to open into Hell.

Men began to scream as the seams gaped wider and more shadow-forms streamed from the gaps, surging upward in the guise of ghostly reivers armed with scythes. Glowing eyes flashed wild in the darkness as the shadows massed and attacked indiscriminately, bright blades flashing. Spectral fingers clutched at living flesh to leave dead-white marks that burned like frostbite. Bellows of primal terror erupted from the ranks of Nogaret's men as, in utter panic, they flung down their arms and bolted for the gates, trampling one another in their struggle to escape, leaving the Templars to stand alone against a host of undead enemies.

And stand they did, as the shadows swooped and dived around them like gorcrows, starting to take their toll of men. The Templars fought with all the ferocity that had made them famous throughout Christendom, but their blades whispered harmlessly through forms insubstantial as mist—until all at once Breville materialized beside Torquil, *his* blade connecting with a flash that let smoke leak from one of the fleeing specters like blood under water.

"Quick! Wet your blade!" he ordered, thrusting a leather flask into Torquil's hand.

"But, what—"

"It's holy water. Use it sparingly and pass it on!"

Ducking to avoid another wraith, Torquil sloshed water on his blade and tossed the flask to the next man. His next sword slash connected with a showering of sparks, causing two wraiths to dissipate like smoke, but half a dozen more surged in to take their place.

Except around Arnault, who suddenly realized that he was the only one not under attack by the wraiths, despite the fact that his sword had not yet been anointed with holy water. In that instant, it dawned on him that he had an even more potent defense at hand.

"Breville, stay and hold the rear guard," Arnault cried, his free hand pressing the Shard to his breast. "Christoph and Torquil, come with me!"

The three of them made a break for the south tower. Wraiths swooped and harried them from all sides, but never close enough to do any harm—proof that the Shard had power to protect. Running, stumbling, the three men gained the shelter of the archway overhanging the tower's guard port; but the door itself was barred fast from the inside.

Torquil rammed his shoulder against the panel, but shook

his head when it did not budge. But Arnault had already sheathed his sword and was reaching into the front of his tunic, drawing forth the fragment of God's Holy Law.

"O Word of God, be thou shield and defender in the midst of our enemies," he prayed, trembling at his own presumption.

The Shard was glowing as he took it out, a pure, cool sapphire that bathed his face in a holy light. Folding his hands around it, Arnault contained the light in a narrow beam, which he directed at the center of the door. As he did so, words came unbidden to his lips, dimly recalled from holy writ:

"Thus saith the Lord of Hosts: Because ye speak this word, behold, I will make My words in thy mouth fire, and this people wood, and it shall devour them. And the word is Adonai!"

The timbers ignited with a searing crackle and a burst of deep blue flame that ate its way outward with blinding speed. In mere seconds, the port was reduced to ashes, its iron fittings turned to slag. Avoiding the smoldering cinders, Christoph and then Arnault and Torquil carefully stepped across the threshold, defenders fleeing before them, Arnault numbly holding the Shard at his side.

"I had no idea," said Christoph over his shoulder, "that you were such a biblical scholar."

"I'm not," Arnault murmured. "That wasn't me."

A short antechamber gave access to a spiral stairway, where several of the defenders had retreated—likely confirmation that Nogaret was up there somewhere—but as the three Templars started up the steps, the impending presence of evil assailed them with the force of a blow. Leading the way, Christoph staggered and nearly fell back on Arnault and Torquil, but when Arnault thrust the Shard aloft, light again blazed from it, this time like a beacon to light their way. As they resumed climbing, words again came to Arnault's lips, weaving ever-stronger protection around the three of them.

"Thy Word shall go before me as a Pillar of Fire by night, and as a Pillar of Cloud shall I follow it by day. . . ."

The sense of evil grew more intense as they ascended, an almost-visible miasma, but it fled before the light of the Shard. Nonetheless, they were finding it more and more difficult to breathe. At the third-floor landing, even Arnault had to stop to catch his breath. Beyond, they could see two of the tower's defenders sprawled dead or unconscious on the stairs.

"Let's go," Arnault urged, after only a moment's breather, not looking to see whether the others followed.

They resumed their climb, stepping warily over the downed guardsmen. Approaching the summit of the stair, they passed another motionless body—and beyond, spied an arched doorway heavily painted across the lintel with arcane inscriptions that wavered and faded before the light of the Shard. Evil emanated from behind the closed door, coming in heavy, pulsing waves, leaving no doubt what sort of thing lay beyond.

"This is where it ends," Arnault whispered, gathering his strength to climb the last few steps.

The three of them halted on the landing before the door, Torquil and Christoph flanking Arnault with drawn swords. Holding the Shard to his breast, to cup his hands around its light, Arnault drew himself erect.

"Guillaume de Nogaret, come forth!" he said in a loud voice. "The hour of your judgment is at hand!"

Only silence answered this command, though they could hear scurrying sounds beyond the door.

"Guillaume de Nogaret, come forth!" Arnault repeated.

"And who might it be who makes bold to challenge the master in his own house?" came a silky, defiant voice from within.

"Frère Arnault de Saint Clair, Knight of the Temple," Arnault responded, lowering the Shard to his side. "You are called to answer for the many heinous crimes you have committed against the laws of God and of man."

The door swung slowly open, spilling a lurid swath of crimson light onto the landing, along with the stench of sulfur and brimstone.

"Enter—if you dare," came the low, dangerous response from the shadows beyond.

Cautiously the Templars advanced across the threshold, Torquil and Christoph with swords in hands, Arnault holding the Shard along his thigh. Within, Nogaret stood facing them across the width of a black-draped table or altar surmounted by magical paraphernalia, garbed in the vestments of an alchemist-sorcerer. Three more black-robed men were ranged behind him. Around them, containing them within the protection of a series of magical squares, Arnault could not fail to notice the magical sigils chalked on the floor—fully charged and activated. The empty eye sockets of the skulls guarding the salients of the outermost square glowed with the ruby light of hellfire.

"Your presumption is quite remarkable, if foolish," Nogaret said coldly, contempt in his voice. "By what authority do you claim the right to judge me?"

"It is not we who come to judge," Arnault replied. "We are here merely as witnesses and messengers. God Himself is your judge. For the manifold perjuries and injustices which you have committed against the Order of the Temple of Jerusalem and others, contravening the Laws of God, you stand in peril of eternal damnation. Will you confess your sins and commend yourself to the mercies of your Creator?"

"Confess to *you*?" A contemptuous laugh creaked from somewhere in Nogaret's chest. "Hardly likely. Will I acknowledge my own success? Certainly. Will I be reconciled to God? Never! He and I are at war; and I will never bow to Him!"

He raised his left hand, where a baleful jewel blazed red like a demon's eye from the massive ring on his index finger.

A grim smile curved at his lips as he laid his hand on the alembic before him and spoke a word of power, answered by a scarlet fire sparking from ring to the curdling gases inside, which ignited and coalesced into the crouching form of a red-skinned manikin with the eyes of a goat, and a fanged mouth.

"You should have stayed cowering with the rest of your miserable Order," Nogaret said mildly, a dangerous smile lifting the corners of his mouth as he quickly backed away.

Growing almost too quickly to see, the demon Ialdabaeoth burst from the alembic in a shattering of glass and a sulfurous stench, already the size of a bear and still growing as it reared up, fanged jaws agape. Instinctively, Torquil and Christoph raised their swords, but in that same instant, Arnault lifted the Shard to point it at the demon like the weapon it was, releasing a beam of cleansing sapphire that enveloped the creature in a blaze of celestial glory and a colossal *boom*.

The backlash of the flash left them all half-blind and staggering, ears ringing. Somehow Arnault managed to keep his feet under him. Torquil and Christoph likewise were still standing, albeit shakily. Clutching at the altar for support, an astonished Nogaret dragged himself upright. His minions had been bowled off their feet, and the demon was gone.

"No!" he cried, though they scarcely could hear him for the ringing in their ears. "*I* am master here! You will die where you stand, you pious wretches!"

With a flick of his wrist, he made a casting gesture with the hand that wore the ring. A gout of crimson flame belched forth from his opening palm, but the Shard in Arnault's hands now seemed to respond of its own volition. Cerulean light blazed from the Shard in a cleansing torrent, filling the room with a heavenly radiance that turned the tide of hellfire back on itself with another cataclysmic *boom*.

Chapter Thirty-six

April, 1313

"TORQUIL! TORQUIL, WAKE UP. TORQUIL—SAY SOMETHING!"

A familiar voice dimly penetrated the crimson-flecked darkness that wrapped Torquil's mind and body in pain. It was the urgency of tone, more than the words, that began dragging him back to consciousness. Surfacing was like trying to swim through quicksand. As someone lifted his head, new pain stabbed behind his eyes and made him wince, groaning aloud.

"Torquil! I need your help!" the voice insisted, urging—pleading.

Groggily he made an effort to open his eyes, feeling nauseous. It took him several confused seconds to recognize Arnault's face swimming above him, looking at least as wretched as Torquil felt. He had a torch in his free hand.

"Sweet Jesus, stop shaking me; I'm awake! What happened?"

Arnault fairly sagged with relief. "We survived—just. Are you hurt?"

"I don't know."

Dazedly Torquil ran a dry tongue over dry lips and drew another cautious breath as he turned his head to look around him—which was a mistake, because the movement almost made him throw up. In his half-stunned condition, it took him a moment to retrieve his last conscious memory.

"Was there . . . an explosion?" he ventured.

"After a fashion. Let me help you up. We have to find Christoph—and the Shard."

"The Shard? But *you* had—"

"I haven't got it now," Arnault said, hoisting him under one arm. "It's possible that someone revived before me, and made off with it. Or it may have been destroyed in the blast."

"Jesus God!"

As Torquil struggled painfully to his feet, he saw that the windows of the tower had been blown out by the force of the blast. Here and there, bits of debris were still burning. The room itself looked like a storm had swept through. A cold wind whistled through the jagged window gaps, but at least the air was clean. A part of him marveled that he and Arnault had survived. Still woozy, he caught his balance against the edge of the black altar as Arnault edged around behind.

"Here's a body," Arnault announced, bending down. "But it isn't Christoph—or Nogaret."

"Thank God," Torquil murmured dully, "—at least about Christoph." Gaining strength, he let his eyes search the wind-battered remnants of the room. "What's that, over there?"

He started hobbling toward what looked like a mound of clothes, still fighting nausea, but Arnault was there first, bending down and then shaking his head.

"Another of Nogaret's minions," he said. "But where the devil is Nogaret himself?"

"Maybe the devil has him," Torquil muttered. "That, or— you don't suppose *he* took the Shard, do you?"

Before Arnault could answer, they were both arrested by the sound of hurried footsteps mounting the stair outside the chamber door. Seconds later, several ragged figures materialized out of a pall of smoke: Breville leading three more knights.

"Thank God!" Breville exclaimed, when he spotted Torquil and Arnault.

"Thank Him, indeed!" Arnault returned, trading handclasps. "I take it that you managed to fend off the wraiths."

"Mostly," Breville replied. "We've four men dead, and several more injured, but it could have been far worse. The wraiths seem to have disappeared when the place went up." He cast another look around. "Where's Christoph?"

"We haven't found him yet," Arnault said. "We're still looking."

With the help of Breville and the other knights, they resumed combing through the debris. Torquil, still shaky on his feet, stayed leaning against the altar, casting his inspection over what lay in his vicinity.

Behind the altar, it appeared that the man lying there had grabbed at the velvet covering as he fell, pulling it and its contents onto the floor. Spilled coals were scattered across the paving slabs and atop the rumpled velvet, burning holes in the rich pile, and the glass alembic was now a jagged splash of greenish shards. The skulls, he noted, had been smashed to powder. But amid this debris, as Torquil poked with his toe at the folds of ruined velvet, he suddenly spotted a glint of bright white and gemstones and gold.

"Arnault?" he called, as he crouched down for a closer look, careful not to touch it. "I've found the Breastplate."

The others came immediately, Arnault handing his torch to Torquil as he dropped to his knees to pick it up.

"The stones seem to be intact," he said after a few seconds, as he held the bank of gemstones to the light of Torquil's torch. "The linen is none too clean, but that can be—"

He broke off as he turned the breastplate to inspect the back, pinching at the twin pockets meant for the *Urim* and

Thummin and then holding the backing closer, ramming his fingertips into pockets that were definitely empty.

"*Christ*," he breathed. "They're gone. The *Urim* and *Thummin* are gone!"

"Gone?" Breville echoed, coming to see for himself.

"They should be stitched into these pockets," Arnault murmured, his fingers still feeling inside, though his eyes were roving unfocused over the floor before them. "They aren't here."

"What's that?" Torquil said, pointing toward a glint in the torchlight, just visible at one edge of the ruined altar cloth. "Could it be the *Urim*?"

Scuffing forward on his knees, Arnault pounced on what proved to be a shard of the shattered alembic, though a closer look under the cloth did, indeed, produce the *Urim*. He heaved a relieved sigh as he picked it up and polished it under his thumb.

"It isn't damaged," he whispered. "At least not physically. Look for the *Thummin*," he ordered, glancing at the others as well. "It's the same size as this, only made of polished onyx."

With six men searching on their hands and knees, they soon located the missing stone, but Arnault's expression became perplexed as he balanced the two in his palms, then closed them in his hands, shaking his head.

"There's something wrong here," he murmured. "Nogaret must have done something to them."

"*Done* something to them?" Breville repeated.

Arnault nodded. "They're dead. I'm not picking up any of the resonances they should have."

Breville shuffled closer on his knees to look at the stones as Arnault opened his hands.

"What could he have done? How is that possible?"

"I don't know," Arnault said. "It may be that, in trying to appropriate their power, he did something to neutralize it. Or maybe this incident drained them," he added, gesturing around the room.

"Permanently?" Breville asked.

"I can't tell—at least not here, where the very air is tainted with evil."

Much disheartened, Arnault slipped the *Urim* and *Thummin* back into their pockets, then wrapped a piece of one of the ruined drapes around the Breastplate before slipping it down the front of his tunic next to the pouch that had carried the Shard.

"I'll have a better look when we've gotten away from here," he said, getting to his feet. "As long as there's some spark left, we might have some hope of restoring it. We've got to find Christoph."

He and Breville found Nogaret first, far at the other side of the room, under a heap of heavy drapes torn from the windows during the storm of power. Though his body appeared to be unmarked, his face was frozen in a rictus of such horror and malice that Arnault dropped the fold of drape he had lifted and hurriedly crossed himself before daring to kneel and turn the drape back fully. Closer inspection revealed that the left hand had been burned off at the wrist. It was nowhere to be seen.

"Interesting," Breville said coldly, as he crouched beside Arnault. "I would venture to surmise that perhaps Guillaume de Nogaret did, indeed, face the Supreme Judge."

"So one might suppose," Arnault replied. "And I think it's clear that *he* didn't take the Shard. But what has become of his hand, and the ring he was wearing? That seemed to be one of the vehicles of his power. He called a demon with it."

"Maybe it was taken by the same powers that overcame him," Breville ventured.

"Or maybe someone was here before we came around," Arnault said, rising to look around. "We've only found the bodies of two of his minions."

At that moment there came a cry from outside the door to

the chamber—Torquil, sounding bereft. Abandoning Nogaret's corpse, Arnault and Breville ran to investigate—and found Torquil kneeling at the head of the turnpike stair, cradling Christoph's broken body in his arms.

"Sweet Jesus!" Arnault breathed, stepping over a dead or unconscious guard and sinking to his knees.

Christoph was still alive, but only barely. His face was a battered mask of abrasions and bruises, his eyes closed, and his breathing had an ugly rasp to it. The bloody fingers of one hand were pressed to a terrible wound deep in his side, from which blood was seeping in an ever-growing blossom of scarlet. One of Torquil's hands was also pressed to that wound, but to little avail.

The bruised and broken fingers of Christoph's other hand were locked tight around a splinter-shaped fragment of stone. Only at second glance did Arnault realize that it was, in fact, the sacred Shard, its light quenched, its power apparently exhausted. Tears were runneling down Torquil's bearded cheeks as he held Christoph close, lips pressed to the dying man's forehead as he crooned soft sounds of comfort.

Behind him, other members of the Templar party had begun picking their way up the turnpike stair, swords in hands, dazed and cautious, only to recoil at the sight of their fallen leader. Wordlessly Breville herded them back a few paces to kneel in vigil as, with a sinking feeling in his stomach, Arnault gently laid one hand over Christoph's on the Shard.

"Dare we move him?" he asked Torquil.

Torquil shook his head, barely able to speak.

"Even if it weren't for the wound," he managed to choke out, "I doubt there's a bone in his body that isn't broken."

At that, Christoph's bruised eyelids fluttered open, pain evident in the pale eyes; but when he saw Arnault's face above him, an expression of relief transfigured his broken features.

"Praise . . . be to God," he murmured. "*Le Cercle* remains yet unbroken. . . ."

He made a struggling move as if to sit up, but both his benefactors gently restrained him, though their very touch obviously caused him further pain.

"Christoph, no," Arnault murmured. "Rest easy, old friend. Save your strength."

Christoph ceased trying to sit, but drew a labored breath, slowly shaking his head. "No need . . . now. I have . . . poured out my life as an oblation, Arnault. In its ending, I have been faithful. . . ." He paused to draw another ragged breath.

"You lay senseless as one of Nogaret's minions took his ring," he went on. "*That,* I could not stop . . . but I gladly paid the price to prevent him taking *this.*" Trembling with the effort, he made his broken fingers relax enough to let Arnault's hand cup over the Shard.

"For a last battle," he continued, his voice growing more threadlike as he spoke, "this was a worthy one, I think. You are senior now. Lead the Order to survival, Arnault. Promise me. . . ." His gaze sought Arnault's with a look of burning urgency.

"I will do my best," Arnault managed to whisper. "You have my word."

Christoph's fingers twitched under his, and a faint smile briefly flitted across the battered lips as he nodded, starting to lose focus.

"Your word . . ." he whispered, "and His. . . . *His Word shall go before me . . . as a Pillar of Fire by night . . . and as a Pillar of Cloud shall I follow it by day. . . .*"

"Christoph . . ." Arnault began.

But the dying man's strength was nearly gone.

"*Non nobis, Domine . . .*" he managed to whisper, his voice trailing into a breathless sigh as he slipped into unconsciousness. But in that instant, Torquil suddenly seized Arnault's arm with his free hand.

"Arnault! Didn't Iskander say that the silk he gave us was a healing talisman?"

Arnault's hand flew to his breast, hand flat against the bulge of the pouch that contained the silk.

"He said we must ask from the heart, if ever we needed to invoke its healing powers," he said, his eyes wide as he fumbled urgently in his tunic for the pouch and pulled it out, wrenching at the silk inside. Breville had moved closer, and was urgently motioning for the others to join him.

"Brothers, come and lend us your prayers and your faith!" Arnault cried, as he shook out the silk. "Torquil, lay him flat. Keep pressure on his wound!"

Christoph moaned as Torquil shifted him onto the stairs, as horizontal as he could manage—still alive, at least. That part of Arnault that must always doubt noted that the healing talisman, with its angels and words of power, might well become Christoph's shroud; but he pushed those doubts from his mind as he spread the embellished silk over the dying man's recumbent form so that angel wings enfolded him, and the images of the holy nails lay over his hands and feet. The Shard of the Law still lay in one slack hand.

Now Arnault must ask from his heart, if he dared to hope for the grace that might still save Christoph, if only their faith was strong enough. The heart with its Crown of Thorns fell over Christoph's heart, and Arnault laid one hand atop it as he laid his other over his own heart, bowing his head in desperate prayer. Under the silk, both Torquil's hands were pressed to the wound in Christoph's side, and his tears were falling onto Arnault's hand. The tears were welling in Arnault's eyes as well as he drew forth the words—inadequate, mere words—or, were they?

"God of Israel, Word Incarnate, Sacred Heart, Chief of chiefs . . . omit not this man from Thy covenant. . . ." he whispered. "Of Thy grace, O Lord, if it be Thy will, restore Thy servant Christoph to Thy service. Not to us, Lord, not to us but unto Thy Name be the glory. . . ."

He paused to swallow, searching for more words, but could find none save for scripture. But they were words of the Word, that he had heard all his life, at the conclusion of every Mass; and with the Shard of the Law beneath his hand, the very Word of God, the words took on new meaning as he spoke them now.

"In principio erat Verbum. . . ."

In the beginning was the Word, and the Word was with God, and the Word was God. The same was in the beginning with God. All things were made by Him; and without Him was not any thing made that was made. In Him was life; and the life was the light of men. And the light shineth in darkness; and the darkness comprehended it not. . . .

And suddenly, as the words whispered from Arnault's lips, light did, indeed, shine in the darkness, coming from underneath the silken talisman that covered Christoph. Arnault heard the soft intake of breath from the others watching, saw Torquil slowly raise his head to gaze in wonder at the light streaming up his wrists from beneath the silk, where his hands were pressed to Christoph's wound.

Then Arnault felt Christoph's chest stir under his hand, rising and falling—once, again!—as the light slowly faded and Christoph's hand moved beneath the silk and drew it back from his face, wonder in his eyes.

"Christoph?" Arnault dared to breathe, as the pale eyes blinked away heavenly visions and then drifted to lock on Arnault's.

"I had the most extraordinary dream," Christoph said.

His other hand also stirred underneath the silk, to emerge with the Shard, now softly glowing. He smiled as he offered it to Arnault.

"This is your charge, I think," he said softly.

Speechless, Arnault held out his hand and let Christoph lay the Shard on his palm. The light faded, but he could feel the tingle of its power, now restored.

"You must use it to erect the Fifth Temple," Christoph

said briskly, sitting up with no sign of lingering weakness. "There lies such survival as is ordained for the Order—in Scotland, with your Bruce.

"As for me, what has happened has made it clear that my work from this point lies here in France, doing what I can to ease the spirits of our incarcerated brethren, and serving That which I took to safety, as priest. I am soldier no longer—but you must be."

Nodding, still speechless, Arnault closed his hand around the Shard and watched Torquil begin methodically folding the silk of the talisman. As he did so, Breville and the other watching knights rose and came closer, the former according Arnault a sober salute.

"We await your orders, *Maître*," he said quietly.

Breville's use of the formal title jarred Arnault to full awareness of what had just occurred, in addition to Christoph's healing. Torquil, too, was watching him through new eyes. Christoph himself was gently smiling, and gave an approving nod as Arnault squared his shoulders and drew a deep breath.

"We have accomplished what we set out to do," he told them. "Nogaret will harry the Order no more—though I would it had been sooner that he was called to judgment. Gather up the bodies of our slain brethren and bring them with us. We will find them an honorable resting place, once we are far from this accursed keep."

"What about Nogaret's men?" one of the knights asked. "Some of them are merely stunned."

A rare expression of anger crossed Arnault's pale face, but his answer was temperate.

"We cannot know if they were fully aware what their master was about," he said, tucking the Shard into the pouch Torquil handed him and then slipping that into his tunic with the Breastplate. "I'll not be responsible for slaying helpless and possibly innocent men—or helping the Devil's own. Leave them where they lie. And let God be the judge."

* * *

The explosion that rocked the turret of Castle Montaigre was audible from several miles away. Approaching by torchlight, Rodolphe de Crevecoeur reined in his horse with a startled oath, as did Bartholeme de Challon. The sudden stop caused Bartholeme's dwarf, Mercurius, likewise to yank his pony to a sharp halt, with the men of their retinue strung out uncertainly behind them.

"Thunder?" Rodolphe ventured, though without conviction.

"I very much doubt it," Bartholeme said. "It's clear tonight. There isn't a cloud in the sky. At a guess, I would propose that de Vesey's fears may have been well-founded."

Rodolphe nodded dispassionately. "You may well be right. Could it be that our esteemed Magister has made a serious error in judgment?"

"Indeed," Bartholeme agreed, with a malicious flicker of a smile. "With any luck, it will prove to be his last."

This observation elicited a bark of laughter from Mercurius.

"We won't know, of course, until we get there," Rodolphe said reflectively, and added, "At this moment, I rather fancy that Nogaret is repenting his decision to exclude us from his secret works. Shall we press on, in case there's something to be salvaged from the situation?"

"Like the High Priest's Breastplate?" Bartholeme flashed his companion a rakish grin. "And perhaps that ring, as well. If Nogaret has inadvertently overstepped the proprieties of dealing with demons, I, for one, shall not be wasting many tears."

The dwarf laughed again—an evil chortle—and Rodolphe grimaced, but he refrained from comment as he signaled the company to move on, their pace now quicker despite the darkness. They were still half a mile from the castle gates when suddenly a tattered, wild-eyed figure staggered into the torchlight ahead of them, arms waving wildly.

The horses in front shied. Mercurius uttered a vindictive hiss. The men-at-arms reached for weapons. Both Rodolphe and Bartholeme took a closer look.

"Well, well, if it isn't de Vesey himself," Rodolphe said mildly.

With his clothing hanging in shreds and his face and hands a mass of cuts and bruises, Lord Valentin de Vesey was scarcely recognizable as the debonair young courtier they were accustomed to seeing. With a low groan, he lurched forward and seized Bartholeme's horse by the bridle.

"You're late!" he rasped. "It's all over."

"So it appears," Bartholeme agreed. "Allow me to congratulate you on making good your escape."

The escapee gave a hysterical crack of laughter. "If only you knew!"

"Get a grip on yourself, man," Rodolphe snapped. "Here, have some of this."

He tossed Valentin a flask and swung down from his horse. Trembling, the new arrival took a gulping swallow and sank down on a nearby boulder. Likewise dismounting, Bartholeme waved their men away out of close earshot, first taking a torch from one of them. Valentin glared at them accusingly as he took another deep draught, sighing as he wiped the back of a hand across his mouth and let himself relax a little, like a wind bladder slowly deflating.

"I gave you ample warning," he said sullenly. "Why didn't you come sooner?"

"Because that would have defeated the purpose," Bartholeme replied, in a voice like silk. "The plan, in case you've forgotten, was to give Magister Nogaret enough rope to hang himself."

"That shows how little you know!" Valentin sulked, after taking another swig. "He had success within his grasp. We had brought Ialdabaeoth to full power. We were ready to refocus the power of the *Urim* and *Thummin*. That would have given us full access to the Breastplate itself. We had even started the process. But then Templars broke into the citadel and disrupted everything."

"*Templars?*" Rodolphe repeated. "You must have addled your wits."

"Don't you think I know what I saw?" Valentin snapped. "It's all their fault. If it weren't for their meddling, Nogaret would still be alive."

"So, he's dead?" Bartholeme interposed.

"Oh, yes. And if you want proof, have a look at this."

He tossed something small and metallic to Bartholeme, who caught it neatly. Holding it to the torchlight, Bartholeme raised an eyebrow as he recognized the demon-ring—except that its great ruby now was a dense, solid black, reflecting no light whatsoever.

"I think you'd better give us the tale in full," he recommended, closing the ring in his fist as he sank down on a rock across from Valentin.

Dully Valentin recounted the events leading up to the explosion, interspersing his recital with gulps from the flask.

"Saint Clair had an artifact that was proof against the ring, the demon, the Breastplate, and even Nogaret himself," he concluded. "I don't know what it was. Peret and Baudoin died in the blast. I was nearest the door. If the back draft hadn't flung me down the stairs, I'd be dead, too."

"How did you come by the ring?" Rodolphe asked.

"I stripped it from Nogaret's hand," Valentin said. With another ragged bark of gallows laughter, he added, "It made it easier that the hand was lying in a separate place from the rest of his body. I'm not sure how that happened. Maybe the demon did it."

Behind Bartholeme, the dwarf sniggered, the whites of his eyes just visible at the edge of the torchlight.

"And what about the Breastplate?" Bartholeme pressed. "And that other artifact?"

Valentin's eyes wavered shiftily, and he hiccuped. "I

don't know. I didn't stop to look for them. Everyone else was dead or unconscious. I was afraid some of them would come around. I just wanted to get out of there."

"So you turned tail and ran away."

"You weren't there!" Valentin retorted. "You don't know how it was. What would you have done in my place? I've told you the kind of power they wield. Are you suggesting that I should have attacked them single-handed, for the pleasure of getting myself killed?"

"That at least would have been heroic," Bartholeme said. "Not that it's difficult or brave to kill unconscious men. As it is, you leave me with a problem on my hands."

Valentin's eyes narrowed suspiciously. "What do you mean?"

"Simply that you haven't proved yourself a very trustworthy acolyte, have you?" Bartholeme replied. "Your services, I think, are no longer required."

He snapped his fingers to the darkness behind him, and men emerged from the shadows. Valentin started up in alarm, only to be seized and pinioned from behind. Mercurius, too, had moved into the torchlight, stubby fingers fondling the ornate hilt of an oversize dagger at his belt.

"Have you gone mad?" the captive shrieked, struggling, as Bartholeme rose. "What are you doing?"

"What Nogaret would have done, *should* have done, if he hadn't been blinded by his own ambition," Bartholeme said.

He nodded to Mercurius. Grinning, the dwarf drew his dagger and, testing the blade against his thumb, advanced on the struggling Valentin. The captive uttered a piercing howl and tried even harder to break away, fighting for his life, but Bartholeme's men held him fast as, with merciless precision, the dwarf deftly slit his throat.

Eyes wide with disbelief, the dying man gave a bubbling moan, then slowly sagged in his captors' arms. Mercurius was still grinning as he stepped back, and Rodolphe's dislike turned to distaste as the dwarf licked the blade clean with his tongue. Bartholeme was unmoved.

"Get rid of the carcass," he ordered curtly.

"Wasn't that a trifle drastic?" Rodolphe remarked, as the guards dragged Valentin's body into the rocks.

"This is war," Bartholeme responded with a shrug. "We can't afford to tolerate any further weakness or divisions in our ranks. Especially not now, when we know that at least some of the Templars are still a force to be reckoned with. Now let's see what more we can learn from this."

While Rodolphe held the torch, Bartholeme carefully polished the blackened stone against his sleeve and breathed on it, whispering a word of power. Most gratifyingly, it gave off a tiny flicker of garnet flame.

"Well, would you look at that!" Rodolphe exclaimed.

Bartholeme nodded. His eyes were very cold and very bright.

"It seems there may still be some life in this little toy of Nogaret's," he mused. "Ialdabaeoth, are you there? Acknowledge your new master. . . ."

Nothing happened, but Bartholeme merely smiled and closed the ring in his hand.

"No matter," he said lightly. "I can sense its presence; it's sulking—*and* it was hurt somewhat by whatever happened. But at least we know that those accursed Templars didn't have it all their own way after all."

"Evidently not," Rodolphe agreed. "The question is, can we make use of the ring now that Nogaret is gone?"

"I'm quite certain I can bargain successfully for the use of its powers," Bartholeme said. "Unless, of course, you intend to challenge me for its possession?"

The question was accompanied by a predatory glare, before which Rodolphe shook his head and gave a mirthless laugh.

"Some other time, perhaps. I rather like being alive. If you feel you have it in you to lead the Decuria against the

Templars, by all means take the helm. If you survive, you will be assured of your place. If not . . ."

"If not, you will be waiting to assume the mantle of command," Bartholeme said. "I quite understand."

"Oh, I'm prepared to be led, for the present," Rodolphe said lightly. "Which reminds me: Valentin implied that some of the Templars survived—which means they may still be in the area. Have you any orders regarding them?"

"Let them go their way—for now," Bartholeme said. "We need time to consolidate our forces and rebuild our strength, to summon the rest of the Decuria."

"Isn't it risky to let them vanish into the night?" Rodolphe asked. "After all, they probably have the Breastplate again—and whatever killed Nogaret."

"Oh, they probably do—but I don't mean to challenge them for either, just now," Bartholeme said. "After all, I know exactly where they mean to go from here."

"You do?"

"Oh, yes," Bartholeme replied. "Tell him, Mercurius."

The dwarf leered, finally sheathing his dagger.

"Scotland, Master. Now that they have their precious Breastplate back, they'll be off to rejoin their puppet king Robert Bruce—and that's where we'll find them, when the time is ripe."

Chapter Thirty-seven

April-November, 1313

"I WISH I COULD BELIEVE WE'VE SEEN THE LAST OF THE Knights of the Black Swan," Torquil said aside to Arnault, when their party paused to rest, several hours after leaving Castle Montaigre. "Unfortunately, though Nogaret's death may slow them down for a while, there's sure to be some ambitious underling waiting to seize control, now that he's gone."

"Aye, this is a serpent of many heads," Arnault agreed bleakly. "It will take more than one blow to kill it."

"At least we've bought ourselves some valuable time," Breville said. "We must put it to good use."

By the end of that day, they had scattered to various assignments, with orders to make their way to Scotland as and when they could. Christoph had already made his own intentions clear; Breville had more active pursuits in mind.

"We've eliminated Nogaret," he pointed out, "but we've only wounded the Decuria. My guess is that Bartholeme de Challon will assert himself, now that Nogaret is gone—and we know that, in the past, he has taken an interest in what transpires in Scotland. If he seems to be doing so again, I will send you advance warning."

Arnault gave his assent, but not without misgivings, for he was well aware that Nogaret's cohorts were not the only adversaries they had to fear. Not content with destroying the good name of the Order, King Philip now seemed bent upon securing its complete and abject annihilation. The papal bull disbanding the Order the previous year had ordered all remaining Templars to surrender themselves to the judgment of the Church or face automatic excommunication and civil outlawry. Papal inquisitors and servants of the crown remained on the alert throughout the realm of France, eager as bloodhounds to sniff out anyone associated with the Temple. As long as Breville or Christoph or any other Templar remained on French soil, the danger of discovery would always be present.

That danger made travel difficult and slow, once Arnault and Torquil parted company with their brethren. They had intended to make for Iona first, for Arnault wished to take counsel of the Columban brethren regarding the Breastplate and the Shard. But faced with travel difficulties and near-run encounters with royal patrols, they were obliged to seize opportunities when and as they could. Thus it was that, after some months' delay, they found themselves at last aboard a Portuguese galley bound for Dublin.

Not that Ireland could offer much in the way of sanctuary for renegade Templars, despite the fact that persecution of the Order there had never been more than halfhearted. Though officers of the English king eventually had made a show of rounding up all the Irish Templars they could find, they had netted only thirty men out of nearly a hundred said to be based on the Emerald Isle. And as for Templar treasure, the vaults at Clontarf Castle, the Order's principal Irish preceptory just outside Dublin, had yielded only a few rusty swords.

The Irish Templars themselves, including the Master of Ireland, had soon been released on bail—and had melted into the Irish countryside. But cautious inquiry by Arnault and Torquil in the vicinity of Clontarf eventually had turned up *le Cercle*'s man in Ireland, Brother Richard of Kilsaren, who readily agreed to secure them transport on to Iona.

"A number of our galleys ended up in the west of Ireland," Brother Richard told them. "I can summon one within a few weeks, to take you wherever you need to go."

Brother Richard was also well informed on the current state of affairs in Scotland.

"There's been good progress, actually—slow but steady. Since you were last in Scotland, King Robert has prevailed decisively over the Comyns and the Balliols. The Earl of Ross has come into his peace, and many other prominent nobles and lairds besides. With internal opposition essentially resolved, Bruce has been able to reinstate the Scottish parliament as a reliable instrument of government. Trade relations have been renewed with the Baltic states, and Scottish law has largely been restored throughout the countryside."

"But . . . ?" Torquil prompted, when Brother Richard did not go on.

The Irish Templar grimaced. "There is still the matter of England. As I told you, King Edward still holds those four pivotal Scottish locations. As long as he continues to do so, he can continue to claim suzerainty over Scotland's domains."

The point was not lost on either of his listeners, both of whom had intimate knowledge of all four strongholds. Arnault slowly nodded.

"I take your point. But we've long known that the Scots must reclaim those castles."

"Stirling is a bit more immediate," Brother Richard replied. "Is it possible you've not heard?"

At the looks of question on both his listeners' faces, Richard drew a deep breath and let it out.

"Dear me. Earlier this year, King Robert sent his brother Edward to besiege Stirling Castle. After several months of stalemate, the commander of the English garrison, Sir Philip Moubray, made young Bruce a proposal by way of securing a truce. Put simply, the bargain was this: If no English army comes to relieve the castle by next midsummer's day, Moubray has vowed to surrender the castle without further bloodshed. Without consulting his brother, young Bruce agreed."

Arnault and Torquil exchanged troubled looks as Richard continued.

"I see that the implications are more readily apparent to you than they were to young Bruce," Richard said. "No doubt, he thought he had hit upon a way to win back Stirling without the trouble and expense of mounting a further assault. But in fact, all he has done is provoke Edward of England into launching a full-scale invasion."

"True enough," Arnault agreed. "Edward can hardly allow such a challenge to pass. It was astute strategy on Moubray's part."

"Indeed," Richard said. "English supporters north of the Border have been clamoring for reinforcements for several seasons now—thus far, in vain. But this bargain puts English royal pride at stake. By next midsummer, Edward Plantagenet must either redeem Moubray's bargain by force or submit to being branded a weakling and a coward. God grant he may prove to be both, but that does not appear likely. My contacts tell me that the English commissioners of array have received orders to raise an army and gather provisions during the winter."

Both Arnault and Torquil were shaking their heads, well aware what such a campaign would mean for Scotland.

"So much for the hit-and-run tactics that have served us so well up until now," Torquil murmured. "This will force the king into the pitched battles he's been trying to avoid."

"Unfortunately, it will," Arnault said. "But here, perhaps, I begin to see a way in which we Templars may lend valuable aid to the Scottish cause—not by our numbers, but by our experience in the arts of war. We have six months. We can do a lot of training in that time."

"Those are mostly winter months," Richard pointed out, "but I agree. And we already have several score of our brethren hiding in the fastness of Argyll—and more have come from France, I hear."

"And more *will* come," Arnault agreed. "There are some on their way even as we speak."

"There is hope, then," Richard said. "Will you go now to Bruce?"

"As soon as possible, with your help," Arnault replied.

Brother Richard had already sent word regarding a ship, and now furnished his brethren with horses to speed them on their way. Leaving Clontarf, they pressed westward, through the flatlands of Offaly and deep into Galway. The vessel that met them at Kinvarra flew the colors of MacDonald of the Isles, one of Bruce's staunchest allies: a sleek coastal galley well able for the cold waters of the North.

They set sail under gusty autumn skies, ghosting northward around Connemara, then skirting the Donegal coast to head back eastward toward Islay and the Mull of Oa. Sunset of a late-November day found them within sight of Mull—and, at its westernmost tip, lovely Iona itself.

The tide was out, exposing a pebbled strand. In the soft light and mist of dusk, the weathered church and outbuildings of the Columban community appeared unchanged to Arnault's yearning eyes. Skillfully handled, the galley coasted to a standstill a dozen yards from shore. As Arnault and Torquil slipped over the side to wade ashore, two white-robed figures trotted down to the beach to meet them—novices, by their youthful faces and earnest manners.

"Father Abbot said that we were to expect visitors before nightfall," the taller of the pair confided. "If you will be pleased to accompany us, we'll take you to him."

Arnault suppressed a smile and glanced at Torquil. Very little went on in the environs of the island that escaped the notice of the Columbans, mystically attuned as they were to every whisper of the wind, every turn of the tide.

"How *is* Abbot Fingon these days?" Torquil asked.

The novices looked somewhat abashed. "Father Fingon

died at Eastertide," the shorter of the two informed them. "Father Ninian is now the head of our community."

The two Templars exchanged glances, taken aback at the news.

"This place seems so timeless," Torquil murmured, as they followed their guides toward the abbey's cloister court, "it never crossed my mind to expect any change."

"Nor I," Arnault replied. "Fortunately, Ninian has been in our confidence since the beginning. I trust his counsel as much as I would have trusted Fingon's."

Their guides showed them into the familiar warmth of the abbot's study, where Ninian laid aside the book he had been reading and came to meet his visitors. Their ensuing exchange of greetings was accompanied by words of condolence regarding Fingon.

"His health had declined, of late, but he went gently," the new abbot said, waving the two to seats. "On the night before Saint Columba called him home, Father Fingon told me that you would return to us before the year's end. The reason, I gather, must be pressing, since you have come here before making your presence known to the king."

Arnault had long ago ceased to wonder how the Columbans came by their knowledge. It was sufficient that they had their own methods of discovery. He was counting on those gifts now.

"We came because we need your guidance, Father Abbot," Arnault said, reaching into his tunic. "Our quest in the Holy Land was successful, in that we brought back what we went for. And it enabled us to recover the High Priest's Breastplate, on our way back through France."

He produced both items: the Shard, now housed only in its leather bag, and the Breastplate, folded inside a length of white linen. It was the latter he began unwrapping for Ninian's inspection. He had left the healing talisman in Christoph's keeping.

"Unfortunately, the Breastplate was in the possession of

Guillaume de Nogaret, the king's minister," he went on, un-folding layers of linen. "He's dead now—and good rid-dance—but he did something to the Breastplate. Probably something vile, because he conjured up a demon while we were there—and that, in itself, is a story worth the telling, later on," he added candidly, at Ninian's raised eyebrows. "In any case, we think the problem lies with the *Urim* and *Thum-min.* We're hoping you can tell us how to reverse whatever it was he did."

He had exposed the Breastplate and flipped it over to ex-pose the pockets as he spoke, and now slid out the two stones. Ninian gazed at them silently for a long moment, folded hands pressed to his lips, then briefly laid his hands atop the *Urim* and *Thummin,* as if touch could tell him more than mere sight. His expression was both thoughtful and grave as he drew back his hands and glanced up at the waiting Templars.

"There is much here which wants clearer understanding," he observed with a shake of his head. "I think we must ask guidance from a higher wisdom."

He slid the *Urim* and *Thummin* back into their pockets, then cradled the Breastplate in his open palms, closing his eyes.

"Holy Michael, whom we hail as Cra-gheal, the Red-White One," he murmured softly, "we have need of your counsel. This instrument of God's Word has been touched by His ene-mies. The Lights and Perfections have grown dim. Can you show us how these may be restored?"

Arnault and Torquil kept watchfully silent as Ninian lapsed deeper into meditation, fingers curling around the relic. A range of emotions—pain, anger, and revulsion—swept over his ascetic features. When he at last roused from his trance, carefully setting the Breastplate on the table before them, his expression was troubled.

"It is as I feared," he said. "Nogaret had attempted to per-vert its powers to his use. This has rendered the Breastplate unclean. Like diseased flesh, it must be purged of all taint of corruption. But the source of that corruption is still present and active in the material world. And as long as this exponent remains at large, the damage wrought through its agency cannot wholly be undone."

"Are you saying that the Decuria still maintain some kind of hold over the Breastplate?" Torquil exclaimed in dismay.

Ninian nodded. "Alas, I am. The evidence suggests that God's enemies were preparing the Breastplate to channel power from the infernal realm. The process involves the conjuring of unclean spirits. Command over these forces is usually vested in a power object of some kind. But what that object might be, I could not determine."

"I think I know," Arnault said quietly, after a beat. "It will have been Nogaret's demon-ring."

Torquil looked at him sharply. "But—wasn't it destroyed?"

"We assumed it was," Arnault said. "But maybe not. We never found his hand, either."

"Then, one of his disciples could have recovered it," Ninian ventured.

"It's—possible," Arnault replied.

Torquil slowly shook his head. "This is my fault. I should have gone back and made a thorough search."

"No, if anyone is to blame, I am," Arnault said. "And if we were distracted, it was in a good cause."

Briefly he told Ninian of the healing of Christoph, and the events that led up to a need for such healing, sparing no detail that he could remember. The recitation left him drained, head bowed in his hands. After a moment, Ninian spoke.

"You both should rest," he said gently. "You have had a long and arduous journey. If you will heed my advice, you should remain here for a few days yet and mend your strength."

"No, we must move on," Arnault said dully. "The king must be told of the danger. And you must be on guard as well. If Nogaret's successors do have his ring, they may be able to follow us here, using it as a focus, and seek a final accounting."

"No harm shall befall *us*," Ninian said gently, "if that is what you fear. And the king shall know within the hour."

Both Templars merely stared at him blankly.

"Brother Fionn and Brother Ciaran are with him," Ninian said, as if that explained everything. "Father Fingon sent them shortly after you left on your quest to the Holy Land."

"But, how—"

"Go and rest," Ninian said, rising. "But first, ask Brother Seoirse to give you something to eat. You will need your strength, when you go to Bruce."

Ninian came to them the next morning after morning prayers, drawing them out into the snowy cloister to walk with him.

"I am informed that the Lights and Perfections can be healed through the power of the Stone of Destiny," he told them, though he made no mention of how he had been so informed. "But before the Stone can be used in this way, I am given to understand that Bruce's agreement is necessary. If we leave immediately, we can be at Dunkeld by the Feast of Saint Andrew. We may seek his permission then."

"Bruce is at Dunkeld?" Torquil said, surprised.

"Not yet," Ninian said with a tiny smile, "but he will be." At Arnault's look of question, he added, "Our survival, like that of your Order, is linked to the Fifth Temple, Brother Arnault. And the Stone of Destiny is the Temple's keystone. I will ride with you to Dunkeld, for it lies there."

The galley that had brought the Templars to Iona had stayed in the lee between Iona and Mull, waiting to transport them where they wished. They sailed at dawn, coasting along the southern shores of Mull and into the Firth of Lorne, then heading around the bluffs of Oban and into Loch Etive. There they went ashore under cover of darkness. At a nearby village, they procured three rough-coated ponies and a guide to show them the route across country ahead of the winter snows.

Throughout the course of their journey, Arnault remained conscious of the twin burdens of the Shard and the Breastplate that he carried. The latter was presently a deadweight, reduced to mere precious metal and gems; he did not wish to contemplate the state of the *Urim* and *Thummin*. He could only hope that the latent power of the Shard might somehow enable the Stone to reignite the mystical Lights and Perfections, for he sensed that the *Urim* and *Thummin*, not the Breastplate itself, were the key to what must be done.

The chilly November dusk was gathering when at last they reached the stone fastness of Dunkeld Cathedral. During the journey, they had learned that Matthew Crambeth was no longer bishop. "Sadly, he passed away, some three or four years ago," Ninian had told them. But the new bishop was William Sinclair, a distant cousin of Aubrey and, even more distantly, of Arnault himself.

"I think I've only met him once or twice, when we were both far younger," Arnault had said, on learning the new bishop's identity. "I can hardly say that I know him, especially as a man."

"Well, thanks to young Aubrey, Bishop William knows a good deal about you and the somewhat special circumstances of your recent journey to the Holy Land," Ninian assured them. "And of course, he is in total sympathy with the plight of your Order. You'll find that he has been a faithful custodian of the Stone in your absence."

Given the new bishop's affiliations, their reception at Dunkeld was cordial; and their dinner conversation quickly assumed an air of easy familiarity as Bishop William acquainted them with the political developments of the past several years—for he also had the king's ear, and a brother and two nephews in Bruce's service.

The three were in the following that arrived with the king the next morning, along with Aubrey, Flannan Fraser, and the white-robed figures of Brother Ciaran and Brother Fionn. The passage of five years had left Flannan looking leaner and more weathered than Arnault remembered, and Aubrey had acquired a scar across his chin and streaks of silver at his temples, but in every other respect, both appeared as hardy as ever.

"Your return is well-timed," Bruce said to Arnault and Torquil, after he and the bishop had exchanged greetings. "I've a situation that has been forced upon me, and I'll be interested to hear what you make of it. Bishop, might we use a room in your house?"

"So, there you have it," Bruce concluded, after he had outlined the situation, ensconced with them before a fire in the bishop's parlor. "My brother thought he would spare us the necessity to continue a long siege of Stirling Castle."

Arnault and Torquil exchanged glances. Bruce's account of the Stirling Castle agreement tallied closely with what Brother Richard had told them, with added details regarding the intelligence the king had gained from agents reporting from London.

"So, what is it that you intend to do between now and next summer, Sire?" Torquil asked.

"Regain as much ground as I can," Bruce replied. "If we harry the English fiercely enough in the next six months, Edward's greater magnates may decide that Stirling isn't worth the trouble. If not"—he shrugged—"I may be forced to fight a pitched battle—in which case, it's going to be all or nothing."

"A dangerous gamble," Arnault said. "It would appear that you'll be needing all the help you can get."

At his faint smile, Bruce sat forward.

"Your tone suggests that you may have a plan. What kind of help did you have in mind?"

"Templar help," Arnault replied. "And not merely as individual observers and advisors, like myself and Torquil, but in a rather more organized manner."

Bruce cocked his head at them in question, but did not speak as Arnault went on.

"I know you're aware of the general decline in the Order's fortunes in the last six years," Arnault continued. "You may *not* be aware that a number of our fugitive brethren have taken refuge in the west of Scotland. In return for even the hope of asylum, when all of this is done, I believe they would fight their hearts out for you, Sire. They have funds as well, smuggled out of France ahead of King Philip's raids, that could be turned to buying weapons. We can bring those in through Ireland, to arm more of your men. And we can turn our military expertise to helping train your Scottish forces to stand against the English host."

Bruce was slowly nodding, wide-eyed. "You give me hope that we can actually accomplish it," he said. "Certainly, I would never withdraw the promise of refuge from men who have lost so much and still are willing to give so much to our Scottish cause."

After some further discussion, it was decided that Aubrey and Flannan Fraser should travel to the west of Scotland, there to organize men, horses, and arms. For safekeeping, Arnault left the Breastplate in Bishop Sinclair's custody.

"Aubrey will have told you of the part this has already played in Scotland's destiny," he said, "and there is more to be done, when this war is won. But it will be safer kept here than with me, with all the places I must go in the next few months."

"It will be well guarded until you return," the bishop promised them. "In fact, it will reside well with what I had already intended to offer the king."

From a hidden aumbry behind a wall tapestry, Sinclair brought out Dunkeld's most precious treasure: the Moneymusk Reliquary. Shaped like a tiny house with peaked roof, and embellished with Celtic designs, the little casket contained relics of Saint Columba himself, and was sometimes carried before Scottish armies like a miniature Ark of the Covenant. It had been present when Bruce was enthroned on the Stone, eight years before.

"The *Brecbennach*," Sinclair murmured, giving it its Gaelic name as he brought it before Bruce. "Let this be your standard in battle, Sire. And may the blessings of Saint Columba, Saint Andrew, Saint Fillan, and all the saints of Scotland watch over you, and all who march beneath your banner."

Quite overcome, Bruce touched his fingertips to his lips, then to the little reliquary, running a reverent finger briefly along the top of its lid.

"I thank you, Bishop. And when the time comes, I shall ask Father Ninian to take charge of this precious object on my behalf."

The Columban abbot set one hand to his breast and bowed slightly. "I will be honored to do so, Sire. And Brother Arnault . . ."

Arnault looked at him in question.

"Seeing the *Brecbennach* has given me an idea," Ninian went on, laying his hand upon it. "May I suggest that you take the *Urim* and *Thummin* from the Breastplate and place one of them inside the *Brecbennach*. Leave the other on the Stone itself, as a link between the two."

"But the *Urim* and *Thummin* are dead," Arnault said.

"No, not dead; sleeping," Ninian replied. "And once the Ring of the Black Swan has been destroyed, they will awaken. At that point, you should be able to use the Shard to activate the link between them, and tap directly into the energy of the Stone."

Chapter Thirty-eight

Early 1314

BRUCE AND HIS ADVISORS SPENT CHRISTMAS LAYING PLANS for a series of offensives. With the coming of the new year, James Douglas, the youngest of the Scottish commanders, was given the honor of assaulting Roxburgh Castle.

On the eve of Ash Wednesday, which fell that year in mid-February, Douglas and his men smeared their faces with soot and donned black surcoats to hide their armor. Then, armed with rope ladders attached to grappling hooks, they crept up on the castle in the dead of night and silently scaled the walls, silencing the sentries and taking the garrison by surprise in the midst of their Shrove Tuesday revelry. By morning the castle was in Scottish hands.

Following on this success, hardly a month later, the king's nephew, Thomas Randolph, took Edinburgh Castle by a similar combination of stealth and bravado. King Robert ordered both castles razed to the ground, for he dared not risk having them taken back by the English.

Early in May, with demolition well under way, in Edinburgh, Arnault and Torquil had been watching the king drill his schiltrons when Luc de Brabant arrived with fresh news from France—ill news, by his grave expression.

"I have good news and bad," he told them, as he drew them aside for privacy. "The good news is that Breville managed to spirit Oliver out of prison. He's stayed in France to join Christoph."

"That *is* good news," Arnault replied. "And the bad news?"

"The king has burned de Molay."

Both Arnault and Torquil stared at him in shock.

"What?"

"And the Preceptor of Normandy. On March 14."

Torquil looked sick, like a man just kicked in the groin. Arnault was reeling with images from his dreams en route to the Holy Land.

"I never thought Philip would dare," he murmured.

"Nor did I, but Breville saw it." Luc grimly shook his head. "Paraud and Gonneville would have been burned as well, but they had already upheld their confessions. It's said they'll be sent to perpetual imprisonment."

Torquil's face was stony as he slowly shook his head. "This doesn't make sense," he said disbelievingly. "It's been nearly seven years since they were arrested, and two since the Order was disbanded. Why burn them now?"

"I don't think that was the original intention," Luc replied. "De Molay and de Charney had made private confessions of guilt, but apparently Philip wanted them to make some grand public confession on behalf of the whole Order—especially de Molay, since he was the Grand Master."

"And they refused?" Torquil said.

"More than just refused," Luc muttered. He drew a deep breath. "Breville says that a high platform had been specially constructed in front of Notre Dame Cathedral. On the appointed day, de Molay and the other three were marched out onto the platform, wearing full Templar habit but also laden with chains, to underline their guilt. There was a huge crowd, come to bear witness to the expected confession—

which was meant to vindicate King Philip, but things turned out otherwise."

"Go on," Arnault urged, when Luc paused.

A pained smile plucked at Luc's lips as he slowly shook his head. "It seems that, in the very depths of humiliation, our late Grand Master found the greatest moment of his life. Breville wrote down his words, afterward."

From the pocket of his sleeve, he took out a much-folded piece of parchment, which he handed to Arnault. Unfolding it, Arnault read the words aloud.

"I think it only right that, at so solemn a moment, when my life has so little time to run, I should reveal the deception which has been practiced and speak up for the truth. Before Heaven and earth and all of you here, my witnesses, I admit that I am guilty of the grossest iniquity. But the iniquity is that I have lied in admitting the disgusting charges laid against the Order.

"I declare, and I must declare, that the Order is innocent. Its purity and saintliness are beyond question. I have indeed confessed that the Order is guilty, but I have done so only to save myself from terrible tortures by saying what my enemies wished me to say. Other knights who have retracted their confessions have been led to the stake, yet the thought of dying is not so awful that I shall confess to foul crimes which have never been committed. Life is offered to me, but at the price of infamy. At such a price, life is not worth having. I do not grieve that I must die if life can be bought only by piling one lie upon another."

Arnault was shaking his head as he handed the parchment back to Luc. Torquil was biting at his lip, his face turned partially away.

"You're right," Arnault said quietly. "De Molay was never greater than in his final hours."

"No, never," Luc agreed. "And de Charney likewise retracted his confession on the spot. Philip was furious, as you can imagine, and ordered them dragged from the platform.

Paraud and Gonneville were hurried away before they could change their minds. By late afternoon, the pyres had been readied."

He lifted his gaze beyond them as he continued, tears in his eyes.

"The wood was dry and well seasoned, deliberately chosen to burn hot and bright, with little smoke. But even in the midst of their death agonies, de Molay and de Charney continued to cry out the innocence of the Order. And at the end, with his dying breath, de Molay called on the king and the pope to meet him before God's throne of judgment within the year, and cursed the king and his family for the next thirteen generations. I should add that the Holy Father has already been called to his accounting, hardly a fortnight ago."

"*Clement* is dead?" Torquil gasped.

As Luc merely nodded, his two companions slowly crossed themselves, stunned, and Torquil whispered, "May God have mercy on their souls."

After another moment of heavy silence, Arnault glanced back determinedly in the direction of the king's camp.

"This severs our last tie with France," he said quietly. "One way or another, Scotland is destined to be the Order's final home."

While the Templars were still mourning the death of their Grand Master, one of their greatest enemies was traveling north from London in the van of King Edward's invading army.

"Tell me, my lord," said the young Earl of Gloucester, plucking idly at the jeweled cuff of his riding glove, "do you really think there could be a significant number of Templars at large in Scotland, fighting for this upstart Bruce?"

"My king is certain of it," said Bartholeme de Challon. "Otherwise, we should not be here."

He gestured over his shoulder at the body of armored knights riding behind him under the banner of the Black

Swan—superbly mounted, expensively caparisoned, a match for any band of English chivalry. Among them rode Mercurius, on an evil-looking black pony, as richly turned out, but in miniature. It was he who had caught the king's particular fancy, thereby ensuring that Bartholeme and his companions were accorded a place of honor among the higher English nobility.

Riding on the other side of Bartholeme, Count Rodolphe leaned forward to address the English lord.

"Recall, my lord Earl, that Bruce is excommunicate. The papal bull disbanding the Order has never been enforced in Scotland, despite your master's efforts to comply. What better place for a remnant of condemned sorcerers to seek refuge than amongst others of their kind?"

"A fair enough comment," Gloucester agreed. He turned in his saddle to scan the colorful array of heraldic devices displayed among the French company. "But, what is it that brings you to our cause? Each of you is a knight of noble birth, bearing his own arms. Why is it that all of you choose to ride under the banner of the Black Swan?"

"It is a sign of our common purpose," Bartholeme explained glibly, "to hunt down and destroy the last remnant of the Templars, and put an end to their sorceries."

"Surely there can't be many of them left," said young Henry de Bohun, who fancied himself nigh invincible on the tourney field.

"Any who survive are dangerous," Bartholeme replied, "and those who have fled to Scotland are amongst the worst. Believe me when I tell you that the inquisitors of France have obtained hundreds of confessions attesting to heresy and the practice of magic—and you must not imagine that the most skilled of them were captured. Many used their magic to make good their escape. And Bruce, another heretic, was only too glad to offer them safe haven, in barter for their talents."

Gloucester laughed uneasily. "Surely you don't expect us

to believe that Bruce's successes can be attributed to magic?"

Riding beside Bartholeme was the exiled John Macdougall of Lorn, who gigged his horse a little forward at the remark.

"How else do you account for Bruce's successes of recent years?" he snapped. "It's no coincidence that, since the suppression of the Order on the continent, Bruce's fortunes have been on the ascendant."

"Whilst yours have declined?" Bohun said, a sneer in his voice. "Well, that's one explanation anyway."

He touched spurs to his mount and rode on ahead, belatedly followed by Gloucester, leaving Lorn bristling furiously in their wake.

"You see what insolence I am compelled to endure?" Lorn said to Bartholeme in an angry undertone. "That swaggering English puppy was scarcely out of leading strings when Bruce and his Templar wizards—"

"Peace," Bartholeme advised. "Your time will come."

"When?" Lorn demanded.

"Very soon now," Bartholeme promised. Lowering his voice, he added, "We will speak of this more fully when there are not so many others present."

Later that afternoon, when they had halted to rest the horses, Rodolphe drew Bartholeme aside.

"That Lorn is a fool and an oaf," he muttered. "I fail to see why you tolerate his company."

"For the same reason a man keeps a mastiff," Bartholeme replied. "To sniff out enemies and give the alarm in case of trouble."

"The aptness of the comparison escapes me, I'm afraid," said Rodolphe.

"My agents inform me that there is a strong likelihood the Templars have established bases in the west of Scotland," Bartholeme said with a touch of impatience. "Lorn knows that country well. While we engage the enemy at Stirling, I propose sending our Scottish mastiff to guard the back door—in case the Templars attempt to summon reinforcements."

"He's no fit match for them."

"He will be," said Bartholeme. "Once I've given him this."

He produced a jeweled pendant set with curiously variegated gems whose colors fluctuated greasily in the light from red to blue to brown to green. The central stone seemed to glow slightly from within.

"I hope you know what you're doing," Rodolphe said.

"The power belongs to one of the lesser demons," Bartholeme said. "The demon itself is answerable to me."

"When do you plan to give it to him?"

"When we cross the Border."

Chapter Thirty-nine

June 22, 1314

$\mathcal{I}$ MAKE IT EIGHT INFANTRY DIVISIONS SO FAR," ARNAULT said, "and they're still coming. It wouldn't surprise me if the final head count for infantry was close to fifteen thousand."

Beside him, from their hidden vantage point in the Torwood, overlooking the English line of march toward Falkirk—and Stirling, beyond—Sir Robert Keith glanced aside at the third of their scouting party, young James Douglas.

"What do you think, Jamie?"

Douglas had the look of a wolf sizing up a herd of large prey.

"Not the odds I would've asked for," he said, "but then, we didn't ask for any of this, did we? And look at them! You'd think they were riding to a bloody tournament!"

Keeping well under cover, the three men had been shadowing the English army for the past hour. Fortunately, the English were sticking to the road, and their outriders did not stray far from the main body, for years of ambush warfare by the Scots had taught them to fear being cut off and destroyed piecemeal.

The knights of Edward's vanguard, commanded by the

earls of Gloucester and Hereford, did, indeed, make a brave show. Sunlight glanced in bold flashes off their polished chain mail and burnished weaponry. Their painted shields and embroidered surcoats made a mosaic of lavish colors, as rich and jewel-like as panels picked out in stained glass. Their spirited destriers were larger and fiercer than any mount ever bred in Scotland, massive hooves kicking up clouds of dust from the dry roadbed.

"How much heavy cavalry do you estimate?" Arnault asked.

Keith pursed his lips. "Well over two thousand; perhaps as many as three."

"Aye, the flower of English nobility, all coming to pay us a visit," Douglas said sourly.

"Enough to outmatch our own horse by three to one, at least," Arnault observed. "But you'd think, by now, that Edward would realize that heavy cavalry isn't the advantage he thinks, where we'll be fighting. I do wish we could tell how many bowmen they have."

Douglas gave a contemptuous snort, but Arnault recalled only too clearly the havoc that English bowmen had wrought upon the Scottish schiltrons at Falkirk, softening them up for the hammerblow of a mounted charge. He and Torquil had barely managed to rescue William Wallace from the ensuing rout.

"Och, there's no way to tell from here," Douglas said, restively fingering the hilt of his sword. "Maybe one of us should ride down there and see how many arrows he takes in his back."

Keith ignored Douglas's black humor. "The point is that they're here in time to prevent Stirling Castle surrendering," he said. "It might be best to withdraw and concede them this round."

"The king's in no mind for that," Douglas said.

Keith tipped a nod at the English host. "He hasn't seen

this yet. Their baggage train is an army in itself. I must've counted at least two hundred carts."

Douglas snorted. "Aye, y'd think Edward's brought his whole palace with him, to set up in the middle of Scotland."

"It takes a lot of provisioning for an army this size," Arnault pointed out.

"Well, if they've come for a banquet," Douglas said grimly, "they'll find blood in their goblets!"

"We'd best report back to the king and see what he says to it," Keith said.

As the other two headed back toward their ponies, tied in a coppice down the other side of the hill, Arnault lingered for another scan of the troops of English cavalry interspersed among the units of marching infantry and bowmen. He was looking for any sign of a band of Black Swan Knights, said by Armand Breville to be on their way from France to join the English army on its northerly march to Stirling. He was about to turn away when a flutter of black-and-white silk caught his eye above a new mass of English chivalry just coming into sight.

He knew the banner could not be *Beaucéant*—not in these times, and not among the English chivalry. But as his gaze quested for definition, darting to those who rode beneath the black-and-white banner, he singled out a small band of about a dozen knights, all wearing black cloaks over damascened armor. In that instant, the breeze lifted their banner enough to display its device: a black swan set against a background of silvery white.

Dimly Arnault was aware of the baffled whispers of his companions urging him to horse, of Keith even starting back toward him, and he made himself shake off the compulsion that had drawn him to the sight he had not wanted to see.

But it was proof that Breville's warning had been timely. Arnault had no doubt that the men beneath the Black Swan banner were members of Nogaret's sorcerous brotherhood, and their very presence confirmed that the Black Swan

Knights remained dedicated to the destruction of the Templars. Undeterred by the death of their leader, Nogaret's successors had pursued the Order even here.

"Saint Clair!" Keith whispered sharply. "If you tarry any longer, then the first battle will be fought right here, the three of us against Edward's whole army."

Finally acknowledging Keith's prompt, Arnault returned to his pony and vaulted into the saddle, falling in behind his companions as they cantered back toward the Scots' lines. But he could not repress a final backward glance, like a man who fears there to see a fiend on his trail.

Bruce had made his camp on the wooded slopes below Stirling Castle. The New Park, as the area was known locally, had been established by previous kings of Scotland as a royal hunting preserve. Bruce had chosen the ground with care. Its trees and hollows provided concealment and protection for the Scottish army while the English approached openly from the south.

On the western fringe of the camp, the horses that comprised Bruce's small force of light cavalry were being fed a last measure of fodder. Leaving their mounts with a groom, Arnault, Keith, and Douglas went in search of the king. They found him sitting outside his weather-stained pavilion, sharpening his long-handled battle-axe. The surrounding encampment hummed with purposeful activity as men whetted their spear blades and strapped on leather hauberks.

Bruce listened impassively as each of the three scouts made his report and gave his assessment of the English muster. Once they had finished, the king surveyed their glum faces and flashed a predatory grin.

"You're forgetting that all this works to our advantage."

"How do you calculate that?" Douglas asked skeptically.

"Just think how confident they must be feeling," the king responded.

"Aye, and with good reason," Keith grumbled, as Douglas made a disgruntled noise at the back of his throat.

Bruce put his grindstone away and hefted the weight of his battle-axe.

"Be of good cheer, gentlemen. The English think the victory's already won, but we know the truth of it—that there's a battle yet to come. And we're ready for it."

"The numbers—" Robert Keith began.

"The numbers don't matter a damn," Bruce interrupted, giving his weapon an expert flourish. "Our enemies are strung out on that road, and we've dug pits on either side to keep them there. How many men do you think they can present on a narrow front like that? It comes down to a man-to-man fight—and that, we can win."

Even the glowering Douglas was infected with Bruce's energy.

"That's true," he agreed with a hungry gleam of anticipation in his eyes. "Man-to-man, we can slaughter them like sheep."

Bruce clapped the younger man on the shoulder. "Gather your men and tell them that."

As Douglas strode off to issue orders to his division of the army, Bruce glanced after him fondly.

"There goes one of the bravest fighters in the whole Scottish army," he said. "I don't know what I would have done without him."

Arnault nodded. Douglas's father had been a loyal supporter of Wallace, and had died a prisoner in the Tower of London—something that was never far from the young warrior's mind. Bruce turned to Keith.

"Sir Robert, muster our horse, but hold them in check," he ordered. "We can't afford to squander them."

With a nod and a crooked grin, Keith rode off to follow his orders. Left alone with the king, Arnault lowered his voice so that no one passing might accidentally overhear.

"Sire, there is another danger that the others aren't aware of," he murmured. "But you must know about it."

Quickly he recounted his sighting of the Knights of the Black Swan. Bruce had experienced enough over the past few years to take the Templar at his word, and his expression darkened at this worrying development.

"I've drilled my spearmen until they're ready to fight in their sleep, if they hear my voice command it," he told Arnault. "They'll stand against anything Edward can throw at them. But what are these Black Swan Knights preparing for us? Some sorcerous attack?"

"I don't know," Arnault answered with a frustrated shake of the head. "Probably."

"Well, can you and the Columban brothers match them?" Bruce pressed him.

"With God's help, we can," Arnault answered.

"I'll take that as a yes," Bruce said. "I leave it to you and Father Ninian to decide how best to deploy your resources."

Waving his esquire over, he called for his horse. Retiring with a bow, Arnault sought out Torquil to warn him what was afoot.

"This battle is enough of a gamble, as it is," Torquil remarked when he heard the news. "What do you think those knights are here for? Bruce or us?"

"Probably both," Arnault replied. "I can only guess that, like their former master, they seek to expand their sorcerous power. So they will do whatever they can to destroy the Fifth Temple before it is established."

Torquil gritted his teeth. "And still no word from Aubrey and Flannan! What can be keeping them?"

"I wish I knew," Arnault replied, "but they'd be here if they could. Let's see what advice the Columbans have to offer."

Even the normally unshakable Ninian was taken aback when Arnault apprised him of the presence of the Black Knights.

"You and I must keep close to the king," he said. "If they do mean to mount some kind of sorcerous attack, we should form an effective bulwark, between us."

"With your permission, Father Abbot," the fair-haired Brother Fionn said, "Brother Ciaran and I will station ourselves among the forward contingents of the army. That will put us in position to watch out for the Black Swan Knights, and relay advance warning if they appear."

Bruce readily gave his consent for Fionn to join the right brigade, commanded by his brother Edward. To Torquil he gave the instruction to join Brother Ciaran on the left flank, commanded by Thomas Randolph.

"That is potentially our most vulnerable position," he noted grimly. "If our enemies attempt an outflanking maneuver, it'll be Randolph's job to get in their way."

"That will leave Douglas's brigade without the benefit of an observer," Torquil reminded the king.

"I'll keep an eye on Douglas myself," Bruce replied. "You stick close to Randolph. If anything should happen to him, I'll be counting on you to contain the English and keep them from making a break for the castle."

Chapter Forty

June 23, 1314

KING EDWARD II REINED IN HIS HORSE AND PAUSED TO take stock of his position.

Eleven miles to the south lay Falkirk, where the English host had spent the previous night. Three miles ahead and to the north lay Stirling Castle, a cluster of turrets perched atop a stony crag. To the west stretched the dense forests of the New Park. To the east, the open fields of the Carse of Stirling made a spongy green island between the waters of the Bannockburn and the River Forth. The burn itself ran like a ribbon of silver across their path. The ford leading across it, and the entry to the forest, lay unguarded.

"So, where is Bruce?" Edward said to Aymer de Valence, the veteran Earl of Pembroke. "Has he taken to his heels?"

"I think it most unlikely, Sire," Pembroke responded. "I recommend that we hold until our scouts can report."

Pembroke's advice carried the weight of twenty years' experience in the field. On this occasion, Edward was astute enough to heed it. A royal order was relayed to the earls of Gloucester and Hereford, enjoining them to halt their advance. Soon Hereford rode back in person, seeking an explanation.

"What have we stopped for?" he demanded. "The way ahead is clear."

"I want to learn where the Scots are," Edward said testily. "We can't beat them if we don't know their whereabouts."

"I think I just saw some movement in the trees there," Pembroke interjected, pointing ahead.

Edward peered hard in that direction. "I can't see anything."

"Look, Sire!" said Sir Giles d'Argentan, the senior knight of the king's retinue. "Riders from the castle!"

Sure enough, a small band of horsemen was cantering toward them across the open ground, keeping well clear of the woods that flanked the road to the west. They slowed to a trot to ford the burn, splashing up spray as they came. Pickets surged forward to challenge them as they reached the other side, but their leader identified himself and was allowed through the lines to approach the king.

"It's Moubray!" Pembroke exclaimed in surprise.

Sir Philip Moubray, the commander of Stirling Castle, drew rein before the royal party and paid his loyal respects to the king, breathless from his swift ride.

"Praise God, you have come in time, Sire," he exclaimed. "I've come to warn you. Bruce and his men lie hidden in the trees of the New Park."

"As I suspected," Pembroke growled. "They're skulking like robbers."

Edward drummed his fingers on the pommel of his saddle. "Is this some clumsy ambush?"

"More likely, they plan to use the woods to cover their retreat," Pembroke said.

"Then we must make haste to deploy our forces and catch them before they can escape," Hereford declared.

"They're not aiming to escape," Moubray cautioned. "Bruce has set traps. From the castle walls, we saw them digging pits on both sides of the road, then concealing them beneath a cover of branches and leaves."

"We need to find out where their main strength lies," Edward said. "Send an advance party to probe the forest."

"I will go, Sire," an eager voice volunteered.

The speaker was Hereford's nephew, Henry de Bohun. A tall, powerfully built young man on a large roan destrier, he clearly was eager to brave the enemy face-to-face.

"Very well," Edward agreed. "Take a party of knights and scout the road ahead. But have your footmen follow behind to secure the way. Don't let yourself be cut off."

With an airy salute, de Bohun wheeled his big horse and galloped off to the head of the line, calling his mounted men-at-arms to gather round him. Pembroke watched their departure with a hint of reservation, hoping the hotheaded youth wouldn't do anything he might later regret.

From his vantage point amid the trees, Arnault peered out at the glittering mass of the English army on the far side of the Bannockburn, along with the other knights of Bruce's household. Too few in number to form a separate division of their own, they had left their horses to the rear and now stood ready to form the core of the king's schiltron, where their commanding presence would lend strength to the formation. From where he was standing Arnault had a better view of the field than anyone but the king himself, who alone remained mounted.

Bruce had organized his army into four divisions, rather than the traditional three—a tactic that would afford him greater mobility and also, at any given moment, the ability to direct his soldiers to where they could mount the most effective attack against the English. In this way, he hoped to counter their superior numbers and block any attempt they might make to outflank him.

Against the advice of his counselors, the King of Scots had decided that he would personally command the leading brigade—a decision about which Arnault had decidedly mixed feelings. He fully appreciated that Bruce intended to set an example for the rest of the army by boldly leading his brigade into battle against the English invaders. But he could not overlook the mortal danger inherent in being the first to confront the enemy.

Muttered curses flew down the line as the men of the king's schiltron caught their first glimpse of a party of English heavy cavalry heading fast toward the burn. Some of the foot soldiers instinctively shrank back into the sheltering shadows of the forest, but Bruce was quick to reassure his troops.

"Never fear, lads," Arnault heard him call with an easy chuckle. "Go for the horses, and the riders will fall at your feet like ripe apples. See, I'll even draw them out for you!"

Before Arnault could call out a word of remonstrance, the king broke from the front lines and trotted out into the open, pulling his axe from his saddle and brandishing it above his head, where the sun made a glittering halo of the golden crown that encircled his leather helmet. It looked for all the world as though he was ready to stand alone against the advancing enemy.

The sight of Bruce's bravado kindled the hearts of his men, his presence drawing them forward like iron drawn to a magnet. Arnault could feel the schiltron starting to stir, ready to back their king, and he knew he could not hold them back—nor should he. A surge of excitement set his crusader's blood on fire.

"Men of Scotland, forward!" he cried, drawing his sword.

Other voices took up the cry as the men of the schiltron began moving forward.

Young Henry de Bohun reached the burn well in advance of the rest of the English company. Hungry for action, he urged his powerful destrier into the water. Halfway across, he turned to shout derisive encouragement to those who hung back.

"Look, Henry! There they are!" one of his friends called, pointing with his lance in the direction of the forest edge.

De Bohun looked. The Scots were, indeed, emerging from the tree line, led by a lone figure meanly mounted on a sturdy, rough-coated gray pony. As he spotted the kingly circlet of gold surmounting the rider's leather helmet, de Bohun's eyes gaped wide. Could it truly be Robert Bruce himself?

Breathing an exultant prayer of thanksgiving—for here was a God-given opportunity to conquer Scotland at a single stroke!—the young knight couched his lance and drove his spurs hard into the flanks of his huge warhorse.

Turf flew as the destrier broke from a trot to a canter, headed straight toward Bruce. Alerted by the rumble of hooves, Arnault looked up and saw the danger, but caught in the midst of the Scottish spear ranks, he was powerless to intervene.

"Sire, take care!" he shouted.

But instead of wheeling about and riding for the safety of the Scots' lines, Bruce reined his pony firmly to a standstill, gloved fingers closing harder around the haft of his axe, watching as the English knight converged at the gallop.

Arnault's blood ran cold. He knew the arms of the charging knight, and he knew the reputation of Henry de Bohun— as did Bruce!—but the king's demeanor was calm, as if he were about to greet a messenger, rather than meet a murderous attack.

Powerless to intervene, Arnault watched the tip of de Bohun's lance drop, aiming directly at Bruce's breast as he braced its weight against his side and leaned forward. The destrier thundered on, gathering speed and momentum at every stride, but Bruce stood his ground as the distance closed. Even as de Bohun let out a bellow of triumph, Bruce was jerking his pony aside to avoid the killing thrust and, with a battle-hardened arm, swinging his long-handled axe aloft. Then, as de Bohun swept past him, he stood straight up in his stirrups and, with a sweeping blow, struck.

His freshly sharpened blade split the English knight's helmet, the clang of metal on metal mingling with a more hollow crack as the axe clove the skull beneath, blood and brain matter spewing everywhere like pulp bursting from a crushed melon. The force of the blow shattered Bruce's axe haft and left him gripping a jagged shard of wood, but his enemy tumbled dead to the ground, the axe blade still embedded in his cloven head.

For an instant, stunned shock and surprise transfixed the fighting men on both sides, until Arnault suddenly shouted, "To the king!"

The Scottish spearmen rallied at the sound of his voice, surging forward to form a defensive screen between Bruce and the enemy. Arnault shouldered his way through the ranks to confront the king.

"What madness prompted you to sustain de Bohun's charge?" he demanded in stricken tones. "What would become of us if you had been killed?"

Bruce didn't seem to hear.

"Would you look!" he exclaimed, brandishing the broken haft of his weapon in disgust. "The battle's barely begun, and already I've lost my best axe!"

The English vanguard was massing on the far side of the Bannockburn. From their movements, a full-scale attack was imminent. Bruce tossed his broken axe shaft aside and drew his sword, bellowing the order to form the schiltron.

Promptly the Scots drew together into bristling hedge-hogs of spears. Scarcely had they formed ranks when the English received the order to advance. Led by the earls of Gloucester and Hereford, several hundred knights plowed impetuously across the Bannockburn and, without pausing to form ranks, charged forward, bent on retribution.

Several English knights fell victim to the ditches the Scots had dug and concealed to the right of the road.

Hemmed in by trees on their left flank, the rest found themselves confined to a narrow front.

Undaunted, they quickened their pace. Heavy hooves drummed the earth like thunder as the forward ranks converged on the Scottish infantry brigade. Formidable in their heavy armor, the English knights loomed large as giants astride their tall destriers, eyes ablaze with battle lust as they lowered their lances for the attack. But from the midst of the schiltron, Bruce's voice rang firm.

"Hold your ground, lads! This is as far as they come!"

The gap narrowed with breathtaking speed, and the knights struck home. The crash of steel split the air, riven by the squeals of wounded horses, but the Scots withstood the impact. The English line broke apart on the spear wall like a flawed blade shattering against a stone.

Gloucester's mount foundered beneath him, impaled on the Scottish spear hedge, and he pitched from the saddle and rolled to the ground. Only a desperate, ignoble scramble saved him from being seized and dragged captive into the Scots' lines. All around him, other knights hurled themselves at the schiltron wall, only to be flung back in disorder. The copper tang of blood was in the air, maddening the horses, and many of them shied away from the hedge of spears. Riders collided, entangling one another's weapons. What began as a charge disintegrated rapidly into disarray.

A derisive roar went up from the Scots as the knights abandoned their efforts and fell back to re-form. Inside the schiltron, broken weapons were hastily replaced and injured men sent to the rear. The front rank retired to catch their breath, and the second rank moved to the fore. A hundred yards away, the English chivalry made ready to charge again.

Gloucester's squire brought him a fresh horse. Flushed with fury, the earl seized a new lance and mounted up. Brandishing the weapon high, he rallied his fellow knights around him.

"That was mere practice!" he shouted out to them. "Now do England proud!"

The English vanguard lunged forward in a body. Seeing them come, the Scottish spearmen leaned grimly forward, presenting a fearsome thicket of steel to the enemy. The air throbbed with the pounding of hooves, and the thunder broke with a rending crash as the English chivalry drove hard at the Scots' line.

Horses were ripped through the gut and collapsed squealing under their riders. Some of the horses stumbled over beasts already dead or dying. The knights tried in vain to press the attack, only to find themselves unable to outreach the length of the Scots' spears. Once again the English were forced to withdraw.

Axemen darted out from the Scottish ranks to dispatch any riders who had fallen. The edges of the schiltron began to fray as men ventured rashly forward to loot the bodies of their enemies.

"Stay your ground!" the king shouted.

The order was repeated throughout the ranks. Soldiers were pulled roughly back into line until an unbroken spear wall once again presented itself to the foe. On the far side of the field, Gloucester and Hereford called up reinforcements, and both sides braced for a third encounter.

Chapter Forty-one

June 23, 1314

FARTHER BACK ALONG THE ENGLISH COLUMN, BARTHOLEME DE Challon watched the melee with growing impatience. The entire army had floundered to a halt, and only the clumsiest efforts were being made to deploy the various divisions into proper battle order.

The French knights were caught between the brigades of Sir Robert Clifford and Sir Henry Beaumont. The latter could only look on as his fellow nobles in the vanguard continued to charge the Scottish spears. The road ahead was too clogged for them to join the fray. The restive stamping and snorting of the horses seemed to echo the evident frustration of their masters.

"The Scots have rendered the direct route to Stirling impassable," Bartholeme said aside to Count Rodolphe. "If the English are to prevail, they must adopt a different approach."

To the west lay the dense woodland of the New Park, manifestly unsuitable for cavalry.

"There is open ground to the east," Rodolphe noted, pointing to the far side of the burn. "And it appears to be quite undefended."

"So it does," Bartholeme replied.

Wheeling his horse around, he forced his way to the side of Sir Robert Clifford.

"What is the point of this skirmishing on the road?" he demanded. "To the east, the way to the castle lies clear."

Clifford regarded the French knight with disdain. "We must keep to the road," he said. "How else are the wagons to reach the castle?"

"Devil take the wagons!" Bartholeme replied. "None of us will reach the castle unless we put the Scots to flight. We must use our superiority in cavalry to envelop them."

"The ground is difficult in that quarter," said Sir Thomas Grey, one of the other senior knights. "And there is no safe ford across the Bannockburn except where the road and the stream intersect."

"We are not riding Highland ponies," Bartholeme reminded the Englishman. "Is this trickle of water a sufficient obstacle to unman you?"

Clifford considered but a moment before throwing caution to the winds.

"Very well, let's hazard it," he said. "With luck, we may strike the Scots in their underbelly."

King Robert's schiltron still held the road through the New Park, despite repeated attacks by the Earl of Gloucester. Temporarily exhausted by their efforts, the English at last abandoned the assault. Casualties among the Scots had been light. A mood of jubilation took hold of the men of the schiltron, to see the enemy turned back at so little cost to themselves.

"This fight is well won!" Abbot Bernard of Arbroath declared. Bruce's friend and chancellor, he had joined Arnault and Ninian at the king's side.

"We've broken Edward's nose all right," Bruce said, "but he can still punch and kick."

"I think there's a punch coming now," Arnault warned.

He pointed to the east. At some distance from the ford, a force of English knights were braving the deeper waters of the Bannockburn. The other members of the king's entourage took a closer look.

"Are they just scouting, do you think?" Ninian ventured.

"No, there must be a good three hundred horse in that band," Arnault replied, and scowled at the strategic implications. "They probably hope to outflank us and attack our left wing."

"It's what I'd do," Bruce agreed. "There's no getting past us through the woods, so what other route lies open to them?"

"They could just turn around and go home," Bernard said dryly.

"Aren't you going to meet them before they bring more troops over?" Ninian asked.

Bruce shook his head. "I'll not let them force my hand before I'm ready. They're just feeling their way as yet, and I trust Randolph to act as my shield."

The men of Randolph's brigade had taken up position among the trees adjoining St. Ninian's Church. From a vantage point of high ground, Torquil had a comprehensive view of the flatland between the Bannockburn and the Pelstream Burn to the north of it. After crossing the Bannockburn, the English chivalry wheeled aside to avoid the boggy flats of the Carse, a stretch of uncertain ground broken up by meandering rivulets—which did not surprise Torquil, for the Carse was difficult country for men and horses alike.

Brother Ciaran stood nearby, his dark eyes narrowed in concentration as he leaned on the staff of Randolph's standard.

"Do you sense anything out of the ordinary?" Torquil asked.

The wiry cleric knotted his dark brows. "I'm not sure," he

whispered, almost as if he feared an enemy might be listening in.

Uneasy, Torquil moved to Randolph's side.

"Is it your intention to let them go by?"

"No, but surprise is a weapon, and we must use it as best we can," Randolph said. "We'll let them get as far from their own army as possible before we show ourselves."

He passed a hushed order along his lines for his men to make ready. The English completed their crossing and set off north, with the boggy ground to the east. Randolph waited until the enemy came abreast of their position. Then, satisfied that he had them pinned, he drew his sword.

"Up, lads, and at them!" he yelled.

The Scots poured out of the wooded churchyard like water from a sluice. As they sped across the open ground, they held their spears high to keep them from becoming entangled with their feet, for speed was vital. If the English found room to charge before the Scots could re-form, the latter would be cut to ribbons.

The possibility of a Scottish infantry charge was the furthest thing from Sir Robert Clifford's mind as he reined closer beside his counterpart, Sir Henry Beaumont. Having mustered nearly three hundred heavy cavalry troops between them, he was confident that they would be able to achieve their objective.

"Not far to go now," Clifford declared, peering ahead with satisfaction. "When we reach the castle, we can lead a sally that will take Bruce in the rear and drive him out of the woods."

Skirting the Pelstream Burn, they struck a stretch of solid ground and lengthened stride. As the troupe set off north toward Stirling Castle, amid the thunder of heavy, steel-shod hooves, Beaumont wondered how the earls of Gloucester and Hereford were faring. The spire of St. Ninian's Church caught his eye, but even as he reined back for a second look, a dense wave of Scots burst from cover and came pelting across the open ground straight toward him.

Clifford saw them, too, and reined short in sudden consternation.

"What madness is this?" he exclaimed. "Common footmen charging knights?"

"Mad or not, they'll regret their rashness," Beaumont cried, as he wheeled his mount to face the onrushing Scots.

An incredulous murmur swept the English ranks as they prepared to mount a counterattack. But Beaumont knew that nothing less than a massed assault would sweep the Scots away before them.

"Hold!" he cried, calling out to his men to restrain them. "Let them come on! Give them some ground. We must draw back, the better to charge."

With the distance shortening, Randolph, too, called his Scots to a halt, for they had run forward far enough to challenge their enemy's progress, and were close enough to rob him of valuable maneuvering room. His lieutenants directed their soldiers this way and that, shoving and kicking them when necessary, until they had packed together to form a new schiltron, bristling with rank upon rank of spears in every direction, ready to receive the enemy's attack.

And amid the advancing enemy ranks, Sir Thomas Grey confronted Beaumont in angry tones.

"They are only low churls, and nothing to us! Why attack, when we can easily bypass them and proceed to the castle?"

"Flee, then, if you're afraid!" Beaumont replied with a sneer.

Grey bristled at the affront to his honor. For a nobleman born and bred, there could be only one answer to such a challenge.

"Fear will not make me flee," he retorted hotly.

Lowering his lance, he spurred his horse forward and galloped headlong at the Scots. Other knights from all along the English line immediately followed suit, pennons fluttering, hooves drumming the earth, making a bold but ragged charge.

On the Scottish side of the field, Randolph watched the enemy converge—and watched his schiltron brace to receive the charge.

"Spit 'em, boys! Spit 'em like rabbits!" he urged.

Grey was the first to dash himself against the schiltron. His horse was skewered by spears in throat and belly. As he slid from the saddle, greedy hands seized him and dragged him into the midst of his enemies, and those who followed him also foundered or were driven back by the barbed array of steel.

Realizing that there was no time now to form up properly, Beaumont and the rest of the knights joined the charge his rebuff had incited. They crashed into the schiltron, only to be driven back, leaving mangled horses and slain men littering the ground at the feet of the Scots.

Clifford rallied his cavalry as best he could and led them in another charge, but once more their momentum could not break the Scots. The knights rode in circles around the schiltron, probing it as they would a fortress, seeking a weak point in the defenses where they might break in. Unable to close with their enemy, they flung knives, axes, and even swords at the Scots as they swept past the forest of spears.

But the Scots held firm beneath the fruitless hail of enemy missiles. Whenever a man fell in the front rank, another stepped forward to take his place, keeping the spear wall unbroken and impenetrable as ever.

The knights charged again. Again the Scottish spears ran red with blood. In desperation, the English redoubled their attack, kicking up a cloud of dust that only added to their confusion.

In the midst of the English chivalry, Bartholeme signaled his own men to hold back.

"We must take a hand in this," he told Rodolphe. "We

cannot allow our allies' incompetence to compromise our own intentions."

Forming the other Black Knights into a circle around him, he drew rein in their midst and rummaged in a pouch at his belt, bringing forth a handful of dust which he cupped in his left hand while he recited an incantation. With a final imprecation, he blew the dust from his fingers and watched it fly across the intervening ground to mingle with the dirt kicked up by the horses. As the dust cloud expanded, it swept across the field toward Randolph's schiltron.

Sir Robert Clifford was wondering whether to abandon the field when his bridle was suddenly seized by a masterful hand. Whirling, he found the French knight, Bartholeme de Challon, staring across at him, a determined glint sparkling in his cold blue eyes.

"You have one last chance to destroy your enemies," Bartholeme told him, releasing his reins, "but you must seize it now. Form up your men for another attack."

Gesturing, he directed Clifford's attention toward the Scots, where a huge wall of dust was billowing up to engulf them. Answering howls of dismay echoed across the field from the Scottish spear ranks.

"Very well," Clifford said, renewed hope banishing his weariness. "Again, my friends! Come to me, and ready the charge!"

From his vantage point on the high ground, Bruce was keeping a wary eye on the action to his left. He had watched Randolph's men fling back a succession of English attacks, and was satisfied that they would hold their position. But a beating of hooves heralded the arrival of James Douglas, who drew up beside the king in some consternation.

"Randolph is hard-pressed!" he announced urgently. "Let me take my men down there to help him."

"We'll all be hard-pressed before the day is won," Bruce

replied. "Randolph knows his task is to hold the flank, and that is what he will do."

"Am I to stand and do nothing, then?" Douglas demanded, his dark face flushed.

"You'll go where you're needed and when you're needed," Bruce snapped. "Now, hold fast!"

A startled exclamation from Arnault made both men look round. To their amazement, they saw the dust raised by the English horses congealing into a single black cloud that rushed down on Randolph's schiltron as though driven by a gale. Forming a line behind it, the English knights galloped forward to attack the Scots once more.

"What devilry is this?" Douglas growled. "Do the very elements rise up against us?"

"There is nothing natural here," Bruce muttered.

Arnault knew he was right. Fixing his gaze on the cloud, his right hand drifting to the slight bulge of the Shard beneath his hauberk, he summoned up his deeper faculties of perception and gradually penetrated the sorcerous murk. With terrible clarity, he saw the contingent of Black Knights advancing through the swirling dust.

Fingers curling harder over the bulge that was the Shard, Arnault called upon its powers—the first time he had so presumed since the Templar assault on Castle Montaigre.

"Lord," he whispered, "by the power of Thy Word, grant me the strength to break the enchantments of our enemies before it is too late."

Standing shoulder to shoulder with Randolph, Torquil was fully alive to the danger. As the cloud bore down on them, the swirling dust formed wicked, leering faces, and an eerie keening dinned in their ears like the lamentations of the damned. Superstitious dread struck fear into the hearts of many Scottish spearmen, and the schiltron ranks began to waver.

White-faced and wild-eyed, Randolph tried to hold his men together.

"Trust your courage and your spears, men!" he shouted. "Don't let this damnable illusion overwhelm you!"

Even as he spoke, the cloud rolled over them, plunging the schiltron into screeching darkness. At Randolph's side, Brother Ciaran grasped the standard tightly and muttered a prayer invoking the aid of Columba and Saint Bride. Even as the words left his lips, a wing of shadow swept over him like an icy wave.

Hearing the Columban brother cry out, Torquil tried to grope his way toward him, but in the next instant, the English charge struck the outer fringes of the schiltron in a catastrophic clang, like sheet metal struck with a hammer. Torquil sensed, rather than saw the Scottish ranks begin to buckle as English heavy cavalry broke into the schiltron like men driving their horses through the surf into a turbulent, hostile sea.

"Cra-gheal, shield and defend us!" he cried out, lunging at a glimpse of heaving horse, for only the English were mounted in this fray.

The press of bodies was too dense for lance play. The English knights used the advantage of height to lay about them with maces and swords, cracking skulls and carving through sinew. The Scots fought back, dragging knights from their saddles and dispatching them with the quick stroke of a dirk or the savage blow of an axe. All around them swirled the inky cloud, stinging their eyes and choking their throats.

No sooner did Torquil aim a blow at an adversary than his target was masked in darkness. Randolph shouted hoarsely at his men to fill the gaps in their ranks and tried to discern through the murk just where the enemy were strongest. A great, dark horse burst suddenly between them. Again Torquil thrust out his sword, but the next instant the enemy had gone.

*   *   *

Up on the hill overlooking the field, not far from where Bruce and Arnault also watched, James Douglas tugged furiously at his thick black beard as he tried to make out what was happening below. The cloud of dust had entirely enveloped Randolph's brigade, totally obscuring the action, but the shrieks and howls and clash of weaponry told their own tale of a desperate struggle in progress.

"Sire, let me go to their aid!" he pleaded of Bruce.

The king glanced at Arnault, whose attempts to engage the power of the Shard were not succeeding.

"Go, then," Bruce ordered.

Douglas sped away. Arnault, seized by desperation, turned to Brother Ninian, who had the *Brecbennach* clasped against his chest.

"This isn't working the way it has in the past," Arnault murmured, urgently fumbling inside the neck of his hauberk to draw out the Shard in its leather pouch. "Maybe I need to touch it directly."

"Or," said Ninian, "perhaps it requires contact with the Stone, or something linked to it, since this work is on Bruce's behalf. No doubt Father Columba can sort it out." He thrust the saint's reliquary between them, in which also lay the *Urim*.

"Take the Shard in your right hand, and lay the other one on the *Brecbennach*!" Ninian instructed.

Arnault obeyed. As he did so, a tingle of power communicated itself through his fingers—from the *Brecbennach*, not the Shard.

"Father Columba," Ninian said in a conversational tone, "we ask you to speak for the Stone, so that the Light of the Law may drive away the darkness."

An answering fire quickened in Arnault's heart and in what dwelt inside the *Brecbennach*, expanding to make his living body a channel of divine light. Energy flowed from the casket, through his hand, and into the Shard, which came to life in response. Before his entranced gaze, the fragment of the Law began to glow, so brilliant a blue that it put to shame the fire of the midsummer sun; and yet, he sensed that it was not with mortal eyes that he perceived it.

Quivering with the flow of energy, Arnault directed the power of the Shard toward the cloud below, piercing it like a sword cleaving rotten fruit. Disintegrating patches of cloud dispersed like guttering rags of burnt cloth to reveal the Scottish schiltron still intact at its center.

There where the cloud had been, momentarily bewildered, Randolph glanced around him for the Scots standard—and seized it from where it lay on the ground. He could see no sign of Brother Ciaran, but he hoisted the banner high in defiance of their enemies.

"For Scotland and King Robert!" he shouted.

His cry enflamed the Scots, rousing them as from a sleep. The sudden evaporation of the cloud had revealed the English knights isolated in small pockets that left them dangerously exposed to attack. At once they began to pull back out of range of the Scottish spears, but seeing them disorganized and demoralized by the failure of their last attack, Randolph seized his opportunity.

"Forward!" he yelled, waving the banner again. "Drive them from the field!"

With a roar, the Scots moved onto the attack, jabbing their spears at any knight who did not spur his horse out of danger in time. Like a great spiny beast, the schiltron began to advance.

The English were stricken with dismay. Never before had they been thrown on the defensive by mere footmen. It had taken weeks of constant drilling to instill the Scottish troops with the necessary discipline to advance in such a fashion without falling into disorder. Now they rolled unstoppably forward, driving through the center of the beaten knights and forcing them to take to their heels.

Approaching from the right flank, a relieved Douglas saw

that the enemy was in flight, and ordered his own troops to halt.

"Let Randolph have the glory of this moment," he told them. "He and his men have done more than enough to earn it."

Himself relieved, and sweating with exertion, Torquil gazed after their scattered enemies. Some fled back to the main body of their army. Others, cut off from that avenue of escape, rode for their lives toward the safety of Stirling Castle, bellowing at the garrison to open the gates to them.

He sheathed his sword and went to help Randolph regroup his cheering forces. Only gradually did it occur to him that he had not seen Brother Ciaran for some time.

Chapter Forty-two

June 23, 1314

THE SCOTTISH ARMY WITHDREW FOR THE NIGHT TO THE forested security of the New Park. After defeating the English on two fronts in one day, the troops were almost giddy with jubilation.

The tale of how Robert Bruce had personally slain the nephew of the Earl of Hereford spread like wildfire throughout the ranks, raising the men's spirits to new heights of faith in their king and their cause. But for Bruce and his inner circle of advisors, the successes of the day were overshadowed by a matter of grave uncertainty.

"Brother Ciaran has disappeared," Torquil reported grimly. "We've searched the battleground three times over without finding any trace of him, alive or dead."

"The last anyone remembers seeing him was just before that dust cloud swept the battleground," Ninian said. "Whatever has befallen him, it seems to have happened then."

"Which does not bode well for Ciaran," Breville said. "Most assuredly, that cloud was conjured up by the Knights of the Black Swan."

"Why would they bother to capture a monk?" Torquil said.

"I doubt that was their original intent," Arnault replied. "If they took Ciaran prisoner, it was probably only as an afterthought, when their main gambit failed."

"Either that, or this Lord Bartholeme has deduced the affinity between the Templars and the Columbans," Breville said.

"So what are we to do?" Torquil asked.

"Pray," Bruce recommended curtly.

"Surely that isn't all, Sire?" Fionn blurted.

"I understand and share your fears," the king said, "but the painful truth is this: If Brother Ciaran has been taken prisoner by the Black Knights, the only folk who might be able to aid him are those I can least afford to spare."

Ninian seconded this view. "His Majesty is right. We can't risk throwing everything away for the sake of one man—however dear to us he may be."

A bleak silence set in. All present knew only too well the crucial stakes for which this war was being waged.

"Can we not at least try to make mystical contact with Ciaran?" Fionn begged.

Arnault shook his head. "Too risky. If Ciaran has been captured by our enemies, they will try to use him as a weapon against us."

"Ciaran would never consent to betray us!" Fionn protested.

"Consent will not have entered into the matter," Breville warned grimly. "From this point onward, we must be doubly on our guard against sorcerous attack."

Uncertainties of an entirely different order dominated the spirits of the English nobility. Exhausted and sweating, still reeling from the shock of their losses, they retired from the field to rest and regroup as best they could. Scouts were dispersed to search for a suitable camping place.

Selection fell upon a spread of level ground a few furlongs to the north of the abandoned peasant village of Bannock, encompassed on either side by branching tributaries of the burn giving the village its name. The streams offered not only ample water to refresh the army's thirsty cavalry mounts and dray animals, but also a protective barrier against the threat of a night attack.

Rude bridges of planks, plundered from the village, were flung across the southern branch of the burn to afford safe transit for the English horses and baggage wagons. Company by company, the various contingents of the army filed across. Tents and cook fires sprang up. All but one of the bridges were then withdrawn, leaving the English host encamped in bristling isolation, like castaways on an island set in monster-infested waters.

While he waited for his servants to prepare his evening meal, King Edward listened sullenly as Gloucester and the other nobles discussed their various failures and setbacks of the day.

"I remind you, gentlemen, that in seven hundred years, no king of England has met defeat on Scottish soil," he said at last.

"Nor shall it happen tomorrow, Sire," Gloucester vowed. "We shall array our forces to overwhelm and destroy these rebels. And there will be no quarter given."

The long midsummer twilight set in, bringing some relief from the earlier heat of the day. The English chivalry spent the evening resentfully contemplating the mortification they had suffered earlier in the day. The English infantry were similarly restless and uneasy. Many resorted to drink and ribaldry in an effort to fortify their spirits, but only added a further element of discord to the already-unsettled atmosphere.

Far on the northern fringe of the encampment, Bartholeme and the other Knights of the Black Swan established their own enclave, their pavilions erected in a semicircle overlooking the burn—a deployment designed to shield them from view of the rest of the camp. With full night still an hour away, Bartholeme called Mercurius to his side.

"How is our prisoner?" he asked.

The dwarf's misaligned features twisted in a malignant grin. "Wishing with all his heart he was back in his holy sanctuary."

"And what does our little man of God have to say for himself?"

"He doesn't respond very well to direct questioning," Mercurius admitted, "but it's clear he's had dealings with the Templars in Bruce's camp. I could smell it on him, the moment you brought him in."

"Were you able to gain any impression of their numbers?"

Mercurius nodded. "There are not many of them. But those who remain have considerable power at their command."

"That was made manifest earlier today," Bartholeme snapped, though he reined in his temper. "Keep questioning the little monk. At the very least, it would be useful to know what relics our enemies hold in reserve. But be careful not to kill him. Even if he refuses to play the role of informant, he can still serve as a Judas goat."

A little later, hearing what their leader had in mind, both Rodolphe and Thibault registered strong interest in the proposal.

"You certainly don't lack invention," Rodolphe acknowledged.

"Not only that," Thibault pointed out, "if we're successful, the results should win not only the battle, but the war itself! It will appear that Bruce and his companions have been struck down by a hand of judgment."

"Precisely my intention," Bartholeme replied. "Come. We have preparations to make."

He nominated Rodolphe, Thibault, and Mercurius to serve as his acolytes, though all of the Black Knights save those on watch would witness and support the working. Before beginning, each of them donned a protective amulet to render them immune to their own destructive enchantments.

On the space of open ground in the midst of their pavilions, the men marked out a sorcerous triangle, fixing its points with staves of ashwood. This was circumscribed, in turn, by a shallow circular trench into which the alchemists set shallow containers of incendiary oils.

The long twilight deepened. As the sun finally dipped toward the horizon, they carefully noted its vanishing point.

"The light of the world has departed!" Bartholeme finally proclaimed, on a note of predatory satisfaction. "Fetch the prisoner! We must make the most of our few hours of darkness."

Wrists trussed behind him and tied to his bound ankles, the captured monk lay shivering in the corner of Mercurius's tent, his white habit besmirched with blood and hanging in tatters about his wiry frame. Chuckling under his breath, Mercurius flung a halter of braided rope around the prisoner's neck and, with the help of two of his master's men-at-arms, dragged his victim outside into the open air.

Bartholeme beckoned them toward the alchemist's circle. Ignoring the prisoner's feeble resistance, his handlers carried him across the trench into the middle of the triangle, where they tethered him by his neck halter to an iron stake driven into the ground at the center of the configuration.

The halter was secured by a loose slipknot that tightened sharply when the captive attempted to struggle, and backed off when the struggles subsided. Choked nearly to unconsciousness, the monk lay curled on his side with closed eyes, his bloodless lips moving in silent prayer.

"Don't think that pious words will save you," Mercurius jeered, making sure of the bonds. "You're already a dead man—the first of many!"

Ordering the subordinate members of their retinue to retreat to a safe distance outside the trench circle, Bartholeme supplied each of his chosen acolytes with a hollow globe of alchemical glass, each containing a different mixture of sorcerous chemicals. He kept one for himself as well, as the four of them dispersed to the four cardinal points of the compass. The three acolytes abased themselves as Bartholeme set his glass globe at his feet and spread his arms wide in a gesture of summoning.

"Great Lucifer, confer upon us, we beseech you, the powers of desecration!" he said. "Let our enemies feel the might of your hand, which brings eternal Darkness!"

He spat into the trench. The oil ignited with a rush, encircling the prisoner in a flickering annulus of fire.

"Behold the Ring of Desolation, the First Mystery of Zosimos!" Bartholeme declared. "Let its boundaries extend to all who profess themselves servants or friends of the Temple."

He indicated the prisoner with a stab of his hand, then stooped to pick up his globe, cupping it in his right hand as he sketched an arcane symbol in the air above it with his left. The gray liquid sealed within the globe began to bubble and change hue, fluctuating from livid blue to venomous green.

"I call upon Gzul, bane of water," Bartholeme said. "By the tears of Kaa, I summon and bind you in accordance with the Third Mystery of Zosimos. Send forth an effusion of vapors from the river of death!"

With these words, he dashed the globe to the ground within the compass of the circle. It shattered on impact, splattering the turf with a greasy rainbow of color that gradually resolved into thin tendrils of fog. Like hungry worms, the tendrils began reaching out toward the prisoner in the circle's center, who recoiled ineffectually, only to be choked short by the noose around his neck.

Rodolphe smiled coldly at his distress, executing a ritual gesture over the sphere in his hand as he cried, "I call upon Zoath, bane of earth. By the spittle of Kuum, I summon and bind you in accordance with the Fifth Mystery of Zosimos. Send forth a contagion of dust from the plain of Sodom!"

He shattered his globe against the ground. From the midst of its shards, a fine scattering of sand spilled across the earth. Like a plague of tiny insects, the grains began to creep toward the prisoner. The monk tried to roll to the limits of his tether, wide-eyed with horror as they continued to advance, his lips still moving feverishly in prayer.

Thibault was the next to speak, lifting his sphere in salute to what they called as he, too, sketched a mystic sign.

"I call upon Ythkar, bane of air. By the breath of Pta, I summon and bind you in accordance with the Seventh Mystery of Zosimos! Send forth an affliction of cries from the mouths of the children of Lilith!"

The splintering of his sphere released neither fog nor dust, but a ghostly keening that set the teeth on edge. The shrilling mingled with the sand and fog, forming a contained storm of elements.

"I call upon Oa, bane of fire," Mercurius rasped in his rough voice, lifting his sphere in stubby hands. "By the blood of Shak, I summon and bind you in accordance with the Ninth Mystery of Zosimos! Send forth a malediction of fevers from the well of the inferno!"

His globe, upon shattering, released a swarm of fiery motes that, like burning wasps, joined the wailing storm. As the swirl of elemental evil spiraled inward to overwhelm the captive monk, he managed only a choking sob of mortal despair. None present could be certain whether the victim heard Bartholeme's final words:

"I name you Shuel, the plague-carrier! Through you shall a mortal pestilence be released upon the Templars and all who stand by them!"

In the leafy depths of the New Park, the greater part of the Scottish rebel army lay in fitful sleep, catching what rest they could while the darkness lasted. Arnault was dozing uneasily when he felt a hand on his shoulder, and roused at once to see Torquil bending over him.

"A deserter has arrived from the English camp, claiming to have urgent information for the king," Torquil said quietly. "I thought you should be present to hear what he has to say."

Arnault flung off his blanket and stood up, buckling on his sword as he followed Torquil to Bruce's tent. Closeted with the king was a grizzled nobleman whose accents proclaimed his Scottish origins.

"There's devilry afoot in the English camp," the man was muttering. "If I hadna seen it with my own eyes . . ."

As the man shuddered and crossed himself, Bruce caught Arnault's eye.

"This is Sir Alexander Seton," he said. "He was with us at Turnberry, but then he lost faith in our cause for a while, and has been serving the English—as have many good Scots. But he has just been telling me about a band of French knights who joined King Edward's service under the banner of a black swan. I very much doubt that he was meant to see what he saw, but—tell them, Seton, exactly what you told me."

Seton gave a nervous nod, hugging his shoulders to suppress another shudder. "It was God-awful," he whispered. "I hope never to see its likes again. I think they were conducting some kind of sorcerous ceremony. They were tormenting a prisoner. From where I was standing, he looked to be a monk of some kind. He was wearing white robes. Or at least, they were meant to be white."

Arnault glanced sharply at Torquil, his blood running cold, for there was no doubt in his mind that Seton was describing Brother Ciaran.

"Three of those Black Swan Knights were muttering charms over a fire pit," Seton continued. "And there was a dwarf with them; he was muttering, too, and the poor monk was writhing on the ground, with a halter around his neck that was choking him if he moved—but he couldn't *not* move, because he was in such pain. If this is how King Edward hopes to win his victory, I want no part in his cause."

He drew a steadying breath and fixed his gaze on Bruce. "My lord King, now is the time, if ever you mean to win Scotland. The English have lost heart. They are discomfited, and expect nothing but a sudden and open attack. I swear, on my head and on pain of being hanged and drawn, that if you attack them in the morning, you will defeat them easily, without loss of—"

At that moment, racing footbeats heralded the arrival of one of the schiltron captains.

"Trouble, Sire," he gasped. "Where is Father Ninian? Our chaplain, Brother Fionn, has taken a fit of some kind! It—don't look natural to *me!*"

Arnault and Torquil set off on the run, Bruce close behind. They found the Columban brother writhing on the ground, his eyes wide-open, staring blankly at nothing. His skin had an uncanny, phosphorescent pallor, and when Arnault bent to examine him, he discovered the other man's pulse was racing.

Other denizens of the camp were drifting over, peering and muttering.

"Keep everyone else away!" Arnault ordered, with a glance up at Torquil. "This is no natural illness."

As Torquil moved to disperse the onlookers, also waving the king back, Father Ninian arrived, white and breathless, the *Brecbennach* under one arm.

"Someone told me that Brother Fionn—dear God!" he breathed, as his eyes lit on the stricken monk. He dropped to his knees and gingerly touched Fionn's forehead, then crossed himself quickly.

"We must seal the area immediately," he murmured. "There is great evil about."

"We'll take care of it," Arnault said. "See what you can do for Fionn. Sire, stay well back—please!"

Yielding his place to the Columban abbot, he helped Torquil set the necessary wards in place. By the time they rejoined Ninian, Breville had also arrived and Fionn's condition had worsened alarmingly. A rash of blisters erupted across his skin, swelling and cracking before their very eyes. He was burning with fever. Blind to their presence, the stricken monk thrashed from side to side groaning in anguish.

"If only we had kept that healing talisman," Torquil murmured, appalled.

"Aye, it's like a disease, but it's advancing far too quickly," Breville agreed. "It's as if some deadly plague were devouring him before our very—"

He stopped short as a dread possibility occurred to him, but Ninian spoke his thoughts aloud.

"It *is* a plague—a plague set upon us by our enemies!" he whispered, signing himself in blessing. "And it must be contained before it spreads to every soul within this camp."

From the folds of his robe he produced the *Brecbennach* reliquary. This he touched reverently to his lips before setting it on Fionn's chest, laying his hands flat upon the peaked lid to hold it in place as he offered up a petition for assistance from the one whose relics were contained therein.

> *"Father Columba, again we have need of your aid.*
> *Speak for us in the councils of heaven.*
> *From flood and fire,*
> *From wind and rain,*
> *From woundings and fevers,*
> *Deliver this, your servant."*

The others joined their prayers with his. Just when Arnault feared they must surely fail, he suddenly felt the breath of a fresh and fragrant breeze brush past his cheek. An unearthly brightness suffused the air in the clearing, and a shimmering Presence took shape.

Or rather, *two* Presences.

In the lesser of the two, Arnault sensed the luminous likeness of Brother Ciaran. The greater Presence he recognized with awe as Saint Columba, who had presided over Bruce's mystical enthronement. As Ciaran looked on, the saint stooped gracefully over Fionn's ravaged body. Hands translucent as pearl reached out in a gesture of welcoming summons.

Like a child awaking to the sound of a loving voice, Fionn's soul arose from its corporeal frame. Graceful as a dove, it ascended into the embrace of its summoner, who received it with a kiss of peace. A fragrance like roses filled the glade, erasing the corruption of disease. The next instant, a shimmering blaze of white fire descended and enveloped Fionn's mortal remains.

A blinding light filled the glade, masking the spiritual forms of Columba and his disciples. The blaze scoured the ground and purified the air, forcing all present to avert their dazzled eyes. When the light abated, there was nothing left of Fionn's corpse but a feathery tracery of harmless ash.

From their encampment on the edge of the Carse, Bartholeme sensed the sudden change in the air and knew, in that instant, that their attack had been thwarted. With a curse, he ordered his men to leap back from the boundaries of their working triangle, himself remaining only long enough to hurl a nullifying alchemical powder over the circle of fire.

The next instant, a blast of invisible energy came searing down like a thunderbolt. The disease-ridden corpse of their prisoner vanished in a rainbow flash of raw power.

Like a blast from a furnace, the same cleansing power roared outward to the boundaries of the enclosing circle, sweeping away the last of Bartholeme's enchantment. The knights nearest the center of the explosion were bowled off their feet. When the air stopped ringing, they found that their working ground had been scorched to the bare earth.

Shaken, Rodolphe turned to confront Bartholeme, who was picking himself up off the ground.

"It seems you underestimated the resources of our enemies."

Bartholeme shrugged, brushing ash from his clothing and stilling the trembling of his hand. "If we fell short of the success we hoped for, we still had the best of the encounter: The Templars and their allies have lost at least a few lives they could ill afford to spare. And we are still at full strength."

"What are your plans for tomorrow?" Thibault asked.

Bartholeme's eyes narrowed, and his teeth showed in a feral grin. "To let the English chivalry bear the brunt of the battle. And then, when the time is ripe, we will strike at the very heart of the Scottish army: Robert Bruce himself."

Chapter Forty-three

June 24, 1314

A FEW FAINT STARS LINGERED AS THE BRIEF SUMMER NIGHT
faded into dawn and the Scottish soldiers were roused from
their rest by the insistent voices and boot prods of their captains. When the men had eaten a frugal morning meal of oat
bannocks washed down with ladles of stream water, they
began arming themselves to prepare for battle.

It was Saint John's Day, the true deadline for the English
relief of Stirling Castle. Here and there, the priests who
marched with the army celebrated Mass for soldiers and camp
followers alike, the former already in their harness. In the
slender ranks of the Scottish cavalry, while the army prayed,
saddles were flung over the backs of the horses as they fed.

Amid the encampment of those close to the king, Arnault
and Torquil also roused in the predawn hour, groggy from all
too little sleep, to douse their faces with cold water and arm
before hearing Mass. Joining Bruce for a last briefing while
they broke their fast, neither Templar said much, for both
were grimly conscious of what had happened the night before, and what was expected of them today, not only by Bruce
but also by their absent Templar brethren.

Breville joined them when they had nearly finished eating, returned from scouting along the forward lines.

"They're arming, as one would expect, but I didn't note anything out of the ordinary," he reported, drawing the two aside. "What are your orders for today, *Maître*?"

Touching the bulge of the Shard beneath his mail, Arnault glanced back at the king, who was arming for the day's affray. "Be our eyes and ears, Armand," he said quietly. "The Black Knights have struck at us twice now. A third blow, the heaviest of all, is sure to follow. Torquil and I must be at the king's side, come what may—for if he falls, all is lost, for us as well as for Scotland."

"I'll not fail you," Breville vowed.

Shortly thereafter, the army began forming up on the edge of the camp. Cooks, servants, and those too infirm to fight were placed to the rear in the shadow of Coxet Hill. To guard them, Bruce had appointed a band of Highland ghillies, wild warriors from the far north who were too headstrong and undisciplined to be part of the highly trained schiltrons. Shock-haired and brawny in their rough plaids, they fingered their weapons and muttered among themselves as Bruce's standing army marched out to take to the field.

Once again the Scots were arrayed in four divisions. This time the king's brother Edward Bruce had the vanguard, with Randolph off his left flank and James Douglas as the third forward unit.

Robert Bruce himself, mounted on his favorite gray pony, commanded the rear guard, from which point he could best discern where and how to commit his men. Posted among the members of the king's personal retinue, Arnault and Torquil had likewise taken to horse for this second day of fighting. The remainder of the lightly mounted Scottish horse had been placed behind them as a reserve, well back in the trees, with orders to attack only on Bruce's direct order.

Standing in his stirrups, Bruce cast an approving eye over his followers.

"They've sharpened their weapons as best they can," he said to Arnault and Torquil. "Now it's time to sharpen their hearts."

Followed by the pair of them, his battle-axe firmly in hand, Bruce rode down into their midst. Abbot Ninian had already gone among them with the *Brecbennach,* imparting its blessing, and held it aloft for Bruce to touch before addressing the army. Behind them, Edward Bruce stood beside a man who held a banner of Saint Andrew, white saltire on a blue field, and another bearing the rampant Scottish lion.

"Men of Scotland," Bruce cried, "you who are accustomed to enjoy that full freedom for which, in times gone by, the kings of Scotland have fought many a battle! For eight years and more, I have struggled with much labor for my right to the kingdom and for honorable liberty. I have lost brothers, friends, and kinsmen. Your own kinsmen have been made captive, and bishops and priests are locked in prison. Our country's nobility has poured forth its blood in war."

He gestured toward the clustering tents and smoky fires of the English encampment, so large it was clearly visible from the wooded slope. The sheer size of the enemy army was only too apparent, but Bruce radiated an infectious confidence born of the righteousness of his cause.

"Those barons you can see before you, clad in mail, are bent upon destroying me and obliterating my kingdom—nay, our whole nation," he continued, his voice rising in challenge. "They do not believe that we can survive. They glory in their warhorses and equipment.

"For us, the name of the Lord must be our hope of victory in battle. This day is a day of rejoicing: the birthday of John the Baptist. With our Lord Jesus as commander, Saint Andrew and the martyr Saint Thomas shall fight today with the saints of Scotland for the honor of their country and their nation. If you heartily repent of your sins, you will be victorious under God's command. As for any offenses committed against the

Crown, I proclaim a pardon, by virtue of my royal power, to all those who fight manfully for the kingdom of our fathers."

With those last words Bruce swung his axe aloft in salute. The army returned the gesture with a cheer that shook the branches of the trees. After their king's example of personal valor of the previous day, they were ready to follow this man wherever he chose to lead.

Flanked by Arnault and Torquil, the king rode back to his own brigade, waiting in the trees. Marching orders were given, and the four brigades moved out of cover in disciplined formation, starting down the slope toward the enemy.

"You know that you're giving up the advantage of the high ground," Torquil said to Bruce, as the three forward brigades passed off the slope onto the flat.

"Aye," Bruce said. "Yesterday we held our ground. Today, we'll take theirs."

"This is no small risk, Sire," Arnault said.

"And it is no small victory we seek," Bruce replied. "Today everything hangs on this one fight, and it will be no chivalrous field of honor." He gripped the haft of his axe with renewed determination, and continued on a lower note.

"I have told you before, my friends: forward is the only way left open to me. It will be a bloody day, one way or the other. But at its end, I will have driven our enemies from Scotland—or I will lie dead upon the field. It is in God's hands."

He drew rein with them to watch the banners advancing. Ahead of Edward Bruce's brigade, they could see the banner of Saint Andrew, and Abbot Ninian beside it with the *Brecbennach* in his hands. When the whole Scottish army was arrayed on the flat, a prearranged signal brought them to a halt where, as one man, they fell to their knees and bowed their heads, planting their spear butts on the grass. Then, in voices rough, noble, and humble, they recited the one prayer they all knew best.

"Pater noster, qui est in caelis . . ."

Even the wind seemed to hold its breath as the words of the

Lord's Prayer whispered in the morning stillness and mingled with the gentle stirring of the banners above their heads. As well as decent, honest men, the Scots army had its share of rogues, drunkards, and cattle thieves; but in that instant, the best part of every soul among them was kindled to a blazing fire, touched by Bruce's courage and the Spirit of the God Whose protection they now relied upon to bring them victory over the host that opposed them.

The sight of the Scots emerging rashly from of their hiding place was met with astonishment and derision by the English, who had stood to arms all through the night, lest the Scots attempt raids during the brief hours of darkness. Come the day, Edward had determined to form a battle line and advance against any Scots foolish enough still to block his way to Stirling. He had, however, anticipated eating a proper breakfast and assembling his troops in battle order before driving back any resistance.

"What?" Edward exclaimed, upon hearing of the Scots' advance. "Will those Scots fight?"

"Evidently, my lord, they intend to," said Sir Ingram de Umfraville, a Scot who had once been guardian of Scotland, now loyal to Edward.

"Well, they are mad to invite us to destroy them," Edward said. "But it would be churlish to refuse the invitation."

He smiled as he languidly stretched out his arms to allow his sword belt to be buckled on, watching the Scottish advance, half-turning in some annoyance as Gloucester rode up on his charger at impetuous speed, not yet armed, and reined in with such vigor that the king had to step back to avoid being showered with dirt and sand.

"The rebels have appeared, my lord," Gloucester reported.

"I can see that," Edward snapped. He was drawing breath for a further comment when, after advancing so far, the whole Scottish army halted in its tracks, the men dropping to their knees like supplicants.

"What is this?" the king declared. "These men kneel to ask me for mercy."

"Aye, they ask for mercy," Umfraville said, "but not from you. They ask it of God, for their sins."

"Well, that's a pretty piece of arrogance for an excommunicate king," Edward replied, with a curl of his lip. "The cheek! God has better things to do with His time than listen to the false penitence of that black-hearted villain Bruce."

But he resumed arming with rather more alacrity as the Scottish army rose and continued forward once more. Watching them, Umfraville began to perceive Bruce's intent—for the English were caught in a restricted position that would not allow them to take full advantage of their numbers. To their right, spread along the river, lay the broad, marshy flatlands of the Carse of Stirling, while the area to their left was honeycombed with holes—treacherous footing for man and beast.

"My lord, perhaps we should consider our position," Umfraville suggested to the king.

"Our position?" Edward echoed, somewhat derisively. "They have thrown down a challenge, and we must answer it!"

"What are your orders, Sire?" Gloucester asked.

The king gave a derisive snort. "We attack, of course, you idiot!"

The English ranks were still stirring sluggishly. Individual commanders were doing their best to muster their followings, but the lack of any formal battle array was evident. Umfraville cast a worried look at the advancing Scots' vanguard. With the Bannockburn right at their backs, the English would have a difficult time withdrawing.

"If we are to attack, then it must be soon," he said, "while there is still sufficient distance to charge."

"We have ample ground yet," Gloucester said belligerently.

"Then go!" Edward shrilled. "I have braggarts aplenty, but I look about me for warriors!"

Stung by the rebuke, Gloucester spurred his horse back to

his men to finish arming. Eight hundred strong, the largest of ten English cavalry squadrons, his company had the distinction of forming the English vanguard—already standing mounted and ready while the other squadrons were still readying their mounts. Still scowling, Gloucester beckoned curtly to one of his equerries, omitting to don the surcoat that would identify him in armor.

"Tell Tiptoft to get his men in order and support us," he ordered. "I mean to smash these upstart Scots at a single blow."

The man galloped off. Gloucester snatched his lance from his esquire and rode to the front of his line of horsemen. Open ground lay before them, and nothing to stand between them and revenge for yesterday's defeat.

A small force of English bowmen, readier than the rest, were sent forward to form a skirmish line—which brought Scottish archers darting out of the ranks to counter them. Flurries of arrows flew in both directions, but the Scots were swiftly outmatched by the power of the English longbows. As the exchange continued, the English arrows ripped through the Scots' padded jerkins as though they were made of parchment, sowing red ruin in their ranks.

Still the Scottish archers tried to hold their ground and keep the enemy bowmen out of range of the schiltrons. But before the English bowmen could follow up their advantage, the heavy rumble of hooves to their rear warned that the cavalry was advancing. Abandoning their fire, the bowmen broke ranks and scattered to avoid being caught in the way of the horses. The Scottish archers, likewise, scurried back to the protection of Edward Bruce's schiltron to await the first attack.

The English chivalry converged in three long lines. Those of noblest birth had claimed the places to the fore: Gloucester, Clifford, and highborn Scottish vassals of Edward like John Comyn, the lord of Badenoch. Lances gleaming and harness jangling, they commenced their advance at a measured pace, flaunting their wealth and power as though they were at a tournament.

They made a daunting sight, for these mailed warriors had been schooled from birth to do only one thing, and do it with supreme efficiency: to smash through the ranks of mere footmen and trample them beneath an unstoppable tidal wave of hooves and steel, grinding their broken bones into the mud. This they knew, as surely as they believed in God and their Saviour.

A blare of trumpets prompted the cavalry to a trot, and the cadence of hoofbeats quickened to a rumbling tattoo. Battle cries rang out, and lances swung downward in glittering arcs as, in a final surge, the destriers broke from a trot to a canter, sweeping across the flat like a rush of boulders spilling off a mountainside.

A sense of godlike power swelled the hearts of the knights. Clad in their heavy steel armor and mounted upon their huge, ferocious warhorses, they felt gigantic and invincible, regarding the ragged spearmen who stood in their path as no more of an obstacle than a weather-beaten hedge on the edge of a field.

Edward Bruce's schiltron drew together and stood their ground, shoulder to shoulder, in bristling, tight-packed array. Scattered throughout the ranks were the armored nobility of Scotland who, in defiance of the pride of chivalry, had chosen to meet their counterparts on foot. Bracing the line with their own devoted men-at-arms, they stood side by side with peasants and herders to face off the fearsome charge.

The English knights closed at the gallop, bellowing and roaring as they braced their lances for the impact. Their great destriers laid back their ears and bared their teeth as their riders spurred them closer, the ground shaking with the rumble of hooves.

Then the enemy struck home.

Chapter Forty-four

June 24, 1314

THE SCHILTRON SHUDDERED AT THE IMPACT, LIKE A SHIELD ringing under the crash of a mace. The destriers plunged and screamed and lashed out with steel-shod hooves; the knights rammed their lances at the enemy. Skulls were cracked and footmen stabbed, but the Scots thrust their spears cruelly into the bellies of the horses, gutting them and bringing them crashing to the ground. Equine screams rent the air along with the mortal groans of dying men. Those fallen knights who were not pinned under their mounts struggled to their feet and drew their swords.

Skirmishers lunged out from the Scots' line, wielding long-hafted Lochaber axes. With sweeps of their heavy blades, they carved through shields and chain mail, cleaving ribs and lopping limbs. Knights trapped on the ground or injured were stabbed or clubbed to death. Those who could still stand had to fight for their lives against spear and axe.

Gloucester drove hard against the forest of spears. He had lost his lance and was laying about him with his sword when he realized he had been cut off from his household knights. His wounded horse buckled beneath him, pitching him forward into a sea of enemy soldiers—without the surcoat that would have marked him for capture and ransom rather than death. The Scots engulfed him, and he disappeared under a rain of killing blows.

Sir Robert Clifford called on his men to avenge the fallen earl, and threw himself at the schiltron in a fury of martial courage. Other knights joined the attack, but the Scots refused to give ground. Clifford shoved his lance straight through the unprotected breast of the nearest spearman, but it gave him only scant respite before he, too, was engulfed and dragged down to his doom.

Randolph's schiltron closed ranks with Edward Bruce's, and Douglas moved up to support him. Thus closely aligned, the three schiltrons formed a continuous wall of sharpened steel. Only the king's division held back, waiting to reinforce any of the schiltrons that began to give way.

The other English squadrons re-formed into battle array. One after another they rushed full tilt into the fray. The huge mass of armored chivalry, nearly three thousand strong, assailed the Scots' line like a colossal mailed fist pounding at a stout wooden door.

When their spearpoints snapped or shafts cracked, the men of the schiltrons drew swords and axes to continue the fight. Troops from the rear pressed forward into the front ranks to replace the dead and wounded. The turf grew slick with the blood of slain knights and the entrails of disemboweled horses. The hands of the Scottish spearmen were dyed with the gore that poured down the length of their spears.

Brutality as much as courage was the order of the day. Highborn nobles entangled in the line were torn from their mounts to be butchered by vengeful peasants. Knives and axes hacked them apart, then the spears rose up again to confront the next wave of knights.

With the failure of the first assault, the English chivalry began to lose their momentum. Every time the tide of horsemen withdrew, the Scots pressed forward, seizing more ground and leaving the knights less and less room to gather the impetus for a charge.

The English infantry formed an improvised line with their backs to the Bannockburn. Many were still eager to join the fray and seize the chance of booty. Others hung back, reluctant to test their mettle against the Scots when they could clearly hear the crazed din of battle and the screams of the dying. But whichever way their feelings ran, there was no way for them to enter the fight unless and until the knights withdrew.

But for the English chivalry, withdrawal was unthinkable. It would amount to an admission of defeat and—even worse—would leave them open to accusations of cowardice. They prized their honor too highly to allow it to be tainted, so they wheeled their horses about, ordered themselves as best they could, and attacked again.

By now, the English dead presented a grisly barrier of their own. The knights rode roughshod over the corpses, trampling the dead into the earth, blind to everything but their hated foes. Umfraville could see that the knights needed assistance, and galloped back to confront the English infantry, galled that they should be standing uselessly to the rear.

"Bowmen!" he yelled. "Bowmen to the fore!"

Given the chance to deploy properly, he knew that the English would have worn the enemy down with missile fire before committing the cavalry. But perhaps it was not too late to give the Scots a taste of the dreaded English longbow.

Most of the archers were stuck at the rear, however, without space to push their way through; and the scattered ranks who could be brought into line were unable to see the Scots over the heads of their own cavalry. They held their arrows nocked to the bowstring, peering through the dust clouds and the surging mass of horses in search of targets.

"Fire!" Umfraville bawled at them. "You came here to fight, so fire, damn you!"

The bowmen obeyed, but with less effect than Umfraville would have liked. Some of the bowmen aimed high and launched their arrows in a lofty arc over the heads of the chivalry. Others knew that such shots would drop on the Scots without sufficient force to do any injury, and tried to shoot straight through the gaps in their own line, hoping to exploit the penetrating power of the longbow, which could snap chain mail and kill an armored man as easily as if he were naked.

Here and there a shaft struck home and felled an unlucky spearman. But just as often, in the murk and confusion of battle, it was an English knight or his mount that fell victim to the deadly missiles. Some of the nobles wheeled about and rode into the midst of the bowmen, cursing them for ill-begotten curs. Flushed with rage, they bellowed at them to desist or be killed on the spot as traitors.

Meanwhile, from their place in Bruce's own brigade, Arnault and Torquil watched the king's battle plan unfold. Elation mounted among the men of the rear guard as the schiltrons up front continued to press slowly, steadily forward.

"This will be a far cry from what King Edward expected," Torquil noted with satisfaction.

"Aye, but our enemies are far from beaten," Arnault replied. "The English still have an infantry of ten thousand in reserve. And we've yet to see the Knights of the Black Swan make their move."

"It's coming," Breville muttered ominously. "I can feel it in the air."

Torquil merely rumbled low in his throat, for all of them had spotted individual members of the Decuria taking part in the fighting, and knew they would not accept defeat gladly.

Gray eyes glinting like Lochaber steel, Robert Bruce drew his companions' attention to the eastern front of the fighting.

"Look you, there between the battle line and the bog! There's enough open space for the English to overrun our flank, if they've got the presence of mind to seize their chance. I think it's time to commit this division as well: one last throw of the dice."

At his command, his standard-bearer inclined the royal banner in that direction. With Father Ninian bearing the *Brecbennach* before him, Bruce led his troops forward. A roar of welcome went up from Douglas's men, as the royal schiltron moved up into position at their side.

At the sight of Bruce's standard, a squadron of English knights launched a fresh attack, knowing that if they could reach the rebel king, they might break the whole Scottish army. The men of the schiltron presented their weapons in defense of their lord, grimly determined in the face of the charge. There came again the ruinous clangor of weaponry against armor as the squadron hurled itself into the wall of spears, but once again, the cavalry broke apart like a wave smashing onto an immovable rock.

The English pulled back and attempted to rally.

"Forward!" Bruce yelled above the tumult of battle. "Take the fight to them!"

The men of his schiltron advanced to meet the next English charge. The morning sun witnessed a prolonged and bitter struggle as mounted knights probed and circled while the Scottish infantry grimly held their formation.

Men on both sides were drenched in sweat, muscles aching under the weight of their weapons. Their eyes blurred with the strain of their exertions, and their ears rang with the din of combat. Yet still they remained locked in combat, trampling heedlessly over the dead to grapple afresh with the living foe.

Observing a momentary lull in the fighting, Rodolphe sought out Bartholeme, dipping his helmeted head close.

"These English are in danger of throwing the battle away," he said. "We must act soon, or not at all."

"Would you have me unleash the puissance of the ring on mere foot soldiers," Bartholeme countered, "and have nothing in reserve when we come face-to-face with the Templars? No, we will win the day as warriors, if we can!"

Beating men aside with the flat of his sword, and with Rodolphe close behind, he forced his charger through the packed English infantry to where companies of archers waited at the rear, impotently fingering their bows.

"You men!" he called, singling out the English captains. "Follow me, if you would strike a blow for England and your king!"

The battered squadrons of English cavalry had pulled together to try yet another assault on the center of the Scots' formation, hoping to break the schiltrons, which had opened several chinks in the English ranks. Urged on by Bartholeme, a number of archers surged forward before the gaps could close again, skirting the English right flank to take possession of a shallow rise that provided them a clear field of fire.

Again, clouds of English arrows blackened the sky. A score of men on the Scots' left flank fell wounded or dying, with goose-feathered barbs protruding from their flesh. Seeing the devastation, Arnault bit back an oath and pressed close to the king's side.

"Look you there," he said, pointing. "The enemy have brought some of their bowmen to bear."

Even as he spoke, the bowmen loosed a second deadly volley. Instinctively Arnault flung up his shield to protect Bruce—and in doing so, opened himself to another shaft that grazed the edge of the shield and embedded beneath his own left collarbone.

The shock of his recoil ripped the barb loose, blood streaming down his shield arm, and the shield sank as he curled forward over his pony's neck, gasping from the pain. But a strong hand seized his sword arm and kept him from falling—Bruce's hand.

"Steady, I've got you!" the king said.

Torquil, too, was crowding his pony close to seize the reins of Arnault's mount.

"Hang on!" he ordered. "I'll bear you to the rear."

"No!" Arnault jerked his reins from Torquil and tried to straighten. "Stay with the king. I'll go by myself."

"You can't—"

"Stay *here*!" Arnault insisted. "Keep fighting."

Bruce resolved the issue by seizing upon two of his nearest retainers.

"Escort Brother Arnault from the field," he ordered curtly. "Find someone competent to tend to his injury. I can't afford to lose this man."

Reluctantly, Torquil surrendered Arnault into their charge, ducking with a grimace as more arrows hissed and thudded about them.

"I want those English archers put out of action," Bruce said to him, gesturing with his axe. "Go slip Keith from his leash. Tell him to set the hounds on the rabbits."

Arrows continued to pepper the schiltron at his back as Torquil turned and galloped back through the trees to where Sir Robert Keith and his five hundred horsemen were mustered.

"The king's orders!" he announced, and pointed toward the formation of archers. "Remove that thorn from his side!"

The Scottish cavalry had been chafing for the chance to join the battle. At Keith's command, they bolted forward like starving men falling upon a banquet. Torquil whipped his own mount around to join the charge. Baying like bloodhounds, the mounted Scots erupted from cover and streamed in a wave toward the enemy archers.

Coarsely bred and undersized by English cavalry standards, their wiry Scottish ponies nimbly covered the broken ground. Seeing them come on, the archer captains frantically ordered their men to redirect and redouble their fire.

The English longbows loosed their shafts with a sound

like the wind booming through a cave. A dozen riders fell at the first volley, but the Scots opened ranks to present more scattered targets, for all knew that they must close the distance swiftly, or be killed trying.

Keith urged his men to even greater speed. Shafts continued to rain down on them, claiming men and horses at every round, but the Scottish charge never slackened, and seconds later they were within striking range of the enemy.

The archers had not been able to fortify their position by planting stakes in the ground. With no knights or spearmen to defend them, they had nothing to stand between them and the murderous spears and blades of the Scottish riders. A scattered few stood their ground and fired off a last desperate volley, but most knew they were staring certain death in the face. Flinging down their heavy bows and quivers, they turned and made a panic-stricken bolt for safety.

Some dashed back toward their own ranks. Others floundered across the boggy ground toward the bend of the River Forth, their unprotected backs presenting easy targets to the pursuing horsemen. Unrelentingly, the Scots swept after them, stabbing and slashing, so that soon the field was clear of all but the dead.

With the archers' threat neutralized, Torquil reined short and turned back to report their success to the king.

"If Edward had brought those bowmen forward earlier in the day, we might have found ourselves in trouble," Bruce commented with a wolfish show of teeth.

"Aye, and it isn't over yet," Torquil agreed. "But if you can spare me, I'd better go see how Arnault is faring."

"Go," Bruce said with a nod. "That arrow that struck him down was meant for me. Let's hope it doesn't prove our undoing."

Chapter Forty-five

June 24, 1314

No LONGER MENACED BY THE LETHAL THREAT OF LONGBOW fire, Bruce's army resumed its advance. The English, first to their chagrin and then to their dismay, were forced to give ground. The schiltrons solidified into a single bristling wall, thrusting inexorably forward. With the battle shifting in their favor, fierce cries rang out from the Scots' ranks.

"On them! On them! Push on!"

The English vanguard steadily disintegrated. Caught between the gorge of the Bannockburn and the treacherous Carse, Edward's forces were further hemmed in by the River Forth. Chaos broke out among the troops to the rear as they found themselves trapped within the shrinking confines of their previous night's encampment—and on the verge of defeat.

From the extreme left of the English army, Bartholeme and his Knights of the Black Swan surveyed the ongoing slaughter of the English chivalry with growing disdain. Mutilated corpses littered the field, with here and there a still-living body twitching and groaning in the bloody mire. Riderless horses careered this way and that in wild-eyed panic, adding to the pandemonium.

"Who would have thought England's king would be such a fool as to squander his every advantage?" Rodolphe said with contempt.

Thibault turned to Bartholeme.

"Why are we here?" he asked. "This battle is as good as lost. Leave the English to their humiliation. There are better ways, surely, to finish off the Templars than to remain and risk being slaughtered by ignorant peasants."

Bartholeme rounded on him with tight-jawed fury.

"The Templars are fewer and weaker now than they have been since their earliest beginnings! If we let this opportunity slip through our fingers, we may not get another. If you fear death so greatly, then be gone! Your departure will not hinder the rest of the Decuria from triumph."

An angry flush suffused Thibault's face, but the response came from Rodolphe.

"The time to prove your words is now, Bartholeme. If this Scottish rabble wins the day, the Templars will be forever beyond our reach."

"They will not win," Bartholeme said coldly. "Scotland stands or falls by her king. I know a spell that will kill a man dead in his tracks. I mean to unleash it at Robert Bruce."

Several of the knights recoiled uneasily, and Rodolphe's expression hardened as he lifted his gaze to Bartholeme's.

"I also know that spell," he said. "The cost is the life of the alchemist who casts it."

"Or some equal indemnity of power," Bartholeme countered. "Why else do you suppose I have been holding the Ring of Ialdabaeoth in reserve until now?"

He glared at each of his men in turn, inviting further challenge. None came. Satisfied that he had made his point, he went on.

"For this spell to succeed, I must have Bruce in my line of sight. After remaining to the rear all the morning, he has since advanced to the fore, the better to be seen by his men.

That ridge over there presents a good eminence. From there, Bruce should be plainly visible to me."

It was the same high ground that the English archers had briefly occupied earlier.

"Getting there could pose a problem," said Guy de Vitry, a recently inducted member of the Decuria. "The Scots have overrun the area. If we must fight our way through, there's no guarantee that any of us would survive."

"Oh yes, there is," Bartholeme said. "Mercurius?"

Hitherto silent, the dwarf today was riding pillion behind his master. Keeping a grip on Bartholeme's belt with one hand, he thrust the other into his belt pouch and produced a yellow glass vial. Inside was a thick, bilious-looking liquid.

"All of you know of the demon that dwells in this ring," Bartholeme said, holding up his left hand, where the dark stone glittered like blood. "A bargain has been struck. None who drink of that elixir can be slain in battle, for Ialdabaeoth will protect him."

"And what is the price for such a victory?" one of the men asked.

"The price was paid after Castle Montaigre, when I brought the demon back from certain annihilation. You need not fear to partake of its gratitude."

Eagerly the Black Knights crowded closer to take the vial from Mercurius and sip from it. When all had done so, Bartholeme stood in his stirrups and brandished his sword.

"Now, Brethren of the Black Swan, are you as keen for killing as I am?" he cried. "Then, let's be off!"

Scarcely had they set out when they clashed with a roving band of Scottish cavalry. The Black Knights were fresh, skilled, and could take no wound, so they cut a swath through the Scots, reveling in their own butchery, leaving carnage in their wake. By the time they reached the foot of the ridge, they had claimed nearly a hundred lives.

"Now for our main objective!" Bartholeme said, as they plunged up the hillside.

Drawing rein at the summit, Bartholeme bade his Black Knights form a circle around him as he thrust his bloodied weapon toward the sky.

"Now throw wide the gates of hell, great Lucifer, Prince of Darkness, and set free the demon hounds of fear!" he cried. "Cast down the vassals of your enemy! Harrow them with visions of your terrible wrath!"

A gust of sulfurous wind swept the hilltop, and a shadow passed over the sun. The Scots attempting to scale the hill were suddenly stricken with unreasoning fear. Riders were thrown to the ground as ponies bolted in panic. Spearmen turned tail and fled as if from the gaping mouth of an inferno. At the sight, a harsh bark of laughter burst from Bartholeme's lips.

"You see?" he proclaimed triumphantly. "We are masters here!"

Casting his gaze farther afield, he scanned the battlefield until he spotted a tall figure on a gray pony, recklessly distinguished by the circlet of gold around his helmet.

"Excellent," he murmured. "Now maintain the interdict of fear, while I prepare the death bolt that will slay the Templars' precious King of Scots!"

Torquil reached the top of Coxet Hill to find the Scottish camp abuzz with excitement.

"What's going on?" he demanded of one of the wagon drivers, as he swung down from his weary pony.

The man grinned.

"We've just been joined by reinforcements."

"Reinforcements?" Torquil echoed blankly.

"Aye, Templars—lots of them!" The man pointed beyond, where scores of men in the Temple's white surcoats with red crosses were adjusting white bardings on tall, clean-limbed steeds that bore the stamp of Templar breeding. Mixed among them, here and there, were men wearing the brown of Templar serjeants.

"Who—?" Torquil began.

"Their officers have been taken to report to Sir Arnault," the wagoner informed him, as Torquil thrust his pony's reins into the man's hand and started in the direction of the Templars.

At that, Torquil headed instead in the direction of the hospital tents, where he found Arnault lying in the shade of one of the supply carts, stripped to the waist and having his shoulder bandaged. Crouched across from the infirmarer were two mailed figures in white surcoats, who looked around as Torquil pounded toward them: Flannan Fraser and Aubrey Saint Clair.

"Sweet Jesu, am I glad to see you!" he exclaimed, as the two rose to exchange hearty handshakes with him. Arnault looked a little pale, but considerably heartened by the presence of their brother knights.

"We'd have been here sooner," Aubrey said with a grin, "but we ran into a little interference on the way. I believe the fellow's name was Macdougall of Lorn."

"Lorn?!" Torquil said, looking concerned.

"Aye." Flannan grinned. "He wasn't so tough. The idiot actually tried to work magic against us."

Torquil snorted. "Well, you're here, so he can't have been very good at it. We think he was one of Bartholeme de Challon's pawns."

"If so, he's a broken pawn now," said Flannan. "He got away with his life, but that's about all I can say for him."

Torquil only shook his head, turning his attention to Arnault. "Are you all right?"

"I will be."

"Hmmm, yes, so he says," Aubrey quipped. "Keeping our esteemed *Maître* out of trouble is clearly too much work for one man alone to handle."

"Aye, well, keeping Bruce out of trouble is a full-time occupation as well," Torquil retorted. "How many men have you brought?"

"Nearly fourscore," Flannan replied. "And more than half of those are knights."

"Excellent!" said Torquil. "Let's get them into action, then."

"We're ready," Aubrey said, producing two white bundles from under his arm. "Would you care to put on proper attire? We may never get another chance."

What unfurled from the bundles was a pair of white surcoats like the ones he and Flannan wore, with the red Templar cross bold across front and back. Torquil grinned as he took one, casting a sharp look at Arnault, who was struggling to his feet.

"Now, just a minute, you! I don't think—"

Even as he spoke, there came a shout from the outskirts of the encampment as Armand Breville came riding up, spurring his horse in their direction as he spotted them, reining short, then, and leaping to the ground.

"I think the Black Knights are about to make their move!" he cried breathlessly. "Somehow, they fought through our lines and gained a position on one of the heights. Militarily, it does them no good, but it's a perfect spot from which to launch a sorcerous attack."

Arnault felt a shiver up his spine, for here, at last, was the full manifestation of the threat he had been fearing throughout the day. Motioning to Torquil to help him rearm, he turned to Aubrey and Flannan.

"Have you any mounts to spare? Good! Summon the rest of your men to join us. We must ride to the defense of the king."

"But, your injury—" Flannan began.

"—is of no account," Arnault said sharply. "Bruce is in deadly danger, and only the power of the Shard can save him."

His subordinates leapt into action. While Templar serjeants ran to fetch horses, Arnault let Torquil rearm him, wincing as he eased back into his bloodstained hauberk and mail.

"How much use have you got in your left arm?" Torquil asked, as he slipped a Templar surcoat over everything.

Arnault flexed the fingers of his left hand and repressed a grimace, but pulled the pouch with the Shard out from under the surcoat.

"Enough," he assured his friend. "I doubt I could manage a normal shield, but I don't think I'll need to, with this. Don't worry. Nothing's broken. It's a flesh wound, and it hurts like hell, but there's nothing I can do about that. I have to be able to ride."

He squared his shoulders, deriving comfort from wearing Templar livery again, and found himself grinning as he walked over to the barded horse a serjeant had brought him, for he had not ridden such a steed for several years. The breath hissed between his teeth as he let the serjeant give him a leg up, but he drew himself upright in the saddle, glancing at the other Templars sitting their barded horses around him as he lifted the pouch that held the sacred Shard.

"My brothers, this and our faith are now our greatest weapons," he told them. "This is the Shard of the Law, by which we shall strive to be the guardians of God Law today. And may He be our guide and our strength in the coming test."

He touched the pouch briefly to his lips before tucking it back into the breast of his gambeson so that it rested secure against his heart, nodding to Sir Hamish Kerr to unfurl their battle standard.

"Now we must issue a challenge to our enemies—force ourselves on their attention," he declared for the benefit of all, as the Order's standard unfurled in a billow of black and white. "Raise our banner high, and let *Beauçéant* proclaim our presence for all to see!"

Chapter Forty-six

June 24, 1314

THE RUMBLE OF A GROWING CHEER FROM THE SCOTS' LINE penetrated the sorcerous barricade the Knights of the Black Swan had erected around themselves. The sound of it yanked Bartholeme back to awareness, out of the depths of his ensorceled trance.

Snarling at the interruption, he made a sweeping survey of the battlefield below—and suddenly stood in his stirrups to stare at the black-and-white billow of a new banner entering the field above a body of white-clad horsemen, moving in disciplined formation along the northernmost fringe of the fighting. The horses, too, were barded in white—tall, clean-limbed horses proudly carrying a contingent of the most renowned fighting men in the known world.

"Templars!" He fairly spat the name, sitting back hard in his saddle with a venomous hiss.

Around him, the other Black Knights muttered and stared in kindred disbelief.

"Where the devil did *they* come from?" Thibault said, sounding vexed.

"Wherever they came from," Rodolphe said scathingly, "it's clear that your precious Lorn failed in what he was ordered to do. I knew it was a mistake to place much faith in that ignorant lout."

"Be silent!" Bartholeme snapped. "While you grope for explanations, our enemies are gaining ground."

"And whose fault is that?" Rodolphe countered. "Don't make the same mistake Nogaret made. Use the power of the ring *now,* to wipe them out!"

Fury flared briefly in Bartholeme's eyes, but then he mastered himself.

"I will do whatever it takes to destroy these self-styled monks of war," he said coldly. "Let all those who are like-minded come with me, and let us put our mettle to the test."

Three quarters of a mile away, the ghillies and the small-folk who supported Bruce's army had been watching the battle from the top of Coxet Hill where, for two whole days, they had respected the king's command to guard the baggage wagons. Now, fired by the example of the Templars, they could no longer contain their zeal for battle.

Yelling and brandishing whatever rude weapons they could lay hands upon, they swarmed down off the hilltop toward the battlefront, others from the encampment following suit. Ghillies and laborers alike hurled themselves in a ragged frenzy at the wavering English battle line, even some of the camp followers snatching up cloths to wave as banners, and pots with which to bang on heads. Faced with a new wave of Scottish fighters, fronted by the hard-driving line of charging Templars, King Edward's army lost what little coherence remained to it. Infantry and cavalry alike flung down their weapons and attempted to flee.

Arnault sensed the beginnings of the rout, but riding in the forefront of the Templar charge, his attention remained focused on the occluded hilltop occupied by their adversaries. English and Scots might stand opposed amid the passing fortunes of war, but the conflict between the Templars and the Knights of the Black Swan was age-old, a clash between good and evil, Light and Darkness.

Not to us, Lord, not to us, he prayed fervently, *but to Thy name give the glory. . . .*

The utterance of this age-old prayer brought the Shard to life. He felt it warming against his heart, filling his whole body with energizing force and banishing both his fatigue and his pain. The foot of the enemy hill loomed ahead, its slopes sheathed in demonic murk, but he was oblivious now to his own condition as he shouted aloud, *"Non nobis, Domine . . . !"*

The Black Knights leveled their swords at the charging Templars, buttressing their position on the high ground with a sorcerous aura of fear. In their midst, their leader raised his left hand, displaying the fiery glint of a ruby ring on his third finger. Power emanated from the ring in baleful waves—the same infernal influence that had darkened the air of Nogaret's secret citadel—but the Templars kept coming. Riding at Arnault's side, Torquil knew the wielder of the ring for the same who had sent the demonic bird against Bruce, so many years before.

And Bartholeme, for his part, recognized in Torquil the Templar knight who had struck him the almost-mortal blow of seven years before, green-eyed and freckle-faced, thwarting the attack that should have taken Bruce's soul. But he sensed that the darker man riding at his side posed the greater danger, and turned his head to mouth an order to the dwarf still perched behind him on the saddle, clinging like a monkey—for the demon ring had yet to reach its full power.

The Templars had reached the hilltop, and surged around the packed mass of Black Knights, now feinting, now striking. Each meeting of blades caused a ringing explosion of sparks. Lighter and fleeter than their counterparts, the Templar horses danced away from the bared teeth and striking hooves of the Black Knights' destriers. Dust clouded the air amid the dissonant clangor of combat; and into this, the dwarf cast a pinch of crystalline sand, at the same time muttering a charm.

The falling sand resolved itself into a filmy curtain, isolating Bartholeme and the dwarf from the general melee. Thus screened, the Magister of the Decuria renewed the deadly invocation interrupted by the Templars' attack.

"I call upon the fury of Gzul the Slayer!" he declared. "I call upon the hunger of Zoath the Devourer! I call upon the lust of Ukur the Ravager! I call upon the pride of Lucifer, the Unhallowed and Unconquered! Let all the powers of Darkness make me gifts of fire. Let that fire be as an arrow from the bow that cannot miss!"

The ring on his hand glowed brighter with each phrase of invocation. The infusion of power made his blood sing. On the battlefield below, King Robert Bruce fought on, oblivious to the imminence of death. Breathless, Bartholeme awaited the moment of climax when he would unleash the forces at his command.

Beyond the sorcerous veil, the battle between Black Knights and Templars raged on. Men had begun to fall on both sides, neither giving quarter. Arnault had the Shard and his reins in his left hand and his sword in his right, and was peering urgently into the swirling dust.

"What's become of Bartholeme?" Torquil panted, from Arnault's left side. "I know I saw him! You don't suppose he's bolted?"

"No, he's here somewhere," Arnault returned. "I have a strong sense of his presence."

"Then *find* him!" Torquil cried. "I'll watch your back."

Wrenching his horse around, he stationed himself on guard at Arnault's left and slightly behind him, ready to fight off all comers as Arnault sheathed his sword and shifted the Shard into his right hand, silently commending himself to the protection of Saint Michael as he summoned up all his deeper powers of perception. Casting his augmented sight this way and that, he at once became aware of an uncanny disturbance in the air some thirty paces back from the hill-top, as if the very light of day were being bent or twisted awry.

Lifting the Shard to his lips, Arnault invoked its power and bent his gaze on the heart of the disturbance—and Saw, beyond the veil, Bartholeme de Challon and his dwarf-familiar mounted together on one horse, in unconscious parody of the knights depicted on the Templar seal. Even as Arnault espied the black magician, a fiery glow began to shimmer around the Frenchman's upraised ring hand in vis-ible token of a killing bolt of energy about to be launched.

Spurring his horse to a gallop, praying he would not lose the Shard, Arnault leveled it like a lance and burst through the alchemical curtain. The Black Knight's diminutive com-panion shrilled a warning, but Arnault was already upon them, his horse colliding hard enough with Bartholeme's to jar the dwarf from his perch, screaming as he tumbled to the ground and vanished beneath the weight of trampling hooves. Arnault shouldered hard against Bartholeme and knocked him flying as well, just as the Black Knight pro-nounced his last syllable of interdiction.

There was a thunderous blast. The field of Bannockburn with all its butchery vanished in a hurricane roar. When the chaos subsided, Arnault found himself crouched on hands and knees in the midst of a far-flung landscape of fire and rock, where volcanic cinder cones rumbled and smoked in the distance and the air was harsh with poisonous fumes. But the Shard was still locked in his fingers—which was as well, because Bartholeme was also there, a few yards away, likewise picking himself up to round on Arnault in fury.

"You pious meddler!" he seethed. "Lucifer's vultures shall devour your soul!"

He made a summoning gesture with his ring hand, and a great airborne shape materialized on the burning horizon, half-bird and half-serpent, striking out across the fire-eaten landscape with massive beats of its leathery wings. Arnault scrambled for safety in the shelter of a nest of boulders as the monster swooped to attack, its fanged jaws gaping wide. A hot gust of carrion breath wafted over him as the creature rammed its snout against the rocks.

Heart hammering against his ribs, Arnault lifted the Shard toward the creature. A blue-white radiance blazed forth in a pure, unsullied beam.

The serpent-bird drew back with a roar, spitting bile and venom. Brandishing the Shard before him, Arnault rose from cover and thrust the light in the monster's face.

The creature's retreat was only momentary. Rearing up to its full height, it mantled its wings and attacked. In desperation, Arnault thrust the Shard toward it again, to fend it off.

This time, like a sword in Arnault's hand, the beam of the Shard's light sheared a slash in one looming wing, carving shadow like substance. Each cut left behind a gaping wound, but the creature itself remained undiminished.

He was dimly aware of Bartholeme inciting the creature to attack, with raving curses. The Shard's light remained his only weapon, and seemed to be growing dimmer as he continued to hold the monster at bay. Watching it flicker and wane, Arnault could only pray for fresh inspiration.

—and was answered by the sudden image in his mind of a rough block of stone: the Stone of Destiny!

Calling upon the sacrificial blood bond he once had shared with William Wallace, Arnault reached beyond himself, tapping into the far-off reservoirs of the Stone's power. At once, fresh energy flowed back into the Shard, which shone forth brighter than ever. And then, in further inspiration, Arnault directed the beam, not at the demon serpent-bird but at the ring on Bartholeme's hand.

The move caught Bartholeme off guard. He recoiled with a howl, but not soon enough, for the beam of holy light lanced through the arid air of the demon realm to strike the demon-ring with a searing crack.

The demon-stone shattered in a cascading shower of

crimson flecks that exploded outward from the shards. Caught in the backlash, without even a chance to cry out, Bartholeme disappeared in a web of corrosive energies that consumed him down to the bone, leaving only a shadow of ash. The ground heaved and cracked, sulfurous smoke belching from the rifts. Then came a rumbling roar, just before fire roared upward with a catastrophic *boom*.

The infernal plain broke apart in flames, and Arnault found himself suddenly spinning through space. Broken images cartwheeled around him in a dizzying whirl. Vertigo took his breath away, and darkness overwhelmed him.

An eternity of numb, ringing silence passed. Floating weightless in a sea of night, Arnault gradually became aware of a distant dawning light that steadily broadened, banishing the darkness to the void whence it had sprung. Then voices began to penetrate the silence, tantalizing snatches of conversation, ebbing and flowing.

". . . English are fleeing. Let me go after them . . ."

"Take sixty knights, no more . . . don't want to risk the enemy regrouping . . ."

". . . found the dwarf trampled to pulp. I doubt any of them escaped. . . ."

Arnault drew a deep breath and smelled the familiar camp reek of cooking, wet blankets, and horse manure. Cracking his lids, he glimpsed ordinary firelight.

"I think he's coming round," said a voice he recognized as Torquil's. "Arnault, are you with us?"

Arnault forced a nod, raking at dry lips with a furry tongue.

"The king—?" he managed to croak.

"The king, thanks to you, is not only uninjured, but victorious," said a second voice—that of Bruce himself.

Arnault forced his eyes wide open, though it was almost too much effort. He was lying, he discovered, in one of the hospital tents—and his right hand was still locked around the Shard. The darkness outside suggested that many hours had passed since the Templars' encounter with their enemies on the hilltop.

"The battle's over?" he asked.

"Not only the battle, but probably the war itself," Bruce said. "The English are utterly routed. From this day, Scotland is once again a free nation—and if you'll pardon me, I have kingly duties to perform."

He took his leave. Arnault turned his head to Torquil. "What about our men?"

"Three killed, a dozen more wounded," Torquil supplied. "The good news is that the Black Knights have been all but eliminated. The few that escaped are on the run. Aubrey, Flannan, and Breville have gone after them, to see them off."

Arnault drew a deep breath, feeling as if a great weight had been lifted off his chest. "I feel as if I could sleep for a week," he murmured.

"Rest easy then," Torquil advised. "We'll talk more in the morning."

Leaving his superior sleeping, Torquil went in search of Robert Bruce. He was told that the king had repaired to St. Ninian's Church, where he found a dozen men from Bruce's retinue keeping watch outside. Entering, he discovered the king kneeling in prayer beside the body of his late adversary, the Earl of Gloucester.

"Sire?" Torquil called softly, before approaching closer.

Crossing himself, Bruce rose and greeted Torquil with a grim smile. Motioning the Templar to remain, he gestured with his chin toward the still figure laid out on a makeshift bier.

"He was only twenty-three years old," he noted reflectively, "a rash, hotblooded youth with more romance than sense in his soul. I'm sorry he died so young. I regret that we had to fight this battle—but Edward's pride and obstinacy left us no choice."

He drew a breath. "For eight long years, I have told the

Scottish people that as long as but a hundred of us remain alive, never will we on any condition be brought under English rule. I have told them that it is not in truth for glory, nor riches, nor honor that we fight, but for freedom—which no honest man gives up but with life itself. I mean to nurture and cherish that freedom as much from this day onward as ever in any time in the past."

Epilogue

June 25–November 30, 1314

Wₕ₁ₗₑ NEWS OF BRUCE'S VICTORY AT BANNOCKBURN WAS
flying to the ends of Scotland, the battered and humiliated
remnants of the English army fled south toward the Border.

King Edward's defeat was abject and total. Harried from
behind by the newly knighted Sir James Douglas and a band
of Scottish cavalry, the English monarch and his escort at
last reached the temporary safety of Dunbar, whence they
were able to escape by sea to Berwick. But there was no escaping the fact that the Scots had struck the deciding blow
in their hard-fought struggle for freedom.

The aftermath of the battle saw a rapid realignment of
loyalties. The astute Sir Philip Moubray surrendered Stirling
Castle, and was allowed to renounce his fealty to Edward in
favor of King Robert. The English Earl of Hereford and his
following applied for sanctuary at Bothwell Castle on the
Clyde, only to be taken prisoner by Walter Gilbertson, the
constable. When Gilbertson subsequently handed his emi-
nent captives over to King Robert, he also was permitted to
change his allegiance.

Many English knights were allowed to go home free of
ransom, and the bodies of the Earl of Gloucester and Sir

Robert Clifford were restored to their families without any conditions or demands. Aubrey Saint Clair and Flannan Fraser were sent on Bruce's behalf to return King Edward's shield and his privy seal, which had been lost in the latter's precipitous retreat.

"I hope Edward appreciates the courtesy," Arnault remarked to Bruce on the morning of their departure.

Bruce shrugged. "He may as well have the baubles back. God knows they're scant use to me."

The King of Scots had another diplomatic commission for his Templar allies. This time the selection fell on Torquil.

"Here's a test of your bartering abilities," Bruce informed him. "The Earl of Hereford seems to think he's worth a great deal to his friends back home. See how many of our own folk you can redeem as the price of his release."

Torquil grinned. "I'll do my best to drive a hard bargain."

He proved as good as his word. By October, he had secured the release of Bruce's queen, his daughter Marjorie, his sister Mary, and Bishop Robert Wishart in exchange for Hereford.

"I'm afraid I couldn't persuade them to let Countess Isabel return home," Torquil told the king, "but I did get them to agree to change the conditions of her captivity. Henceforth, she'll be decently treated while we continue negotiating for her freedom."

With so much work to be done, and so many diplomatic imperatives to fulfill, it was early November before Bruce was once again able to convene the Scottish parliament. But then, satisfied that the work of government was now advancing smoothly, his Templar advisors at last were able to turn their attention to their own imperative: the erecting of the Fifth Temple. As soon as parliament was in session, Arnault and Torquil retired to Dunkeld, where Ninian had been communing with the Stone of Destiny since shortly after the victory at Bannockburn. They found him in the crypt where the Stone was kept, kneeling at a prie-dieu set before it, chin resting on folded hands. Atop the Stone were set the High Priest's Breastplate and the *Urim* and *Thummin,* with the *Brecbennach* on a stand a little to one side.

"In case you had any doubt," Ninian said, not looking up as they approached from behind, "we were entirely right to separate the *Urim* and *Thummin.* They called to one another during battle," he went on, "and carried the messages of the Stone, but now they are glad to be reunited."

He roused and stood at that, turning to exchange a fraternal embrace with each of them, smiling at their looks of wonderment.

"You speak as if the *Urim* and the *Thummin* were alive," Arnault said.

"Of course. I told you they were but sleeping. And with the destruction of the demon-ring, the Breastplate, too, was revived. Father Columba introduced me to them, when I brought the *Brecbennach* back to Dunkeld. We have become well acquainted in the past few months. I believe you wished to consult with them regarding the placement of the Fifth Temple's cornerstone?"

Arnault and Torquil exchanged amazed glances, but by now, they had become somewhat accustomed to the Columban abbot's easy and informal relationship with his saintly patron. Still, Arnault had expected that guidance would be rather more dearly bought than merely given for the asking.

"Er, yes," he said tentatively. He gave Torquil a puzzled look. "Ah, just ask?"

Ninian gestured toward the Stone, with the Hallows lying atop it. "You are in the presence of old friends," he said quietly. "You have but to speak from your heart. And I would invite the Shard to attend, as well. You carry it with you, do you not?"

Nodding, wordless, Arnault withdrew the Shard's leather pouch bag from the front of his hauberk and removed the Shard, laying it between the *Urim* and *Thummin,* just above the Breastplate, as he knelt before the Stone. Torquil sank to his knees beside Ninian, wide-eyed.

A little awkwardly, Arnault inclined his head to the *Brecbennach* as if Saint Columba did, indeed, reside in its symbol in some real way. Gently, tentatively, he laid his hands over the *Urim* and *Thummin*, forefingers touching the Shard and thumbs lying along the top edge of the Breastplate, so that it lay within the compass of his arms. Unbidden, words came to his lips, which he allowed himself to utter.

"Thank you, Father Columba, for being the friend of the Stone, and the Breastplate, and the *Urim* and *Thummin*," he found himself saying. "You know that we need guidance today. I have been instructed that the Stone of Destiny is to become the cornerstone for the Fifth Temple, to be erected here in Scotland. Now that Scotland is free, I have come to ask where we should lay this cornerstone, to provide the strongest possible foundation for God's Holy Temple."

For a long moment, nothing seemed to happen, but then the Shard began to glow, until its brightness filled the room. At the same time, a warm tingling began under Arnault's fingertips, spreading up his arms and throughout his whole body, infusing every nerve with vibrant energy and surrounding the Breastplate with that energy.

His body became a living vessel, his arms a living bridge. Kindling to his touch, the magnetic properties of the *Urim* and *Thummin* began to assert themselves, diverting the flow of energy so that, like empty vessels, the twin stones began to fill with power. As this occurred, the gems of the High Priest's Breastplate awoke to radiant new life.

Instinctively, Arnault slid his hands around it and lifted it up as an oblation and a thanksgiving. As he did so, a sense of rapture stole over him, centering on his heart and then spreading through all his being as the gemstones of the Breastplate blazed forth in twelve rays of bright light. They converged in a rainbow beam that splashed across the ceiling above their heads, forming moving images.

First came the jagged silhouette of a rude hill fort scowling over the brooding waters of a long and narrow loch. He heard Torquil's soft gasp of wonder at a group of Pictish warriors gathering on the shore of the loch, blue-stained with woad, watching as a white-clad monk stepped out upon a rock just above the water. A monstrous, serpentine head broke the surface of the loch, rearing up with hostile intent; but at a stern injunction from the cleric, the creature bowed its head in submission and withdrew into the depths. This image faded as the ripples of the creature's descent spread outward.

Then a second set of images took form: Arnault himself, standing on the deck of a small galley, the Stone of Destiny before him and the Shard of the Law in his hands, kneeling to raise it above the Stone in both his hands, point downward—and lowering the Shard to press it into the very rock until it disappeared from sight. Then this image, too, faded.

When it had gone completely, the rainbow beam died away and Arnault slowly lowered the Breastplate, a look of wonder on his face as he turned to glance at Ninian and Torquil.

"What *do* you make of that?" he asked softly.

"Which part?" the Columban abbot answered, with a whimsical smile. "The first is clear enough, I think. We all know the tale of how Father Columba dispelled a faerie water-beast that had been troubling King Brude of the Picts. By this sign, I would say that we are to take the stone to Urquhart Castle and commit it to the waters of Loch Ness."

"We're to sink it in the loch?" Torquil asked incredulously. "Beyond retrieval?"

"What better place to keep it safe until the end of time?" Ninian replied. "It is Scotland's anchorstone, and the Temple's cornerstone. Guarded by the secrets of the loch, none shall dare to try and take it from us, ever again.

"As for the second part," he went on, again resting his chin on his folded hands to gaze at the artifacts spread atop the Stone, "the image of the Shard piercing the Stone recalls for me the legends of the sword in the stone. In English, the very word for sword embodies the Word. Thus it seems to me that the Shard, which is the very Word of God, is to be united with the Stone of Destiny before it is sent to its watery resting place. Thus will the Word of God help to anchor His Fifth Temple here in Scotland."

His brow furrowing, Arnault picked up the Shard and looked at it, then touched its point to the Stone.

"I don't understand. How is this to be done?"

"I can only assume," said Ninian, "that this will be made clear at the appropriate time, as have other things. I suggest that the Feast of Saint Andrew would be the most auspicious time to carry out this task."

"That's less than a month away," Torquil said. "And it's a long way to Loch Ness."

"Aye, the first snows already lie on the hills," Arnault said, looking at Ninian in question. "But you obviously have something in mind, or you wouldn't have suggested so near a date."

Ninian summoned a faint smile. "I have had several months to prepare, my friends," he said, "and Brother Flannan was most helpful. Two of your Templar galleys will be at Dundee by the time we can transport the Stone south."

His listeners only nodded, by now well accustomed not to question anything that had to do with the abilities or information sources of the Columban brethren.

The next day, they began the slow process of bringing the Stone out of its hiding place in the crypt below the cathedral and transporting it down from Dunkeld by wagon, by way of Scone, Perth, and the River Tay. True to Ninian's promise, the galleys were waiting for them, one for transporting the Stone and one to provide an armed escort. All of the remaining Templars of *le Cercle* still in Scotland were part of

the escort party—Aubrey, Flannan, Hamish Kerr, and Breville, along with Arnault and Torquil—and even Luc, who
had come over from Argyll, where the rest of their brethren
had retired after Bannokburn.

"It's good to see you, old friend," Arnault told him, as
they clasped hands on making the rendezvous at Dundee.
"You and I are the only ones left who were present at that
council on Cyprus. It's only fitting that we both should witness the fulfillment of that prophecy."

The Templars crewing the galleys were all known to Arnault and Torquil, and asked no questions. Ninian and
Brother Seoirse, a young monk from Iona, joined them, their
Columban robes most welcome among men so long denied
the right to wear the white habit of their own order.

"We expect fair winds, with you along!" Torquil said
aside to Ninian, grinning, as they sailed out of the Firth of
Tay and headed north.

And fair winds they had, day after day. Skirting the coast
past Arbroath and Aberdeen, then along the sandy shoreline
to round the points at Peterhead and Kinnaird, the galleys
made good time. It was the end of the third week in November as they passed Burghead, where, after the slaying of
Red John Comyn, Arnault had led a band of Templars in
rooting out what they believed to be the last vestiges of the
Comyn family's links with Scotland's pagan past. Glancing
at Flannan Fraser, standing farther along the rail, Arnault
wondered if he, too, was remembering that day, and perhaps
reflecting on developments since then.

The wind shifted as they entered the Moray Firth, coming
directly from where they wished to go, so they were obliged
to drop sail and resort to oars. The weather worsened as the
wind rose, and even the prayers of their Columban brothers
were to no avail, though Ninian had a thoughtful expression
on his face as he came away from the bow of the ship.

They continued up the firth, rowing against the wind and
hidden by the rain and the mist. Three days before Saint An-

drew's Day, they pulled into a hidden inlet, where they took an extra turning of the tides to transfer all unnecessary supplies and extraneous crew to the escort vessel, which would not attempt the transit into Loch Ness. There they also winched the Stone up onto the deck, covering it with a heavy blanket of tartan wool. Arnault sat beside it, occasionally reaching out to touch it, for all the long day it took them to row out of the bay and proceed up the firth, with the coasts drawing in on either hand.

They slipped past Inverness that night, under cover of sleet and hail. Dawn found them at the mouth of the narrow sea estuary that connected the firth and the loch, with the Feast of Saint Andrew but two days away. During the night, the temperature had plummeted below freezing, and a rime of ice clung to the rocks inshore and all across a raft of sea weed clogging the mouth of the stream. Ice likewise adorned all the ship's rigging.

"Are you sure the channel is navigable?" Arnault asked the captain of the transport galley.

"No, not at all sure," came the response. "But Brother Ninian tells me that Saint Columba will take care of it. Meanwhile, the best time to try it is at the high tide."

They waited until nearly noon to attempt a transit, more than an hour before the expected high tide. Timbers creaking in protest, the galley nosed her way cautiously into the mouth of the stream, with a crewman sounding the depth from the bow and oarsmen occasionally fending them off from obstacles. The channel was close, the depth variable. Now and again the ship's keel scraped along a sandbar. They had been at it most of the day when the galley softly grated to a standstill.

"It's too shallow, and there's ice clogging the channel ahead," the captain informed Arnault, before hurrying forward to investigate.

Going with him to peer ahead from the bow, Arnault saw that the previous night's intense cold had constricted the brackish waters of the stream to an ice-bound trickle mid-stream.

"Can we cut through with axes?" he asked.

"We could try," the captain agreed, "but this late in the day, we wouldn't get very far. The tide's turned, and the temperature will drop again with nightfall."

"What can we do?" Torquil whispered to Arnault, as the captain directed men overboard to try with the axes anyway.

Arnault slowly shook his head. "I don't know what will happen if we miss the appointed time."

He asked the Stone, laying his hands upon it and offering up his plea for guidance, but none was forthcoming. He knew the Stone was still alive, but he could get no response from it. Nor could any of the others who tried, either Templar or Columban brother.

The short winter day drew to an early close, and they could do nothing more. Again the night was bitterly cold and crystalline clear, the sky bejeweled with stars. Bringing an extra blanket from below, Arnault bedded down beside the Stone, pillowing his head upon it as Jacob had done, worrying and listening to the creak of the ship's timbers as she squatted aground. Eventually weariness got the better of worry or listening, and he dozed off.

But his sleep was fitful, and after a while he became dimly aware of a far-off rushing sound, like the roar of the sea heard through a seashell. The roaring became mingled with other noises—a strange, deep-throated chorus of hoots and groans that sent a faint tingle up his spine, though it was not the tingle of fear. Puzzled, his dream-self stood up to investigate.

Gone were the wintry stars. The galley lay softly swathed in a blanket of silvery fog, though far at its bow he could sense a white-robed form standing with arms outstretched into the milk-white blankness. Beyond, he sensed huge primordial shapes swimming just at the edge of vision, long serpentine necks cresting and dipping as the creatures converged on the galley in a herd, calling out to one another with eerie, moaning cries.

A broad, glistening back broke the fog off the galley's port flank; a second creature surfaced to starboard. A series of heavy bumps from below caused the deck to lurch and shudder, and Arnault clutched at the railing as the ship suddenly lifted beneath him—though he could not seem to move farther, or to summon up enough will even to try.

But the ship moved. Borne up on the creatures' backs, teetering and swaying, the vessel slowly began to edge forward. Other long-necked beasts flanked the ship on either hand, propelling themselves with supple sweeps of their long tails. The rolling surge of their movement was hypnotic, soothing, and carried Arnault back into heavy sleep.

He woke to the cries of excited voices, and rolled free of his blanket to scramble to his feet, hand reaching for his sword. To his astonishment, the galley was floating free on a broad sweep of open water that stretched mirror-silver into predawn mist. Torquil was standing at the railing nearby, and glanced back at him in wonder.

"I have a feeling you won't be at all surprised," he said, "but I do believe we've found our way into Loch Ness! The captain says that some freakish turn of the tide must have moved the jam of seaweed and ice and carried us through."

Remembering his curiously vivid dream, Arnault only smiled faintly.

"Stranger things are possible, I suppose."

They rowed southward down the loch while the daylight lasted. Arnault stayed with the Stone, one hand resting lightly upon it as if in reassurance—whether to it or himself, he could not have said. All the day long, Ninian stood gazing ahead in the bow of the ship like the apparition of the night before, though Arnault sensed it had not been Ninian then, but the saint the Columban brother served.

Toward dusk, they at last caught sight of the slighted towers and walls of ruined Urquhart Castle, emerging from the shadowed shoreline to their right. The water before it was still as a mirror, its bottomless depths reflecting the castle ruins and the snow-covered peaks to the north and east. Behind them, the *V* of their gentle wake followed like a trail of glory, embellished with the rhythmic ripple the oars made. Gazing out across the water, Arnault could almost imagine that he stood on the brink of some strange rift in the fabric of the material world, where sprites and faeries and other creatures, far stranger, could pass freely back and forth into the realm of spirit. He wondered again what had carried the ship into the loch, and whether it—or they—still followed in the depths below.

Just before sunset, they put the bulk of the crew ashore at Urquhart, retaining only half a dozen to man the oars—Templars, all, the captain among them. From the ship's stores, preserved against this hour, Torquil brought out two white Templar mantles, which he and Arnault donned after girding on their swords—God's monks of war once more, ready to do Him service, for the glory of His name. A chill haze was settling above the water as the crew remaining on land gave the galley a push to send it on its way from shore, as winter shadows edged across the loch and the short day began slipping into twilight.

"Not long now," Ninian murmured to Arnault, gazing out across the black mirror of the water.

Clumsily, those remaining bent to the oars, less than a dozen of them, propelling the big galley slowly into the center of the loch. They reached the appointed position just as the sun was dipping behind the hills. A deep blue twilight rolled across the landscape and the surface of the loch as the rowers shipped their oars to let the craft glide to a halt.

As Arnault and Torquil began winching the Stone high enough to clear the rail, and let it balance there, the crew came from below to line up along the opposite rail—except for the captain, who went to the mast with a bundle of something under his arm and ran up a sea version of *Beaucéant*:

a long, swallow-tailed pennon of black and white, horizontally divided, that lifted briefly on a faint breath of air and then was still.

In the silence, it seemed that all creation held its breath, waiting. Quietly Arnault and Torquil stood to either side of the Stone, hands upon it as they waited for the rising of the moon. Ninian stood between them, behind the Stone, gazing out at the lunar glow building beyond the mountain peaks to the east.

Presently, a shimmer of silvery brightness broke behind the eastern horizon as the disk of the rising moon began to emerge. In that first flush of moonlight, Ninian raised his hands in invocation from their Celtic heritage.

> *"In name of the Holy Spirit of Grace,*
> *In name of the Father of the City of peace,*
> *In name of Jesus Who took death off us,*
> *In name of the Three Who shield us in every need,*
> *Be thou welcome, thou bright white moon of the*
> *seasons."*

In the silence that followed these words, Arnault took the Shard from inside his tunic, clasping it between his hands, point downward, and raising it above the Stone as he likewise lifted his eyes and his heart.

"In the beginning was the Word," he murmured, "and the Word was with God, and the Word was God. . . ." He drew a deep breath and let it out.

"Lord, may Your Holy Word ever be our foundation, and Christ Himself our chief cornerstone." He slowly brought the Shard down so that its point rested against the center of the Stone.

"Non nobis, Domine, non nobis, sed nomine Tua da gloriam," he said boldly—and was not surprised when the Stone yielded before the Shard of the Law like ice melting under the sun's warmth, or a bride welcoming her beloved.

When he lifted his hands, he could see no sign of the Shard, but when he laid his hands on the Stone again, he could feel the puissance of their union as a quickening that filled his heart with gladness.

He let Torquil help him steady the Stone as they lifted it enough to swing out over the side. His voice rang true and clear as he spoke from the heart.

"Except the Lord build the house, they labor in vain that build it; except the Lord keep the city, the watchman waketh but in vain," he said, quoting from the Psalms. He could feel the cosmic connection as he lifted his face to the glow that would be the rising moon, as a focus for the prayer he now offered.

"Glorious Chief of chiefs, and captain of my soul—By Your command, the great Solomon raised up the First Temple to be a sign of faith and wisdom. Though physical Temples have come and gone, their ideal has endured down through the ages.

"Now, in accordance with that mandate You gave to Hugues de Payens, our founder, we pledge to raise Your Temple yet again, not by human hands but by faith, and we here lay down the cornerstone of what will become, by Your grace, the foundation for a new Temple, stretching between Heaven and earth. May its walls be an abiding bastion of Light, and its chambers a treasury of wisdom for the ages. And may this Stone of Destiny, which was Jacob's Pillow—the seat of Scotland's Sovereignty—no longer be that alone, but Scotland's anchorstone, as well, and the anchorstone of Your Temple."

He gave a nod to Torquil, who drew his sword, then turned his face again toward the approaching moonlight.

"Thus saith the Lord," he declared, again quoting from scripture. *"Behold, I lay in Zion for a foundation a stone, a tried stone, a precious cornerstone, a sure foundation . . . and the waters shall overflow the hiding place."*

In that instant, the moon broke free of the line of hills,

burnishing the surface of the loch to a silvery sheen. Arnault could feel the Stone throbbing beneath his hand, and he backed away and gave a nod to Torquil, who saluted the Stone with his sword, and murmured, *"Non nobis, Domine!"*—and slashed the cable.

The strands parted, and the Stone of Destiny plunged toward the water below, breaking the surface in a hollow *plunk* and an explosion of silver droplets. Just a glimpse they had of the cut end of the cable fluttering after it as it sank into the darkness, accompanied by a trail of tiny bubbles and a brief phosphorescence in the water—and then a brief flurry of coiled tails and sinuous necks that followed it into the unplumbed depths below.

Speechless, Arnault turned his startled glance to Torquil's, intending to ask what he had seen, but in that instant he became aware that a profound hush had arisen behind the sound of the Stone entering the water, as if time itself held its breath. Torquil looked equally awestruck, as did the crewmen who had just witnessed the Stone's departure, standing motionless at the opposite rail. Ninian was still gazing at the ripples spreading from where the Stone had disappeared, not so much with awe as expectancy.

An expectancy apparently well justified, for suddenly a diamond-mote of white light erupted from the water amid an explosion of bubbles and a shimmer of silvery bells. More lights whizzed skyward, leaping and sporting like shooting stars. Ribbons and streamers of light followed, soaring toward the moon in radiant arcs.

Soon the whole surface of the loch was dancing with light, as far as the eye could see. Great beams and ribs of light took shape as they watched, enraptured, soaring skyward to shape a luminous edifice of columns and architraves, arches and buttresses, shining against the night sky—a whole divine geometry expressed in angelic form, dazzling and joyful.

As his gaze yearned upward toward the Temple's soaring

vault, Arnault caught a shining, exalted glimpse of a wondrous city of adamant and pearl, encompassed by concentric bands of crystal. A fragrance like roses suffused his senses, and a great melodic paean of joy rang out across the heavens—caught only in echo, by mortal ears, but Arnault knew it for the music of the spheres.

A moment only it lingered, leaving but the whisper of roses on the still night air—that and a memory that no one present would ever forget. Yet even as the vision faded before their dazzled eyes, those privileged to have witnessed it—and to have made it possible—knew that the foundation for a new Temple had, indeed, been laid on this, the Feast of Saint Andrew, and that a new Temple would, indeed, arise to bridge the span between Heaven and earth.

Historical Afterword

THIS TALE IS FAR MORE CONJECTURAL THAN OUR PREVIOUS book about the Knights Templar, but the historical under-pinnings are mostly accurate as to the timeline, the various historical events and persons, and the general case against the Templars. We have tried to avoid taking too many liber-ties with historical personages.

Guillaume de Nogaret was a natural for our villain, and didn't require a great deal of embroidery to make him really despicable. And it seemed like a good idea to extend the no-tion regarding demons that he invented to discredit Pope Boniface VIII, and to make this his vice as well.

Of the historical Templars mentioned, in most cases little is known of them save their names and, sometimes, their of-fices, though we have a bit of information about Jacques de Molay. The principal officers of the Temple in Paris fall into this category—and also Oliver de Penne: the only other Templar to be named by name as having his judgment re-served solely to the pope himself, along with de Molay, Geoffrey de Charney, Hugues Paraud, and Geoffrey de Gonneville. We find no other mention of Oliver in historical documents, and nothing is known of his ultimate fate, but he must have been a man of some importance, to have been so named—so he was a likely candidate for membership in *le Cercle*—which is conjectural, of course; but it *could* have existed.

Hardly a month after the burning of de Molay and de Charney, on April 20, 1314, Pope Clement V died of a sudden onslaught of dysentery.

King Philip IV of France died on the Eve of Saint Andrew's Day, November 29, 1314, perhaps while the Stone of Destiny was being carried into Loch Ness to find its final resting place.

When Louis XVI died by the guillotine in 1793, the last of his line, a man is said to have leaped onto the platform and dipped his hand in the dead king's blood, flicked it out over the crowd, and cried, "Jacques de Molay, thou art avenged."

> —Katherine Kurtz and Deborah Turner Harris,
> Ireland and Scotland, 2001

Partial Bibliography

Addison, Charles G. THE HISTORY OF THE KNIGHTS TEMPLAR. Kempton, IL: Adventures Unlimited Press, 1997. (Reprint of 1842 London edition.)

Andrews, Richard and Paul Schellenberger. THE TOMB OF GOD. London: Little, Brown and Company, 1996.

Adomnan. LIFE OF COLUMBA. Alan Orr Anderson and Marjorie Ogilvie Anderson, trans. London/Edinburgh: Thomas Nelson and Sons, Ltd., 1961.

Baigent, Michael and Richard Leigh. THE TEMPLE AND THE LODGE. London: Jonathan Cape, 1989.

Barber, Malcolm. THE TRIAL OF THE TEMPLARS. Cambridge, England: Cambridge University Press, 1978.

Barber, Malcolm. THE NEW KNIGHTHOOD. Cambridge, England: Cambridge University Press, 1994.

Barron, E.M. THE SCOTTISH WAR OF INDEPENDENCE: A Critical Study. Inverness: Robert Carruthers, 1934.

Barrow, Geoffrey W.S. ROBERT THE BRUCE & THE COMMUNITY OF THE REALM OF SCOTLAND. Edinburgh: Edinburgh University Press, 1965, 1994.

Bower, Walter. SCOTICHRONICON. (15th century chronicle) General Editor: D.E.R. Watt. Aberdeen: Aberdeen University Press, 1989.

Burman, Edward. SUPREMELY ABOMINABLE CRIMES: The Trial of the Knights Templar. London: Allison & Busby Ltd., 1994.

_____. THE TEMPLARS: KNIGHTS OF GOD. Wellingborough: Aquarian Press, 1986.

Burnes, James. A SKETCH OF THE HISTORY OF THE KNIGHTS TEMPLAR. Edinburgh: William Blackstone and Sons, 1857.

Carmichael, Alexander. CARMINA GADELICA. Edinburgh: Floris Books, 1994.

Crome, Sarah. SCOTLAND'S FIRST WAR OF INDEPENDENCE. Alford, Lincolnshire: Auch Books, 1999.

Gerber, Pat. THE SEARCH FOR THE STONE OF DESTINY. Edinburgh: Canongate Press, 1992.

Knight, Christopher and Robert Lomas. THE SECOND MESSIAH: Templars, the Turin Shroud, and the Great Secret of Freemasonry. London: Century Books, 1997.

Kurtz, Katherine, ed. TALES OF THE KNIGHTS TEMPLAR. New York: Warner, 1995.

_____. ON CRUSADE: MORE TALES OF THE KNIGHTS TEMPLAR. New York: Warner, 1998.

Laidler, Keith. THE HEAD OF GOD: The Lost Treasure of the Templars. London: Weidenfeld & Nicholson, 1998.

Partner, Peter. THE MURDERED MAGICIANS. [Also published as THE KNIGHTS TEMPLAR AND THEIR MYTH.] Oxford, England: Oxford University Press, 1981.

Paterson, Raymond Campbell. FOR THE LION: A History of the Scottish Wars of Independence 1296–1357. Edinburgh: John Donald Publishers, Ltd., 1996.

Picknett, Lynn and Clive Prince. THE TEMPLAR REVELATION. London: Bantam Press, 1997.

Prebble, John. THE LION IN THE NORTH. London: George Rainbird, Ltd., 1971.

Prestwick, Michael. EDWARD I. London: Methven, 1988.

Robinson, John J. BORN IN BLOOD. New York: M. Evans, 1989.

Robinson, John J. DUNGEON, FIRE, AND SWORD. New York: M. Evans, 1991.

Rosslyn, The Earl of. ROSSLYN CHAPEL. The Rosslyn Chapel Trust, 1997.

Runciman, Sir Steven. HISTORY OF THE CRUSADES, Vol. III, The Kingdom of Acre and the Later Crusades. Cambridge University Press, 1954.

Simon, Edith. THE PIEBALD STANDARD: A Biography of the Knights Templar. Boston: Little, Brown, 1959.

Upton-Ward, J.M. THE RULE OF THE TEMPLARS. New York: Boydell Press, 1992. (Translated from the French of Henri de Curzon's 1886 edition of the French Rule, derived from the three extant medieval manuscripts.)

Young, Alan and Michael J. Stead. IN THE FOOTSTEPS OF ROBERT THE BRUCE. Stroud, Gloucestershire: Sutton Publishing Limited, 1999.

About the Authors

KATHERINE KURTZ is the author of the internationally bestselling Deryni books and other historical fantasies. Katherine Kurtz lives in Ireland.

DEBORAH TURNER HARRIS is the author of the Mages of Garillon trilogy, and coauthor with Katherine Kurtz of the Adept series, including *The Templar Treasure*. Deborah Turner Harris lives in Scotland.

About the Authors

KATHERINE KURTZ is the author of the internationally bestselling Deryni books and other historical fantasies. Katherine Kurtz lives in Ireland.

DEBORAH TURNER HARRIS is the author of the Mages of Garillon trilogy, and coauthor with Katherine Kurtz of the Adept series, including *The Templar Treasure*. Deborah Turner Harris lives in Scotland.

About the Author